Reading is the
REAL
Super Power!

Raceboy and Super Qwok
Adventures

Glad to support the
Paws to Read Program
Have a "reading filled" summer

Gwen Hopkins Group

RACEBOY

&

SUPER QWOK

ADVENTURES

Andrew Winkel

Illustrated by Christopher Brault

HIEROPHANTASM
CLIFTON, ILLINOIS

HIEROPHANTASM
P. O. Box 792
Clifton, IL 60927
hierophantasm.com

Flesch-Kincaid Reading Grade Level: 5.0

For my children:

Alex, Bryan, Katherine, and Anna

The objection to fairy stories is that they tell children there are dragons. But children have always known there are dragons. Fairy stories tell children that dragons can be killed.

Terry Pratchett,
Paraphrasing G. K. Chesterton

TABLE OF CONTENTS

INTRODUCTION

Good. If you're reading this, you realize you're not ready for this book. And you're right. To really enjoy this collection of stories, you need two things: a willing suspension of disbelief, and this introduction.

It begins with an admission: I did not create Raceboy and Super Qwok. They are the inventions of my sons, Alex and Bryan.

At five, Alex imagined his superhero alter-ego, Raceboy. Raceboy's main characteristic was his super speed: he could race like the wind or move like lightning. He could get things done fast: faster than you could say, "Raceboy!" Sometimes he used high tech gadgetry or a utility belt. At other times he managed to manifest nearly every other superhero quality, from laser eyes to stretch power.

Bryan, at three, came up with his own superhero name, Super Qwok. No one could figure out what he was trying to say. I tried, "Super Quack?"

"No," he shook his head.

"Super Quake?"

"No," he stated resolutely.

"Super Clock?"

"Uh-uh," he declared.

At last I managed, "Super Qwok?"

1

"Yes," he agreed. "Super Qwok."

Super Qwok's main characteristic was his strength; he was a tiny titan.

Around October 2006 I began to tell the boys stories about Raceboy and Super Qwok as they used their superhero powers to defend the Village of Clifton from an expanding cast of bad guys, monsters, dastardly difficulties, and diabolical plots. These adventures were primarily bedtime stories, though we did sometimes tell stories on car rides home from a family visit, or the zoo, or the museum.

Many stories in *Raceboy and Super Qwok Adventures* were not simple narratives; rather, they were exchanges between the boys and me. The stories would flow or stall based on the boys' moods and input. The boys would add embellishments. I might ask them what they thought should happen next. I didn't always do what they suggested, but many of these stories are a fusion of all of our ideas and creativity.

Since the majority of the adventures in this collection were told in 2006-7, my daughter Katherine was still the one-year-old baby of the family. The boys began to include her in the action as Racegirl. Her powers were Alex's powers; the only difference was that she wasn't Alex. Much later, she decided to rename herself Flowergirl, with mysterious powers that are thought to include an affinity for both plants and animals.

Anna, the youngest in the family, came into the world around the time Mom discovered the boys' secret identities. She did not make it into any of the early stories, but she did get her own superhero alter ego around the same time she hit her terrible two's. Her ability to dismantle all things Lego, block, or train track earned her the name Dr. Destructo. Her powers of chaos and cacophony give her the ability to destroy without effort and channel that

2

destructive energy against the forces of evil.

The stories collected in *Raceboy and Super Qwok Adventures* were gathered from a number of sources: my not-entirely-reliable memory, obscure sentences scrawled on index cards, summaries typed into computer files, audio recordings, and two full-fledged printouts of story drafts. A few stories received the literary equivalent of a paint job; many more required extensive repairs and needed to be taken down to the studs; at least one was rebuilt on what I believe to be its original foundation; and still others were so far gone that they could not be revised and do not exist here.

From the beginning I had vague designs to collect the stories into an anthology for my children, but it was easier to procrastinate and wait for "some day." If I opened my desk drawer to get the stapler and saw the stack of audiocassettes, I would close the drawer and think *Some day I will sit down and transcribe all of those recordings.* Or if I was shuffling through the story files in my filing cabinet and flipped past *Raceboy and Super Qwok Adventures,* I would tell myself, *Some day I will collect all these notes and write them into a draft.* If I happened to be opening a file on my computer and found the folder titled "Stories," I would reflect for a moment and and say, "Some day I will pull everything together into a book for Alex, Bryan, Katherine, and Anna."

Some day.

Then one day I noticed: Alex was growing up. Nine is nearly ten, and ten is nearly teen, and teen is nearly been and passed and past, and some day I would look back and realize: some day was yesterday, no longer tomorrow. With this realization I knew: someday must be right now.

That was September 2010. As I write this, I have been working on *Raceboy and Super Qwok Adventures* for more than one year. I started out with a single objective: to produce an anthology of

Raceboy and Super Qwok Adventures

Raceboy and Super Qwok stories, and I can say finally that my objective is now complete.

Finally, a word of caution. This book isn't for everybody. If you can't stomach tales about talking noses, alien invasions, walking dinosaur bones, mad scientists, robot krakens, and pre-teen superheroes, stop reading right now. If the idea of a five-year-old and three-year-old sneaking out to drive superhero vehicles and face rampaging monsters makes you cringe, close this book and pick up something else. If you refuse to believe that two boys from Clifton can have a secret base, jet-packs, laser-swords, and clone-bots, then this book is not for you, because *Raceboy and Super Qwok Adventures* has all of these things, and more.

And now, with introductions done, it's time to suspend your disbelief, and enjoy *Raceboy and Super Qwok Adventures.*

Andrew Winkel
Clifton, Illinois
December, 2011

5

PIRATE CAPTAIN BLUE-AND-GREEN

"The end," Dad said and closed the book. He sat on the carpeted floor of the boys' bedroom, his back against a stack of colorful pillows. From his spot leaning against Dad's left side, Alex said, "I love superhero books!"

"Yeah," agreed Bryan from Dad's right side. "Read it again, Daddy!"

Dad laughed. "Not tonight! It's already past your bedtimes. If I don't hurry—"

A woman's voice interrupted from the room across the hall where Mom was dressing one-year-old Katherine in her pajamas. "Lights out!" Mom warned.

Dad shrugged apologetically, pulled himself to his feet, then lifted Bryan from the floor. With the practiced efficiency of a juggler or a father of three, he slid the sheets down on the bottom bunk, rearranged pillow from the floor to the head of the bed, and tossed Bryan atop the pillow. Bryan giggled as Dad pulled the covers back over him and planted a kiss on his forehead.

Alex climbed the ladder and wiggled under his sheets of the top bunk. "I wish we could have another story," he sighed.

"Me too," Dad agreed and kissed him on the cheek. "But it's bedtime now. There will be time for more superhero stories later. Maybe tomorrow night."

1

"It would be awesome to be a superhero," Alex mused.

"You think so?" Dad asked.

"Yes!" said Bryan. "We could fight bad guys and pirates and robots and monsters."

"And save people," Alex said. "Superheroes have costumes and save people."

"Wow, monsters, robots, pirates, and bad guys! You two heroes will need your sleep to face that scurvy bunch," Dad looked out the second-story bedroom window and paused. The backyard stretched away, bordered in the distance by a row of trees. The edge of a corn field could be seen to the west; metal grain elevators rose along the nearby road stretching south. Something caught his attention on the horizon. Dad squinted, watched for a silent moment, rubbed his chin. "Hmmm."

"What?" asked Alex, leaning over the protective rail of his bunk, trying to follow the direction of Dad's glance.

"Just thinking...maybe it could be a story," Dad said.

Bryan sat up. "A story? Tell us! Tell us!"

Dad laughed again and ruffled Bryan's hair. "Go to sleep, buddy. I'll tell you soon." On his way out the door he flipped the light off. "I love you both!"

Dad's footsteps faded across the hall. The boys heard Mom's voice, then Dad's in reply. Mom sailed in and out of the room one final time, finishing the nighttime routine with extra tucking of sheets, extra kissing of cheeks, and one last admonishment to the boys to remember their prayers.

Alex said, "NowIlaymedowntosleepIpraythelordmy—" and Mom put a finger to his lips, "Slow down!"

After she left, Katherine cried for a while, a soft wail that was silenced with a pacifier and the creaking rhythm of the rocking chair. Footsteps again, this time two sets, as both Mom and Dad made their way downstairs. Both boys wriggled and twisted beneath covers until finally their breathing came in the steady pattern of slumber. The house passed into silence.

A grinding rumble woke Alex and Bryan. Sunlight glowed through the bedroom curtains. Alex rubbed his eyes. "What is that? It doesn't sound like any train I've ever heard!"

Both boys leapt from their beds. Bryan pulled back the curtains, and they stared into the morning.

A giant boat rumbled into Clifton. It was a large wooden structure with tall masts and giant sails visible above the tops of the houses. It rolled over the ground on wheels; it crossed road and field, blown by the power of the wind in its sails.

"We'd better get to the Qwok Tower," Bryan said, but Alex had already raced from the window to the closet door. He opened it and flipped a hidden switch. There was a mechanical crinkling and popping and the interior of the closet was replaced. The closet door now opened into a large room filled with work tables, computer equipment, and shelves. Immediately inside the portal hung two superhero costumes.

Alex stepped through the door and grabbed his costume from its hook. He turned on his speed, and in less time than it takes to blink, Raceboy stood clothed in his gray suit with blue boots, gloves, mask, and cape. A blue R was emblazoned on his chest.

Bryan rolled his eyes. Although he would never admit it, he found it annoying that his brother's super power was so convenient for pulling on superhero garments. Bryan stepped through the portal to the Qwok Tower and hit the switch that severed the connection to the bedroom closet. Grabbing his costume from its hook, he proceeded to pull it on. It was a white suit with an exploding SQ on its chest, a red mask with red gloves and boots. Super Qwok pounded his gloved hands together. Sure, Raceboy had his speed, but Super Qwok had power.

Raceboy looked up from a glowing electronic display on a work-table. "I can't find any records about wheeled ships in the Race-computer." He tapped the keyboard and pressed enter. He shook his head. "But, I've got satellite imagery showing it's stopped at the bank."

A sudden blaring alarm sounded. "And there's the Race-alarm," Raceboy said. "Let's go!"

"The First Federal Bank?" Super Qwok asked as the engine of the Race-mobile revved to life. He looked around for Raceboy, and realized that his brother had already zipped ahead in his super-hero vehicle. Super Qwok rolled his eyes again. Sometimes talking with Raceboy was like holding a conversation with someone in a different timezone. Or timestream. He trotted over to the

Qwok-cycle and started it. Then he accelerated and followed the Race-mobile through the second portal, the one that teleported them out of the Qwok Tower to one of a dozen carefully chosen spots around Clifton.

* * *

People all around Clifton had heard the sound of the land-born ship as its many wheels rolled over the ground. They had came running to look at the mysterious sight. They had seen, at the top of the masts, in what's called the crow's nest, a figure with a spy-glass looking around the town. And on the deck at the wheel they had been able to discern a man with a beard. On his hat there was a skull and crossbones.

What kind of man was this? A treasure man, he was; what's more commonly known as a pirate.

The look-out in the crow's nest had looked left and right and had finally yelled, "Bank ahoy!"

"Drop anchor!" shouted the bearded pirate at the wheel.

A chain had rattled; the anchor had fallen to catch on one of the concrete flower planters adorning Main Street. The boat had ground to a halt.

People watching saw a horde of angry buccaneers swing from the ship. Pirates of every shape and size: short pirates, long pirates, tall pirates, fat pirates, wide pirates, all of them wearing tattered clothes, brandishing pistols, snarling with teeth that clenched wickedly curved knives as they roared toward the bank.

Believe it or not, this was a very effective way to rob a bank. No one expected a pirate ship to attack a bank, especially not a bank in the middle of Illinois.

Inside the First Federal Bank of Clifton, the tellers were flab-bergasted. Yes, they hit the secret distress button to alert the po-lice, but that didn't stop the pirates from cleaning out the vault, removing the cash from each teller's drawer, and even collecting the proof sets of commemorative pennies that were on display.

As swiftly as the pirates had descended, they ran back, pulled themselves up to the deck of the boat, and raised the anchor. The boat began to creep away, building speed as the wind filled the sails.

The Police Captain came racing towards the bank in his squad car; he had his red and blue lights flashing.

The pirate captain pointed his cutlass, his curved sword, towards the Police Captain and yelled, "Ahoy there, mates! Let's show them what we're made of. Arm the cannon!"

Hands raced to and fro on the deck, and with trained precision the pirate crew pointed the cannon towards the Police Captain. The cannon's name was "Escape."

The wick was lit. It hissed and burned into the barrel of the cannon. The Police Captain opened the door and leapt from his car just in time: the cannonball crashed straight into the front of his car. It didn't roar through the car like a traditional, solid cannonball would have, and it didn't explode either. Instead it went *SPLAT!* It was like a giant, wet, water balloon. The cannonball contained an acid that began to eat the car: *CRUNCH, CRUNCH, CRUNCH* went the acid as it sucked the metal of the car and turned it into a liquid. Within minutes there was nothing left of the car but a puddle of colorful acid on the road. The Police Captain looked at the spot where his car had been and realized how very lucky he was to have escaped in time.

And who should also be on the scene? That's right: Raceboy and Super Qwok. The Race-mobile squealed to a halt with the Qwok-cycle immediately beside it. The heroes stepped up to the Police Captain as he looked back and forth between the oozing puddle of his car and the pirate ship rumbling away from Clifton.

"Captain?" asked Raceboy.

The Police Captain said, "It was some sort of acid cannonball. I've never seen anything like it!"

"What do we need to know?" Super Qwok asked.

"Bank robbery. Possible hostages. I haven't been able to secure the scene, yet."

"Thanks, Captain," said Raceboy.

Both boys looked at the ship crunching over the ground as it made its getaway. Super Qwok said, "Raceboy, let's use teamwork. Would you still be able to run fast if you carried me on your back?"

"Certainly!" answered Raceboy.

"Good. Then my idea is that we use teamwork to create a new superhero named 'Race Qwok.'"

Raceboy said, "That's very interesting, Super Qwok. How does your idea work?"

"I'll get on your back. You race fast. I'll use my powerful strength while you use your powerful speed to make us Race Qwok!"

"Jump on!" Raceboy bent slightly. Super Qwok climbed onto Raceboy's back in piggy-back fashion. Raceboy held Super Qwok's legs with his arms, shifted slightly to get comfortable, then burst into Race-mode. In an instant they were beside the ship.

Super Qwok punched the side of the boat. *CLANG!* Although the ship looked like it was made out of wood, it was really a very strong metal. He punched it again, and despite his strength, the metal did not bend, and he could not find any fingerholds to tear it apart.

"We're not getting in that way," he told Raceboy. "Use your jet-pack!"

Raceboy fired his jet-pack and lifted Super Qwok and himself onto the ship. They landed near the main mast.

One of the pirates, a short figure in ragged clothing, pointed and shouted, "Look, Pirate Captain Green-and-blue! We've been boarded!"

The pirate captain shook his fist at the crewman and bellowed, "Pirate Captain Blue-and-green! How many times do I have to tell you scurvy knaves...It's Pirate Captain Blue-and-green!" He swatted the air a final time. "Take the wheel, Mr. Brown," growled the pirate captain, and released control of the ship to his first mate.

Raceboy and Super Qwok stood back to back in the center of the deck. Pirates surrounded them. The captain flipped himself over the rail to land with a solid smack on the deck. "Look lively, lads! We have guests! Let's give them the *royal* treatment!" The pirate captain laughed, "Ha ha ha ha ha." Both heroes thought there was something mysterious about the way this pirate captain laughed. Indeed, as they stared into the eyes of the crew, they began to realize that these were not normal pirates. For one thing, they didn't look quite right. Yes, they looked evil. They looked like bad guys, but there was something about the way they looked, as though each pirate was really a manufactured device, a machine created to look like a pirate. Even as the boys stood surrounded by the pirates, a fog rose up from holes on the ship's deck. The pirates smiled wicked, mechanical smiles as the green, putrid fog surrounded them.

Neither boy wanted to inhale the green fog; they tried to hold their breath; they tried to move away from the fog. It was too late. The fog had gotten to their lungs, and even the smallest amount was enough: both boys were suddenly weak and disoriented. They wobbled and fell to the deck, struggling to keep conscious. The last thing they heard was the diabolical laughter of Pirate Captain Blue-and-green. The last thing they saw was the rapscallions of his crew moving forward with ropes. Then all was dark.

The boys awoke to find themselves tied with coils of metal rope.

Raceboy tugged against his bonds to no avail. He turned to see Super Qwok struggling as well. Despite his great strength, the ropes were unbreakable. They appeared to be made from the same metal as the hull of the ship.

Pirate Captain Blue-and-green roared to his crew, "Now, scallywags, it's time for the prisoners to walk the plank!"

From the robot crew rose a ragged cheer.

Raceboy and Super Qwok could see that the ship was nowhere near Clifton. Indeed, it had sailed somewhere far away. There was no land anywhere in the distance; they could only see the blue of the deep ocean stretching as far as the eye could see. The air was filled with a sound like a tornado, but neither Raceboy nor Super Qwok were sure what this meant. All they knew was that this amazing ship was able to drive on roads, off roads, and even had the ability to fly great distances.

The pirate robots scurried around the deck. They readied the plank, extending it from the side of the ship. Raceboy and Super Qwok looked at one another as though to share the same thought: *How are we going to get out of this?*

Super Qwok flexed his muscles. He hoped he could get the metal to stretch, but the powerful coils would not loosen and would not release him.

Pirate Captain Blue-and-green laughed and said, "Hah hah, matey, you think I haven't thought of that? Aargh, I've created the strongest bonds just for you! And don't you go thinking you can sneak some extra power on me I've never heard about like laser vision to burn your way free, 'cuz these bands are impervious to lasers also.

"Now, Raceboy, walk the plank!" He took Raceboy by the back and led him to the edge of the boat where the plank extended from the deck of the ship like a diving board. Raceboy stepped onto the plank and as he passed over open space he discovered what the roaring sound was. Calm ocean did not wait below; instead the ship hovered in the open air above a giant whirlpool that spun like water going down Poseidon's kitchen drain or maybe his toilet.

This is not the sort of problem that superheroes want to have. No superhero wants to look down from the plank of a pirate ship into a swirling, whirling whirlpool. Raceboy knew that he was going to be made to jump into the whirlpool, and within such a powerful natural force even a superhero is in trouble.

Pirate Captain Blue-and-green brandished his cutlass in one hand, a wicked double-edged knife in the other. He waved the two weapons and said, "Now, avast there, Matey. Jump into the depths of the whirlpool!"

Raceboy had gone off the diving board at swimming lessons, so he knew about bouncing. A plank is just like a diving board, after all, and as it would bounce, bounce, and bounce, he would fly higher, higher, and higher. And having practiced gymnastics, because he was a superhero, Raceboy bounced, and he bounced. Then, using his racing powers of speed, and his gymnastic talents, he back-flipped over the heads of the eager robot crew and also Pirate Captain Blue-and-green.

He landed on the deck of the boat, and proceeded to use the only weapon he had available: his feet. He did ninja kicks left and ninja kicks right. He spun around, knocking into robots with his knees and his feet and his toes.

Super Qwok, likewise, began to use his strength to push robots with his feet and his knees. Super Qwok even bent over and charged them with his head, knocking robots to the left and right.

The superheroes met in the middle of the boat. Back to back they faced the horde of pirates. They said to one another, "How are we going to escape?"

That was when Pirate Captain Blue-and-green yelled, "Bring out the monster!"

There are few things that you want to hear when you are tied up with unbreakable metal rope. One of the lowest on the list is, "Bring out the monster!" which is exactly what Pirate Captain Blue-and-green yelled.

There was a rumble from below the decks, then a trapdoor opened, and from the cavernous depths of the ship reached a purple metal tentacle. A long, slender tentacle with electro-suckers reached out from inside the deck. Then another. And another. Andanotherandanotherandanother.

How many tentacles are there? wondered Super Qwok.

Raceboy was thinking, *What kind of creature can this be?*

The long metal arms waved in the air as the machine pulled its central shape up, and they could see the beak-like mouth, the hideous, misty, foggy eye of an enormous robot kraken. It was like a giant metal squid. With an echoing thunk the kraken pulled its bulk onto the deck and roared from its beak.

The kraken pulled its way toward Super Qwok and Raceboy, who were both trying desperately to fight against their metal bonds. Now, though, they were trying to get the metal rope off one another. Super Qwok leaned over to Raceboy and grabbed hold of the rope with his mouth and pulled as Raceboy sank to the ground. The rope loosened. Raceboy slid into super speed and wiggled free of the rope.

As the kraken reached for him it discovered nothing in its tentacle but a single strand of silver rope. Raceboy had sped away, except that the tentacles had slammed down all around him like the bars of a prison. Raceboy used the tentacles to leap from, bouncing, rolling backwards in a dodge, slipping forward in a somersault. The kraken waved the rope around and between its tentacles.

18

Meanwhile, Super Qwok knew that he had to do something to save himself from the kraken. He jumped as high as he could, up and down. The powerful thud of his feet stomped the deck, rumbling the entire ship with the earthquake of his power. Again and again he jumped, and the ship began to come apart at the edges.

Raceboy bounced backwards and saw his salvation was that strand of metal rope still tangled in the kraken's tentacles. He grabbed the strand, then raced to Super Qwok, who bent over as though bowing after meeting a famous king. Raceboy grabbed Super Qwok's rope as he passed and pulled it, uncoiling his brother. Super Qwok unwound like a bobbin on a sewing machine, then began (somewhat shakily, for even superheroes get dizzy when they are unwound at super speed) striking the metal tentacles of the giant kraken.

Raceboy now had the ends of two coils of rope, and he had a plan. He raced a knot to bind the two lengths together. "Super Qwok! Take an end!" He passed one end of the rope to his brother.

Although his crew had stayed away from the kraken, Pirate Captain Blue-and-green yelled pirate phrases and pointed a weapon at Raceboy and Super Qwok. It was shaped like a giant blunderbuss cradled against his shoulder. He kept tracking the heroes, but didn't fire because the arms of the kraken were always in the way.

Super Qwok took the rope and went one way; Raceboy used the rope and went the other. The two began to weave and wrap the kraken's arms in giant knots. When both boys met at the other side of the kraken, Raceboy handed his end of the rope to Super Qwok, who wrenched it tight and tied the only knot he knew how: the one he used to tie his shoes.

"Faster!" exclaimed Raceboy.

"Hold on! I always have a problem with this part!" said Super Qwok as he tried to get the rabbit ears through the hole. Or something like that. He added a couple more loops just in case and said, "There."

Raceboy cried out as he was unexpectedly flung high into the rigging, where his shirt caught above the crow's nest. He saw that although they had tied many of the kraken's limbs, still others were spilling out. One had batted him like a baseball and sent him high. He watched as another batted Super Qwok.

"No!" Raceboy screamed, struggling to free himself, and the tentacle slammed Super Qwok in a line drive straight into the mast of the ship, which gave a horrendous crack like thunder. The mast began to fall on Super Qwok. With Raceboy still caught above, he and the falling mast plummeted toward the deck and Super Qwok.

Super Qwok knew the mast was falling; after all, he'd broken it with his back. He twisted and lifted the base of the mast to make certain it didn't crush him. He swept the deck of robot pirates, slamming them aside like they were the baseballs and he was the batter.

Raceboy took advantage of the momentum to leap from the mast and attack Pirate Captain Blue-and-green. He knocked the blunderbuss from the pirate's grip and embraced him in a hug. Without the mast, the ship began to tip dangerously low toward the whirlpool. Raceboy and Pirate Captain Blue-and-green slid down the sloping deck to the rail of the ship. Raceboy held the pirate above the swirling waters, and yelled, "Is this what you want? Do you want me to drop you in the whirlpool?"

Nearby, Super Qwok took hold of two of the kraken's arms and began to spin. His legs were planted firmly on the deck of the ship as he swung the kraken around and around. Its lone enormous eye stared in confusion and the beak squawked angry rants until Super Qwok let go, and the many-armed creature flung high into the sky then straight down into the whirlpool, where its body surfaced once to spin around and around while the limbs waved frantically, before being sucked down into the swirling depths.

Raceboy and Pirate Captain Blue-and-green watched the kraken sink out of sight, watched as the ship sank closer and closer to the whirlpool. Once caught in its swirling grip, there would be no escape.

Pirate Captain Blue-and-green shook his robot head, "No!" he cried. "No, I don't want you to!"

"You're lucky I'm a good guy!" Raceboy said, and in a burst of speed he ran to the back of the ship and fired his jet-pack. The burst of the jet-pack pushed the airship away from the whirlpool, maneuvering it above the open ocean.

Pirate Captain Blue-and-green was so ashamed that he offered to take the heroes back home and return all the money he had stolen from the bank. He vowed to never cause any more harm. His robot crew repaired the mast and the damage to the ship, and the pirate ship traveled back to Clifton, where Pirate Captain Blue-and-green returned all the loot from the bank then dropped Raceboy and Super Qwok on Main Street. The two superheroes congratulated each other as they watched the ship rumble away over the corn fields and disappear into the distance.

A Sticky Situation

The Race-mobile stopped so suddenly both Super Qwok and Raceboy yelled in surprise.

"I knew I should have taken the Qwok-cycle! What happened?" said Super Qwok.

"I don't know," replied Raceboy. "It just stopped."

"Something's all over the road," pointed out Super Qwok. Sure enough, the entire stretch of the road was covered with a cream-colored goop. Other vehicles appeared to be caught in the goop ahead as well.

Super Qwok opened his door and stepped out.

"Wait!" said Raceboy.

Super Qwok yelled, "Yikes! I can't move!" He pulled on his foot, but the boot was firmly attached to the gooey roadway. Super Qwok looked at the road's edge, to the gravel and grass. The glue stopped at the end of the blacktop.

He unlaced his boots and carefully stepped atop them, then he bent his knees and leapt with all his force out of the glue.

"Super Qwok?" said Raceboy, standing on the inside ledge of his door and looking around.

"Here!" came a voice from above.

Raceboy looked up. "What are you doing in those trees?"

"I forgot how powerful I am when I jumped!"

"See anything?"

Super Qwok looked around. "Over there!" He pointed ahead of them on the roadway. A large wheeled laboratory was painting glue on the road. Atop the laboratory stood the white coated figure of-

"A mad scientist!" Super Qwok exclaimed.

"Dr. Devious?" asked Raceboy.

Super Qwok nodded, "It's Dr. Devious, all right. He's looking through a telescope. In fact, it's like he's watching the accidents he's causing with his glue-making machine."

"Let's put an end to this sticky situation," Raceboy said. He climbed onto the roof of the Race-mobile and leapt to the side of the roadway. Super Qwok dropped to the ground, landing with a bend of the knees. The two ran along the roadway toward the rolling laboratory.

Raceboy sped up, quickly outdistancing Super Qwok. Ahead of him, Dr. Devious set the telescope down and picked up something else: a long cylinder that he set atop his right shoulder. He pointed it straight at Raceboy. Instead of a bang, there was a splat as he fired. A glue ball! Raceboy ducked out of the way as the glue ball splattered a wide splotch of grass and gravel.

Dr. Devious fired the Gluzooka at Super Qwok, and unfortunately the barefoot superhero wasn't able to get out of the way. The glue ball hit him squarely on the chest, knocking him to the ground.

Raceboy neared the platform of the rolling laboratory as another volley of Gluzooka blasts splattered all around him. His only hope was to avoid the blasts and make it onto the platform to confront the scientist. He decided on a ruse to outthink Dr. Devious.

He dropped his speed to make himself more visible, then acted like he was going to head straight toward the platform and leap.

Just as he crouched to leap, he blasted into Race-mode and turned, running around the platform. A blob of glue splattered where he would have been if he had jumped. To Dr. Devious, it must have looked like Raceboy had disappeared. From the back side of the platform, Raceboy climbed up and approached the mad scientist from behind.

As though sensing some trickery, Dr. Devious activated a device, and was immediately surrounded in an orb of swirling yellow glue...a glue shield!

Super Qwok struggled against the glue ball that covered his body. His hands and feet extended from the edges of the glue ball, but he looked like a walking pom-pom. He neared the rolling laboratory and was close enough to hear Raceboy yell, "Why are you doing this?"

Within the glue shield, Dr. Devious's voice screeched in barely controlled fits of laughter. "At last, a plan worthy of my intellect! My glue will give me control over the world! No one can stop the power of my glue!"

Raceboy drew his laser-sword. "I can," he declared. He struck the swirling, oozing shield of glue. The laser-sword hissed and the glue smoked. Although pieces of glue hardened, blackened and fell to the ground, the shield held, and Dr. Devious laughed triumphantly. A smell like burnt grilled cheese or scorched noodles hung in the air.

As suddenly as he began, Raceboy quit the attack, and instead tossed the laser-sword to Super Qwok, who managed to catch it. Super Qwok ignited the energy blade and began to hack pieces of the glue ball from his body.

Raceboy turned back to Dr. Devious. "You seem to have forgotten something."

Dr. Devious's voice inside the glue shield asked, "What? My

plans are perfect."

"While you're in that shield, you're helpless. It may protect you, but it also imprisons you. And more, what happens if something hits you hard? Something moving very fast?"

"Eh?" Dr. Devious asked.

Raceboy backed up, intent on the swirling glue shield. Then he charged full-speed straight into it. Maybe he couldn't get through the sticky field, but then, that hadn't been his intent. The shield surrounded Dr. Devious like a swirling balloon of glue, and like a balloon, the sides seemed to bend under pressure. The shield was no match for Raceboy's velocity. As he pushed into it; the side bent, distorted, and the battering ram that was Raceboy collided with Dr. Devious, who found himself trapped by the wall of the glue shield.

"No!!!" howled Dr. Devious, his face stuck opposite Raceboy's.

After a few tense moments of staring at one another through the

swirling glue, Dr. Devious howled sharply and switched off the shield. This didn't remove the glue from either Raceboy or Dr. Devious, but it did get rid of the bubble holding them together.

Super Qwok climbed onto the laboratory as Dr. Devious sobbed, "No! It can't be! Everything was so perfect, so wonderfully sticky!" There was a click as Super Qwok stuck Dr. Devious to the laboratory with some good old fashioned non-glue based Qwok-cuffs.

Raceboy, covered in the yellow glue, looked at Super Qwok, who was still mostly covered with glue from the Gluzooka. Raceboy said, "I hope the Police Captain gets here soon. I've got to get out of these clothes."

Raceboy's communicator beeped. "Raceboy," came the voice of the Police Captain.

"Ah, good! There's the cavalry." Into the communicator he said, "Come in, Captain."

"Uh," came the Captain's reply, "it's going to be a while. I've got to get my car out of this glue..."

THE BIRTHDAY BANDIT

The Birthday Bandit had struck at least a dozen times in the last week. Alex looked at the most recent update from the Police Captain and discussed it with Bryan. "Let's go over the facts about this case again. Where does the Birthday Bandit strike?"

Bryan said, "Birthday parties. Only birthday parties."

Alex nodded. "An odd choice. That's how he got his name, obviously, since he's never stopped and introduced himself. Okay, what is his objective?"

"He steals presents. Just the presents. Nothing else."

"Again, an unusual choice. What is his modus operandi?"

"Come again?"

"Modus operandi?"

Bryan frowned. "What's that mean?" he asked.

"I don't exactly know. I guess it means 'the way he does it.'"

"Sounds technical. I like it. All right, his modus operandi is to wait until everyone is singing 'Happy Birthday' around the cake with candles burning. Then he strikes. If the presents are in another room, *BAM,* no one notices they're missing until the last bit of the song gets done. If the presents are in the same room, he races in on his electric horse, swipes the presents, and races out while everyone stands with their mouths hanging open. At least, that's what we looked like at the two parties we've been to when

he's struck."

"It's frustrating to be at a crime and unable to pursue a villain without revealing our secret identities." Alex shook his head.

"But," reminded Bryan, "it's given us some insights into the Birthday Bandit. And we can use those insights to capture him. All we need now is a birthday, and you don't have to be a mind reader to know what I'm thinking."

"Yes, Mom's party is tonight, but we can't exactly slip out!"

"There's only one solution when we need to be in two places at once."

"The clone-bots? But we've only experimented with them at night when we're supposed to be sleeping! During the day someone may notice that they're not us, that they're robots."

Bryan was resolute. "The clone-bots will work. No one's going to pay any attention to them, anyway. All of the attention will be on the Birthday Bandit and us. Besides, I've got an inkling that we should be at the party as Super Qwok and Raceboy. With the string of birthday robberies, it would make perfect sense."

Although it wasn't a surprise party, Mom was very surprised to have two costumed superheroes enter the kitchen.

"Super Qwok! Raceboy!" she said. "Why are you here?"

Raceboy explained, "With the recent string of birthday robberies, we felt it necessary to be nearby in case of an emergency."

"Yes, but how did you know it was my birthday?"

Super Qwok said, "Your sons contacted us, Ma'am." He nodded in the direction of the living room, where the robot versions of Alex and Bryan were sitting very still on the couch, side by side.

"Don't mind them," Mom told the heroes. "When there's a television on, they can't focus on anything else. They get that from their Dad."

"But it's a commercial!" Super Qwok said.

"For Diaper'n'Cry dolls!" Raceboy added.

"We're going to have to work on them," muttered Super Qwok.

Mom nodded. "I know. It's almost a sickness. If I'm lucky, they'll snap out of it long enough to sing Happy Birthday."

The party grew to a happy throng, including all of Mom's family who lived nearby. Super Qwok and Raceboy stayed out of the way, but it was impossible to completely ignore a pair of costumed superheroes guarding presents.

As Dad opened a box of matches, both boys looked at one another meaningfully. Dad struck the match and lit a candle, which he then used to light the remaining candles on the cake. Then he broke into the first notes of "Happy Birthday."

Everyone joined in, and their voices rolled together and became louder, clearer. Suddenly a tall metal shape clattered into the room: the unlikely figure of a mechanical horse, and astride the robotic device, the Birthday Bandit.

The mechanical horse was not the same size as a real horse; it was more of a mechanical pony. It was silver all over, except for its saddle, which was padded red leather. Instead of a saddle horn it had a controller stick. And instead of regular eyes, it had red lights that glittered and flashed.

"Yee-haw!" yelled the Birthday Bandit. He wore jeans and a flannel shirt. He had a wide brimmed cowboy hat and a bandana that covered his mouth and nose, leaving only a slit between the brim of the hat and the red bandana where his eyes could peer out.

People moved aside for the mechanical horse, and the Birthday Bandit leaned down to the table near Mom to grab her presents.

"Stop!" yelled Raceboy. "Leave those presents."

It was as though the Birthday Bandit recognized that he had company for the first time. He picked up Mom's cake from right in front of her and threw it straight at Raceboy. With his super

speed, Raceboy ducked out of the way. Super Qwok wasn't so lucky; the cake covered his face and ran down his shoulders, onto his chest and back.

Super Qwok sucked a candle off his frosted face, chewed once, twice, three times, and rolled it into a ball with his tongue. Then, *P-TOO,* he spat it straight at the Birthday Bandit. It hit the Bandit right on the cheek, and it hit with such force that the Bandit's head was tipped straight back, and he toppled from his horse.

That didn't stop him. In an instant he had a Birthday Candle Cannon, which he fired at Raceboy. It was no ordinary cannon; rather, the long, twisting barrel shot flames out like the roaring mouth of a dragon. Raceboy ducked again and felt the hair on his head getting warmer and warmer, and he started to really get nervous that it was going to burst into flame at any moment. Then he felt a wind, and turning, saw that Super Qwok was combating the Birthday Candle Cannon with his own superhero breath. Blowing furiously, Super Qwok was stopping the flame as it came out of the cannon, which finally fizzled and was extinguished.

From another holster the Birthday Bandit drew his Frosting Blaster. He aimed it at Super Qwok and pulled the trigger. Super Qwok couldn't evade fast enough, and the Frosting Blaster stopped him in his tracks. It wasn't cake frosting; it was a freeze ray! Super Qwok stood covered in a white layer of frost. In a moment cracks began to appear on the surface of his frozen coating. Chips of ice fell away like molting snake-skin, and he shook. The chips fell to the ground with a tinkle like tiny bells.

Raceboy had an idea. He began to sing, "Happy Birthday to you…"

The Birthday Bandit looked around the room, down at the presents that he hadn't quite swiped yet, then back at Raceboy, who continued, "Happy Birthday to you…" Other voices joined in,

31

aunts and uncles and grandparents, all those family members who had come to celebrate with Mom. Raceboy noticed that even the Clone-bots were trying to stand at the doorway and sing while keeping an eye on television commercials.

The Birthday Bandit shook his head. The Frosting Blaster fell from his hands and he tried to cover his ears with his hands. "No," he gasped.

"Happy Birthday dear Bandit!"

"It's not my Birthday!" screamed the Birthday Bandit.

"Happy Birthday to you!"

Like a child in a tantrum, the Birthday Bandit stamped and stomped. His eyes were closed. "Not my birthday! You can't sing to me!"

"But I do have a present for you," explained Super Qwok as he snapped the Qwok-cuffs onto the Birthday Bandit. "Except I suppose it's not much of a present because you have to give them back."

"Not my birthday!" mumbled the Birthday Bandit.

Sirens sounded outside the house and the Police Captain's car pulled up. The Police Captain rushed up the sidewalk, up the stairs, and into the kitchen. He skidded to a stop on the tile and looked around the room. "Raceboy! Super Qwok!" he said. "You've caught the Birthday Bandit!"

The Police Captain stepped forward and removed the Bandit's hat. He slid the bandana off the Bandit's nose to reveal a thick nose with a dainty moustache and wide lips.

"Dr. Brick?" Super Qwok and Raceboy asked at the same time.

For indeed, it was Dr. Brick, the very same villain who had plagued Clifton in the past, and now his stint as the Birthday Bandit was at an end. Or was it?

Polidori's Legacy

Afterward Dr. Devious would never discuss the experiment. He would only snarl, "Ask Dr. Brick."

And Dr. Brick was similarly close-lipped. When the subject came up, he might recite Italian sonnets, list Kasparov's chess moves against Topalov in their famous 1999 game, or conjugate Russian verbs. But he never would explain.

Neither one would divulge the truth. It was only careful reconstruction of the evidence by Raceboy and Super Qwok that revealed these facts:

Drs. Brick and Devious had unearthed handwritten notes from 1814 written by John William Polidori. While a medical student at the University of Edinburgh, he had assisted an unnamed professor in an experiment that was so controversial that it was done under the veil of darkness. The notes were very specific, including procedures and observations.

Drs. Brick and Devious took steps to reproduce the experiment detailed by Polidori. First, however, they needed source material to carry out the procedure. Receipts recovered in the investigation show that some of the experiment's materials came from internet science supply companies. The rest are presumed to have come from the Clifton Cemetery, though no conclusive evidence was found and neither doctor was charged.

The experiment was carried out on the ninth of October. Recreating Polidori's experiment required lightning, and the night proved perfect: a storm spilled cold rain and blasted bolts of lightning at the ground.

What happened? What went wrong? Without witnesses willing to discuss the subject, all that remains are conjectures. Raceboy and Super Qwok talked about it:

"The straps holding the creature snapped. It must have been stronger than Dr. Devious and Dr. Brick thought," Raceboy said.

"Or maybe it was the lightning. The electricity could have given the creature great strength," said Super Qwok.

"Or maybe it was shock—"

Super Qwok stared disgustedly at his brother.

"What?" asked Raceboy. "I didn't mean to pun! I just meant, maybe it was the shock of awareness … The shock of coming to life like that, in an instant …"

"I guess we'll never know," Super Qwok sighed.

The first accounts of the creature came from people on Main Street, who saw a human shape illuminated by lightning raging down the street. The figure stopped at every window and pressed its face against the rain-streaked surface. The bartender in St. Bartholomew's Pub reported that the face looking into the pub window was so awful in the neon glow, so horrible and fearsome, that people cried out, ducked beneath tables, and even dropped their beer bottles.

Next, the creature ran into the Clifton Public Library, where it ripped the posters from the walls and pushed books off the shelves. Alex and Bryan's dad was working at the library that night, and they listened to him explain later over dinner that the creature was the scariest sight he had ever seen: "It looked like a man, but it had to stoop to push through the door. It looked at me with its mismatched eyes, one green and the other a striking blue, and I felt like I was looking at a clay version of a man or a golem or a jigsaw puzzle that was man-shaped."

Alex and Bryan's dad placed the first 9–1–1 call at 6:43 PM. By that time the creature had gone next door to the grocery store, where it continued its rampage. In the store it stomped on cereal boxes and shattered syrup bottles. It pushed over stacks of soda and tossed bananas at the cashier, who ran shrieking out the door and bumped into the Police Captain.

The creature followed the cashier through the door into the rainy evening. The Police Captain, sizing it up in an instant, drew his pistol and aimed. "Freeze," he ordered. Thunder rolled in that moment, and the Police Captain wondered briefly if he had awakened his true nature as a Norse god.

Newly born and completely uneducated, the creature could not understand this simple command. It kept moving.

The Police Captain shot the creature in the arm, and the creature howled. The bullet didn't have the same effect as it would have on a normal, living, pre-dead person. With a cry that split the rain-filled night, the creature charged the Police Captain, yanked the gun from his fingers, and threw it against the brick wall of the grocery store. It then picked up the Police Captain and threw *him* against the brick wall of the grocery store. *Nope,* realized the Police Captain as he slid upside-down into some prickly evergreens. *The thunder was just a coincidence.*

Running down the next block, the creature discovered that it was surrounded. Its creators stood behind it: Drs. Devious and Brick. Before the creature stood Raceboy and Super Qwok, newly arrived at the scene in response to the Race-alarm.

In the downpour, the creature looked back and forth between the costumed heroes and the plain white lab coats of the mad scientists. As if deciding that the scientists were less dangerous, it raged at Dr. Brick.

Dr. Brick yelled, "No, no! That's bad! Bad—" Dr. Brick's protests changed to shrieks as the creature lifted him by the feet and began swinging him around like a baseball bat. "Bad! Not bat!" he screamed.

The creature proceeded to use Dr. Brick to bat Dr. Devious, not unlike Raceboy and Super Qwok's own early attempts at hitting a baseball from a tee.

Raceboy said, "It seems a shame to stop it. I think it's really getting the hang of stepping into its swing."

Super Qwok exhaled sadly. "Even though they deserve it, we should probably save them while they still have some chance of recuperating."

Raceboy zoomed past the creature. It looked at its hand, which was suddenly and unexpectedly empty of Dr. Brick. Before it could react, the creature found itself lifted high above Super Qwok's head.

The creature howled, the sound something between a pipe organ's throaty bellow and a nail wrenched from a stud. Then it flipped into the air, twisting from Super Qwok's hands, knocking him back.

Raceboy grabbed the creature's arms, twisting them behind its back and pinning them so it couldn't move. Except the creature had been assembled from body parts and was not constructed in entirely the same way that most humans are. It lifted its arms, with Raceboy, upwards over its head and down in the front. Raceboy found himself upside down and suddenly twisted in a hug from a huge, undead monster. Raceboy's nose pressed against the monster's belly button.

The creature squeezed, and Raceboy howled. It wasn't the pain that hurt, it was the smell. This was the worst smell Raceboy had ever smelled. Although he tried to struggle, he found himself disoriented, weak, and ready to pass out.

Super Qwok ran, leapt, and planted a solid punch right into the creature's bent nose. The blow made a smacking sound, and Raceboy slid free, fell head-first into the mud, where he breathed in the clean air and tried to regain some equilibrium.

Anger shot through the monster. It made a noise unlike any that has ever been heard on this Earth before, unless it was once the sort of thing heard during the days of the dinosaurs, when a fearsome tyrannosaurus found itself foiled by the sharp horns of a triceratops.

The creature flailed its arms like a windmill, trying to hit everything and anything it could.

Super Qwok kept out of its reach, but then decided on a new strategy, a new distraction. He ripped some flowers from a nearby flower pot ("Impatiens," his mother explained later when he asked about them), and held them just in front of the creature's face. Perhaps it could smell the soft scent of the flowers? Or perhaps it was soothed by the colors? Whatever the cause, the creature began to calm down. Using the flowers, Super Qwok began to lead it. But where could they go? For a moment Super Qwok thought the creature might have smiled at the flowers; the edges of its mouth turned upwards. But it wasn't the lips that made him think the creature was smiling; it was the eyes, the green and the blue, which seemed to have softened. *This creature isn't evil,* Super Qwok realized. *It's confused. It's like a wild animal out of its element, or maybe it doesn't have an element at all; it's just doing the best that it can until it understands.*

By this time Raceboy was trying to stagger to his feet, except the more he moved, the more the rank smell made him nauseous.

It clung to him, leeched into the folds of his superhero costume, saturated his being. If he moved too fast he knew he was going to throw up. He looked around and saw that Dr. Devious and Dr. Brick had regained their feet and were both wobbling toward the monster. Dr. Brick groaned, "Come home with us!"

Super Qwok heard the voice before he saw the doctors. He knew the voice, of course, but he hadn't taken his eyes from the creature. He saw the transition as the creature's eyes shifted from serene to hate-filled, saw the creature turn and look one last time at the flowers before shrieking a brief, sharp cry. It flung its arms out and ran into the night.

Super Qwok followed and wished again that he had Raceboy's speed. He ran as fast as he could, his boots splattering through mud puddles. He wiped his eyes, always trying to keep the shadow of the creature in sight. Behind him he could hear footsteps, and knew that either Dr. Brick or Dr. Devious or both trailed him and their creature.

Raceboy also followed, but he was unable to use his super speed. Each time he tried he had to stop before he got sick all over the place. This put him, for the first time he could remember, in last place. He couldn't even keep up with Dr. Brick, who'd been swung around and beat against Dr. Devious.

Super Qwok stopped at the edge of the towering form of a grain elevator as it rose round and tall into the rainy night. Above him he could see the lone ladder that reached to the top, and on it, the figure of the creature climbing. He hesitated, unsure whether it would do any good to chase it up the grain elevator. After all, there was nowhere for the monster to go once it reached the top, and besides, the rain made the ladder dangerously slippery. As he looked up lightning illuminated the sky and he could see in that instant the creature step to the top. Standing atop a tall metal structure

during a lightning storm was not a good plan, he decided.

"Move, brat." Dr. Devious pushed him aside and began to climb after his creation. Dr. Brick arrived a moment later, panting and wheezing.

Super Qwok backed up, trying to see the creature on the sloping roof of the elevator. Raceboy met him just as he was able to make out the creature as it reached the peak of the grain elevator.

"Oh, there's a—" Raceboy said to no one in particular. In fact, both he and Super Qwok knew, having lived so close to the grain elevators for so long, that hawks nested atop the structures. He was interrupted by a shriek. A hawk exploded straight into the night sky, its form lost amid the storm clouds and rain. The creature's arms swirled, and it teetered.

"Noooo—" both boys yelled together as they saw it topple backwards and slide down the angled roof. The arms and legs reached for something, but the smooth surface had no purchase to slow its descent. The body pitched from the edge of the elevator and fell past Dr. Devious and Dr. Brick. Its landing was oddly silent except for the groan of a thunder strike rolling heavily in exclamation. The pitter-patter of rain remained.

Raceboy and Super Qwok approached. For once Super Qwok was able to move more quickly than Raceboy, and, ironically, he didn't even notice. At the top ledge of the elevator the pair of scientists stared down for a moment, yelled at one another, and began their descent on the ladder. They joined Raceboy and Super Qwok to stand over the creature. It lay still and was no longer breathing. The long fall had knocked its parts back to the death they had previously known.

The news media made a great spectacle of the ethical question of the experiment. Talking heads discussed the circumstances and the repercussions of an attempt to reanimate life. Editorials scolded the scientists with headlines like, "When Science Lacks Sense" and "Look How Far Science has Fallen." Major news magazines like *American News* dedicated entire issues to the subject. And Dr. Devious and Dr. Brick were criticized by everyone: college professors, medical doctors, churches of every denomination, public librarians, rural grain cooperatives, and numerous organizations, including the Society for Ethical Experimentation, who called the entire affair, "irresponsible and unfortunate."

One night, just before bedtime, Alex stared for the umpteenth time at the handwritten notes from 1814 that were recovered as evidence from Drs. Devious and Brick. Although Polidori had not named his professor in his notes, Bryan and Alex had used the Race-computer to do research, and they had a very good guess that literature knew his name, even if history did not. Because John William Polidori had finished his studies, and had gone on to become a doctor; in fact, he became the physician to George Gordon, Lord Byron. This, in turn, brought him to attend a very famous dinner party in 1816 with the poet Percy Bysshe Shelley and his even more famous wife, Mary Shelley. Of course, she wasn't more famous at that dinner party. She was a young sixteen-year-old girl.

It was only after that night that she began to write the story for which she would become known through the ages, eclipsing her husband's legacy; on that night she found the inspiration for her book *Frankenstein*.

"I can't believe Polidori told her," Alex said, waving the papers.

"It stands to reason," Bryan replied.

"It's just, well, it happened before. I worry that it will happen again."

"You've seen the news: same stories with new faces and new places."

"I know, but it seems so senseless to create something that can't be, that shouldn't be, that doesn't fit—"

"People do it all the time," Bryan said. "They act like they don't

know it, but every time people choose to be selfish, every time they choose to ignore the consequences of their actions, every time they fail to think about how their actions affect others, it's like they've created another creature and let it free in the world."

Alex thought about this. "I guess we see it all the time, don't we?"

"Every time the Race-alarm goes off."

Both boys looked expectantly at the small light that was hidden above the closet door. For once it stayed mute.

Bryan said, "I think he could have been happy as a landscaper."

Alex looked at the twisting scrawl on the paper. "I wonder," he murmured, and put the notes back in the evidence file.

THE MAGIC CAULDRON

"We're too late," said Super Qwok, looking down the street at the Halloween trick-or-treaters. Up the street children in costumes cried while holding empty trick-or-treat bags. The bottom of each bag still smoked from spell-fire burns. A shrill voice cackled in the distance.

"Not so fast," said Raceboy. "She hasn't escaped yet. Follow me in the Race-mobile." He activated a homing beacon before he zipped after the Wicked Witch's laughter.

At the end of the block Raceboy peered around the corner of the house. Sure enough, he could see the Wicked Witch with her three guard monkeys as she led them down a street. Each of the giant monkeys carried a large sack with them — presumably all of the candy they had stolen from the neighborhood kids. As they walked, the Wicked Witch waved her broom and in the next instant all of them, Witch and monkeys alike, disappeared.

Invisible or not, the Witch's monkey guards couldn't be absolutely quiet. They snorted and hooted as the Witch led them toward the edge of town.

Where is she going? Raceboy wondered. He knew the Wicked Witch had a secret hideout. Would she really lead him to it?

Maybe if he hadn't seen them disappear Raceboy wouldn't have been able to follow their trail. Since he had, it was easy to follow

the monkeys and the shrill-voiced witch. Her magic must have allowed her to still see the monkeys, because every once in a while her voice rang out and she swatted one or another of them for goofing around and a smack would echo. "Seamus!" she would snap, or "Amos!" she would roar, or "Remus!" she would chide.

The Witch and her monkeys led the still sneaking Raceboy down the road by the grain elevators and the railroad tracks. The road bent at a ninety-degree angle and led into the open country. Not far along the road they turned up a lone lane to a dilapidated barn. The barn door opened and clanged a couple of times while Raceboy hid in the ditch at the end of the lane and waited.

Moments later dust from the gravel road plumed near Raceboy, and he heard Super Qwok's voice say, "Is this it?"

That's when Raceboy realized Super Qwok had turned on the Race-mobile's cloaking device, so that he, too, had been as invisible as the Witch's magic spell.

"Yes," Raceboy said. "Program the Race-mobile to idle on autopilot until I signal for it. Leave it cloaked."

Super Qwok appeared when he stepped out of the cloaked Race-mobile. Gravel dust rose once again as the Race-mobile moved quietly down the road on autopilot.

"Surprise is our best weapon," said Raceboy. "We'll go in together." Although Raceboy could have raced up to the barn and gone in alone, he moved at regular speed with Super Qwok so the two arrived at the door at the same time.

The boys looked at one another, then Raceboy mouthed the count: "One, two, three... Go!"

He opened the door lightning fast, and Super Qwok barreled in. Raceboy followed.

Suddenly the ground fell away beneath his feet, and he found himself pulled tight against Super Qwok in a thick-roped net: a trap! The net swung gently back and forth above the dirt floor of the barn.

"Surprise!" cackled the Wicked Witch. Three monkey voices chorused with hoots of excitement.

The barn was remarkably empty for all the noise. That's because the Witch and her monkeys were still invisible. Both Raceboy and Super Qwok could see a very un-invisible giant cauldron in the middle of the floor of the barn. Its gray metal sides were coated with the ashes of countless fires. Near its lip were squiggly shapes: spell-runes. The cauldron rested on an eagle's nest of timber and branches which were smoking with the beginnings of a fire.

"I don't like the look of that," mumbled Super Qwok, and Raceboy had to agree with him. The cauldron was easily large enough for two superheroes to bathe, but it seemed unlikely that the Wicked Witch was interested in anything to do with soap.

Raceboy lit his laser-sword and cut the ropes. Both boys tumbled from the net to land in a heap on the ground. Raceboy was on his feet and moving full speed, laser-sword still in hand, except he wasn't sure where to move. His speed was useless without a visible target. As he spun around with his laser-sword extended there was a flash that he felt behind his eyes; it felt like lightning had just crashed into his brain. As the handle of his laser-sword slid from his fingers, the electric blue of the blade fizzled and disappeared. The handle hit the ground with a crack. Raceboy's body slumped and fell atop it.

Super Qwok saw his brother fall. He had also seen the flash like lightning from where it had erupted near the wall of the barn. The Witch! Her spell had stunned Raceboy; Super Qwok imagined that she must be targeting him next, which meant that he didn't have much time. He dove to the left and was proven correct as a spell blasted like white energy behind him in the exact place he had leapt from.

He rolled and felt his body crash against the feet of a monkey. The invisible creature let out a loud, "Oook!" Super Qwok grabbed hold of the monkey's leg and didn't let go. He had an idea that the Witch wouldn't blast him if there was a chance that she might hit one of her precious monkeys. Of course, there was also a chance that she wouldn't care and would blast them both to smithereens. Either way, the monkey was his best bet, and he knew it.

Raceboy groaned and tried to lift his head. It felt so heavy. He thought he felt a presence, a shadow-something small-flitter away from his cheek. His muscles strained to lift as he opened his eyes and realized that he was in a dream. He knew it was a dream because Super Qwok was flying around a barn, and Raceboy knew his brother didn't have the ability to fly.

No. That wasn't it, he realized as he tried to blink his bleary eyes. It *was* Super Qwok, that was true. And he was floating, but it looked more like Super Qwok was bouncing on the back of an invisible bronco in a rodeo: up he'd go as his head kicked back, then down with his head coming forward. Again and again, up and down.

Only when noise broke into his stumbling brain did Raceboy register what was going on. He recognized the voice of the Wicked Witch yell, "Get him off, Remus! I can't get a clear shot!"

Everything came back to Raceboy in that moment: the barn, the trap, the cauldron. Super Qwok needed his help! The Witch yelled again, "Amos, help him with that measly boy!" Raceboy followed the direction of the Witch's voice. There, against the wall—He was sure of it. There was an ever so slight ripple in the shadows of that spot.

Although his body felt every bit as heavy as his head, Raceboy burst at full speed up to his knees, took a step, then another. He caught his laser-sword and stuck it to his belt as he felt the world around him downshift into stillness, like a still-life landscape. His power allowed him to speed up so quickly that regular time ticked by hardly at all, or at least, so imperceptibly to him that it was like roaming through a hall of statues.

Within steps he was to the spot where the Wicked Witch had been, and he grabbed, catching hold of something, a garment, maybe a shoulder, and wrestling against it, feeling her limbs like gnarly branches in his grip and hearing her bellow and smelling something that he imagined was her breath though it reminded him of a ditch filled with green water, stagnant and putrid. He backed away but tried to turn her away when —

She was visible! Somehow Raceboy had broken the invisibility spell.

The Wicked Witch was visible, and she was furious.

It was a simple fact that neither Raceboy nor Super Qwok would ever hit an elderly woman. They had been raised the right way and respected their elders. However, there are moments in the life of a superhero that defy the acceptable rules of civility for polite company. These are the moments when manners must give way to survival, when politeness must take a backseat to the greater good, when being civil simply isn't going to cut it, when, in short, a witch who is about to cast a spell capable of turning you into a toad needs a good whack so the spell will miss. This was one of those times.

Raceboy punched the Wicked Witch in the stomach.

She exhaled with a *WHOOF* that proved his suspicion: her breath was the source of the unpleasant smell.

Fast again, Raceboy pulled his Race-cuffs from his utility belt and snapped them over the Witch's wrists.

His brother, meanwhile, did not have the advantage of speed.

Thanks to Raceboy, however, Super Qwok had regained something that for him was nearly as important: the ability to see the monkeys.

When Raceboy broke the Wicked Witch's spell of invisibility, not only was the Witch visible, but her three monkeys became visible as well. Super Qwok saw that both Seamus and Amos were trying to get close enough to wrench him off Remus. *Let them try,* he thought. With Raceboy grappling with the Witch, Super Qwok didn't need to play cowboy anymore. Instead he pushed hard on Remus's back, knocking the monkey off balance and onto the ground. As he stood on the ground, he caught both Seamus and Amos by the scruffs of their necks and brought the two skulls together with a solid crash. It was something like the crack Mom had taught him to break two eggs against one another but with more *oomph.* Both monkeys fell, splayed atop Remus, who let out a whimpering, "Ook."

Super Qwok saw that Raceboy had cuffed the Witch, but she was pointing at both boys and shouting, "Get them! Put them in the cauldron!" Both boys thought this was odd, since her monkeys were lying on the ground at Super Qwok's feet, unable to get a banana into the cauldron, let alone the superheroes.

That's when the entire inside of the barn broke loose.

Swarming shapes slid from crevices and shadows. They moved across the floor and chittered. Super Qwok stared. Had the witch cast a spell on blowing leaves? But the sound…No…Not leaves…Rats? An army of rats summoned by the witch? Then he noticed the black fabric, like an army of crumpled black handkerchiefs making their way across the floor. The chittering noises they made almost resembled words: "Getta, gedda, gat! Getta, gedda, gat!"

In an instant the swarm was upon him, and try as he might

ANDREW WINKEL

to kick them or pull them or shake them or smash them, there were too many. What were they? Witchlings. Tiny scraps of mud and fabric animated through the Witch's power, capable of following her every instruction. Dozens…Hundreds…Thousands! They were small, but they were innumerable. As he turned around to dislodge some, more took their place. Super Qwok slapped, but the Witchlings held on and chittered, "Downy, down-on, downer!" and like living clothing, began to swarm over his entire body and drag him to the ground.

He fought. He destroyed Witchlings, broke them to dust and scrap, but for every one he shattered, a dozen took their place. He found himself being carried, pulled, like a boy trapped in the tide, to a hill of Witchlings beside the cauldron, and they lifted him up to drop him into the cauldron right on his head.

"Ow," said Raceboy. "You've got a hard head."

Super Qwok rubbed his left ear. "Yours isn't exactly a pillow. How'd you get in here?"

"Same as you. About two seconds before you did. Witchlings."

They both looked up at the lip of the cauldron.

Super Qwok shook his head. "Well," he mused, "this could be worse."

Raceboy hopped a little. The fire in the wood outside was definitely making the cauldron hot, and the heat was working its way through the metal into the superheroes' boots. "How?" he demanded, and he puffed towards his feet in what was basically a useless attempt to cool off his toes.

Super Qwok said, "It could be full of water."

Raceboy sneered and said sarcastically, "Well, there's the cauldron half full!"

At another time he would have expected some comment on how clever this was, but Super Qwok only shrugged and said matter-of-factly, "It's probably harder for you to run in water is all."

"Why would I run? Where would I run? We're in a cauldron surrounded by thousands of Witchlings, three insane monkeys, and a witch who wants to cook us!"

Water splattered against the side of his face. He looked up, sputtering. One of the Witchlings peered over the lip of the cauldron, a bucket the size of a coffee mug in its hand. It chirped, "Wada-wata-wawa-wata."

"There's your water!" Raceboy spat at Super Qwok.

"I'm tipping this thing—" water splashed Super Qwok in the face, "—and you be ready to run—"

Raceboy wanted to say, "Huh?" but Super Qwok was already in motion, running to the left and leaning, then running back to the right and leaning. The cauldron wobbled first in one direction, then more steeply in the other direction. Super Qwok dashed and pushed, dashed and pushed. Just as the cauldron began to tip onto its side, Raceboy recognized Super Qwok's plan. He began to run.

There are still, in the parks of rare rural towns, giant barrels that spin when you run around inside them. Set atop wheels and rails, sometimes built into enclosures the size of a standard shed, these amusing inventions have mostly been done away with to protect children from the alarming combination of centrifugal force and gravity. Although Raceboy couldn't quite remember where he had played in one of these barrels—at a family reunion, or maybe at one of his soccer games—he knew that he had, at least once in his life, stood inside and run while the barrel spun faster and faster. Rolling the cauldron was exactly like running inside the barrel. With his augmented strength and hyper-speed he was able to set the cauldron rolling forward, and once he had the momentum it was easier to adjust the direction of the rolling cauldron by stepping left or right on the curved surface.

There was nowhere for Super Qwok to go to get out of Race-boy's way, so he simply lay down and was carried around and around like the car of a roller coaster traveling in loops and spirals. Raceboy stepped over him when he could manage it, stepped on him a few times when he couldn't. "Oof," said Super Qwok. And, "Ouch."

"No!" shrieked the Wicked Witch from somewhere ahead of them. "Don't let them get away! Don't let them—" her voice broke in a high-pitched exclamation. "Get away! Get away! Get out of the way!" and the cauldron rolled past a rolling witch who was visible for an instant—black robes, pointed-hat, Race-cuffs and all—on the barn's floor.

The door crashed open from the heavy cauldron and its devastating momentum.

"Not my cauldron!" the witch bellowed from behind. "Don't let them take my cauldron!"

It was too late for the monkeys or the Witchlings to stop them. Raceboy wheeled the cauldron down the lane and away from the Wicked Witch forever.

Without her cauldron, the Witch was never again able to create Witchlings, and the tiny helpers that she had fashioned were nothing more than temporary homunculi, who inevitably withered

into dust. With the loss of her cauldron, she lost a large part of her powers.

Some people claim that Raceboy and Super Qwok used the metal from that cauldron to fashion a new protective suit. They claim that the suit was impervious to magical assault and many other types of attacks. It's even said that Raceboy wore the suit before he was rescued by his and Bryan's friend, Logan, who had donned the suit to save him from yet another life-threatening plot of Dr. Devious. And that's how Logan became Knight-in-shining-armor-boy and began to help Raceboy and Super Qwok. Or so they say.

BLOBULOUS

Last Halloween, Bryan got loads of bubble gum: sticks of gum, and gum tape, and little pink nougats in twisty wrappers, and gum balls. He had scads and gads of gobs and blobs. Bryan loved his gum, but every time he chewed a piece, he swallowed it. Chomp, chomp, chomp, gulp.

Mom warned him, "Bryan, do not swallow your gum!"

The result was that Bryan didn't get to chew gum any more. Neither Mom nor Dad would let him.

"You'll turn into a big blob of gum, Bryan," Dad said.

Mom explained, "And as sweet as you are, there is such a thing as too sweet."

There was, however, another boy in the neighborhood whose mother did not stop him from chewing and eating all of the bubble gum in his trick-or-treat bag. This boy's name was Harold.

Oh, his mother thought she tried, but you must understand: she was one of *those* mothers. She said, "Now Harold, you shouldn't eat all that gum, dear. It's not good for you."

Chomp, chomp, chomp, gulp. Even though he'd heard his mother, Harold unwrapped, chewed, and swallowed every piece of gum in his Halloween trick-or-treat bag. All that gum slid down his throat and hung out in his stomach. He looked into his bag for another piece of gum. He was hungry for more gum. He loved

gum, and wanted to keep eating it.

He noticed with disappointment that his bubble gum was gone, but he did discover a can of pop in his trick-or-treat bag. It wasn't a brand he'd ever heard of before. The picture on the side looked like pink popcorn. Words beneath the picture declared, "Like a Cotton Candy Explosion in Your Mouth!"

"Harold," said his mother, "you shouldn't drink soda at this time of night."

Harold heard, but he didn't want to listen. He cracked open the sugary-sweet concoction and drained it into his mouth. He finished with a refreshing belch.

"Ahh," sighed Harold. "That was good." All he could think about, however, was that his gum was gone, and his soda pop was gone, and his—

Wait. What was that? A rumble. Was that an earthquake? No—It had come from inside his stomach!

The rumble struck again, this time more violently, and Harold's body shook left, then right, as though a roller coaster were blasting back and forth along the tracks of his guts. It was a chain reaction, and it moved through his body.

By this time the chemicals in his body were making mysterious noises, and Harold's thoughts weren't so clear. He turned and raced out of his house, disappearing into the night. Behind him, his mother's voice said, "Harold, you shouldn't go out after dark..."

The next morning when the sun rose, it did not find Harold. Harold had disappeared, swallowed up from inside by a giant, pink, sticky monster. An angry pink monster. The blob raged from within, filled with violent bubbles that oozed and popped across its surface in volcanic ranges of rage.

The monster could change like putty or clay. It lacked a human shape, unless it used what remnants of a mind remained to force a human shape upon it.

The boy Harold was forgotten in the creature that called itself Blobulous.

Blobulous brought new meaning to the term "sticky fingers." It used its sticky fingers to steal. It had an insatiable desire to take things, especially valuable things. It began to terrorize Clifton. Its monstrous form struck fear into the hearts of all who saw it.

Of course, it wasn't long before…

The Race-alarm went off. Raceboy and Super Qwok leapt into action, racing off to the scene of the crime: the Main Street Diner.

Raceboy turned the wheel of the Race-mobile and slid the car into a parking spot alongside the diner. Super Qwok pulled to a stop on the Qwok-cycle.

"Are you coming already?" Raceboy asked.

Super Qwok rolled his eyes and tried to hustle a bit faster. He knew there was no point trying to move as fast as Raceboy, but at the same time, he didn't want to miss out on any action.

Both boys approached the door of the diner. It opened, and out stepped Blobulous. The creature had to stoop to leave the diner, it was so tall. It had a vaguely man-like shape, walking on thick, gooey trunks. Its head was merged with its shoulders. It had ab-sorbed the money from the theft within limbs that on a human would be called arms. Two heavy money-bags filled with bills and loads of change hung at the ends of the limbs.

"We've caught you red-handed," Super Qwok declared, then noticed Blobulous didn't have hands. "Um. Oh, make that, um, red…armed? Red-limbed? Red-appendaged?" Raceboy elbowed him. Super Qwok finished, "Come with us peacefully, or we will take you by force, if necessary."

Blobulous laughed a thunderous laugh. "You can't stop me with your puny powers! I am Blobulous!"

Super Qwok stepped forward and swung one of his fists at the monster. Blobulous changed his shape, contorting his body to disappear where Super Qwok's blow should have struck. Instead of hitting the monster's body, Super Qwok found the momentum from his ferocious blow carrying him past Blobulous, who laughed and immediately punched the hero with his heavy, cash-filled limb. The blow sent Super Qwok spinning head-over-heel in a cartwheel.

Raceboy zoomed into action. He sped towards Blobulous, who changed its shape into an archway, letting Raceboy fly through its center to pass onto the other side.

By this time Super Qwok was ready to attack again. Super Qwok punched Blobulous. This time the creature did not change shape; instead it let the blow strike home. Super Qwok's fist rammed straight into the gelatinous shape and stuck fast.

"My fist!" exclaimed Super Qwok.

Blobulous chuckled while Super Qwok's fist was pulled deeper into Blobulous's slimy, slurpy body.

"Help me, Raceboy!" Super Qwok shouted. "I'm being absorbed!"

Blobulous writhed and wriggled with laughter as Super Qwok sank deeper into the giant pink shape. Raceboy did not dare to strike Blobulous. Rather he pulled on Super Qwok's leg in what became a desperate tug of war for his brother. Even Super Qwok's enormous strength and Raceboy's speed could not stop the absorption. At last there was a bubbling pop, and Super Qwok was entirely surrounded within the form of Blobulous. The superhero could be seen inside, trapped. It was as if Blobulous was a suit which Super Qwok was wearing, except that the wearer had no control of what the suit was doing.

Now Raceboy had a problem. He had no way to attack Blobu-lous, unless he wanted to harm Super Qwok as well.

He picked up a stick and swung it. Immediately after he hit the gelatin form of Blobulous, the creature sucked the stick into his amoeba shape. This gave Raceboy an idea.

Maybe he couldn't hurt Blobulous himself. Maybe he had to trick the villain.

Raceboy pulled his laser-sword from his utility belt. The energy blade crackled with bright blue fire. He knew that he was playing a desperate game for Super Qwok's life. If he actually hit Blobulous, the fiery sword could cut Super Qwok as well. He had to trick Blobulous into believing that he really was going to fight him with the laser-sword so the villain wouldn't expect what was going to happen next.

Raceboy swung his laser-sword to the left. Blobulous slid to the opposite side. Raceboy swung the laser-sword right. Blobulous slid aside again. Raceboy moved in a slow feint. Blobulous curled forth two pseudopods and wrapped them around Raceboy's laser-sword, snatching it away and shutting it off.

"Let me take that from you," it blurbled in its bubbling voice. Raceboy sped backwards out of Blobulous's reach and watched as the laser-sword was absorbed in the giant pink shape.

Blobulous had fallen for his plan!

Super Qwok didn't need to have Raceboy tell him what the plan was. All he had to do was see the laser-sword come within his reach to know he was meant to use it in the one place Blobulous couldn't protect himself from: his own inside!

Super Qwok turned on the laser-sword with a smoking crackle. Blobulous's eyes suddenly grew large. It may have realized the mistake it had made. With a hissing, squealing of laser-sword fury, Super Qwok spun in a circle, opening Blobulous with the energy blade.

Raceboy helped pull his brother from the gelatin.

Blobulous roared in rage. It collected itself together and reformed from the smoking, oozing, charred gobs. In its anger, it grew larger and larger. The bubble gum inside took in air and grew, grew, and grew until Blobulous towered above the street, a vast bubble an entire city block in height. And all the while it burbled with rage.

Both Raceboy and Super Qwok backed up, staying ahead of the rapidly growing monster.

"Super Qwok!" Raceboy called, and Super Qwok caught the shape his brother had tossed. He didn't need to look at it to know what it was; the shape and texture were enough: a Speederang.

Super Qwok, still backing up, cocked his arm back and threw,

sending the Speederang straight at the spheroid shape of Blobulous. The blue-black V spun so rapidly that it appeared to be a
spinning O as it punctured the side of the raging blob.

With a giant *POP* Blobulous exploded, raining pink, gooey gum
over Main Street, the diner, the concrete flower pots, the Race-
mobile, Super Qwok, and Raceboy. Throughout the entire town,
in fact, tiny bits and pieces of sticky bubble gum rained down,
sticking to roofs and messing up landscaping.

Harold lay stunned on the sidewalk, pink as a newborn. He was
the only thing in a four block radius that was not covered with
gum. Blobulous was never seen again.

Raceboy and Super Qwok returned home to get cleaned up.

Some time later Bryan realized that he no longer had the urge
to swallow gum when he chewed it. Looking back, he never could
decide if his taste buds had changed, or if he had just gotten wiser,
or if he had been traumatized by his stay inside a gum monster. It
really didn't matter which. "Anymore," he explained to Alex, "it
just tastes too sweet."

THE BIRTHDAY BANDIT STRIKES— AGAIN!

Raceboy and Super Qwok traveled in a camel-mobile to the desert, where they found a city of tents and a group of people who gave away Christmas presents on Valentine's Day.

"What are you doing?" asked Super Qwok.

"Giving Christmas presents," answered the people.

"But it's Valentine's Day!" Raceboy explained. "Most people give valentines on Valentine's Day."

The people explained, "No, here we do things differently. But something has happened. Our Valentine's Day presents have been stolen! Someone has taken them, and we think it was the Birthday Bandit."

"The Birthday Bandit!" said Super Qwok and Raceboy. "We captured him a long time ago. Why would he come here?"

Raceboy asked, "What sorts of presents do you give each other?"

"Oh," explained an elderly man with a long gray beard, "we give magic things to each other."

"Magic?" Super Qwok looked from the old man to the rest of the people to see if anyone was laughing. No one was.

"That's right," the man explained. "All of our Valentine's Day gifts have magical powers."

"That explains it!" said Super Qwok. "That's why the Birthday Bandit would travel all the way here. He wants those gifts. If he

could collect all your magic items, he could put them together to create a powerful magical artifact."

People gasped or swore. Another man said, "That's true! And we've never thought about that before. Our ancient cult has always practiced the mystery of giving magic gifts on Valentine's Day. In this way we are able to share our magic with one another. We never could have imagined such a terrible plan as to steal all of the magic items and use their magic together."

Super Qwok looked at Raceboy. Each boy knew that he must stop the Birthday Bandit before it was too late.

Not only had Raceboy and Super Qwok invented the camel-mobile, but they had also created an elephant-mobile. This latter invention was very clever because when the door was closed it looked just like a real elephant. The trunk was a periscope that could see far and sense magic artifacts.

Raceboy and Super Qwok began to travel the countryside in their elephant-mobile, using its sensors to check for magical items. Sniff, sniff here. Sniff, sniff there. Nothing. They did not find any hint of magic.

"Where could the magic items be?" asked Super Qwok.

"They've got to be somewhere," Raceboy said. "I can't imagine that the Birthday Bandit stole all those gifts and got very far."

All of the sudden both boys' wrist receivers sounded. Raceboy activated his wrist receiver and said, "What's going on, Race-computer?"

BEEP-BEEP-DIP-DIP-DIP-DIP, the Race-computer chirped. It explained, "I have detected a mysterious seismic disturbance 1.4 miles from where you are currently traveling in the senso-meter elephant."

Raceboy said, "We've got to check that out! A strange seismic disturbance? Maybe we're looking in the wrong spot."

Following the Race-computer's coordinates, the boys traveled across the land in the elephant-mobile. When they arrived at the empty place, the trunk of the elephant brushed the ground. *BUP…BUP…BUP BUP-BUP-BUP BUPBUPBUP.* Sure enough, the sensor was sensing magical items. They discovered, as they looked through the trunk-periscope, that there was a section of the ground that appeared to have been dug up very recently.

Super Qwok and Raceboy decided to do some quick digging of their own. Between Super Qwok's muscles and Raceboy's speed they could dig very quickly indeed. Raceboy took a shovel and left the elephant-mobile while Super Qwok hurried after.

The boys stood near the recently disturbed dirt and began to dig and dig and dig. As they dug deeper the elephant began to *BUP* louder and faster as it began to sense more and more magical artifacts. The deeper the boys dug, the wider the circle, until suddenly Raceboy's shovel clanged against metal.

They continued to dig the metal out, and discovered that it was the roof of a mysterious building, a building that had been buried underground.

Dropping his shovel, Raceboy lit his laser-sword and used it to trace a square on the ceiling of the building. The metal slowly turned orange in strips of fire as he melted the seams to create an opening.

Once the square was drawn, Super Qwok punched the door open, and the metal fell into the room. From within was a mysterious blue glow.

Super Qwok and Raceboy jumped into the room, landing on their feet. Surrounding them were all sorts of magical devices: boots and lamps and necklaces and crowns, rings, wands, and everything you could imagine that was magic.

The boys looked for the Birthday Bandit, but he was nowhere.

As they looked above to the hole they'd cut to break in, they saw a face looking down. A face that laughed. "Whoo-hoo, ha, ha, ha! I have you now!" it said.

Without warning the room moved. Both boys fell. The giant building rattled and shook and began to rise into the sky.

"Oh, no!" said Super Qwok. "We're being launched in a rocket into space!"

"We have to do something and quick!" Raceboy urged. If that rocket-powered magical-device-laden craft flew into space, they would be able to float, sure, in the weightlessness of space, but they also wouldn't have any air to breath. That would be a terrible problem, even for superheroes.

The building rumbled upwards.

"What are we going to do, Raceboy?"

"Well, we could just get out of here and jump."

Super Qwok said, "I'm powerful, but I can't really bounce. Bouncing isn't one of my powers."

"I know, but I have the Race-parachute that's built into my uniform. You know that!"

"Yes, and I have my parachute, too, but that doesn't stop the problem of all these magic items. We have to figure out how to get this craft back to the ground with the magic items."

"Super Qwok, we've got to move fast. Let's just jump out!"

"We can't leave the magic items." Super Qwok crossed his arms.

There was a moment's pause as the two heroes stared at one another. The room or ship or whatever it was that they were in continued to rise higher and higher. Then something clicked and Raceboy said, "Wait! What are we thinking? These are magic items! Certainly with all the rings and vases and chests and crowns there has to be some sort of bag, a magic bag!"

Super Qwok caught on. "Like in fairy tales!"

Raceboy continued, his excited voice gaining energy, "A magic bag that you can put stuff in, and it can hold all of the things that you put into it."

"Yeah! Let's look."

They moved around the room, pushing through piles of magic items. It didn't take them long to find a bag; it was roughly the size of a garbage bag. It was made of a velvet cloth and was a bluish color (because, if you remember, all of the magic items were a bluish color).

Super Qwok took it. "I'll hold the bag. Raceboy, you go into Race-mode and grab everything and put it inside the bag."

Raceboy cleaned faster than he'd ever cleaned before. He raced around the room picking up, throwing and scooping. You've never seen a room get cleaned as fast as Raceboy cleaned that room of magic items. He put all of the items into the bag.

You might imagine that Super Qwok would have moved around a little and tried to help. But he didn't. He was too worried about how fast Raceboy was going, because Raceboy was going so fast that Super Qwok couldn't even see him. Sometimes he'd see a hint of color as Raceboy went back and forth and held something bluish and glowing in his arms. It happened so quickly that before Super Qwok expected it, the room was clean and the bag had all of the items in it.

You might also think that the bag would have gotten bigger, since Raceboy had just stuffed a room's worth of magic items into a bag the size of your standard kitchen garbage bag. Super Qwok thought that, despite his great strength, he wouldn't be able to lift a bag, even a magical bag that had been stuffed with so many magic items. So he was surprised when he pulled the tie-strings on the bag and lifted and discovered that the bag didn't weigh anything at all; it was like carrying an empty bag. "Let's go," he told Raceboy.

They both looked up at the hole in the ceiling and jumped as hard as they could. Super Qwok's leap took him clear of the flying vessel; Raceboy landed on the roof and skipped off after Super Qwok.

Both heroes pulled the cords to their parachutes and floated down, down through the clouds. Super Qwok held onto the bag. Finally they landed on the ground near one another within sight of their elephant-mobile and the crater that had been the storage area of the magic items.

Both boys were folding their parachutes when an insidious voice near Raceboy said, "I'll take this!"

Before either Raceboy or Super Qwok knew what was happening, the bag of magic items, which they had left on the ground while they were rolling their chutes, was in the hands of the Birthday Bandit. Except he was no longer in his Birthday Bandit guise. He wore his customary mad scientist outfit once again: Dr. Brick.

Rocks all around began to crunch and grind and as the boys looked, they discovered that they were surrounded by an army of golems. Do you know what a golem is? It's a creature that is shaped like a man but is made from dirt or clay. And sometimes it can be made out of rock. Dr. Brick, with his scientific knowledge, had created a process to turn plain old dirt and rocks into soldiers to follow his every command. These creatures were completely silent, completely faceless, and completely obedient to his will.

Raceboy and Super Qwok stood back-to-back, completely surrounded by the creatures.

"Any ideas?" Raceboy asked.

Super Qwok answered, "I haven't quite put my parachute away."

Raceboy said, "Um, yeah. I was thinking more about the army of dirt creatures that is surrounding us."

"So was I," replied Super Qwok. "I think you'd better use your jet-pack."

There are times when one brother will question the other, maybe doubt him. This was not one of those times. Raceboy ignited his jet-pack and shot straight upwards just as the first of the golems charged at him.

Super Qwok yanked on his parachute and ran straight by the golem, dragging the parachute so it caught the golem like a rock in a sling. Then yanking with all of his might, he began to swing the parachute around and around in large circles. The weight of the golem within the parachute caused it to spin with such force that when Super Qwok directed the parachute straight into another golem, it was shattered into dust from the impact.

Overhead Raceboy let out a whoop and was thankful he wasn't

on the ground trying to jump over the swinging parachute lines. He watched the scene below as Super Qwok smashed through the army with his parachute mallet. Around and around he swung the loaded parachute, cutting through the line of golems like the blade of a lawnmower. If the golem in his parachute was reduced to small fragments or dust, he simply swept up another of the creatures and began the process all over again.

Raceboy buzzed down with his jet-pack to swoop low over the creatures. As he did they lifted arms and charged after him. He shifted his direction and led them straight at the spinning parachute. Then he pulled above the spinning parachute and heard the crash and crunch of the golems that were no longer following him. Again and again he did this, helping Super Qwok.

As he prepared to do another dive and lure the creatures against his brother he saw a sight that stopped him cold—not literally, of course. Dr. Brick had concluded that his army was no match for Super Qwok, and he was holding a giant laser cannon. He set the cannon on his shoulder and aimed it straight at Super Qwok.

It's one thing to be on the ground and have the power of super speed. It's quite another to be flying a jet-pack and know that you can only move as fast as the contraption strapped to your back. Raceboy needed to dive straight and fast if he was going to sweep Dr. Brick off his feet before he could shoot Super Qwok.

Raceboy leaned into his dive, pushed his jet-pack as fast as it would go, and held his arms out. But he was too late. There was a startling flash as the laser blasted purple lightning. Raceboy struck Dr. Brick's waist, the gun slipped, and the lightning first blasted upwards then stopped. Raceboy clutched the villain tightly. He turned to stare at Super Qwok, at where Super Qwok should have been. All he could see was a rocky explosion.

"No!" he screamed from the air as pebbles and bits of dirt from the explosion below bit into his thigh and the backs of his legs. Raceboy careened right and lifted higher, feeling his breath coming in short bursts as he looked again for Super Qwok. Dr. Brick shouted and ranted, trying to swing free from Raceboy, who ignored him and looked at the cloud of dust and saw a hint of white from Super Qwok's costume.

The dust cleared and Raceboy could see now. Super Qwok stood holding strings, but his parachute was nowhere; it was obliterated. Spread out in front of him was a triangle of gravel and dirt where Dr. Brick's laser cannon had blasted straight into the parachute weighted with golem pieces, spreading the shrapnel in a triangular debris field that would have killed the scientist if Raceboy had not yanked him out of the way in the nick of time.

Before the raging scientist could free himself, Raceboy dropped him straight into Super Qwok's arms. Then Raceboy landed, took the remaining parachute rope, and ran circles around Dr. Brick until he was wrapped up like fly in a spider's web.

The boys collected the bag full of magic items and returned the bound Dr. Brick to the village of the people who give Christmas gifts for Valentine's Day.

The people gathered to confront the thief, and the elderly man gasped and said, "Dimitri Stonemason! You have returned after all these years! But why?"

"Wait," said Super Qwok. "This is the Birthday Bandit, also known as Dr. Brick. You know him?"

"Know him," laughed the man, though his laughter was one of sorrow. "Of course we know him. He once lived among us, shared our traditions, gave magical Christmas gifts in February as do we all."

"Not all," growled Dr. Brick. "You skipped me one year, remember? Valentine's Day came, and no gift for Dimitri! No one else cared. Everyone running around with their invisibility cloaks or their flying amulets, and poor Dimitri left out, ignored. I swore then that I would do everything in my power to destroy this ridiculous practice so that no other child had to feel the sorrow of being left out. I studied for years to perfect my skills of science until the day when I could steal all of your magic items and blast them far off into the sky where you would never be able to pass them on again!"

The crowd of people hissed and booed. Rock clods rained down and struck Dr. Brick, who did not bow his head, but instead took the blows with a ferocious glare at the elder.

The voice of the elder was whisper soft and frail. "All this because of an accidental oversight? For all these years you've lived with such anger and hatred? An entire life, so full of potential, wasted on retribution..." He shook his head sadly.

"I've waited for thirty years for revenge," sneered Dr. Brick. "I will wait thirty more if need be."

Later, at a special ceremony, the elder presented Raceboy and Super Qwok with gifts of appreciation for their help. To Raceboy he gave seven-league boots. These powerful boots allowed Raceboy to leap seven leagues with each step. To Super Qwok he gave a magic bag of holding. This was similar to, but not identical to, the one the boys had used to save the magic items. Super Qwok folded it with great care and tucked it into a pouch on his belt.

This was the end of the Birthday Bandit, but not the end of Dr. Brick. Both boys knew he would be back.

DINO STICK-UP

Anyone who has ever visited the Field Museum of Natural History in Chicago knows *There will be dinosaurs!* Both Alex and Bryan were fascinated by dinosaurs. But it was Alex especially who would seek out books about dinos, memorizing their bones structures, or unique characteristics, or their Brobdingnagian names (yes, Brobdingnagian means "huge" and "gargantuan" as in pachycephalosaurus, archaeopteryx, or carcharodontosaurus). If anyone asked what Alex was going to be when he grew up, the list—though it was a long one—always began with "Paleontologist."

While Bryan didn't have his brother's zest for dinosaurs, he did like monsters. And there was nothing so monstrous as giant lumbering reptiles from the world's primeval past.

"At least we don't need to worry about villains today," Alex told Bryan as Dad parked the family van near Soldier Field.

"Yeah," smiled Bryan. "We'll be on superhero vacation."

Entering the museum from the south entrance, the first thing the boys could see, aside from the lines to get in, was the lunging shape of a tyrannosaurus rex skeleton.

Mom pushed Katherine's stroller to an elevator while Dad held Alex and Bryan's hands and followed. "I want you two to stay close," he explained. "There are a lot of people here and it would be very easy to get lost."

Neither boy said anything. They were too busy looking at the exhibits lining the vast central hall of the museum: towering totem poles, elephants frozen forever.

"What smells hot?" Alex asked.

Dad sniffed and directed the boys to a freezer-sized machine. "Oh, it's a Mold-A-Rama. They have these at the zoo. It's a machine that molds plastic. That's why it smells hot here."

"It makes a tyrannosaurus. Can we get one, Dad?" Bryan said. "It's only one dollar and fifty cents."

"No, we're not buying Mold-A-Rama. Besides, we just got here."

On their way to the second floor entrance to the hall of dinosaurs, the family passed the science lab where the museum's scientists cleaned fossils for preservation. Within the glass-walled lab, white-coated workers prepared the museum's specimens; the public could watch them work through the windows. Alex was fascinated. The scientist's hands worked back and forth between an unlabeled brown jar and a fossilized dinosaur bone, brushing yellow goop over the surface.

"I think he's cleaning it," Dad said, comparing the scientist's work to a display profiling the steps scientists followed as they handled fossils.

Alex had his nose against the glass when he heard Bryan inhale sharply and whisper, "Don't look now, but that's Dr. Devious."

Immediately Alex looked up at the scientist's face.

"I told you, 'Don't look now'!" Bryan muttered.

Dr. Devious continued coating the bone with the yellow goo. He did not acknowledge the two boys peering through the glass that surrounded his lab. He showed no awareness that he was a museum exhibit and that everything he did was observed by passersby.

As they walked away, Bryan said, "What is he doing here?"

Alex turned and looked back. "He's working with the bones." He hesitated. "Maybe he's finally turned good?"

"Ha!" Bryan countered. "If he's here, there's trouble. We need to be ready."

Entering the Evolving Planet exhibit, the family passed through the ages from single-celled life forms until they were surrounded by more recognizable skeletons and drawings of fish.

"Wow, look at the sharp-edged teeth on this one!" Dad said, but Bryan didn't hear him. He was staring at a spiny dino within a glass display case that was being serviced by another scientist. And this one was none other than —

"Dr. Brick!" Alex blanched.

The boys looked at one another.

Dr. Brick carefully brushed goo onto the skeleton. Like Dr. Devious, he seemed oblivious to the spectators watching him.

"Both of them together here … This can't be good," Bryan said.

"And I was looking forward to seeing dinosaurs," Alex moaned. "I can hardly wait to see what we'll find in the next room."

Guarding the entrance to a wide, brightly lit hall was a pair of raptors: one a skeleton, its partner an artist's life-size model complete with staring reptilian eyes.

"Yikes," said Mom, leaning over the handles of Katherine's stroller. "It even looks hungry."

Murals lined the upper wall of the room, portraying long-necked dinosaurs munching grasses in lakes, bat-winged pterosaurs soaring through the skies, and the ever-popular face-off between a roaring tyrannosaurus and a triceratops.

Behind a rail a large apatosaurus dominated the room. Against it, on a ladder facing the long neck of the apatosaurus, a jump-suited workman dusted the bones.

"Oh, no," said Bryan. "He's not dusting it."

Alex looked closer. Bryan was right. The workman was not dusting. He was coating the skeleton with something gooey. He had a baseball cap on his head, but they couldn't make out his face because his back was to the boys. They watched him finish all of the bones he could reach.

"It's probably just a coincidence," Alex said.

Bryan shook his head. "No, I don't think so."

The workman descended his ladder and turned around.

This time, neither boy gasped in surprise. Mr. Mischief grinned his bubbly, effusive grin at the world, as though laughing at a joke only he had heard. His vision passed over the whole Winkel family and all of the other families in the hall.

"What are we going to do?" Alex asked.

Dad overheard him. "Don't tell me you're bored already!"

Alex snorted. "Bored? Hardly."

"Do you feel all right?" Mom asked. "You look sick."

Alex watched Mr. Mischief fold his ladder and climb over the railing, whistling as he departed. "No, I'm fine. Just all the excitement, I suppose," though there was nothing excited in his voice.

While Mom, Dad, and Katherine stared at a Stegosaurus skeleton, Bryan whispered, "What are we going to do? Dr. Devious, Dr. Brick, and Mr. Mischief are all here! And they're all putting goo on the dinosaur bones. We have to do something!"

"We can't act yet without revealing our identities," Alex grumbled. "But at least we know to expect something. We'll just watch for it."

The tour for the Egyptian exhibit began at 11:00. Dad explained, "We'll go through Egypt, then it will be lunch time." He pushed Katherine in the stroller and looked at his watch. Mom held Alex and Bryan's hands and tried to keep up as Dad turned and bumped Katherine down the wide marble steps. Dad reached the main floor and turned to watch Mom and the boys when a scraping, clattering sound rattled from the stairway behind them. The boys could see Dad's face transform: his smile melted like candle wax while his squinting eyes grew wide like rising flames. The color in his face drained.

Mom followed his look. She screamed. A giant dinosaur skeleton shaped like a tank clattered down the stairs, racing from the upstairs exhibit to the main hall. It made no noise except for the crashing of its bones as they struck marble. Mom yanked both boys out of the way of the dinosaur's three sharp horns. As they fell, Alex whispered to Bryan, "This is it! Grab on."

Bryan snagged an anklebone. Alex grabbed a leg bone. The two boys slid along the ground as the skeleton pounded the rest of the way down the stairs, then headed for the south exit.

"Triceratops," Alex explained to Bryan as they were pulled down the main hall. "From the Cretaceous period."

Behind them, the boys could see both Mom and Dad's looks of horror and helplessness as they watched their boys get further away in the claws of a prehistoric skeleton.

One thing both Alex and Bryan realized was how much more efficient it was to travel through the crowded hall of a museum when you are a walking triceratops skeleton. Where before they had weaved their way through people and tried to squeeze in for a look, now their path was empty as people yelled and raced to get out of the way of the three sharp horns.

The triceratops skeleton flipped aside the railings that had once directed the lines of entrants queuing up for admission, then shattered the glass door frames and broke free of the Field Museum of Natural History to stand in the daylight facing Soldier field. The lawn was filled with people who, upon seeing the walking dinosaur skeleton, stopped and let the image sink in before turning to run with a shriek.

Both boys let go and rolled away from the creature. It walked down the steps and stood on the lawn, then froze. Almost immediately a second dino skeleton came through the broken entrance to join it. This skeleton was far smaller than the triceratops; it was short and squat, with a battering-ram head and a thick collarbone.

"Bradysaurus," Alex said. "Permian."

The bradysaurus was followed by a third skeleton, also smaller than the triceratops, but with a wicked set of sharp teeth and long, lethal spines on its back. All of the skeletons stopped beside one another and became still.

"Dimetrodon. Also Permian," Raceboy said. "It's like they're parking."

Bryan scowled and looked at his costumed brother. "You could have warned me that we were changing into our superhero costumes."

Raceboy raised an eyebrow. "We just hung onto a triceratops skeleton that broke through the museum's door! If that's not a cry for Raceboy and Super Qwok, I don't know what is! Hurry, there's some bushes over there, along the museum wall."

Rolling his eyes and grumbling under his breath, Bryan wiggled between the bushes and the wall.

The lawn filled with more skeletons from the museum's exhibits. Not all of them were dinosaurs, however. Some were fearsome mammals and there was even a terror bird, nearly six feet tall and with a viciously sharp beak. Three by three they came from the broken door and lined up on the lawn.

Once they stopped, people started to get comfortable with the skeletons, perhaps imagining it to be some kind of museum ploy to drum up business. A couple boys with skater shoes and baggy t-shirts touched the bones and laughed. A woman with black braids took a picture of them with her cell phone.

Each new wave of skeletons would send the people scurrying, but as soon as the skeletons went motionless, the people would return. It was like watching flies around a flyswatter at a family reunion.

The final three skeletons to leave the museum through the broken door were the largest to assemble:

"Mastadon," said Raceboy. "Tyrannosaurus rex, and apatosaurus."

"I know already!" Super Qwok said with a frown while tucking in his shirt. I was in the darn exhibit with you!"

"You have a twig in your hair," Raceboy pointed out.

Super Qwok ran a gloved hand over his head.

Atop the skeletons, riding triumphant, were the very three villains

Alex and Bryan had seen in the Evolving Planet exhibit. Dr. Brick rode the mastodon, Mr. Mischief rode the apatosaurus, and Dr. Devious rode the tyrannosaurus rex. Each of the villains carried a box-like device with knobs, sliders, and a single long metal antenna.

Mr. Mischief cackled. "Remote controlled glue! You really are as ingenious as you claim to be!" He punched a switch on his gizmo and the tail of his apatosaurus curled to the side like a whip.

"Yes," explained Dr. Devious. "Yes, I am. Though to be quite fair, Dr. Brick's polymer experiments to create golems were my inspiration." He inhaled sharply and pointed, "Now, gentlemen, let us take control of the city. It is time to conquer the Sears Tower!"

Mr. Mischief snickered. Dr. Brick smiled. Then Raceboy stepped from the edge of the building. Super Qwok followed his lead and tried to pose heroically. Raceboy yelled, "It isn't called the Sears Tower anymore, Devious!"

"Gak!" Devious choked. "You two! Here?" He bowed his head slightly, as though performing some rapid mental math. Then he recovered. "Of course it's still called the Sears Tower. It will always be the Sears Tower! What do you call it?" he asked Dr. Brick.

Dr. Brick shrugged. "The Sears Tower."

"You?" Dr. Devious looked at Mr. Mischief.

"It's the Sears Tower, of course."

Smugly, Dr. Devious nodded at the superheroes. "There, you see? Sears Tower. It's just the difference in our generations. You call it what you want, we'll call it the Sears Tower."

Super Qwok cracked his knuckles. "I call it 'time to crunch some bones.'"

"No!" Raceboy grabbed Super Qwok's glove. "Those are fossils from the Earth's prehistoric past! They're irreplaceable."

"I know one bone, at least, that's not original. I read the signs.

The original t-rex skull is up on the second story. This one," he pointed at Dr. Devious, "is a cast." He bounded straight at Devious's t-rex skeleton, leapt, cocked his arm, and delivered a resounding blow to the center of its snout. The plaster skull shattered to shards and dust with an anticlimactic puff.

"Gak!" Dr. Devious yelped a second time.

"Like a headless chicken," Super Qwok mused as he landed, surrounded by the cloud of his destruction. That was the exact moment the whip-like tail of the apatosaurus smashed into his stomach and spun him down the stairs like a Slinky in Race-mode. Super Qwok twisted and somersaulted until he was able to get his feet braced to stop. Then he bent his knees and prepared to take a power leap straight at Mr. Mischief and the apatosaurus.

Raceboy appeared at his side and caught his shoulder. "Wait. We need to plan. If we go in swinging now, we'll cause more senseless damage. We need to take out their remote controls."

All three villains charged down the stairs. The mastodon lowered its curved tusks; the apatosaurus leveled its head; the t-rex wobbled uncertainly without the weight of its cast skull.

Raceboy went into Race-mode and danced onto the apatosaurus's head, then raced along its vertebrate like a tightrope walker. As he neared the still-smiling, still-confident Mr. Mischief, he unhooked his laser-sword from his belt, activated the flashing blade, then jammed it into the remote control. Raceboy shifted from Race-mode long enough to watch Mr. Mischief's face realize what just happened. The pleasant smile became an uncertain smirk. The curved eyebrows became lines of confusion. The lips curled in an angry pucker. And finally he yelled, "Hey, that—What—But—" as his skeleton mount stopped moving.

Super Qwok waited for Dr. Brick to reach him on the mastodon, then he stepped on one of the tusks and jumped. This time he brought a powerful punch straight into the remote control unit. There was a sizzle and a pop as Dr. Brick's remote died. "No!" roared the mad scientist. The mastodon stopped so abruptly that it toppled forward on the stairs, the bones of the body rolling over its tusks and scattering both Dr. Brick and Super Qwok.

Super Qwok lay on his back a moment and stared at the sky. He grumbled, "I hate these stairs," before he grabbed the still stunned Dr. Brick and drug him by the collar of his lab coat back up the stairs.

Raceboy, meanwhile, yanked Devious's t-rex by the tail. The skeleton stopped. "Face it, Devious! You're through! You've only got one remote control unit left."

Devious smirked. "Actually, the glue may be set at different frequencies, but my controller unit can transmit over them all, so —"

Devious smacked his remote control and every skeleton on the lawn snapped to attention. Then, collectively, as a single army marching in lock step, they began to close in on Raceboy and Super Qwok.

"Yikes," said Super Qwok. "That sort of backfired."

"Not if I can help it," Raceboy said and shifted to Race-mode. The world paused. He leapt at Dr. Devious.

The mad scientist was still smirking. He did not look uncertain. Raceboy noted that there was no fear on Dr. Devious's face, and as he rose through the air with his hands outstretched, he wondered: why is Devious so confident? There is nothing between us to stop me from taking his remote and destroying it?

That was the last thing Raceboy thought before everything went black.

Here is what Super Qwok saw:

Raceboy said, "Not if I can help it!" and disappeared. Immediately a flash of lightning erupted from Dr. Devious and, for the briefest of instants, it was possible to see the lightning rotate around Devious in a sphere. Raceboy appeared and bumped away from the t-rex, his body rolling over the museum's stairs as slack as a rag doll.

Smoke rose from Raceboy as he lay on the steps.

Super Qwok let go of Dr. Brick and ran to his brother. He knelt at Raceboy's side and felt his cheek. Raceboy was still breathing.

Dr. Devious laughed triumphantly. "Foolish, foolish boy! I conceived of a shield of glue, but when that failed, I conceived of a shield of electricity! A kinetic shield capable of stopping anything that moves quickly! Only the slow-moving object can pass through it, so I am fully protected from every Super Qwok and especially Raceboy attack! You will not be able to defeat me!"

Dr. Brick scrambled up the stairs and pulled himself onto the t-rex back with Dr. Devious. Mr. Mischief joined him. Dr. Devious adjusted the shield, opened it, enlarged it, until the three rode together inside it. Now that he knew to look for it, Super Qwok could see the faint crackle of its edges around the villains, almost like the film of a soap bubble.

A rush of air flew over his head and he saw the sharp edge of a beak. The terror bird. Super Qwok looked around and realized that the skeletons were still attacking.

"You knocked out the wrong brother," he growled and punched the terror bird's skull straight off its neck. Then he took hold of the neck and flipped the entire terror bird at Dr. Devious. The kinetic shield flashed lightning again and the bones from the fossil skeleton scattered in a pile beneath the scientist.

"I'm not," said Super Qwok as he flipped over the spines of the dimetrodon and grabbed the horns of an Irish deer skull, "going to," he leapt again, spun the entire deer skeleton like a discuss and pitched it at Dr. Devious, "try saving the bones," the kinetic shield blasted the bones, "for science."

The pile of bones surrounding Dr. Devious, Dr. Brick, and Mr. Mischief grew as Super Qwok dismantled the skeletons one-by-one against Dr. Devious's kinetic shield. After the terror bird and the Irish deer, Super Qwok hurled a stegosaurus, a giant ground sloth, a short faced bear, the bradysaurus, and finally the dimetrodon. Atop his headless t-rex skeleton, Dr. Devious sat enthroned upon a pile of bones.

"There," said Super Qwok, and he brushed his gloved hands together. "Your move, Devious."

To Super Qwok's surprise, Dr. Devious laughed. "You have no comprehension of the power of my glue. Combined with the kinetic shield, I am unstoppable! I will take over the Sears Tower, and with it, this city. No one — not you, not your zippy brother — can stop me!" Dr. Devious pulled his lab coat from his shoulders and revealed a black nylon suit with a metal exoskeleton. He activated a red glowing button on the center of his chest. Immediately the bones around the three villains began to quake and come alive. Even the bones of the mastodon and the apatosaurus trembled. Then, like a stop action movie of a flowering plant sped up to super speed, the bones assembled upwards into an entirely new being. This was no recognizable dinosaur, but a giant shaped entirely from fossil bones. It had long limbs like flexible pillars. The right arm ended with the terror bird's beak; the left arm ended with an assortment of razor talons. Its head combined all of the different skulls, and they rolled together like lottery balls that spin atop one another before the friendly lady doesn't pick your number. Each mouth opened in a silent scream. The antlers of the Irish deer topped the creature, while the mastodon's tusks protruded from the front. There, in the center of the bone monster, exactly where the red dot glowed on Devious's chest, was the circle that contained Dr. Devious's kinetic shield and with it, Dr. Devious, Dr. Brick, and Mr. Mischief.

Dr. Devious moved an arm and the bone monster moved an arm. Dr. Devious took a step and the bone monster took a step. Dr. Devious leapt and the bone monster leapt.

Super Qwok grabbed Raceboy's collar and had just enough time to yank his brother's unconscious body before the bone monster landed — right where they had been. Raceboy moaned.

The bone monster caught Super Qwok around the waist and hung him from a light pole by his utility belt. Then it picked up Raceboy and did the same to him. Three villains laughed from within their kinetic shield as the bone monster strode away from the Field Museum to head north on Lake Shore Drive. Horns honked. Tires squealed. Super Qwok heard at least one crash. Then another. A pigeon landed on the lamplight. "Coo," said the pigeon, turning its head to look sideways at the masked hero dangling beneath.

"Well, this could be worse," Super

Qwok told the pigeon with a sigh. His utility belt chose that moment to prove him right by snapping. Surprised, the pigeon lifted off. Super Qwok twisted in mid-air and tried to keep his feet on the bottom half of his falling body. When he struck the ground he managed to cushion his fall with a roll.

Raceboy, still unconscious, hung from his own light pole. Super Qwok scratched his head for a moment, pondering the best method to get his brother down. He looked at Lake Shore Drive and heard more honking in the distance. Shrugging, he grasped the light pole and bent it in half.

"Raceboy," he said, "you've got to snap out of it!"

Raceboy shook his head. "Eh?"

Super Qwok took Raceboy's shoulders. "Snap … Out … Of … It!" he shook.

"What?" Raceboy asked. He clutched his masked head between his hands. "Oh, it's like a dinosaur just chewed on my brain."

"It was worse. Dr. Devious has a kinetic shield. Nothing that moves fast can pass through it. If you try, it will react and blast you."

Raceboy pondered this. "Huh," he said at last. "I wondered what all those stars were."

"C'mon," Super Qwok tugged on Raceboy's arm. "Devious's bone monster was heading down Lake Shore Drive. He's going to try to take over the city."

"Bone monster?" Raceboy asked.

Super Qwok explained as he helped Raceboy get untangled from the light pole, then the two jogged after the bone monster. "Oh, if only the Race-mobile were here," moaned Raceboy, who was still shaky from the blast of the kinetic shield.

"Wouldn't have mattered," Super Qwok said and pointed. He was right. The road ahead had become a parking lot. Cars had twisted at odd angles to avoid the monster's path, and the result was a horn-honking headache that was accented by the yelling voices of drivers screaming at one another while shaking their fists as exclamation points.

"We'll never get through that mess."

"Let's go over!" Super Qwok said and tramped up the trunk of a car, leapt to the top and began to leap from car hood to car roof to car roof like a frog that leaps across the water on lily pads. Although Raceboy momentarily considered how unhappy the people who owned those cars would be to have two superheroes hopping around on top of them, he could also hear the sound of grinding metal in the distance. He knew that a dent in the roof of a car would be nothing compared to life with Dr. Devious in charge. He climbed up the trunk of a Chevelle and skipped off the roof.

Clunk. "Hey!" Clank. "What the?" Clunk. "What!" Clunk. "Hey!" The sounds, both cause and effect, continued as both boys clunk-clank-clunked their way after Dr. Devious and his bone monster.

"I'm going to speed up," Raceboy warned his brother. "Meet me at the Sears Tower," he said, and before he'd realized his mistake, he switched to Race-mode and took off. Even moving at his blazing fast speed, Raceboy was too late. The scene that confronted him at the tallest building in Chicago showed exactly how powerful Dr. Devious's bone monster was: the only police lights were *beneath* upside down police cruisers. The police officers had scattered but continued to plug away with their pistols at the bone monster, a useless practice that they couldn't know was useless. The bone monster, rather than try to deal with the inconsequential humans, was instead climbing the exterior of the building.

Super Qwok caught up when the monster had reached the halfway point of the building. He bent over, panting to catch his breath. "Got…an…ax?"

Raceboy glanced at the monster overhead. "That's no beanstalk," he grumbled. "And it's not coming down after us."

"We've got to stop it," Super Qwok wheezed. "That remote control glue has to be the worst invention Devious has ever come up with!"

"What are we going to do?" Raceboy asked as he looked past the bone monster to the antennas at the top of the building. "Wait—" he said. "That's it—"

Super Qwok looked up at the bone monster on the building. "What's it?" He asked the empty street because Raceboy was gone.

Within the glass entrance Raceboy blasted past the metal detector and security guard station, both of which were already on lock down. There was an instant where he imagined taking all 105 flights of stairs in Race-mode; it lasted until he realized navigating the labyrinth of staircases would likely eat up all of the time he needed. Raceboy held the button for the express elevator, which he decided was the Willis Tower equivalent to Race-mode.

The ride to the Skydeck could have been exhilarating were it not for the pressing concern of Devious's bone monster. He had only seen the thing from the outside as it gripped the sides of the building, but it was big, and there seemed to be no offense capable of penetrating the kinetic shield. The thought of Dr. Devious in charge of the Willis Tower and Chicago gave Raceboy a momentary shiver.

Stepping from the elevator, Raceboy faced another security guard. This man was middle-aged and stern, one hand on his walkie-talkie, the other on a pistol that he held pointed right at the center of Raceboy's chest. "Freeze," said the guard. "The elevator's aren't supposed to be running. You're not supposed to be coming here. And it's not…" He looked Raceboy up-and-down with a snarl, "Halloween yet."

Raceboy explained, "I need to get access to the antenna control rooms!"

The man spoke into his walkie-talkie, "Skydeck here. I need the Police. I have a mover."

"No, wait!" Raceboy protested. "I'm not the one you need the police for! It's the thing outside, on the building." He pointed behind the guard to the glass windows.

The guard rolled his eyes. "Right. Like I'm gonna fall for that old trick."

"I just need to get upstairs!"

Shaking his head, the guard said, "You can't get upstairs without a keycard," he fingered the name-badge hanging from a lanyard around his neck. His eyes snapped quickly between one of the elevator faceplates and Raceboy. Another express elevator was on its way to the Skydeck. Raceboy knew the second one would contain a carload of Chicago's finest, which would be great if he were actually part of the problem.

A clank from the outside of the building forced the guard's attention away from Raceboy for the merest of seconds, but Raceboy didn't need the distraction to switch to Race-mode and yank the lanyard from the guard's neck. He didn't have time to wait to see the guard's reaction when he stood face to face with the bone monster on the outside of the building.

Using the keycard he opened the service stairwell and climbed to the top story of the Willis Tower. He used the keycard to open a final door and stepped into a floor full of computers and electrical stations. Still in Race-mode, he found the first person he could, a slender man with a necktie and curly hair. He sat at a desk, his eyes focused on a computer screen with stacks of green numbers. As Raceboy dropped out of Race-mode, it was as though he appeared from thin air beside the man, who let slip a shriek like a young girl before putting both hands over his mouth in embarrassed horror.

"You didn't hear that," he said, cheeks red.

Raceboy ignored the comment and said simply, "There's an emergency. I need you to amplify the signals in both antennas to cover every possible frequency you can."

"Whoa, whoa! I can't do that! That would turn the Sears Tow—I mean, Willis Tower into the biggest RF jamming device in the history of radio!"

"Exactly," Raceboy said. "So do it."

The man shook his head and waved his hands, "No can do, little costumed person. The FCC doesn't take kindly to people playing with radio frequencies. They're sacred. They're protected by triplicate forms and government bureaucrats. It takes months to—"

The light coming from the long windows was suddenly gone as the bone monster appeared, its many hollow eye sockets staring in.

"What is that!" the tech gasped and pointed a bent finger past Raceboy.

"That's the Future Chicago Controller if you don't jam every frequency available right now."

The tech must have figured out the FCC reference. He looked from the bone monster to Raceboy before him, then abruptly grabbed a series of dials and turned them all the way up.

The bone monster pulled itself just high enough for Raceboy to see Dr. Devious, Mr. Mischief, and Dr. Brick within the ovular shape of the kinetic shield when the antennas on the top of the Willis Tower began their barrage of radio frequencies. For the bone monster, the effect was instantaneous: it came apart. The remote control that Dr. Devious was using could not compete with the antennas powering the tallest building in the continental United States. Within the kinetic shield, the faces of all three

villains went from "Chicago will soon be ours!" to "How many feet above the ground is 105 stories?" to "We are going to fall 105 stories without a parachute!" in an instant.

*   *   *

"The kinetic shield bounced," Super Qwok explained with a laugh. "It didn't break; it was like Dr. Devious, Dr. Brick, and Mr. Mischief were trapped inside a bouncy ball. They hit the ground and bounced around and around. I think they bounced into Lake Michigan." He looked east to the blue horizon.

Raceboy grimaced. "So they got away."

Super Qwok shrugged. "Today. But I don't think they'll try that again. Even though nothing could penetrate the shield, it still looked like they could feel gravity. I don't think it felt very good to bang around downtown Chicago like a pinball."

"But the bones!" Raceboy said. "The bones were irreplaceable! Can you imagine the Field Museum without dinosaurs and skeletons!"

"Those bones?" Super Qwok pointed behind Raceboy, who turned and saw the bone monster, complete but motionless on the ground.

"But—" He shook his head. "But—I don't understand!"

"When you jammed the signal, they all came apart. But as they fell and the jamming stopped, the remote controlled glue pulled them all back together. Dr. Devious's kinetic shield wasn't remote controlled; he was the controller, so it wasn't pulled to the glue. It didn't reform; it just kept falling, with Devious and Mischief and Brick inside it. But the bones came back together, and I figured I better catch that thing, or I'd have to hear you whine the whole way home about the irreplaceable loss for science or something."

Raceboy's eyes remained focused on the bone monster. "But all the bones are jumbled..."

Super Qwok rolled his eyes, looked heavenward as though to ask, "Why me?" He pointed out, "They're still covered with remote controlled glue, right? So figure out what frequency each skeleton is set at, and ta-da! You can sort the bones back out. It's not really such a big deal after all."

"Are you sure you're not really a scientist?" Raceboy asked.

Super Qwok frowned. "Me? Pshaw. I'll just be happy if we can get one of those plastic dinosaurs from the museum."

"Dad will never buy you a Mold-A-Rama. He's too cheap."

"Maybe," Super Qwok shrugged. "But I'll ask anyway. We did get drug out of the museum by a triceratops skeleton."

Super Qwok was right again. When Bryan and Alex turned up in the museum information desk and were returned to their frantic parents, Dad not only bought all three kids a Mold-A-Rama, he and Mom even stopped in the museum gift store and bought each boy a book and a dinosaur poster.

"Well, one good thing," Alex whispered to Bryan on the way home, "is that they didn't try to use mummies."

Both boys imagined for a second the shriveled shapes wrapped in desiccated rags tramping down the steps of the museum, and they shivered.

"That is a sight I never want to see," Bryan agreed.

Professor Solaris

Once upon a time there was a scientist from the moon whose sole desire was to create a paradise on Earth for his fellow Lunans. He was known as Professor Solaris. He lived on the moon, where he researched, experimented, and planned to take over the Earth.

His studies led him to invent a device that he called, "My Solar Flare Generator." He planned to use his invention to create a massive solar flare that would destroy all electronic equipment on Earth.

Professor Solaris's plan had one problem: the Solar Flare Generator was useless unless it was on the surface of the Earth, beneath the Earth's protective atmosphere. While traveling from the moon to the Earth was not a significant challenge with Lunan technology, there was a problem doing so while avoiding detection, especially from the NORAD satellites.

Professor Solaris needed to work in secret and take his time, bringing one or two pieces of the Solar Flare Generator with each trip. He found an abandoned house that suited his needs near the town of Clifton. For two years he patiently assembled his generator. Finally the new day for Lunan paradise was at hand, for Professor Solaris had brought his final shipment to the Earth...

"What was that?" asked Bryan.

Alex shook his head. "I don't know," he replied. "It looked like

a meteorite, maybe."

"We should check it out," said Bryan, pulling the covers off and sitting up in his bed.

Alex looked at the bedroom door. "We're supposed to be asleep." The sky outside was dark, and Alex's cheek was still warm from Mom's goodnight kiss.

"Let's use the clone-bots. I've got a hunch this is important."

Moments later, two Alex and Bryan shaped mannequins rested peacefully in Alex and Bryan's beds, and the boys were suited up and heading north in the Race-mobile.

Raceboy drove north, left Clifton, and came to a section of the road that was bordered by a deep ditch and some thick trees. Lights glowed from behind the trees.

"That's weird," Raceboy said. "I always thought this house was abandoned."

"Not so abandoned tonight," Super Qwok agreed. "I wonder if there's a relationship between that meteorite and this house?"

"Only one way to find out!" Raceboy said.

Leaving the Race-mobile cloaked, the heroes snuck down the overgrown driveway.

"It's not the house," Raceboy pointed. The house remained dark, its white siding peeling paint, the green shingles of the roof decayed and sagging on rotten joists. Instead the light was coming from the barn at the back. One sliding barn door was open just enough to let out a bright beam of light.

Super Qwok crept toward the barn. Raceboy followed, and the two peeked into the door.

A giant machine hummed from its pedestal in the center of the barn. Two humanoid shapes stood off to the side in the shadows. They appeared to be uniformed but the bright light from the pedestal hid them in darkness. Alone at the machine stood a single figure who wore a pair of mechanical goggles and a white lab coat. His hair was stereotypically white and crazy, sticking out at every angle and direction.

"That's a mad scientist if I ever saw one," explained Raceboy.

Super Qwok nodded, "But I don't recognize him. He isn't Dr. Devious, though I'm sure he's up to no good."

At that moment a speaker crackled to life and a computerized voice spoke: "Professor Solaris, provide status report."

The scientist growled and shook his arm at the control panel before flipping a switch and answering, "Solaris here. The Solar Flare Generator is at 75% charge." He turned the communicator switch off.

The voice said, "Once the Solar Flare Generator reaches full charge, engage power. Confirm."

Professor Solaris waved his fist at the control panel again. He yelled, his voice breaking with anger, "Those buffoons act like I don't know the plan!" and then he flipped the switch. His voice was completely different, pleasant and conversational. "Acknowledged," he said. As soon as he broke the connection he began to rant again. "They act like I don't know what to do! Ten years of my life spent in study to develop this generator, two years ferrying the parts down to the Earth's surface, sneaking and hiding to evade NORAD satellites. I have camped in this house without a fellow Lunan for company—no offense to you cyborg soldiers, but you're more machine than Lunan. No one knows the plan better than I do! Power up the Solar Flare Generator, then turn on the generator to create a massive solar flare electrical surge and destroy all of the electrical devices on Earth. Once I flip this switch we can take this world for the People of the Moon!"

"Well, we've arrived in the nick of time," murmured Raceboy. "Looks like we're the only hope to prevent the destruction of civilization as we know it."

"Just another day in the life of a superhero," Super Qwok agreed. "If my eyes don't deceive me, that gauge on Professor Solaris's equipment is approaching 90%." He grabbed the door to the barn and slid it open. The door groaned.

Professor Solaris looked up and his goggles flashed red. "Get them!" he yelled and pointed one hooked finger at the heroes.

Immediately the two uniformed shapes leapt into action. They charged the heroes. Both were encased in metal and looked like robots. While once they may have been Lunans like Professor Solaris, they retained very little of their Lunanity any longer, having become robo-soldiers.

Raceboy threw a super-speedy punch. The first Lunan cyborg countered it. Raceboy kicked, but the cyborg had already spun out of the way. What was going on? Normally Raceboy's speed allowed him to easily out-fight bad guys. Raceboy realized that the Lunan cyborg was using its processing power to predict where the blows would fall. Thus the cyborg soldier was actually blocking Raceboy's kicks and punches!

Super Qwok found himself similarly engaged, but with a difference: his enormous strength. He let the Lunan cyborg soldier punch; he blocked the blow and sensed how much strength the cyborg had. Then he delivered a solid strike to the center of its plate-mailed chest. With a resonant *CLANG* the Lunan flew backwards through one of the barn walls, spilling dust into the air.

The readout on the control panel read 97%. Professor Solaris hovered at the button, his finger hesitating, waiting for the exact moment when he could activate the Solar Flare Generator.

Super Qwok did not have time to spare. He grabbed the Lunan fighting with Raceboy and threw with all his might. The surprised soldier cartwheeled through the air and crashed straight into the

Solar Flare Generator's control panel. With a crackle of electricity, the control panel exploded. Immediately a blast of bright light erupted and the entire Solar Flare Generator turned to vapor, leaving behind a faint trickle of smoke.

Professor Solaris stood dazed, his face black and sooty, his hair smoking at the ends.

"No," he whispered, then said more loudly, "No! My life's work! You have destroyed it!" He buried his face in his hands and sobbed. "Destroyed," he cried. "Everything."

Raceboy and Super Qwok did not turn Professor Solaris over to the Police Captain; instead they contacted Dr. Kensington, a scientist for NASA.

Later, Raceboy asked Dr. Kensington, "Is Professor Solaris going to be okay?"

The doctor's voice crackled through the speakers of the Race-computer. "He has adjusted very well. Most of his anger was simply frustration at being controlled by the Lunan authorities. We've been able to share some of our research and technology with him, and he is simply bubbling over with great ideas. We think his research will be invaluable in harnessing the energy of the sun to generate renewable power for Earth. Thank you, both of you. If NASA can ever be of service," the doctor concluded, "you have only to ask."

Raceboy and Super Qwok smiled at one another. "We will, Dr. Kensington," they said. "You're welcome."

SUBSTANCE Q

No one knew anything about the Bio-wizard company. They only made a single product, and it was so top secret that it was only known as "Substance Q."

Raceboy and Super Qwok learned much later that Substance Q used nano-technology and brain cells. Even with their additional research that was as much as they could find out.

One day Substance Q, this mysterious experimental substance, was being hauled in a tanker truck that was being driven by a hard-working truck driver. The truck driver had been working so hard, and he was so tired, that he managed to doze off. Just for a second, mind you, but it was the worst second to nod, because at that instant he was passing another tanker truck, this one filled with a petroleum product, being driven by another hard-working truck-driver, who happened, at that moment, to be noticing the picture on his global positioning system. It showed him where he was at on the interstate. He was near Clifton. Because he was looking at the GPS, he didn't notice the tanker in the other lane moving over at him.

The collision of the two trucks was loud and violent. Fortunately, both drivers—I'll tell you this up front—were just fine, but their tankers were spread and mangled across the road. Substance Q was thoroughly mixed with the petroleum, creating a thick, tarry,

gooey substance on the road. And you might think that that was bad, and it was, because as cars went through the gloppy mixture, they spun out of control, and they roared into the nearby ditches and crashed. Again fortunately, the people were safe because they were wearing their seat belts.

But the weirdest thing was that when Substance Q came in contact with the petroleum, it began to move on its own like gelatin with a brain. It began to coagulate and collect itself into a giant blob. You might think that's scary, too, and it is: a giant, intelligent blob on the interstate. That's scary, but what the blob began to do next is even scarier: it began to reach for cars as they went by. Those cars were hurting it, rolling over it. It didn't know why they rolled over it; it only knew they hurt. And its response was to throw the cars. This was fearsome and terrible.

Of course, Raceboy and Super Qwok saw the Race-alarm, and they were on their way to fight the blob.

The Race-mobile and Qwok-cycle raced to the scene of the accident. There they found that the giant blob had left the road and was moving across the countryside. Both boys stared at the monstrous, oozing gelatin.

Raceboy said, "We fought a blob before, but it sure wasn't that big!"

Super Qwok remembered Blobulous and shivered; he had been inside that blob for a time. "No, it sure wasn't."

The blob was heading straight for Clifton. As it rolled, dirt from the field stuck to it. Its amoeboid shape was coated with muck and mud, which sucked into its body and was used for fuel.

"We have to stop it!" Super Qwok yelled.

Raceboy agreed, went into Race-mode and zipped after the oozing Substance Q. He pulled out his laser-sword. With a crackle of electricity he swung the laser-sword and struck the ooze. The gelatin hissed and smoked. A dirt-crusted pseudopod—a thick tendril like a reaching arm—oozed from the giant creature and wrapped itself around the laser-sword. No one had ever put out Raceboy's laser-sword before, but the blob put it out like a birthday candle. The energy weapon fizzled in Raceboy's hand. He raced backwards, surprised.

Super Qwok, unable to move as quickly as his brother, had also advanced. He threw a punch straight into the side of the splorching shape. The blob splattered and drops sprayed onto the ground. Then the little drops of splatter sucked back into the main form, which splorched forward without pause.

The blob quivered, and Super Qwok felt that this was no giggling jiggle but rather an angry quake. The blob gathered its ooze together, sucking itself up into a single giant pile that was as big as a train car or a house. The mystery to the boys was how the thing could see, or if it could see; after all, it didn't have any eyes.

Raceboy tried to run around the blob, but even as he ran in Speed-mode a pseudopod snaked out of the massive creature to splat against his chest. He somersaulted backwards on the ground, regained control and spun to his feet. He shifted to a cartwheel and dodged away from a second pseudopod.

Meanwhile there was a tap on Super Qwok's shoulder. He turned and discovered that there was no one behind him—just a giant pseudopod that knocked him to the ground. The long tendril wrapped itself around his leg and began to suck back into the giant blob.

Super Qwok grabbed at the dirt of the field, but it fell apart in his hands. The small plants that were left-over from the last summer were rotted, rootless wraiths of their former green selves. They came out of the ground between his fingers. Super Qwok tried punching at the ground, but like the blob, it only splatted when his fists struck. He was getting closer and closer to the giant creature, and he didn't know what to expect. There was no mouth; the monster couldn't chew him. Then he saw the impression in the blob like an opening as though he was going to be pulled inside the giant, purple, gelatinous, mucky blob.

Raceboy saw Super Qwok being drug by the tendrils. Although his laser-sword had been extinguished once, he fired it up again and swung it in a very quick arc, racing as he ran, spinning it so the blade appeared like a disk or the wheels of a bicycle or the blade of a circular saw. He blitzed past the pseudopod holding his brother and severed it from the main body. Super Qwok kicked the severed goo away. The oozing remnants, though separated, squiggled back to the body of the creature.

Again the blob seemed to gather itself, to shudder and shake.

Both Super Qwok and Raceboy thought that perhaps this was because the creature was angry. *WHOOSH!* There was a giant explosion!

The blob was in a thousand globs flying like fat purple drops of rain. It coated both boys and the ground around them, dripping and plopping.

There were so many of them that neither Super Qwok nor Raceboy were sure what to do. Both boys hesitated, realizing that the blob, in a split second, had both coated and surrounded them. Raceboy spun his still burning laser-sword. It hissed through a small blob, cleaving it. The blobs didn't seem to care at all. They continued to wiggle towards him.

Super Qwok tried stomping on the blobs. As he stomped the mucky blobs splatted around. But they didn't even create mud.

Both boys were in trouble. As far as the eye could see was the residue, and it was gathering on them.

They needed extra help. They needed the help of another hero.

Raceboy clicked his wrist communicator. He called a message out: "Knight-in-shining-armor-boy, hurry! We need you! Knight-in-shining-armor-boy, hurry! We need you!"

The blobs and ooze surrounded the boys, converged on the duo, with their slimy surfaces crawling and creeping up the heroes' legs.

Super Qwok kept stomping; Raceboy kept swinging his laser-sword to cut the blobs of Substance Q smaller and smaller, but even the little pieces would keep moving towards him until they were clinging to the boys' feet and climbing up them.

Although normally in control, both boys were beginning to get nervous. Though they kept knocking globs off themselves, the substance was still oozing closer to them, surrounding them. It seemed to be trying to encase them.

Raceboy knew that they had only so much time before they were going to be in terrible, desperate trouble. He thought about using his jet-pack to pull Super Qwok and himself away from the ground. He was deciding on what he should do when both boys

heard a strange clattering noise.

The boys looked up to see Knight-in-shining-armor-boy. And you know what kind of vehicle Knight-in-shining-armor-boy rides? A robo-horse! That's right, the robo-horse that had once been used by the Birthday Bandit. It matched his armor perfectly.

The horse clattered nearby. *KA-KUCK, KA-KUCK, KA-KUCK, KA-KUCK.* As the horse neared them, Knight-in-shining-armor-boy jumped from the horse, did a flip, and landed in the slime near Raceboy and Super Qwok.

Without hesitating he ordered, "Raceboy, use your jet-pack and lift Super Qwok off the ground!"

"What are you going to do, Knight-in-shining-armor-boy?" Raceboy asked.

Knight-in-shining-armor-boy said, "You just watch and see! I've done some work to my warhammer." He drew the warhammer from where he normally kept it, strapped to his back. It was as long as a baseball bat, and nearly as thick, but the head of it was a

solid rectangle of bright metal. "When I say, 'now,' go! Just a short burst. You need to come down almost immediately."

Then Knight-in-shining-armor-boy brought the warhammer back over his head and yelled, "Now!"

He swung the warhammer forward. Raceboy grabbed Super Qwok in a hug and activated his jet-pack. The jet-pack lifted both boys up into the sky. Up they went. Raceboy turned off the jet-pack and felt himself falling down.

Raceboy and Super Qwok had a clear view of the scene below. Knight-in-shining-armor-boy's warhammer struck the ooze with a powerful blast that echoed like a concussion. There was an enormous *BOOM* and the ground shook all around Knight-in-shining-armor-boy. A jolt of electricity catapulted through the air in a shockwave. All the globs, even the ooze, were struck by the electricity and began to sizzle and fry. The nanocircuitry that had given Substance Q its ability to think and reason was burned by the powerful glow of Knight-in-shining-armor-boy's electrical current. Immediately all of the Substance Q ooze began to turn a terrible charcoal black, and then it began to fall apart into tiny dust particles.

Raceboy pulsed the jet-pack to slow their descent, and the two boys landed on a field covered with ash.

Super Qwok cheered, "You did it, Knight-in-shining-armor-boy! You saved us! But what happened?"

Knight-in-shining-armor-boy shifted his warhammer. "I modified my warhammer so that it can sense whether the target is alive or not. If something is not alive, it will be a regular hammer. But if something *is* alive, it will deliver a powerful electric shock to stop it. I guess this slime was alive, but I didn't know that my hammer would do this." He motioned to the black dust.

Raceboy said, "The sad thing is, though, that that creature never knew if it was good or evil. It was just trying to figure out what was going on, and we had to destroy it. I feel bad about that."

Super Qwok agreed. "I know, but there's no telling what terrible disaster could have happened if we had let it go. It didn't have any sense of what it was supposed to do."

Knight-in-shining-armor-boy put away his warhammer, slinging it over his shoulder. "We had to do what we had to do. A superhero sometimes makes hard choices. At least we know that everyone is safe."

"That's right," Raceboy said. "Everybody is safe." He put an arm around his brother and their good friend. Then the three boys trekked back to the road to help clean up the accident site. They hoped they would never see another mysterious glob-like creature again.

Substance Q Won't Quit

The ash that was left from Substance Q blew across the dirt. You would think that the blob creature was dead, that it was gone. But as the wind blew, that ash began to pull towards itself, to gather. The tiny particles of ash began to group themselves, attach themselves, collect, combine, and coagulate until they formed a shadowy shape without definition. It was a pile of ash. It moved by stretching out a limb of dust and pulling the remainder of itself forward. The dust flowed toward the road, and it saw, or rather sensed, using whatever mysterious powers it had, an automobile pass on the road. It sensed that the method the automobile used to travel was with wheels, which spun around and around.

The ash pile changed its shape, flattened its sides and turned itself into a giant wheel. It rolled along, attempting to mimic the vehicles nearby. Even so, its balance was precarious. The wind could nudge it, and it would tip over. Each time it fell, it had to reshape itself into a wheel and begin rolling again. The giant wheel realized that this was not a particularly good way to travel. Plus, it didn't know where to go. It did, however, come to a realization: it was very angry. And do you know what it was angry about? It was angry that what it had been was destroyed. It wished more than anything to get revenge on the ones who had destroyed its beautiful shape. And do you remember who that was?

Knight-in-shining-armor-boy, Raceboy, and Super Qwok.

The ash creature knew that it wanted to get back at them, destroy them. Only a moment before the giant wheel had halted, wondering which direction it should go. Now it had a direction. It sensed the wheeled devices moving, and it knew that if it followed those devices it would go somewhere. And if it searched enough, somewhere it would find the ones who had robbed it of its beautiful squiggliness.

The creature kept rolling. If you looked at the map you would have discovered that the ash creature was rolling straight toward Clifton, where Raceboy and Super Qwok lived. It rolled right into town and ran straight into a building. *POP!* The ash scattered like a burst balloon, and fell to the ground to form a thick layer of dust. The creature realized that if it was going to destroy the ones it sought, it would need to become stronger than that. Those things that took away its beautiful movement would be able to scatter it to the winds. Instead of loose particles of ash, the creature condensed itself into a tightly bound form. No longer did it look like a giant cloud. Now it was a solid shadow.

It stood nearly fifteen feet tall, was completely black and smooth without ripple or reflection, like a statue of charcoal. Now when it tried its powers to reach out against the wall of the building, it punctured a hole through the cinder block wall. When it pulled its pointed limb from the hole, it felt a strong joy. It knew that with such strength it could destroy the ones who had changed it.

If it had been able to smile, or if it had known what a smile was, the ash creature would have smiled.

In its earliest memory the creature had thrown things. It had actually thrown cars, but it did not know that. All it knew was that throwing had brought them, had brought the ruiners. The creature understood. There was no need for it to try to find the ruiners. The creature could simply lure them; it began to call.

People driving down the street didn't know what hit them. A shadow leapt beside them, and the next thing they knew, their cars were being lifted into the air and thrown. They flew through the air as though they were on a carnival ride. They crashed to the ground. Everyone was very lucky to have their seat belts on, or they could have been very badly hurt. One driver called 9–1–1, but not before the Race-computer had registered the crash and sent an alarm to Raceboy and Super Qwok and Knight-in-shining-armor-boy.

The Race-computer could not prepare the heroes for what to expect; all they knew was that there was trouble on Main Street in Clifton.

Raceboy drove the Race-mobile, Super Qwok steered the Qwok-cycle, and Knight-in-shining-armor-boy rode his robo-horse. They were prepared for mad scientists or wicked witches. They were ready for giant blobs or dancing monkeys. They did not expect to see a mysterious charcoal-like creature in the shape of a man that looked like a walking shadow.

Even as Raceboy parked the Race-mobile, Super Qwok bounded from the Qwok-cycle, and Knight-in-shining-armor-boy leapt from his horse, the creature began to change. The man-shape twisted and became something like an octopus with numerous arms radiating from its center. The arms extended, reaching for the boys. The creature spun very quickly at the heroes.

Super Qwok and Knight-in-shining-armor-boy tried to dodge, but the creature was full of arms and full of speed and full of power. Although Raceboy was moving very fast, and although he twisted and spun, it was impossible to avoid at least one of the arms. He was surprised to discover that the creature was very strong, far stronger than he had expected. Super Qwok took a blow to the chest. Knight-in-shining-armor-boy, clad in his silver armor, took a blow that rattled him backwards. He fell on the street.

In the distance the Police Captain stopped traffic to keep people from traveling near the creature.

The creature, inside whatever part of its body housed its brain, felt very pleased to know that it had lured the ruiners once again. Now all it had to do was ruin them, to get rid of them.

The creature recollected itself, pulling in the tendrils so that it was no longer shaped like an octopus. It was nothing more than a fifteen-foot tall ball, a charcoal ball sitting in the middle of Main Street doing nothing.

Each of the heroes approached it carefully.

"What is it?" asked Knight-in-shining-armor-boy.

Raceboy said, "I've got a bad feeling we've met it before." Before he could say anything else, the ball changed shape. It was like an ink explosion: it spewed arm after arm that collected around Super Qwok, pulling tight like coils of thick rope all around him until he looked like a spool wrapped in black thread. Then the coils flattened and spread like a coating to absorb him.

"Hurry, Knight-in-shining-armor-boy!" yelled Super Qwok.

Tendrils reached Knight-in-shining-armor-boy's leg, wrapped and spread, tripping him. "I can't hit it with my warhammer! It will shock Super Qwok, too!"

Raceboy said, "Try my laser-sword," and he threw it straight to Super Qwok's outstretched hand. Electricity popped as he activated the laser-sword and flipped it in a circle, severing a section of the tendrils. The ashes fell to the ground like powder, puffing in a delicate cloud as they struck the ground. Then they came back together and slowly sucked into the creature's shape. Even the laser-sword was useless against such a powerful creature.

Raceboy didn't not know what to do; his laser-sword had no effect on the ash. Knight-in-shining-armor-boy did not know what to do. His powerful warhammer, which was normally very effective against villains, would also hurt Super Qwok. It was Super Qwok who yelled, "Don't worry about me! I can take the electricity, even if it knocks me out! I'll be okay—" before the inky coating covered his mouth and forced his mouth shut. His eyes behind his mask were wide with helplessness. Knight-in-shining-armor-boy realized that Super Qwok was right. The electricity may knock him out, but the creature had nearly absorbed him.

Knight-in-shining-armor-boy wound up and swung his warhammer with all his might. When it struck Super Qwok, the amazing weapon was not solid metal that would break bones or cause pain; it was an electric cushion that electrified Super Qwok. The jolt sent Super Qwok into seizures. It also passed a ferocious, powerful surge of electricity into the creature, which released Super Qwok.

"I'm sorry, Super Qwok!" yelled Knight-in-shining-armor-boy as he watched his friend topple to the ground.

Leaving Super Qwok, the creature slid toward Knight-in-shining-armor-boy. It didn't come straight at him, as he might have expected. Instead it split in two. The top half flew toward him like two fists fired from a cannon. He couldn't see the bottom half as he fought the top, swinging his warhammer to block the attack. He was surprised to discover that the bottom of the creature had shifted behind him, and it slugged him in the back. He was dealt such a powerful blow that he was sent reeling and fell to the ground, rolling. If you've ever rolled in a suit of armor you will know that this is not a very comfortable thing to do at all.

While Knight-in-shining-armor-boy faced the creature, Raceboy zipped up to his fallen brother and lifted him, dragging him away at full speed. Although this had taken only a split-second to complete with his super speed, he turned to see Knight-in-shining-armor-boy fall beneath the force of the blow. The charcoal shape moved to cover the fallen hero like a blanket.

Raceboy recognized the need to move quickly, and since Raceboy was Raceboy, he did. He lifted Super Qwok and carried him beside Knight-in-shining-armor-boy. He let go of his still-unconscious brother, who would have toppled to the ground a second time, except for one thing: Raceboy could move fast. He opened a pouch on his utility belt and unfolded his magic seven-league boots. The amazing boots took shape, and he slid them atop his own superhero boots. All this he did so quickly that, to you or me, it would have seemed that the boots simply appeared on his feet. He did this so quickly, in fact, that he was able to catch Super Qwok before he even slid an inch down. Then, careful not to take a step in the magic boots, he pulled Knight-in-shining-armor-boy from the grip of the charcoal creature, bent his knees, and leapt straight up.

Some people may have used the boots to jump seven leagues to the west, or seven leagues to the east. But not Raceboy. Holding the unconscious Knight-in-shining-armor-boy with his left arm, and the unconscious Super Qwok with his right, he rose seven leagues straight up. He was launched like a rocket high into the heavens. He rose, passing through the clouds, passing through the atmosphere, higher, higher, until Clifton was a tiny speck below him.

He reached the apex of his leap. Super Qwok and Knight-in-shining-armor-boy seemed to grow light as he held them tightly. Then he began to descend. Like a rocket he sank. Heat built against the bottoms of his shoes. The shoes, which were magical, of course, deflected the heat from around Raceboy, Super Qwok, and Knight-in-shining-armor-boy as they plummeted through the Earth's atmosphere to streak like a comet, like a ferocious falling

star. Raceboy shifted the angle of his boots slightly, and his course changed. He guided his trajectory straight toward Clifton, toward Main Street, toward the creature.

Below him the creature had fused together and become a shadowy shape. It had no eyes, so it did not look around for Raceboy. It used other senses to recognize that the ruiners were gone. Whether it thought that it had succeeded in destroying Raceboy, Super Qwok, and Knight-in-shining-armor-boy will never be known because Raceboy struck the creature smack-dab on its top. The force of the blow was like an explosion or a thunderclap or a detonated bomb. The creature wasn't just flattened. The heat from Raceboy's boots burned its cinder body. The concussion of the force of his fall rattled the Earth and created a crater right in the middle of Main Street. Rocks spewed from Raceboy's collision.

Raceboy, protected by the magic of the boots, stood gently in the pit which he had created, which had once upon a time been black top with yellow stripes and was now nothing more than a hole in the ground. He looked at the road and discovered that he had created such a deep crater that his head was beneath the level of the road.

And where, you may ask, was the shadowy cinder creature that had been there before? It was nowhere to be seen, apparently vaporized to dust by the force of Raceboy's descent.

Raceboy let go of Super Qwok and Knight-in-shining-armor-boy. Still moving with super speed, he took the boots off (he knew

that an accidental step had unexpected results) and placed them back in his utility belt. They folded up tightly and fit snugly in a pouch, which Raceboy closed with a snap. He grabbed the two boys at his sides before they fell, and discovered that they were both shifting their own weight. They both appeared to have been knocked from senselessness by the shock of the fall. Both Super Qwok and Knight-in-shining-armor-boy shook their heads and stared at the crater surrounding them.

Super Qwok asked, "What power did you use, Raceboy, to do this?"

"My seven league boots. But I didn't travel far. Instead I jumped straight up and came straight down on the creature. When I landed, it destroyed our enemy. We are safe now."

Knight-in-shining-armor-boy said, "I don't understand that creature, what it was after, and why it fought us so. It destroyed for the sake of destruction."

Raceboy said, "I suppose it's like trying to understand a plant. We just aren't that sort of a creature. It wasn't a human, and we are not a mysterious creature made from nano-technology and a petroleum based substance that had been electrified into walking ash."

Knight-in-shining-armor-boy said, "Well, yeah. That's true. We're not, are we?"

"No," said Super Qwok, and his voice had a distant, thoughtful quality to it. "We are stranger stuff; we're the stuff of stardust and miracles." He reached down and picked up a stone.

Both Raceboy and Knight-in-shining-armor-boy looked at him oddly. At last Raceboy asked, "Where'd you hear that? Shakespeare?"

Super Qwok shrugged. "I just made it up." He tossed the stone and caught it in a gloved hand.

"Huh. I'd have sworn it was Shakespeare." He climbed out of the pit, turned and reached a hand down to help Super Qwok out. Super Qwok placed the stone in Raceboy's hand.

"What's this?" Raceboy asked as he held out the piece of solid black shininess to the reflect daylight.

Super Qwok drug himself beside Raceboy while saying, "I found it in the debris." Then both Raceboy and Super Qwok yanked Knight-in-shining-armor-boy out of the crater.

Together the three boys looked from the black gem to the crater in Clifton.

Raceboy chuckled. "Stardust and miracles." He put the stone black gem back into Super Qwok's glove.

Thus the heroes finished another adventure, saved the day, and saved themselves.

THE ORIGINS OF RACEBOY AND SUPER QWOK

DEUX EX MACHINA

Raceboy and Super Qwok were not always superheroes. There was a time when they were simply boys like any other boys who lived in the community. They were born, they grew up, and for a couple of years, they lived normal lives. In fact, some of their favorite things in the world were to read about superheroes in books and comics and watch superheroes on TV. They loved to see the costumes the superheroes wore and hear stories about superheroes with amazing speed and powerful strength.

In those days the only powers the boys had existed in their imaginations: as they played in their back yard on swings, they pretended to fly; as they climbed the play-yard ladder, they pretended to achieve the peak of a towering skyscraper; as they slid down the slide, they pretended they were swooping into action to fight off bad guys.

So what happened? How did two average boys in an average town become something more?

One night, Alex and Bryan relaxed in their beds trying to go to sleep. It was difficult, though, since Dad had just finished reading an exciting story about the Amazing Spider-man. At Christmastime these boys might have had visions of sugar plums; on this night they had visions of villains, of excitement, and of saving the day.

At that same moment, outside their window, they saw a giant blue flash from the backyard. It was like lightning, but it came from the ground.

"What was that?" asked Bryan.

"I have no idea!" replied Alex.

"Let's go look," Bryan suggested. The two boys snuck out of their bedroom and down the dark stairs to the sliding door that led into the back yard. Without a sound they crept out onto the deck under the starry nighttime sky.

They walked along the fence.

"Look, over there!" Bryan pointed. Smoke rose from a spot behind the apple trees.

The moon glowed through thin strips of clouds. Both boys trotted through the moist grass, approached the smoke, and discovered a hole.

"Do you think it's dangerous?" Bryan asked, sneaking closer.

"I don't know. Maybe. Yes, we could fall in and maybe get hurt."

The boys moved closer to the hole, until they could peer over the edge. It was a crater. Its diameter was larger than a garbage can and equally as deep. The edges sloped, almost like a funnel. In the middle, half-buried in the dirt, was the source of the smoke: a basketball-sized rock.

Bryan was the first to slide a leg over the lip and skid into the crater. Around him crickets chirped in the trees and lightning bugs flashed.

"Careful," said Alex, "it could be hot!"

Bryan held his hand out and shook his head. "I don't think so. The sides are hot, but not that thing at the bottom."

Alex put a hand out, hesitated, pulled his feet over the lip of the crater and cautiously wiggled until his feet touched the dirt. He kept his hand extended, waiting for some sign of heat. Like Bryan, he could feel some warmth from the ground, but nothing from the rock. "I think it's a meteorite," he said.

"What's that?" Bryan asked.

"You know, a rock from space, a rock that was flying through space and fell through the sky to strike the ground. Dad says most of them burn up before they hit the ground, and that's what we look at when we watch the shooting stars every year."

"Whoa," Bryan said, looking at the silver shape at the bottom of the hole. "So this thing is a shooting star?"

"I'm not sure, but that's my guess."

The boys kneeled beside the meteorite. The dirt was still warm, but the shape itself did not radiate heat.

"I always thought shooting stars had five points like a, you know, star."

"Real stars don't! That's just a symbol."

"Let's wipe it off," Bryan suggested. "I want to see what this otherworldly stuff looks like."

Crouching above the shape, lit only by moonlight, Alex and Bryan brushed their fingers across the meteorite's face. Dirt coated the object in a rocky crust. Alex rubbed one spot and the dirt fell away. "It's just a coating!" he said.

Bryan scraped some of the dirt off, then rubbed more and more as the smooth surface beneath began to shine through and reflect the moonlight.

"Is that the moon's reflection? Or is this glowing?" Alex asked.

Bryan peered closer to the mark he'd scraped clean. "I don't know. It might be glowing, or it might be the moon."

Working together, the boys were able to rub off all of the residue that was coating the sphere, for indeed, it was a sphere. But that was the only thing about the shape that was certain. It may have been metal, for it certainly seemed to be silver. Yet it had a blue

cast to it that appeared to be something entirely different, almost like plastic.

All over the sphere were mysterious etchings. There were lines that ran circles around the sphere, and on the lines were symbols and more shapes. Alex pointed, "These look like the letters I'm learning in preschool. Except not any kind of letters that I know."

Bryan said, "Maybe they aren't the kind of letters that we learn in our country."

Alex said, "Maybe they aren't the kind of letters that we learn in our world!"

Both boys looked at the sphere, their attention drawn to a single symbol that either glowed itself, or reflected the moon brightly. It was a wings upon wings upon wings all stacked atop one another in a geometric progression like a nautilus shell. The wings seemed to unfold with a flutter, and stretch, and shift, and transform in front of them, and the sphere slowly grew in size and spread out and opened to reveal that this sphere was really a container.

"Crystals?" asked Bryan.

Both boys peered more closely at the crystal innards of the sphere. "They're moving!" Alex said.

"I think the crystals are machines," Bryan said. "Do you think we should touch them?"

Alex looked carefully at the crystals. "I think…no, I feel like it's okay…"

The two boys reached into the sphere and touched the crystals. All at once there was a bright flash of light.

When the bright flash disappeared, Alex and Bryan were asleep.

*   *   *

Bryan urged, "Alex, Alex! Wake up!"

Alex sat up and looked around. The sun was up in the eastern sky behind one of Clifton's grain elevators. Both boys were still beside the crater. Oddly enough, the grass all around them was moist with dew, but neither boy's body nor clothing was the least bit wet.

"What happened?" Alex asked. "It's morning! Why are we still lying in the grass?"

Bryan said, "Do you think it was because we touched something inside the meteorite?"

The boys climbed back into the hole and looked. The sphere no longer glowed or reflected the daylight. Within the sphere, the crystals were faded and dull. They no longer moved, no longer looked like tiny moving machines.

Bryan said, "We better get back into the house before Mom and Dad notice we're out here."

"Good idea. If they think we slept outside they probably won't be very happy."

"Why don't we race?"

Alex said, "Okay," and before Alex even finished saying, "Okay," he was back at the house.

Bryan forgot that he didn't want Mom and Dad to know he was outside. He yelled, "How did you do that?"

Alex looked around and frowned. "I don't know! How am I at the house while you're back there still? It was almost like I tele-ported."

"So come back here," Bryan said.

WHOOSH! Alex once again stood next to Bryan. He said, "That's amazing."

Bryan shook his head and stopped by the play yard. He sat on the steps for a moment and thought. "We came outside and saw that meteorite, then we touched it. And now you can like blast super-fast." He thought about this some more. "But why can't I blast super-fast? It's only you." He was still thinking about this when he leaned against the play yard to pull himself up. As he pushed, the play yard moved.

For most play yards this would probably not have been that big of a deal, but Alex and Bryan's play yard was pretty big, as play yards go. Dad had designed it himself and built it when Alex was two. It was so large that although Dad designed it to be modular, the pieces, when separated, took three grown men to move each of the three parts. It had three levels, two slides, a ladder, a staircase, and an entire fort clubhouse, and Bryan was able to move it with a shove. He looked at it again suspiciously.

Alex said, "What?"

"It's strange," Bryan replied. "I think I just moved the play yard when I leaned against it."

"But that play yard is so huge that Daddy can't even budge it when he pushes on it!"

"And you know what? I think I could lift it up." Bryan bent his knees, bent over, and gripped the base of the play yard. The whole thing clattered as Bryan lifted it above his head. He carefully set it on the ground again, lining the base up to set upon the stones Dad had used to level it.

Alex's mouth hung open. "Holy cow! You just lifted the entire play yard; I just ran super-fast in the blink of an eye. What has happened to us?"

"I think it has something to do with the meteorite. I feel different, almost powerful."

"Maybe we should do something with that meteorite before anybody else touches it," Alex suggested.

"I should be able to carry it," Bryan said.

"And I should be able to fill the hole in with dirt in no time flat."

Back at the crater, Bryan fidgeted with the sphere and managed to get the container closed. He dug around the edges with his fingertips, then pulled. Although he was able to wrap his arms all the way around the shape and hug it to his chest, he could tell that it was very heavy, at least, would have been very heavy if he didn't have such powers. With his powers, though, he was able to set the meteorite outside the crater and then pull himself out onto the grass.

Alex stood nearby with one of Dad's shovels that he had claimed from the garage. "You know, I don't think Dad's going to be very happy when he discovers this giant crater in the back yard."

Alex went to work with the shovel, scooping dirt from the edges down into the hole. Working at super-speed, the hole filled in right before Bryan's very eyes. At last it was nothing more than four feet of plain dirt.

As Alex finished Bryan said, "You're cleaning our room from now on. I'll vacuum."

"Ha, ha," Alex replied.

Sirens wailed in the distance. Something was happening on this early morning. Something dangerous, they knew, because you didn't often hear sirens in Clifton.

"What's going on?" Bryan asked.

"Let's hide that somewhere and go look."

Bryan looked at the basketball-sized silver sphere. "Where can we put it?"

Alex thought for a moment. "How about the garage? With all Dad's stuff in there, no one will notice it."

"Of course! We can put it on the bottom shelf of the ball rack. When we get back we'll hide it somewhere better, like the dormer attic in our room."

Sirens continued to sound as Bryan toted the meteorite into the garage and slid it onto the ball rack that Dad had built from scrap wood. He stacked three cans of paint and some baseball bats in front of it. As he stood back he had to admit that it was completely hidden.

"You ready?" Alex asked Bryan as they opened the gate.

"Sure," said Bryan.

Alex started to run. He didn't notice anything particularly unusual about running, though later he would begin to recognize how sounds differed, and even events around him appeared to stop. He reached the First Federal Bank of Clifton; he saw the police cruiser, saw people standing as still as statues. When he came to a stop they began to move their arms and heads at regular speed. Looking around, he discovered that Bryan was nowhere near him. He raced back to Bryan and said, "Something is going on at the bank. There's a police car and people and everything."

Bryan stared at his brother. He looked over Alex's shoulder. "You really were all the way uptown that fast? It was like you didn't even leave!"

Alex tried again; he raced to the end of the street and back. Although he didn't feel that time had changed in any way, the rest of the world slowed almost to a standstill. As Alex returned down the street he could see Bryan's body frozen mid-step, like a still photograph of a boy walking. When he stopped beside his brother, however, Bryan's foot fell to the ground naturally.

Alex said, "It's like I'm a race boy."

Bryan laughed, "That's for sure. I can't even see you. A race boy."

"Yeah, that's what I am! I'm a race boy. I'm Raceboy!" And *PA-CHOO*, he was gone again, back to the bank.

Alex zipped back two then three times to check on Bryan's progress. "Come on," he would say, "aren't you there yet?"

And each time he would bring Bryan additional information about the crime scene.

"There's a strange man. He's wearing some kind of a costume

with a mask," he said, "and he has a hostage. Do you know what a hostage is?"

"No," answered Bryan, who was not quite old enough to go to pre-school, where they still didn't teach you about things like hostages.

"Me either. I just heard somebody say it." *PA-CHOO*, Alex disappeared, then reappeared again. "Okay, I think I figured it out. It looks like the bad guy is holding a gun and a person. Even if he doesn't say, 'This is my hostage. If anyone comes close to me, then I'm gonna hurt her,' everyone just sort of knows what the bad guy is doing."

"So it's sort of like when Mom and Dad keep our toys until we do something we're supposed to do?"

"I guess." *PA-CHOO.*

"The Police Captain is there by his car, but he can't do anything because of the hostage. Hurry up!"

When Bryan followed Alex to the bank parking lot, he already knew what to expect. Near the front of the building, his back against the glass doors, stood a short, round man with a mask of strange silver metal. It was smooth, an inverted teardrop of reflective material. He wore a jumpsuit of crumpled aluminum foil, or perhaps it was an exotic space-age material. In his hand was a silver gun. Alex and Bryan both recognized that it's shape was very similar to the kind of bubble-guns Aunt Gwen was liable to bring to family gatherings. With his other hand the gunman held the arm of a woman. He kept the strange gun pointed at her. The tears on her cheeks and the frantic slant of her eyes clearly indicated that the gun was no grocery store toy aisle bubble blaster, but something more nefarious.

People surrounded the man, watching hesitantly, frozen with helplessness. The Police Captain stood near his own car, careful to hold both his hands open and up, as though making a public declaration that he meant no harm. The Police Captain looked very frazzled.

"Get back!" raged the man in the shining mask, and he directed the silver gun at a bystander who had crept too close. A strange, muted whirring sounded from the gun, and the bystander shrieked an inhuman cry and covered his ears. His eyes rolled back in his head and he collapsed to the ground.

"That's temporary," the masked man explained in a nasally drawl. "But I can make it permanent with the flip of a switch. So don't try anything!" He pointed the gun at the Police Captain in emphasis.

Both Alex, who was now thinking of himself as Raceboy, and Bryan, who was not really thinking of himself as anything yet, stood and watched. A second later Alex said to Bryan, "I think I can do something about this."

"Like what?" Bryan asked. He blinked, and in that split second he noticed a sort of flutter or breeze.

Alex said, "Like this."

"What'd you do?"

"Here," said Alex. "Here's his gun."

Bryan said, "You grabbed the gun from the bad guy?" He looked at the thick barrel and the leather grip. "But he's all the way over there!"

Alex shrugged. "I know. I can move so fast."

Meanwhile, the masked man was staring back and forth between his now empty hand and the hostage. His face wasn't visible through the metallic mask, but his body language radiated absolute surprise. How could the gun have disappeared from his hand? In one instant, a breeze; in the next instant, his gun was gone. Like magic.

Bryan turned from his brother. "All right. That was pretty great, but watch this!" No one noticed him; neither boy had caught any of the bystanders' attention; they were all focused on the now-befuddled hostage-taker. Bryan jumped one time and came down with a powerful thump on the ground.

The ground rumbled, and a crack broke open at his feet in the blacktop of the parking lot. It rolled all the way to where the bad guy stood, and the crack split him away from his hostage. She fell one way; he fell the other.

Alex said, "Wow! That was a super crack you just made! I can't believe you just cracked the ground! You were like an earthquake."

"Yeah, a super crack, an earthquake…Super Qwok! That's my name. I'm Super Qwok."

"What's a Qwok?" Alex asked.

"I just made it up. It's like a word that means crack, quake, and everything else all in one. It's just like total strength."

Alex handed the gun to Bryan, who bent it in half, then threw it into the cracked earth.

The boys watched the Police Captain swoop in on the dazed bad guy and snap handcuffs on him and pull the shining mask from his head. The face that had been hidden beneath the mask was contorted in rage. Short black curls covered his head. He had tiny eyes and porcine jowls, thick lips with a slender mustache beneath a button nose.

"You think you've stopped me," snarled the man, "but you did nothing! Whatever providence saved your skin will not protect you next time. This is only the beginning!"

Alex and Bryan stared uncomfortably at the man. It was the first time they had seen such strong, fiery emotions distort the face of an adult. Sure, they had seen Katherine throw a fit, but she was one, and one-year-olds often shriek when they don't get their own way. Later they would learn his name was Dr. Brick, but for now he was only a man in a strange suit with a strange mask and a strange gun.

The Police Captain put the man in the back of the police cruiser. Some of the people who had been nearby comforted the hostage, and the Police Captain returned to lead her away gingerly. Other people were looking at the crack in the ground, trying to understand what it meant. No one imagined that the crack was created by one tiny boy standing at the edge of the parking lot.

Alex and Bryan's minds were racing almost as fast as Raceboy as they walked home together. Alex said, "If we have powers like this, we should have costumes."

"Superhero costumes," agreed Bryan. "That's exactly what we need: superhero costumes for Super Qwok and Raceboy. But no one can know our secret identities."

"That's right," said Alex. "Not even Mom or Dad. If they found out our secret identities, they'd never let us fight crime. They'd probably worry about us."

"Yeah, Mom especially. She would probably try to stop us, or worse, fight crime herself."

Alex laughed. "That's funny, Mom fighting crime."

The Newspapers tried to report the truth. The headline, "Earthquake Stops Hostage Situation" was partially true. The boys listened as Dad read the article at the dinner table the next night. The newspaper reporter explained that a freak earthquake caused the hostage-taker to drop his gun and get separated from his hostage.

Alex and Bryan looked at each other across the table. They knew that the facts were out of order, but were otherwise substantially accurate: the bad guy had lost his gun and had been separated from his hostage by a crack in the earth. What was missing from the article were the motive forces that took the gun and cracked the ground. The reporter didn't know it, the newspaper publisher didn't know it, and neither Mom nor Dad reading the article knew it, but they had just read the first news story in which Raceboy and Super Qwok saved the day. And it certainly wouldn't be the last.

Alex and Bryan removed the meteorite to their dormer attic. The strange container with its mysterious crystals never glowed for them again, though it did glow at least twice more: once for Katherine, and another time—even later—after Anna was born.

Neither boy ever learned exactly how the crystals had transformed them. Like the newspaper reporter, they had the facts, just not the motive force. They had suspicions, but like many things in life, the result was the only thing that was clear. As they got older, Alex would develop an interest in science, and he would theorize that the tiny crystals were either aliens or robots (or alien robots) that had disassembled each boy's cells and reassembled them in a way

that was completely superior to the way they had been configured before. Bryan would shrug when he heard Alex explain this. His own theory was less mechanical. He thought that the crystals had somehow tapped into their imaginations, allowing their minds to configure their bodies with powers. He thought that the difference in their powers related to the difference in their personalities. Alex would listen to Bryan's explanation with a condescending big-brother look on his face that could be translated as, "Yeah, but I know better so you should listen to me."

Maybe they were both right? Maybe neither was right? It didn't matter, really, because the result was the same: Alex and Bryan were now Raceboy and Super Qwok.

THE TROUBLE WITH TEE-BALL

Raceboy and Super Qwok had a super problem. No, it wasn't another monster come to destroy Clifton; it was not a mind-bending scientist with plans to take over the world; nor mechanical pirates with plots to steal money from the bank. No, this problem was more personal in nature. You see, Raceboy and Super Qwok couldn't turn off their powers. Raceboy wasn't an outfit that Alex put on to make himself run faster. Super Qwok wasn't a pair of gloves with powerful strength. It took all of their energy and concentration to not use their super powers when they weren't being superheroes, which brings us to tee-ball.

Tee-ball season was about to begin, and Alex and Bryan needed to prove that they weren't super powered. They decided to practice their skills in the backyard.

First they tried to play catch with the baseball. Alex picked up the first of the baseballs from the bucket of balls, patted it against the inside of his glove, then threw it at Bryan. The ball flew so fast it punctured a hole in the grain elevator next door. "Oops," said Alex.

Bryan yelled, "Use less speed for Pete's sake!"

Alex pulled another ball from the bucket and fingered it thoughtfully. "Okay, one slow-ball coming up." He cocked his arm and tossed the ball gently. It struck the fence, knocking the panel from

the fence-posts.

"You're going to have to practice that," Bryan said. "And don't hit the garage! The whole thing will fall over!

"Here, you back up and I'll hit the ball to you off the tee." He dropped his glove, set another ball on the tee, then picked up the red wooden bat.

He tapped the dirt from his shoes with his bat like he'd seen the professionals do, or at least the older boys from the traveling league. Then he lined up with the plate and swung. *BOOM!*

Both boys watched the ball shrink smaller and smaller and smaller in the sky. So small, in fact, that it disappeared totally in the distance.

Alex remarked, "I think that one went into orbit." He shrugged. "I guess it's a good thing we have extras." He tried to throw a ball toward Bryan again and was pleased to watch it arc gently and land at his brother's feet.

Bryan set the ball on the tee. "I'll hit this one softly."

BOOM! The ball knocked over another section of the fence.

"Oh, Dad's not going to be very happy with us," Alex said. "What are we going to do about our game tonight?"

Bryan said, "I guess we'll just have to do our best to do our worst."

"Humph! Easy for you to say. I've got to run the bases, and do it so everyone can see me!"

The sky looked like rain, so they did a rain dance and sang, "Rain, rain, go away. Alex and Bryan want to play...TEE-BALL!"

The rain didn't stop the tee-ball game, however. Something else stopped the tee-ball game.

As Dad and Mom parked the van at the ball diamond behind the elementary school, both boys' secret super power senses stirred. They looked at one another. Something wasn't quite right. First of all, there were no people playing tee-ball. Second of all, kids were crying while adults walked around with slumped shoulders and tried comforting their children with hugs and pats on heads.

Alex and Bryan leapt from the van and carried their gloves up to their coach. She said, "Sorry, guys, we can't have a game. All the balls have been stolen."

"What do you mean the balls have been stolen?" asked Dad.

The coach shook her head and frowned. "We don't know. It was mysterious. Everybody was ready to start playing. Next thing we know, no balls anywhere. No one can play tonight!"

"That is mysterious," said Dad. Alex and Bryan agreed. Beyond disappointment, the boys felt a prickling of suspicion. Someone was up to mischief, and if experience was any indicator...Well, there was a certain villain with a history of mischievous antics who came to mind.

The second tee-ball game was different. For starters, everyone brought extra balls. There was no way any coaches or parents were going to miss another game simply because the balls disappeared.

Alex and Bryan took the field and listened as their coach told them where to stand. Around them kids were adjusting their shirts or hats or gloves or shoes. They found themselves squinting at home plate while the coach set up the tee and carefully placed one of the dozens of extra balls atop it. Then the coach yelled, "Hey, where are all the bats?"

It was like a volcano erupting in Clifton. Parents knocked over lawn chairs as they blasted toward the spot they'd last seen their children's bats. Voices rose in oaths and exclamations. Some of the words that came from adult lips should not have attended a children's tee-ball game. While balls may only cost a couple of dollars, bats can cost a lot of money. And they were gone. Every last bat had disappeared from the fields. This caused the second cancellation.

Alex told Bryan, "At this rate we are never going to test how well we can hide our super powers. I think this is a job for Raceboy and Super Qwok."

Bryan nodded, "I think so, too."

The next game every kid had a new bat. Moms and Dads had gone out and bought new bats, or found other bats at home in their garages or basements or closets, or bought them at garage sales. There were plenty of bats. There were plenty of balls. But when it got to be time for the game, there were no gloves.

Raceboy and Super Qwok had been at the fields early. They had seen the first coaches arrive with buckets of supplies. They'd watched as the bases were laid out and the tees were set up and the first few kids slid their fingers into gloves and took the fields. And they had also seen how, for no apparent reason, the gloves had disappeared. Not all at once, but one at a time, randomly, a kid would have a glove under his arm, then *POOF*—gone. A kid would have his arm extended to catch a ball, *POOF*—gone. A kid would throw his glove into the air, *POOF*—gone.

For the fourth game even fewer parents and kids showed up. Those who did, the ones who still believed there was going to be a tee-ball season, showed up with numerous balls, extra gloves, and brand new bats.

"Wait a minute!" said one of the coaches. "How can we have a tee-ball game without any tees? It's not tee-ball if we don't have tees!"

Someone else said, "Let's play baseball, then!"

The first tee-ball game of the season was held, but it was not tee-ball. It was baseball. The coaches tried pitching with the result that the first game of the season was a terrible disaster. These kids had never practiced hitting a pitched ball; they'd only practiced hitting a ball off a tee. Coaches were throwing ten, sometimes twenty pitches at kids with the hopes that the ball and the bat would, through some miracle of physics, share the same spot long enough to project the ball into the field. One of the coaches, after the twenty pitches, had his kids hold the bat straight out so he could pitch at it. The innings stretched on until the games had to be called because the sun had set.

That night Raceboy and Super Qwok decided to run some tests. Alex used the Race-computer to chart electrical consumption over a two week period. He discovered that at 6:00 PM on the nights of the tee-ball games, there was a surge in the electricity being consumed in Clifton.

"That means," Alex told Bryan, "that someone is powering a device at that time. And if there's someone powering a device at that time, it most certainly has to be associated with the disappearing tee-ball equipment.

"Now what we need to do is cross-check these records from the electric company. I'll tap into their database and pull the records on electric meters for the last sixty days."

Bryan nodded and looked over Alex's shoulder, "So basically, we know electricity is being used to power the shenanigans, and we're going to figure out which house is using an extraordinary amount of power."

"Yup."

It took three hours of computing and cross-checking, but the boys were finally able to isolate a one block area where the power was being used during the time when the tee-ball equipment was disappearing.

"Therefore," Alex explained, "we will scope out that block before the next game."

Although the boys had performed reconnaissance during the intervening time, they hadn't seen anything out of the ordinary. On the night of the next tee-ball game, they noticed one house with a tall fence around the back yard. Inside the fence was a mysterious device. It had been pushed out of the shed and wheeled into the middle of the back yard. It looked something like a giant cannon pointed at the sky. It had a spot for a person to sit, straddling the cannon.

"That's got to be the device," said Raceboy. "It sure looks like it would suck a lot of electricity."

Super Qwok shook his head. "I can't believe that anyone would have that in their backyard! What can that thing have to do with tee-ball?"

As the boys watched, a man came out of the shed and climbed onto the machine. It was none other than Mr. Mischief.

"I thought so!" whispered Raceboy. "I knew he was behind this mischief!"

Super Qwok peeked through a hole in the fence. "I don't get it. What could he possibly want from tee-ball things?"

"I don't know, but we are going to find out."

The two heroes snuck over the fence at the back corner behind some bushes. Bushes running the length of the fence allowed them to stay hidden as they got closer to the machine. It hummed and also made a faint *POP-POP-POP-POP*. Then the side of the machine opened up, and it dropped baseball hats onto the yard.

Where had the baseball hats come from? Neither boy needed to see to know. As the kids were coming to their games, Mr. Mischief was using this machine to suck their hats right off their heads and bring them to this yard where he was collecting them.

"But what is the point?" asked Raceboy. "All he's doing is causing—"

"Mischief?" asked Super Qwok.

A screen door on the house slammed and another figure approached the machine. His face and hair was hidden by the barrel of the machine, but his feet were visible. His voice, his very recognizable voice said, "Have you conducted the fifth and final test of my matter transporter?"

"Yes, I have, sir. Everything is working splendidly," Mr. Mischief giggled.

"Good, good," said the voice, and the figure moved around the cannon until they could see his hands rubbing together in satisfaction, and at very last, his face: Dr. Devious—the only scientist capable of both creating a matter transporter and working with Mr. Mischief.

"Argh," growled Dr. Devious as he approached the pile of hats on the ground. "When are you going to do something diabolical? Stealing tee-ball things is not diabolical in the least."

Mr. Mischief guffawed and answered, "Yeah, but think of how much mischief I'm causing!"

Dr. Devious said, "I asked you for five tests ... five tests of my device before I put it to use to take over the world! And you test it by stealing tee-ball paraphernalia?"

"Sure," said Mr. Mischief. "First off, I made lots of kids sad. They had five games and they didn't get to play."

"Kids?" Dr. Devious's voice rose shrilly. "This device is capable

137

of so much more! With it, I will make the leaders of the world sad! I will steal the guns from the armies, the tanks from their troops. I will use my invention to shift power by shifting matter. With it, I will take over the world!"

Hearing this, Raceboy and Super Qwok realized that with such a machine, Dr. Devious wouldn't stop at stealing weapons. He would find new ways to use the matter transporter for even greater evil; he might steal money straight from the vault of the First Federal Bank of Clifton, or maybe even steal people from families, then charge a ransom for their return. No, clearly Dr. Devious would never use this invention for good.

Raceboy and Super Qwok stood up. "Dr. Devious! This experiment is over!"

Mr. Mischief started to laugh. This is not the normal reaction superheroes are looking for when they stand up and reveal themselves in the presence of their villainous arch-enemies.

Dr. Devious directed his sarcasm at the boys. "As if I couldn't have guessed: Raceboy and Super Qwok. Clifton's protectors come to stop me. I suppose you think I will simply listen to you and go away?"

Raceboy answered, "That's right. We know what you're up to, and it's not going to work."

Super Qwok said, "We're going to make sure you're in prison."

A sharp laugh burst from Dr. Devious's lips. "For stealing little league equipment?"

"Tee-ball," corrected Super Qwok.

"Give me more credit than that. If I am going to prison, it will be for something far more grand than baseball hats." He paused, then barked abruptly, "Now, Mr. Mischief!"

Neither boy had paid attention to Mr. Mischief astride the matter transporter. At the order from Dr. Devious, Mr. Mischief flipped a switch. It was as though the world exploded in white hot light and the boys felt themselves being sucked through a funnel: *BWEOOP!*

The next thing they knew they were standing in the middle of a bean field with the sun on their left and a small creek meandering in the distance. The young plants spread around them in fist-sized clumps.

"Huh," said Raceboy. "This is embarrassing."

Super Qwok kicked a dirt clod. "I can't believe we fell for that. It must be one of the oldest tricks in the book."

"So the matter transmitter can both pull matter to it, or push matter away from it. Interesting."

Super Qwok grabbed Raceboy by the arm. "We have to get back to Clifton and stop them before they use that machine to do something even more evil."

Raceboy said, "I can race very quickly. Why don't you take my seven league boots? He opened a pouch on his utility belt and pulled the boots out, unfolding and handing them to Super Qwok.

"Remind me how to use these again."

"Just put them on, and for every step you take, you'll jump seven leagues."

"How far?" Super Qwok asked.

"Ah, it's one of those standard units of measurement. I don't know, something like, um, uh, I don't have any idea. I have to look it up in a dictionary or on the Race-computer."

"Just another reason why we should switch to the metric system."

Raceboy said, "I don't know. It just wouldn't be the same to have thirty-five kilometer boots—" but Super Qwok didn't hear because he'd already taken a step and disappeared east.

Raceboy kicked into Speed-mode and blasted after his brother, leaving a trail of dust behind him, first black from dirt, second gray from the dust of the gravel roads he found.

The two arrived at the house at the same time. Raceboy's speed was so fast that even Super Qwok's gigantic steps did not leave Raceboy behind. Super Qwok handed the boots back to Raceboy and said, "Those things were about to make me motion sick."

The truth was that both boys expected to return to the house and discover that Dr. Devious and Mr. Mischief had taken the device and disappeared, maybe even transported themselves somewhere far off where it would be difficult to find them. Thus it was with some surprise that Raceboy and Super Qwok found that the villains had done nothing. Inside the fence, Dr. Devious and Mr. Mischief discussed their plans for the matter transmitter. The heroes listened for a moment before Dr. Devious said, "You may as well come back into the yard, Raceboy and Super Qwok."

The boys looked at one another in surprise. For the second time Dr. Devious had taken them unawares.

"That's right," Dr. Devious said, "I knew you would be back. I'm quite pleased with the accuracy of my estimations about your speed, Raceboy, though I must say I did not predict Super Qwok would be back so soon. I believe a variable has been introduced to the equation that affected the results. Hmm."

When neither Raceboy nor Super Qwok entered, Dr. Devious added, "I believe the gate is the preferred method of entering a yard, though doubtless you assume I am going to zap you with my matter transmitter ray again. And in this you would be very close to ascertaining my actual intentions, however, procedurally, I am uninclined to—"

Raceboy jumped the fence and Super Qwok followed. Neither took Dr. Devious's suggestion of using the gate.

"Of course, I expected that as well. The gate was merely a decoy to get you into position for the next stage of my plan."

Raceboy and Super Qwok stared at Dr. Devious, Mr. Mischief, and the machine. It appeared that Mr. Mischief was not close enough to activate the machine, but with Dr. Devious's apparent predictions about where and when the superheroes would arrive, they couldn't simply leave everything to chance.

Dr. Devious continued, "If you thought that the little demonstration I just gave you about the capabilities of my transmitter showcased its limitations, you would be wrong. I simply gave you a taste of what this can do. You see, we are going to take over the world, and you two are going to help us!" He laughed.

"Ha," said Raceboy without humor. "We are not going to help you. We are going to help you to jail; that's where we are going to help you."

Super Qwok said, "Why would we help you?"

Mr. Mischief chuckled. "You tell'em, boss."

Dr. Devious cleared his throat and continued, "You are going to help us because my matter transmitter can do more than transmit matter. It is also a control device. With it, I can control you."

Raceboy said, "You're pulling my leg."

Dr. Devious snarled, "Pulling your leg? What do you mean, pulling your leg? I'm nowhere near you. How could I pull your leg?"

"Quit being so literal," said Raceboy.

Meanwhile, Super Qwok said, "So, this machine," he had edged closer while Dr. Devious ranted, "this machine right here, you're saying," he patted the side of the barrel of the machine, "can control people?"

Dr. Devious explained, "That's right. It has the ability to—" and before he could say anything else, Super Qwok reached up and bent the front of the machine in half.

"Noooo!" howled Dr. Devious. "My machine!"

Super Qwok asked, "Does it work now?"

Mr. Mischief sputtered, stared with disbelief. "You broke it!"

Dr. Devious punched the air with a clenched fist. "All that work! It was going along so beautifully and, and…you bent my matter transmitter!" He fell to his knees and moaned.

Mr. Mischief did not fall to his knees. Instead he drew a laser pistol from a pocket. This he pointed at Raceboy and Super Qwok, who figured that it wasn't any ordinary gun. First of all, it looked silvery and science-fictiony. Second, Mr. Mischief was always getting gizmos from Dr. Devious after the mad scientist had created then forgotten about them. Mr. Mischief said, "All right. We're getting out of this place. I'm not going to jail just because I had some fun with tee-ball stuff. I'm taking Dr. Devious, and we're out of here."

Super Qwok and Raceboy both said, "You're not going any-where." As they were in the middle of the line, Raceboy kicked into Speed-mode and finished the word "where" with the gun in his hand while Mr. Mischief stared down at his fingertips now empty of the gun, wondering what had happened to Raceboy.

Raceboy said, "Looking for something?" as he dangled the gun in front of him. He tossed it to Super Qwok, who caught it and squeezed it until it looked like a silver walnut, round and wrinkled. Super Qwok tossed it back at Mr. Mischief.

"How d'ya like them nuts?" Super Qwok asked.

Mr. Mischief's lip began to quiver. He looked at Dr. Devious. "Boss! Do something! You've got to do something!"

Dr. Devious growled, "All that hard work. I'll get you for this. You and You! Argh!" He didn't say anything else. He just disap-peared. And Mr. Mischief followed, like the Cheshire Cat, all of him was gone and his mouth followed a split second after.

"What kind of matter transmitter did they use?" Raceboy asked.

"I don't know since this machine's broken."

Immediately after, the house began to glow a strange orange. It started to incinerate from the inside out. It glowed, then slowly blew into pieces as the wind swept it away, like a newspaper that burns to ash and disintegrates. Dr. Devious's machine, like the house, disintegrated until there was nothing left but a puddle of metal that quickly became a solid. The lot was empty except for the slab foundation, some lonely green shrubs, and a pile of base-ball hats in the middle of the back yard.

Super Qwok looked at the lot. "I think they'll be back."

"Of course," said Raceboy. "Devious wants his revenge. They'll be back."

"On the other hand, our game should be starting any minute. We should go play."

Raceboy said, "Finally! Let's collect these hats. I'll race them over. You change and meet me there."

As Alex and Bryan arrived late for their first real tee-ball game, they were thankful to Raceboy and Super Qwok, who had returned the missing ball caps and explained that there would be no further "delays of game."

"All right," and, "Yeah," and, "Cool," each boy agreed as he waited his turn to bat. Since Bryan was number ten and Alex was number eleven, they were at the bottom of the tee-ball line-up. As number nine smacked a ground-roll straight into the coach's left ankle, Bryan muttered, "Oh, man, what am I going to do?"

Alex said, "You'll figure something out. I hope..."

Bryan got up with his bat and sauntered over to the tee. He tried first to spread his hands apart, but another coach corrected his grip and reminded him to strike the ball. He wiggled the bat, swung, and missed on purpose. "Phew," he said, frustrated, and behind him Mom shouted, "Don't worry, Bry! You can hit it. Just concentrate on the ball."

"If she only knew," he mumbled. For most kids, the challenge was to hit the ball so far it would be a home run. Bryan had the opposite challenge. He needed to keep the ball from either circling the globe or hitting one of the players and sending them to the hospital. *Okay,* he thought, *I've just got to swing as gently as possible.* He swung high again, missing on purpose.

Wait, he thought. *Here's a better idea: I will hit the ball as gently as possible right where it sits on the tee. That will knock the ball forward.* He tried this—gently, gently—he let the bat hit the tee, not the ball. Bump. The ball popped from the tee and rolled casually into the field. A dozen gloves carried by stubby legs raced through the grass to grapple for the ball, then throw it to first base.

Bryan was so excited that he didn't knock anybody out that he stood at home plate jumping up and down watching the action. He had forgotten to run. Everyone began screaming, "Run, Bryan! Run to first base!"

"Oh," he said, and ran to first, where he continued hopping.

Alex picked up the bat Bryan had dropped and tried to talk himself up. "Here goes nothing!" He lined himself up beside the tee and readied his stance. As one of the older members of the team, he had three pitches before the coach resorted to the tee. The first pitch came; he swung as slowly as he could. A miss. The next pitch came and he swung. *THUNK,* the ball rolled past the coach.

All the outfielders raced past the infielders attempting to be the first to retrieve the hit ball. Alex was so excited he ran all the way around the bases and back home to the same spot where he'd started. He did this in less time than it takes to blink, so if anyone noticed it, they may have also imagined it was an optical illusion, a momentary flutter, a shadow from a bird. "Oh, my goodness! I've got to slow down!"

Alex half-skipped to first base, where he stayed on it until it was time to run. And then he half-skipped again.

The rest of the game was pretty easy. It wasn't until the end, when they had to clap hands with the other team that they worried. What if Super Qwok clapped some kid with his powers and knocked his arms clean off? Alex suggested that they resist the desire to clap and simply be clapped. "Let them hit you," he explained. And that was what they did.

As they sat cross legged on a blanket afterwards enjoying the obligatory tee-ball snack of a juice-box and some cookies, Bryan said, "Well, we did it. We just have to keep doing it."

"You did great," agreed Mom. "That was a super first game!"

"Un-super," Alex chuckled, but only Bryan got the joke.

"Oh, Alex," Dad said. "You just need to stretch your legs out when you run. I really think you could run faster if you'd just stretch those legs out. You know, put a little energy into it!"

JACKYL

Although superheroes know that it's very important to take medicine after visiting the doctor, one little boy who lived near Alex and Bryan refused to follow this advice. This little boy was named Jack.

"Time for your medicine," said Jack's mother.

Jack put his hands over his mouth and said through tight fingers, "It tastes yucky."

Jack's mother sat on the edge of his bed. "Now, Jack," she admonished, "if you don't take your medicine you will get very sick! It's important for you to take your medicine."

Jack refused. A mysterious alteration began to take place. First, hair grew all over his body. Second, his teeth grew longer, sharper. Third, his body swelled to an enormous size, and his pajamas ripped and hung in slender shreds from his shoulders. Without his medicine and its ability to contain his sickness, the sickness had taken over Jack's body, turning him into...the Jackyl.

Jackyl ripped the front door from its hinges and threw it aside. It clattered against the wall, then rattled flat on the floor. With a howl Jackyl stepped into the dusk.

On the porch, Jackyl looked around. He could still feel the vibration of the door as it had broken from its hinges; he liked that feeling, to destroy. It made him swell with strength. He ran claws

against railings as he descended the stairs, splitting the spindles into splintered strips of painted wood.

Jackyl uprooted the bushes in the landscaping and howled before throwing them straight into the neighbor's windows. Glass shattered, and a voice screamed inside the nearby house.

Jackyl raced up and down the street, and screams followed him.

His sickness gave him enormous strength; he overturned a car, uprooted a tree, and beat it against a house. He left destruction behind.

That was before Raceboy and Super Qwok arrived.

Neither hero tried to talk sense into Jackyl. Super Qwok simply stepped in Jackyl's way.

Jackyl responded with a beast's ferocity: he punched Super Qwok in the shoulder. From a normal man such a blow would have had no effect; but such a blow from Jackyl actually knocked Super Qwok backwards.

Raceboy raced at Jackyl, but the sickness had also given the monster lightning-fast reflexes. Jackyl caught Raceboy by an arm, pivoted, and threw Raceboy onto the roof of a nearby porch, where the boy hero bounced against the second story wall.

Super Qwok shook off Jackyl's punch, stepped forward and threw a punch of his own. Knocked off balance, Jackyl recoiled and roared. As the cry died away, another cry could be heard in the distance. Both boys wondered: was another creature coming to spread destruction?

Jackyl caught Super Qwok in his powerful grip, wrapping his arms tightly around the hero. He leaned in, trying to use his sharp jaws to bite Super Qwok.

Super Qwok ducked and writhed, wriggled and bent to avoid Jackyl's sharp claws and sharp teeth.

Raceboy leapt from the porch, and as he landed a woman appeared

at his side, took his sleeve and exclaimed, "My little Jack!" Her voice revealed that she had been the cry the boys had heard in the distance. "Help me, Raceboy! He needs to take his medicine!"

Raceboy looked at the woman. She stood on the front lawn with a silver spoon extended in front of her. Its mirrored bowl was filled with something that looked like a mix between grape juice and tree sap. "Eww, that looks gross," Raceboy said.

"Help me!" the woman pleaded. "It's Jack's medicine. He needs

149

to take his medicine!"

"All right," Raceboy said, and he took the spoon and balanced it before him as he tried to approach Super Qwok and Jackyl.

The two still clenched one another, arms and hands locked around shoulders and necks, lower limbs digging into the ground as one, then the other vied, for a superior position, for the ability to toss his opponent off balance. This was no rapid karate barrage, with either side batting blows like kung-fu ping pong; no, this was like sumo wrestling when the competitors are locked with one another, and each is seeking a small, decisive advantage.

Super Qwok groaned as he strained. Jackyl snarled, snapped his fangs.

Raceboy yelled, "Super Qwok! This boy needs his medicine!"

Super Qwok was able to squeeze his response through clenched teeth, "I know what to do," and the figures continued their struggle, two plates on the surface of the Earth, colliding to form a mountain range or an earthquake.

Suddenly Super Qwok shifted his hold, gripped lower. He lifted Jackyl in a bear hug and squeezed with all his might. Jackyl howled in surprise.

That was all the time Raceboy needed. With his super speed he sped to Jackyl and shoved the contents of the spoon down his throat.

Jackyl gagged and released his grip on Super Qwok. His claws reached for his own throat. There was a noise, *GLUG,* and Jackyl's eyes watered as the medicine traveled down his throat.

Suddenly his body lurched with a jerk; he spasmed, seizured, fell to the ground. The hair on his face thinned and disappeared. His body shrank. He shriveled up and became a small boy whose torn pajamas fell from his naked frame to sit in a useless pile on the ground.

"My little Jack!" cried Jack's mother as she rushed forward to embrace him. "Thank you so much for saving him, Raceboy and Super Qwok!"

Raceboy and Super Qwok made sure Jack and his mother got back to their house safely. Afterward, Jack always took his medicine when his mother asked, no matter how bad it tasted, because he knew that being sick was worse than tasting the terrible medicine.

HYPNOVISION

Snow swirled. Wind blasted. Drifts piled up faster than snow plows could move them. School was canceled. Businesses closed for the day. In fact, nearly everything in Clifton was shut down because of the storm.

In houses across the town, people tuned into their televisions to watch storm coverage or waste some time relaxing while dreading the inevitable work shoveling sidewalks and driveways.

Suddenly a mysterious signal appeared on the televisions. It didn't matter if the television was hooked up to cable or satellite. It didn't matter if the television was simply playing a DVD or video game system. At the same time, every television set that was switched on in Clifton changed to a series of strange symbols that shimmered and shook.

Anyone looking at those symbols grew serious, and their jaws slackened. Their eyes grew distant.

A voice came from every television at the same time. It said, "Go to the police station. Let Dr. Devious and Mr. Mischief go." The two had been captured following the great train fiasco. The voice continued, "Bring only your valuables that are small enough to carry. Bring them to the station. Let Dr. Devious and Mr. Mischief go..." The message repeated itself.

Oddly enough, the hypnotized people did what the voice told

them. They didn't even stop for a coat or mittens or hat or even shoes, but instead collected handfuls of cash, jewelry, savings bonds and, in one case, an autographed picture of Liberace, and walked straight to their doors, pushed them open over the snow, and tramped out into the cold.

For Alex and Bryan, the first sign of trouble was the sight of their mom walking out the front door without a coat. If there was one thing they could count on for certain, it was that Mom would not be going out into the storm without a coat. In the split second that the two boys looked at one another with wondering glances, the Race-alarm went off on Alex's wrist.

Both boys immediately changed into their uniforms and jumped into the Race-mobile. Although the snow had shut down most of Clifton, the Race-mobile had extra-large tires and four wheel drive. Raceboy was able to accelerate onto the road and barrel over the drifting snow. On the way they encountered a tree that had fallen over the roadway. Fortunately the Race-mobile had rocket boosters, and the press of a rocket boost button jetted the Race-mobile over the fallen tree.

They arrived at the police station amidst hundreds of people standing in the bitter cold unaware that their skin was exposed. The people swayed and moved like a sea breaking against the beach. They pushed against one another and the doors to the police station. They flowed all the way up to the police station and into the front door.

Raceboy and Super Qwok left the Race-mobile and pushed into the crowd. Super Qwok said, "Go home!"

"Must release Dr. Devious..." said a woman.

"Go home!" urged Raceboy.

Ahead in the throng the boys made out the recognizable figure of their mom. As they watched, both boys saw Mr. Mischief pass by her dragging a bag filled with...no, it was *being* filled as he passed the people and they threw their valuables inside! The boys saw their mom pull something from her finger and throw it into the bag with the rest of the collected valuables: her wedding ring. "No!" yelled Raceboy. His voice was indistinguishable from the voices of the rest of the people and the howl of the wind. Even moving at super speed he couldn't break through the mass of people to stop his mom.

Both Dr. Devious and Mr. Mischief were able to move through the people with ease, but those very same people blocked Raceboy and Super Qwok, keeping them from closing in on the villains.

The two villains got into the police captain's car and drove away into the snowy night. Before they had traveled a block the car was lost in the blizzard, and though Raceboy and Super Qwok wanted to follow, there were hundreds of people who needed to be returned to their homes.

Raceboy found the Police Captain locked in a jail cell, furious. Townspeople, the very people he knew and protected, had come into his police station and thrown him into his very own jail cell! As Raceboy and the Police Captain stepped back outside, it was clear that the hypnosis was wearing off. People had begun to lose that distant look in their eyes. Raceboy saw the Postmaster looking around and shivering. The lady from the bank looked straight at the boy who bagged groceries at the store, and their eyes met in mutual confusion. The bank teller said, "Oh, it's so cold! What am I doing? Where am I? Why am I standing in the cold outside the police station?" Those and a hundred other comments just like them rolled over the street around Raceboy.

Super Qwok's voice carried over the people, "It's all right ma'am. It's all right, sir. You've just awakened from hypnosis."

"Hypnosis?" someone questioned.

"I thought it was all a dream," said another.

"I thought it was a nightmare," added a third.

"I think it's still a nightmare," shivered someone else. A rumbling of agreement greeted this last.

Super Qwok continued, "I'm afraid that you've brought your valuables to the Police Station and now they've been taken by Dr. Devious and Mr. Mischief. Raceboy and I will try to retrieve them for you, but first we have to find Dr. Devious and Mr. Mischief. You all need to go home now and get out of this weather."

After returning everyone home, and returning home themselves, Alex and Bryan were discussing their next steps.

Alex said, "We have to move fast! Otherwise all of the loot they took will be gone!"

"The trail's gone cold." Bryan looked out the window at the falling snow. "Ha! That's a good one!"

"This is no time for jokes!" Alex said. "We've got to figure out where they went. Maybe if I do some checking with the Race-computer..."

Truth be told, the Race-computer was not going to come through. Not this time. Oh, maybe it would have been able to calculate the location of the villains if they had chosen a different location. As it was, Dr. Devious and Mr. Mischief had left the police station in the Police Captain's car and just as quickly abandoned the car, using one of Dr. Devious's clever inventions to hijack a van from the next block over. Then Mr. Mischief put the police car in gear and jammed the accelerator down with a snow scraper. The car crunched down the unplowed street before rolling off the road and bumping into a tree.

"Oh, that was a disappointment," grumbled Mr. Mischief, who liked to crash things or make them explode, especially big crashes or bigger explosions.

On Main Street they watched a snow plow pass, and although Mr. Mischief voted for hijacking the snow plow, Dr. Devious convinced him that following the snow plow was safer in order to keep their escape route a secret.

"Besides," said Dr. Devious, "A snow plow is harder to get rid of than a van. There are lots of vans on the road, and very few snow plows."

Mr. Mischief grumbled some more, but had to admit that going behind the plow was better than without it.

"We will simply follow this plow and make a base of operations," explained Dr. Devious.

The snow plow led them out of Clifton and then south to Ashkum. In Ashkum it turned east and traveled into the country. Finally it stopped totally, and Mr. Mischief asked, "What is it doing? Is it backing up?"

"Those are reverse lights!" agreed Dr. Devious, who jammed the stolen van into reverse and tried to back out of the way of the snow plow. He drove backwards until he found a driveway that had been slightly shoveled, and turned into it. Looking down the street he realized that the reason the snow plow had begun to back up was because they were on a dead end street.

"It's a dead end," he explained.

"Could be as good a place as any for us to make a base," said Mr. Mischief.

Dr. Devious and Mr. Mischief kicked their way through the snow to the front door and barged straight into the house. They knocked their shoes against the carpet to remove the snow, which, if you think about it, didn't seem to make much sense, since it wasn't their house, and they were planning to take it over, which just goes to show that habits are strange things.

The same moment these two pulled into the driveway of this

house, Raceboy and Super Qwok were having their discussion about the trail growing cold (remember, they had to help people get home out of the storm). And as these two stepped into the house without knocking, Raceboy began keying some instructions into the Race-computer. That computer never got the chance to figure out where those villains were, though, because of all the houses in the world, or in the United States, or even the county, Dr. Devious and Mr. Mischief had picked this house. It was the house that the snow plow had led them to. It was the house on a dead end street. It was the house that luck or fate or karma led them to. It was the house that belonged to Alex and Bryan's Grandma and Grandpa Winkel.

Grandpa Winkel was not home. He had shoveled the drive and left for work the night before and was still stuck there. Grandma Winkel was home alone, working on dusting her living room furniture. She had spent many years driving a school bus, and she knew a pair of trouble-makers when she saw them. Even as she looked at the door opening unexpectedly, even looking into the faces of two men she hadn't invited into her home, she didn't flinch. She yelled, "What are you thinking!" in her most ferocious grandmother voice, which normally could stop bus-riders as though they had been zapped with a freeze ray or a Gluzooka.

Mr. Mischief and Dr. Devious were not men who helped little old ladies across the street, and it had been a long time since either of them had respected their elders. Mr. Mischief simply handcuffed Grandma Winkel.

"How dare you!" exclaimed Grandma Winkel.

Mr. Mischief laughed and pulled out duct tape which he stretched over Grandma Winkel's lips so she couldn't talk. This was not particularly surprising. Mr. Mischief was an avowed disciple of duct tape and generally had at least one roll on his person at all times.

He was fond of saying, "You never know when you'll meet a duct with a leak," which was an example of figurative language. Mr. Mischief had never actually used his duct tape on ductwork. But he had used it to keep people quiet, as he did now with Grandma Winkel.

Afterward he taped Grandma Winkel around her chest to her comfy rocker. Her arms, handcuffed still, rested on her lap.

"Now let's take a look at our loot!" Mr. Mischief rubbed his hands together, then opened one of the bags and dumped the contents on the carpeted living room floor.

Dr. Devious stared around the room and rubbed his chin. "We need to secure this house." He tramped through the halls and made sure Grandma Winkel was the only one home before he opened the other bag. Together, the two men began going through their collected goodies.

Kneeling on the ground they looked like two kids going through their Halloween bags. Grandma Winkel watched them silently, which is the only way to watch when your mouth is taped shut with duct tape.

"I can't believe how many diamonds we have," giggled Mr. Mischief as he scooped a pile of wedding rings together. He held one up and Grandma Winkel recognized the familiar glint of Alex and Bryan's mother's ring. All of these things, she realized, were other people's valuables.

"What is this?" asked Dr. Devious, waving a framed picture.

Mr. Mischief examined it and shook his head, "Next time, Devious, you need to be more specific! Valuables indeed!"

Dr. Devious tossed the picture aside. "Even so, Mischief, you must admit my escape plan was brilliant, simply brilliant! Setting up the Hypnovision before we left, and putting a timer on it to activate in case we didn't return! I simply amaze myself!"

Grandma Winkel knew that she had to do something to make sure those valuables were returned to the people they belonged to. She needed to escape from these villains. The villains needed to be returned to jail. In short, what she needed was to get a signal to Raceboy and Super Qwok. And though the villains did not know it, Grandma Winkel had a way — if only she could reach it!

Near her heart she wore a patch. It was heart-shaped and stuck to her skin like a sticker. Looking at it no one would realize that it was more than a simple skin patch; indeed, it was a transmitter that, once activated, would send a signal to Raceboy and Super Qwok. The heroes had given it to Grandma Winkel for extreme emergencies. Although they had explained to her that they had passed out many such patches, the truth was that they had only given patches to a certain few people, especially family members.

Grandma Winkel lifted her handcuffed hands, pretending to scratch at her neck. She brushed her hand across her chest and pressed her heart patch with a gentle tap. There was no sound as the transmitter was activated. No noise. Dr. Devious and Mr. Mischief didn't even budge, it was so quiet.

Yet somehow, someway, the scientific mind of Dr. Devious knew that something had just happened. It was as though he had a special sense. He looked up from the pile of hundred dollar bills he was counting and said, "What did you just do?"

"Nothing," lied Grandma Winkel, except she couldn't really

say it because she had tape on her mouth, so what he heard was, "MMMMMM."

"I think you just did something," said Dr. Devious, his eyes narrowing on her suspiciously. "You don't seem trustworthy to us. Well, we can take care of you, can't we, Mr. Mischief?"

Mr. Mischief grinned a crooked smile and said, "Huh, huh, huh, yeah!"

Grandma Winkel was worried. She knew that she had pressed the heart, but had it worked? There was, after all, no sound. And this didn't look good. How long would it take for the Race-mobile to make it to her house in the storm? What if the heroes were busy handling other problems?

Dr. Devious said, "We'll take her with us. Whatever she's done, we need to get away from this house. Let's clean up this loot and go."

Both men hurriedly collected the valuables, returning them to the bags they'd brought with them. Mr. Mischief opened a long, skinny knife and sliced the tape holding Grandma to the rocker. He grabbed one of her arms and Dr. Devious grabbed the other. Mr. Mischief used his duct tape to secure her arms straight down so she couldn't lift them or move around. Then the villains led her into her garage, where they dumped her into the back seat of her sport utility vehicle. She tried to sit up, but Dr. Devious said, "Stay down! I don't want to have to explain why you're wearing tape."

Mr. Mischief made two trips inside, returning each time with one bag of loot, which he loaded into the back of the vehicle.

Dr. Devious opened the garage door, which clanked open. A cold blast of snowy wind swept into the garage.

"Brr!" said Mr. Mischief when he closed the passenger door behind him. "Turn the heat on full blast!" Mr. Mischief watched his breath swirl for a moment before disappearing.

Dr. Devious looked in his rear-view mirror. He could just squeeze past the van they had stolen from Clifton, except—"You need to shovel out behind us so I can drive to the road," Dr. Devious said.

"No way!" said Mr. Mischief. "It's too cold for that! Just turn on the four wheel drive and gun it."

Dr. Devious grunted. He put the SUV in reverse and jammed on the accelerator. The vehicle moved quickly back, then hit the snow and stopped abruptly. He turned to Mr. Mischief, "See, the snow's too thick."

What neither he nor Mr. Mischief could see was that it wasn't snow stopping the SUV; it was a three-year-old superhero with powerful strength. Super Qwok pushed against the vehicle's bumper so the tires spun on the concrete floor. He walked the vehicle back into the garage.

"What's wrong with this piece of junk?" Mr. Mischief asked.

Dr. Devious had a sinking feeling in his stomach. He caught a blur of motion from the corner of his eye before his door opened. On Mr. Mischief's side, the entire door was ripped off the SUV.

Raceboy pulled Dr. Devious from the vehicle. Super Qwok yanked Mr. Mischief. The heroes were so strong that they pulled the villains out even though they were still seat-belted. Then at the same time, they let go, and the seatbelts sucked the two back into the seats to rattle around. Now the heroes unlatched the buckles and pulled the villains out into the snowy blizzard.

"What have you done with the poor lady who lives in this house?" demanded Raceboy.

"You better tell us," added Super Qwok, "or you'll be sorry."

"What are you going to do?" laughed Mr. Mischief. "You can't hurt us because you're the good guys. We're the bad guys. We're the ones who hurt people!"

Both boys nodded to one another. It was time to show the villains exactly what good guys could do: they began to juggle. They didn't juggle balls. They didn't juggle knives. They didn't juggle flaming torches. They juggled Mr. Mischief and Dr. Devious.

"Aaaah!" screamed Mr. Mischief as he flew through the air and Raceboy caught him.

"Ooooh!" gasped Dr. Devious as he landed in Super Qwok's arms.

"Faster," said Super Qwok.

Both villains soared back and forth, screaming as they went: "Aaaah!" thunk, "Ooooh!" thunk, "Aaaah!" thunk, "Ooooh!" thunk. Their bodies rustled and wooshed in midair.

"This is too easy," Raceboy said as they passed the villains back and forth. "Why don't you grab that snow shovel?"

"Good idea!" said Super Qwok. "And Grandpa has a sledge hammer over by you. It won't hurt too badly if we miss."

"Well, not us, anyway," agreed Raceboy.

Now Dr. Devious, Mr. Mischief, a snow shovel, and a sledge hammer were all zipping back and forth in an arc between the two heroes. And they were going faster and faster. Finally Dr. Devious broke down and said, as he flew away from Super Qwok toward Raceboy, "Okay! Fine! I'll tell you!" Raceboy caught him and threw him back to Super Qwok just in time to catch the sledge hammer. As Dr. Devious flew back the way he came beneath the snow shovel he yelled, "She's in her suv! We trapped her in the back seat! We give up! We give up!"

Neither Super Qwok nor Raceboy made much of an effort to catch the flying villains, and both Dr. Devious and Mr. Mischief found themselves on the ground, feet sticking out of piles of snow.

While Raceboy freed Grandma Winkel, Super Qwok attached Dr. Devious to Mr. Mischief with his Qwok-cuffs.

"Is the Police Captain on his way?" Super Qwok asked.

"He'll be here soon," Raceboy said.

Ten minutes later the Police Captain arrived following a snow plow. He drove a special heavy duty armored car.

"You two don't get to stay in my jail after your jailbreak today," he explained as he led Dr. Devious and Mr. Mischief into the back of the armored car. "I'm going to have to transfer you to a high-security facility."

He collected the bags of loot and waved to Grandma Winkel, Super Qwok, and Raceboy as he followed the snow plow back down the road.

"Would you like to stay for some hot chocolate?" Grandma Winkel asked the heroes.

The shivering boys smiled. "Absolutely," they said.

RACEBOY AND SUPER QWOK, BABYSITTERS!

Raceboy and Super Qwok had fought monsters, mad scientists, witches, and genies, basically an entire bestiary of opponents, but they faced one of their most difficult challenges the night they tried to babysit Katherine, their little sister. This was while Mom was still pregnant with Anna, when Katherine was the baby of the family. She was around two years old, could use some words, was nearly potty-trained, and was gifted with the super power of being ridiculously cute, which is true of most two-year-olds.

Mom and Dad had plans to go out for dinner. They had asked Aunt Amie to babysit for the evening. Everything went as expected, with Aunt Amie arriving on time, taking down instructions on food, bibs, bath toys, and potty habits. Then Aunt Amie waved at the front picture window with Alex, Bryan, and Katherine as Mom and Dad drove away in the family van.

That was when Aunt Amie's cell phone rang. She answered, then her eyes grew wide. "What? What do you mean? Oh, no!" She looked around the room. "What am I going to do?" she asked the room, because really, Alex and Bryan didn't have an answer for her.

"What's wrong, Aunt Amie?" Alex asked.

"It's an emergency!" she answered. "I need to go. What am I going to do? I can't just leave you alone!"

Alex and Bryan looked at one another meaningfully. Alex whispered, "We could change into Raceboy and Super Qwok and babysit. That would help Aunt Amie out."

Alex pulled Aunt Amie's pant leg. "Aunt Amie? I think somebody's at the door."

Aunt Amie looked down at her nephew, took her attention away from the phone for an instant. "What? But—But I'm in a—It's an emergency! I've got to get you guys—I've got to hurry up!"

Alex said, "I don't know. Check the door."

Aunt Amie hurried to the door, and there, outside the door, was Raceboy. Now, reader, you may be wondering how Raceboy could be outside the door when Alex was just in the living room. And you might think it is a trick, that this wasn't the *real* Raceboy. But the truth is that Raceboy could move so fast that in the time it took Aunt Amie to walk from the living room to the front door, Alex was able to change into his Raceboy outfit and run out the back door, then around to the front of the house.

Raceboy said, "I hear you have an emergency. Would you like me to watch the kids for you?"

"Oh, Raceboy! Of course! You're such a hero I know I can trust these kids with you! But you have to put Katherine to bed."

"No problem. Super Qwok's right here with me," and sure enough, Super Qwok was hustling his butt around the corner of the house, still tucking in his superhero shirt into his superhero trousers.

Super Qwok said, "We can sure get her to go to sleep. That shouldn't be a problem, Miss."

Aunt Amie said, "Okay, thank you very much," and raced down the front steps, across the sidewalk to her car.

Raceboy and Super Qwok stepped into the house and closed the front door. Raceboy said, "Whew, all right. Now we just have to get Katherine to bed."

"Where is Katherine?" Super Qwok asked. He called, "Katherine?"

"By-by," they heard, but it was coming from upstairs. The boys looked at one another. While most people would have expected "By-by" to mean that Katherine was waving good-bye to Aunt Amie, Raceboy and Super Qwok knew that "By-by was the way Katherine said Bryan's name. The next thing they knew, there was a flash of blue-white light in the upstairs hallway.

Both boys gasped.

Raceboy turned to Super Qwok. "You did close the closet door, didn't you?"

Super Qwok's eyes grew wide behind his mask. "I was in a hurry!"

Raceboy raced up the stairs. Super Qwok climbed as fast as he could. And this is what they found: Katherine asleep on the floor of the Qwok Tower, her body immediately beside the silvery meteorite that had once upon a time fallen from the sky in the boys' backyard and transformed them into super powered heroes.

"Katherine?" Both boys said at the same time. They knelt at her side and tried to shake her awake. Her blue eyes opened and she blinked. "By-by," she said, looking straight at Super Qwok.

He cleared his throat. "No, little girl, I'm Super Qwok."

She giggled and said, "By-by." Then she turned to Raceboy. "Adex."

"It's not working!" Super Qwok said. "She knows."

"Do you think she touched it? Do you think she's been changed?" Raceboy asked.

"I hope not. Can you imagine if she has super powers? Mom says she's in her terrible two's. Would she become, like, a super villain? Maybe the Terrible Toddler? We could have to fight her to save

Clifton because she would take everybody's stuffed animals and then we'd have to put her in jail—"

"Hold on!" interrupted Raceboy. "Just because she's two doesn't mean she's going to be a villain. She's our sister! She can help us and be a hero."

"Where'd she go?" Super Qwok asked. The Qwok Tower was empty. He looked back through the portal to the bedroom.

"She touched it," Raceboy answered. "She has race powers, like me," and he, too, disappeared.

"Great," mumbled Super Qwok. "Everybody else can zip around like it's nobody's business, and leave the slow guy to clean up." He closed the closet door and tried to follow the trail of sounds that would lead him to his super-speedy siblings. Super Qwok found Raceboy and Katherine in the bathroom.

"First things first," said Raceboy. "It's bath night. We've got to give her a bath."

Super Qwok turned on the faucet to the tub. "Okay, why don't you give her a bath since you are Raceboy and can do it really fast." He tested the water temperature and pushed the plug down.

It appeared, from the look on Raceboy's face, that he really wanted to protest with a reason for Super Qwok to be the one charged with giving the bath, but since there was no part of the bathing process requiring super strength, Raceboy's mouth simply moved up and down a couple of times like a puppet with no voice. At last he said, "Okay," and began to help remove Katherine's t-shirt.

"Oh, I forgot bubbles. She always likes bubbles," said Super Qwok. "Can you blend the water a bit to make bubbles?" He dumped a capful of bubbles into the tub.

Raceboy stuck his fingers in and using his super speed mixed the

water in the tub in circles. Bubbles quickly filled the tub.

After Katherine was in the water she giggled and wiggled her fingers, just as she'd seen Raceboy do. The bubbles grew and grew.

"Katherine, stop!" said Super Qwok.

She giggled and did a super kick. Bubbles flew everywhere, coating Raceboy, Super Qwok, and the dog, Maddie. Raceboy yelled, "Katherine, no!" and managed to sputter more bubbles across the bathroom. Super Qwok, meanwhile, scooped the turbans of bubbles from his own and Raceboy's heads.

"Oh, no!" said Super Qwok. "There's water everywhere! Now we have to clean it all up!"

"And she's not even clean yet!" Raceboy grumbled.

While Super Qwok tried toweling the floor and wall, Raceboy sudsed a rag and tried to reach for his little sister. She zinged out of his reach with a giggle. He reached again. She zinged out of his reach again. Finally he used his super speed. In this way he was able to keep up with her. He lathered her hair and her body and rinsed her off. "I'm not worrying about conditioner," he explained as he lifted her from the tub and stood her on one of the towels Super Qwok had draped across the wet floor.

A few more race-moments later and Katherine was dried off,

clothed in pajamas, and lying on her bed. "Whew," said Raceboy. "That's done."

Katherine said, "Teeth! Teeth! Teeth!"

Super Qwok ran his own tongue across his own teeth. "I think that means she needs to brush her teeth."

Raceboy said, "Oh, brother!"

The boys led Katherine back to the sink and got the toothpaste out.

"I'll hold the toothbrush. You squeeze the toothpaste," Raceboy explained.

"Me, me!" shouted Katherine.

Super Qwok shrugged and handed the tube to his sister.

Raceboy said, "I don't think that's—" as Katherine gave the tube a super-powered squeeze and toothpaste shot all over Raceboy's face. He howled in aggravation. "Super Qwok! I can't see!"

After Super Qwok got out another towel (*Mom's going to be mad about this laundry,* he thought) and scrubbed Raceboy's face, Raceboy said, "Where's Katherine?"

"I don't know. I thought you had her."

"I had the toothbrush!" Raceboy roared.

They found Katherine downstairs, dancing around the living room, falling down and giggling, "Watch this! Watch this! Watch this!"

Once they'd led her back upstairs to the bathroom, they gave her the prepared toothbrush and said, "Okay, brush."

She stuck the toothbrush in her mouth and sucked on it.

"No, no, no!" said Super Qwok. "That will make you sick. You've got to scrub!" He reached for the toothbrush.

"You better not do it," said Raceboy. "You'll scrub her face right off with your super powers. Here, let me brush her."

"If you do it, you'll brush so fast that you'll scrub them right off, too."

"So what do we do?" Raceboy asked.

"Wa-wa," Katherine answered.

"Let her rinse," said Super Qwok.

"All right," said Raceboy. "I'll get her a cup of water." He zipped downstairs for a cup, filled it with water, and was back upstairs in the blink of an eye. Katherine pulled the toothbrush from her mouth and giggled.

"You have to spit, Katherine," encouraged Super Qwok.

She took the water, put it in her mouth, and swished it around her teeth. "Good job, Katherine," said Super Qwok. "But you have to spit." So she did. All over Raceboy's face.

"Aaaaaaah!" yelled Raceboy.

Super Qwok giggled and got out another towel.

Afterward, they put her in her bed and covered her with her blankets. "There," said a still-damp Raceboy. "It's bedtime."

"Potty," said Katherine.

"Aaaaah!" said Raceboy and Super Qwok together. The process of pottying required removing her diaper and setting her on the toilet.

"I don't want to do this," said Raceboy. "Tell you what. Super Qwok, you take her diaper off, and I'll put her on the toilet."

"I'm not taking her diaper off! You're the fast one! I've got the powerful strength. I'll lift her up and set her on the toilet while you do the super-fast thing and whip the diaper off in Race-mode while I hold her."

"All right," grumbled Raceboy.

"But don't wipe her super-fast. That probably won't work."

"I'm not wiping her!" argued Raceboy.

"My hands will be full!" argued Super Qwok.

"So who's gonna?" Raceboy asked.

"We'll just let her air dry."

"Okay."

Super Qwok lifted Katherine atop the seat of the toilet; Raceboy undid the diaper and slid it from her behind in super speed; everybody waited and looked at one another. Katherine focused for a moment, and there was the sound of tinkling water.

"Yay!" everyone cheered. Katherine clapped her hands. "Katherine went pee-pee in the toilet like a big girl!"

Katherine giggled happily. Raceboy did the super-fast diapering, wrapped her up double-plus quick, and everybody washed their hands. They didn't hurry because they knew washing their hands slowly would kill the germs and keep them healthy.

Once again Katherine was placed in the bed, tucked in, and the boys were ready to tip-toe from the room.

"Story? Story?" asked Katherine.

"Oh, no!" said Raceboy and Super Qwok.

"I'm not reading it! I can't read!" said Super Qwok.

Raceboy said, "Yes, you can. Well, you might not be able to read, but you can remember the words. You pick one, and I'll pick one."

"All right." Super Qwok looked through the book shelf and at last came back with a worn-out board book. He read *Goodnight Moon*, and just as Raceboy had said, he knew the words.

Raceboy chose *Brown Bear, Brown Bear*.

At last the lights were off, and the room was still. The boys looked at one another expectantly, and prepared to sneak from the room when Katherine interrupted loudly: "Waaaaaaah! Waaaaaaaah!" she cried.

"Now what?" said one boy.

"What can we do now?" said another. Both boys were pulling the ends of their hair wishing Mom hadn't cut it so short so they could yank it out.

Raceboy said, "I know. I'll turn on music. That always helps us."

He pressed play on the CD player, and soothing instrumental music poured from the speakers like liquid sound.

"Waaaaaah! Waaaaaaah!" shrieked Katherine.

"I'm feeling like an old man," said Raceboy.

"Me, too," agreed Super Qwok. "This kid thing is crazy. Who would have kids?"

"What if I rock her?"

Super Qwok hesitated, "I don't know if that's such a good idea."

Raceboy held Katherine on his lap and began to rock. Katherine wiggled. Raceboy shifted to get a better grip. Katherine wiggled more, and when she wiggled this time, she was moving super-fast. Raceboy rocked faster, and faster, and was so intent on keeping his hold on Katherine, that he didn't notice he was rocking the chair in Race-mode. There are certain daily activities that it is not safe to do in Race-mode; it turns out rocking a baby to sleep is one of them. The rocking chair rolled over backwards in a somersault.

Raceboy groaned.

Super Qwok took the chair and set it back up. "You rock too fast. Here, let me do it. You hold Katherine."

While Raceboy held his little sister, Super Qwok pushed the chair forward and pulled the chair backward to the soothing strains of the music.

"Dink, Dink," whined Katherine.

"You don't need a drink," explained Raceboy. "You've already brushed."

"What if we just give her a sippy-cup of water?"

"Fine," groaned Raceboy, and he wiggled out from under Katherine and raced downstairs again, returning with Katherine's sippy-cup so she wouldn't spill all over her bedroom. "All these stairs are making me tired!"

"Katherine's making me tired," agreed Super Qwok.

Katherine slurped on the water. The quiet lasted for just enough seconds to give the boys hope that the quiet was going to last. Then, "Waaaah!"

Raceboy shook his head. "I can't handle this!"

"How about her blanket? She always likes her blanket."

The pink blanket was found after Raceboy frantically searched the bedroom. "I'd rather fight a super villain than put a toddler to bed! How do Mom and Dad do this every night?" Katherine cuddled up with the blanket against her cheek on Raceboy's lap.

Super Qwok pushed the rocking chair. "I think parents must be the original superheroes."

Katherine's wiggles slowed, and her whimpering and whining finally muted to a stream of inhales and exhales. Her eyes closed and she sighed.

She had her blanket. She'd had her drink. Music was playing.

She'd listened to stories, gone potty, brushed her teeth, and taken a bath with bubbles. Everything was as it should be. At long last, Katherine fell asleep.

Aunt Amie returned before Mom and Dad. When she came in, she discovered the house was quiet. She found Raceboy and Super Qwok sitting in the rocker upstairs, asleep, with a sleeping Katherine on their laps.

Very gently she moved Katherine to her own bed, then whispered, "Raceboy, Super Qwok! Why are you two asleep?"

Raceboy said, "Putting Katherine to bed? That would wear anybody out!"

Before Aunt Amie even noticed, Raceboy and Super Qwok disappeared, swapped their clothes for Alex and Bryan's pajamas, and crawled into their own beds. When Aunt Amie checked, she found her lovely nephews asleep and snoring peacefully in their own superhero sheets.

The Green Light

When Dad walked in the door, he didn't say, "Hi." Instead he walked straight down the front hall, set down his work things, and walked to the kitchen table.

Alex looked at Bryan and Katherine with a raised eyebrow. It wasn't like Dad to ignore the kids.

Dad did not crack a smile, or even acknowledge any of the other family members during dinner. Instead he chewed his food mechanically and afterward sat on the couch and stared at the television. This fact alone was unusual, because Alex and Bryan could count on one hand between the two of them how often their Dad had sat down to watch television on his own.

When Alex or Bryan or Katherine said something, Dad would respond, but his voice was always distant and disinterested. He held Anna while she slept, but the instant she cried he passed her off to Mom.

He went to bed at the same time as the kids, got up the next morning and left before they woke up.

Alex said, "Did you notice how strangely Dad was acting? I mean, it was almost like he wasn't even here. He was so quiet, and he didn't say anything. And when he did talk, it was so flat and emotionless. It just wasn't like Dad at all."

"I know," Bryan agreed. "It was really mysterious. We're going

to have to keep an eye on him."

That night, the same Dad came home from work. Like a robot he walked through the front door. He strode through the house without a glance sideways. He didn't say, "Hello." He didn't speak unless spoken to, and his voice had the same flat, toneless quality as the night before.

While Dad stared at the television screen for the second night in a row, Alex and Bryan came to Mom in the kitchen as she scrubbed the dishes in the sink.

Alex asked, "Mom, why is Dad acting weird?"

Mom only said, "Well, he's been under a lot of pressure, you know, working and stuff, so I'm sure it's because of that." But Alex and Bryan thought that was an excuse, and the look on their Mom's face told them that she was worried about Dad and really didn't know what to say.

The next day Alex and Bryan decided it was time for Raceboy and Super Qwok to do some spying and see what was going on with Dad.

They followed him the whole day. And he didn't do anything mysterious, except he never acted normal. But what was most mysterious was that Raceboy and Super Qwok noticed that Dad wasn't the only one who was acting weird; there were a lot of people who were acting emotionless as they went about their lives in Clifton. They especially noticed it while Dad was working in the Clifton Public Library. The boys watched smiling people walk into the library, then walk out with blank, robotic stares.

That evening at home, Alex and Bryan told Mom that they thought Dad wasn't the only person who was acting unusual. Mom said, "I'll tell you what. Aunt Amie's here right now. I'll run up to the library and just check it out myself just so you guys don't have to worry." She ruffled the hair on both boys' heads as she walked toward the door. But both boys knew that it was because she was worried that she went.

Fifteen minutes later, Mom was back. She walked through the living room and into the kitchen. Aunt Amie asked her something. Mom grunted in response. After two or three more grunts, Aunt Amie decided she would have better conversation at home with her own woodwork. She said as much and left. Mom cleaned up dinner and sat waiting for Dad to get home. When Dad got home, the two of them sat side by side on the couch and stared at the television.

Bryan took Katherine's tiny hand in his.

"Now I'm really scared," said Alex as he held Anna. "I get it, though. If you go in the library, you act like a robot. I guess we'd better not go in there."

"But how are we going to figure out what's going on if we don't go in there?" Bryan asked.

"We don't know what we are up against. What kind of shield do we need? What kind of force is this? Is it radio waves? Is it hypnosis? Is it some kind of mind-virus?"

Bryan argued, "But we have to go. Whatever is going on, we need to stop it. And we know to expect something. It's up to us." He squeezed Katherine's hand and looked at his emotionless parents.

After everyone was asleep for the night, Raceboy and Super Qwok borrowed Dad's library keys and snuck out of the house.

At the library, Super Qwok unlocked the door and opened it. The inside of the library was dark except for the lone light that was always left on when the library was closed.

"I don't feel anything from here," Raceboy explained, standing before the open door.

He raced in, then out, in Speed-mode.

Super Qwok examined him carefully. "Smile."

Raceboy did.

"Hmm. Laugh."

"Super Qwok, I'm fine. I feel the same."

Raceboy burst into the library a second time. He flipped the main lights on.

Super Qwok braced the front door with a doorstop. Then he joined his brother.

The boys looked at one another. "Still nothing," said Raceboy.

"What's that?" asked Super Qwok. "That glow?"

There was a greenish light emanating from the back of the library.

Raceboy said, "I didn't turn any lights on back there."

"Careful," said Super Qwok, and together the two approached the back of the library. There, up above the shelves on the very back wall, out of sight of the front doors, was a device. It glowed green, a sickly glow that covered the room, gave everything a green cast.

Raceboy said, "That's it, right there. That's what it is."

What kind of device was it? It was hard to tell. It resembled a lantern: the center was a glowing sphere, while the top and bottom appeared to be dark metal.

Super Qwok took a single step forward into the green glow when something happened. He turned and ran straight at Raceboy. And before Raceboy could even imagine such a thing possible, Super Qwok punched him right in the face.

The power in that punch knocked Raceboy down the row of books, out the door, and into the brick wall of the building across the street.

As he lay against the wall of the building, Raceboy tried to figure out what had just happened. It's not easy to take a superhero with speed power by surprise, but it can be done, as Super Qwok had

just demonstrated. Raceboy remembered the brief instant Super Qwok turned from the light before he ran and punched Raceboy. He remembered his brother's eyes: distant, far away, emotionless. Just like Mom and Dad.

Whatever had taken over Mom and Dad's thoughts had taken over Super Qwok's.

Raceboy gained his feet and raced back to the library. Super Qwok stepped from the door, ready for him. He held his fists up and stared, but it wasn't an angry look or a mad look. It was a va-cant look, a placid look.

Raceboy needed a plan. He couldn't very well hurt Super Qwok, especially since it was clear something had taken over Super Qwok, something that was using him, controlling him. Super Qwok was the car, but something, or someone else, was in the driver's seat.

Super Qwok punched at Raceboy, who ducked. Raceboy knew that in a fair fight between the two of them, his speed more than made up for Super Qwok's strength — unless one of Super Qwok's punches or kicks connected, because then all the speed in the world didn't matter if he was lying in a pile of rubble beneath a collapsed building. He didn't use his speed to attack, only defend, and he allowed Super Qwok to swing and kick his way forward, away from the library, into the street.

Raceboy looked at Super Qwok's utility belt, to see if he could find the spot where Super Qwok stored his magical bag. It was a very powerful magic bag, about the size of a garbage bag, but the thing was you could fill it and it would never get bigger. Raceboy let Super Qwok continue his attack, then using his super speed, he charged Super Qwok on the left. It was as though Super Qwok was paused; Raceboy zipped under Super Qwok's left arm, lifted the flap of his utility belt, and pulled the bag out. As Raceboy dashed past, he flapped and unfolded the magic bag, shaking it out to its full size.

Without breaking speed, he turned a circle to Super Qwok's other side and leapt. He lifted the bag like a parachute above his head and brought it down right on top of Super Qwok, and with a deft flick of his wrist, twisted just right so Super Qwok tipped over as Raceboy yanked the bag's mouth closed.

Just to make sure, Raceboy peeked in the mouth of the bag. Sure enough, Super Qwok was inside, but he was tiny, no larger than a piece of corn. Raceboy secured the drawstring on the magical bag, folded it up, and put it in one of his own utility belt pouches.

Raceboy could think of only one hero with a suit that might be powerful enough to resist the rays of the green light. He sent a message to Knight-in-shining-armor-boy.

While he waited for Knight-in-shining-armor-boy to arrive,

Raceboy tried testing the range of the light. He discovered that the light made a very clear circle on the carpet of the library. It was only as Super Qwok passed over this circle that the light, or whatever force controlled it, was able to take over Super Qwok. And presumably, it was this circle that all the people in Clifton like Mom and Dad had crossed to be taken over as well.

The clip-clop-clip-clop of horse's hooves announced the approach of Knight-in-shining-armor-boy. Raceboy waved to his friend. The robo-horse slowed and stopped beside the library door.

Raceboy explained the situation. The two approached the green light while they talked, and Raceboy showed Knight-in-shining-armor-boy the green circle on the floor. "This is as near as we can get without feeling the effects of that mysterious light. Another step and I think the light can overpower us."

The two heroes stood looking at the green device hanging high up the wall. At last Knight-in-shining-armor-boy said, "So Super Qwok is stuffed inside a magic bag in your utility belt?"

"Yes."

"Can I see?"

Raceboy unfolded the bag and opened the drawstrings. He let Knight-in-shining-armor-boy peer into the opening.

Knight-in-shining-armor-boy said, "He really is in there! What do you think it feels like?"

Raceboy peeked again. "It looks like being in a sleeping bag, except it's a sleeping bag the size of a warehouse."

Knight-in-shining-armor-boy slid his visor down, covering his eyes. He gripped his warhammer. "Well, if it does the same thing to me as it did to Super Qwok, then stick me in the bag. Maybe you'll figure out how to free us at some point. But whatever you do, don't let me free if I'm under the control of that light!"

"I understand."

Knight-in-shining-armor-boy crossed the circle of light on the floor.

Raceboy held the bag ready.

Knight-in-shining-armor-boy tromped to the back of the library, all the while looking up at the green light. He got closer and closer. When he was finally close enough, he swung his warhammer with all of his might, brought it crashing against the light.

The green light broke. Tiny shards of green glass shattered in the air and fell to the ground. As the tiny green flecks fell, they disappeared like lightning bugs when they turn their glow off. All that was left on the ground was a broken mechanism and black ash.

"It's fine," said Knight-in-shining-armor-boy. "The light is gone."

Both boys looked at the broken device. Raceboy said, "Your suit was strong enough to resist the powers of the device."

"Thank goodness!" said Knight-in-shining-armor-boy.

Raceboy asked, "You are really you, aren't you? You're not some creature pretending to be you?"

Knight-in-shining-armor-boy laughed. "Do you think I would have broken that light if I wasn't really me?"

"It would be pretty diabolical to take control of you, then destroy the lamp. But I can tell from your laugh that you're really you. I wonder if breaking the light freed Super Qwok?"

Raceboy opened the end of the magic bag and looked inside. "Super Qwok," he whispered into the bag, though he wasn't sure why. It was almost like seeing a small Super Qwok meant that the volume should be small as well. "Smile at me, buddy." Raceboy looked up. "He's just staring. I guess destroying the light isn't enough."

The heroes examined the remains of the light. The dark ends were an unfamiliar black metal. The glass, or transparent shell, was gone, but the light's guts were still visible. In fact, they were a stringy knot like overcooked spaghetti.

Raceboy picked the clump up. "This doesn't look like any technology I've ever seen." It was about the size of a closed fist.

Knight-in-shining-armor-boy shook his head. "Maybe a mad scientist?"

"Or," replied Raceboy, holding the unusual knot, "another planet." He tried to separate the strings.

"Could it be?"

"The meteorite that gave Super Qwok and me super powers crashed into Earth from space. Perhaps this comes from the same place. Or maybe someplace else. I just don't know."

"What could they want?" Knight-in-shining-armor-boy mused.

Raceboy shook his head and turned the blob over and over. "Who can understand the mind of an alien race?"

"That's weird," Knight-in-shining-armor-boy said. "What's it doing?"

"It's vibrating. Shaking a bit."

"Set it on the table. Let's see."

Raceboy placed the blob-like shape on the library table. It didn't move. And then it did, a rhythmic, pulsing jerk almost like—

"Is it a heartbeat?" asked Knight-in-shining-armor-boy.

"Or a signal?" asked Raceboy. "Maybe we'd better destroy it completely."

Knight-in-shining-armor-boy said, "All right. Set it on the ground. I'll destroy it once and for all."

Raceboy set the coiled mess on the ground at their feet. Knight-in-shining-armor-boy lifted his warhammer above his head and slammed it straight onto the pile of spaghetti. The stringy stuff was flattened and smashed.

The heroes looked at one another expectantly. "That didn't stop it," Raceboy said.

All of the sudden, from outside the library, they heard a loud roar, louder than the loudest freight train to ever travel the train tracks of Clifton. It was the roar of a thousand freight trains or tornados or dinosaurs screaming together.

"What is going on?" Knight-in-shining-armor-boy asked.

Raceboy raced from the library faster than you could say, "Raceboy." He looked to the sky and saw a giant silver shape—a spacecraft—descending with pedestal legs extended. It hissed steam as the shape settled onto the street in front of the library. The train-like roar immediately began to fade.

The craft was large, so large that the massive legs held its bulk above the tops of the two story buildings, where it covered at least four blocks of Clifton's downtown. Had it not been night already, it would have blocked out the sun. Smoke issued from vents on its surface.

The fading roar changed to a whine as whatever engines powered the ship shut down. A circle glowed on the bottom of the ship, then the circle became a cylinder stretching toward the library's entrance. With a clunk, the cylinder stopped high above the street, and a hatch opened. Stairs extended like a dog's tongue reaching toward the ground.

The hatch was illuminated with a dim light like far-off flames. Then two shapes descended the staircase. And they were not human.

The first and strangest being to descend from the ship was metal, though whether it was a robot or a robotic shell, neither Raceboy nor Knight-in-shining-armor-boy knew. It had three snake-like legs of metal that clunked upon each step of the silver staircase. At its waist, or at least, the place where you and I think a waist should be, there was a silver belt. This was no ordinary belt, however, because it had tentacles that reached from it and wriggled. These weren't metal tentacles like the legs; instead, they looked like octopus tentacles that had been hooked up to a machine. Not only could the tentacles move about, grab things, and wave, but the belt could spin in a circle around the creature's waist.

As if this weird machine or alien couldn't get any stranger, it did, because on the other side of the belt, the top, it had three long necks. The necks, like the legs, were also metal, but each ended with a round bulb. Each bulb was nothing but a sphere that glowed green, the same green as the light in the library, the same

green that had taken over Mom and Dad and Super Qwok.

In any other story, the second being to descend the ship would have inspired fear or caused riots. Walking behind the first creature, however, it looked downright normal. It had the more familiar two legs, and they stepped in the same manner that legs usually do. They were covered with a suit, a cushiony, padded, reflective suit of the type worn by our own astronauts as they make space-walks. The two familiar-looking boots stretched up to knees and a waist, and even a chest and arms that carried a gun-like device. That was where the familiarity ended. There was a flick of motion and the boys saw that the space suit had a tail. And a glass helmet: a strangely-shaped glass helmet that displayed a long snout, big teeth, and beady green eyes. In fact, it looked like—

"A crocodile?" said Raceboy. "In a space suit?"

"Or a dinosaur," said Knight-in-shining-armor-boy.

Both beings, the mysterious three-legged, three-headed robotic monstrosity and his space-suited dino-friend reached the ground and faced Raceboy and Knight-in-shining-armor-boy.

Sound came from the three legged machine. "You have meddled in our affairs for the last time. It is now our judgment that you will be destroyed."

"Who are you?" asked Raceboy.

"We are beyond the ability of your isolated brains to fathom. To use a poor equivalent from your limited schema, we are Overlord. All are one; one are all. We will collectivize your planet. We will teach you the beauty and purity of sharing."

"I don't think it's called 'sharing' if you have to force us to do it," Raceboy answered, clenching his fists.

"Sounds like fighting words to me," agreed Knight-in-shining-armor-boy.

"We are Overlord. You cannot stop us. You will share, or you will not exist."

The space-suited lizard-man pointed the barrel of its weapon at Raceboy. Before it could pull the equivalent of the trigger, Raceboy used Speed-mode to zip to the side. Smoke and lightning crashed in the spot he had stood a moment previous. It cleared to expose a crater in the asphalt of the street.

Raceboy raced past the lizard-man and whipped the weapon from his hands (or claws or whatever). Although not as strong as Super Qwok, he did have enough super strength to break the weapon, which he threw at the feet of Overlord.

Overlord's tentacled arms twittered and raced circles around its waist like the blades of a fan. The three glowing orbs writhed. "You anger us. You are ignorant of your ignorance. Your non-compliance will be punished. We will punish those you love."

As if on cue, the street around Raceboy and Knight-in-shining-armor-boy filled with the very same people who had recently been acting strangely. Dad, Mom, and dozens of other people from Clifton marched to form a circle around Overlord, the lizard-man, Raceboy, and Knight-in-shining-armor-boy.

The threat was clear. Submit or those you love will be harmed. Knight-in-shining-armor-boy didn't wait another moment. He struck the lizard-man with his warhammer. The device, which normally could sense a living creature and would only shock it, instead stayed rock-hard as it crashed into the glass helmet of the space suit. With a crunch and a crash, the helmet shattered. A green gas puffed from the broken helmet. Within, the lizard-man choked and gasped. It tried to reach its own head, but there was nothing it could do to replace the air it was breathing with the air it wanted to breathe. At last its beady black eyes stopped blinking, and the lizard-man slipped to the ground.

The Overlord's heads swayed and wiggled. The green orb-like

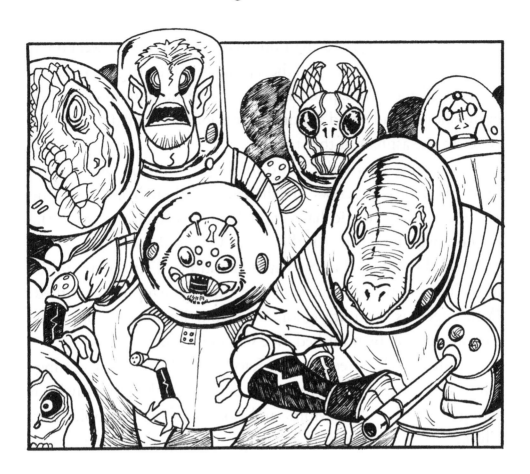

eyes took in the scene of the fallen lizard-man. The voice echoed again. "You see now how useless isolation is. One attacks; one falls. The difference is that if you fall, you are finished. When we fall, we continue."

As if to reinforce his point, the stairs of the spacecraft filled with the marching feet of additional lizard-men and more. Creatures of many shapes descended the stairs. The count of their appendages varied; the count of their heads varied; some had tails; others had long necks. Each wore a suit of the same material as the first lizard-man without any embellishments to tell one another apart. Each was also armed with a weapon similar to the lizard-man, though varying in operations to match their hands or tentacles or claws.

"There are too many for us," Raceboy said. Rarely before had he felt such a heavy burden; his entire existence as he knew it hung in the balance of this moment. *Action,* he told himself. *I must act. If I fail, I fail everyone: Mom, Dad, Bryan, Katherine, Anna, Logan, everyone. They will all be turned into glazed-eyed creatures in the thrall of Overlord, just like those creatures from the ship.*

Indeed, the menagerie of creatures had lined up alongside Overlord.

"I'm going to attack the Overlord," Raceboy whispered. "For all his talk of 'we,' I think *he* is controlling everything else."

Knight-in-shining-armor-boy grunted. "I understand."

Raceboy inhaled and felt that momentary rush of excitement he always felt as he stepped out of regular speed into super speed. The world around him slowed to a standstill and he shifted from stillness to a sprint while unhooking his laser-sword from his utility belt and flipping the switch to activate the crackling blue energy extending from the handle that he held with both hands as he sped along the weapon-toting alien creatures. He passed each and sliced clean through its weapon with the sparkling blue energy blade so swiftly that the sound of each cut was a solid buzz of severed metal. Overlord stood still, like all the others, locked in the familiar time of sixty seconds to a minute while Raceboy was moving through a different time, the time where a single second stretches on and on and on. His feet pounded over the ground, his heart pumped, his lungs sucked in air while Overlord's round eyes cast a glow, a green glow. Raceboy held his laser-sword sideways, ready to slice through all three of the metal necks when he stepped into that green light.

Knight-in-shining-armor-boy was used to Raceboy's speed; at least, he was as used to Raceboy's speed as anyone who can only move at regular speed can be. He was used to seeing Raceboy shift into Speed-mode, and then all bets were off because everything would happen so quickly! After Raceboy told Knight-in-shining-armor-boy that he was planning to attack, there was a moment when Raceboy was there, and then a moment when he wasn't and a crackling of blue energy shot through about half of the alien creatures' weapons in a path straight at Overlord. It was like a lightning bolt had erupted from the right and was racing toward Overlord. The lightning sputtered out. It was as though Overlord had a shield that protected him and the lightning didn't touch him. Raceboy stood still, no longer moving fast, though he did still have his laser-sword in hand. The green light! Knight-in-shining-armor-boy realized. The glow from the green light of Overlord's three heads had touched Raceboy!

"Only you remain," explained Overlord. "We versus you. You cannot defeat us, for we are united. You are isolated. Prove your worth: join us."

"No," said Knight-in-shining-armor-boy as he clenched the handle of his warhammer tightly.

The three heads waved with displeasure, and the rippling passed through the line of space-suited aliens, and even into the circling people of Clifton. Knight-in-shining-armor-boy looked around and saw that the people were moving closer.

Standing beside Overlord, Raceboy opened the magic bag and shook it. Super Qwok spilled out, caught himself, and stood between his brother and Overlord. With the rest of the circling bodies, both heroes walked in a daze toward Knight-in-shining-armor-boy.

Overlord explained, "Submit, and you will be treated well. You will share a place of distinction among us."

"If everyone is the same, how can you set me above the others?" Knight-in-shining-armor-boy asked.

"We are all equals," explained Overlord. "Some are more equal than others."

"That doesn't make sense," Knight-in-shining-armor-boy yelled.

The ring of people and suited aliens tightened. Knight-in-shining-armor-boy thought about Raceboy's last words, that Overlord was controlling the rest of the people. He knew that he didn't have Raceboy's speed, but he did have a pretty heavy warhammer and a

heck of a throwing arm.

He slung his right arm backward, moved his left arm forward to help keep his balance, and threw the warhammer. It sailed over the ground, and it did not twist end over end like a knife; instead the heavy head plowed the air, broke the air, pushed the air with deadly force. The brick-shaped head crashed right into Overlord's tentacled belt. *BZZZZH!* There was an electrical explosion, and two of the three heads sagged. The green light faded. The third head began to spark and smoke.

Overlord's legs buckled, and the entire creature or machine or robot collapsed on the ground.

The effect was immediate. Both humans and aliens shook their heads as though coming out of a sleep.

Lizard-men rasped, "We-uh-goo-da-woo-da-wee-a-we-eh," which in Lizarding meant, "Where are we? What are we doing here?"

Other lizard-men answered, "Oo-ah-blah-eh-blah-bleh," or, "We don't know."

Similar conversations went on with other creatures and even humans.

Super Qwok said, "The last thing I remember I was in the library."

Raceboy said, "I was under control of the Overlord, wasn't I?"

Knight-in-shining-armor-boy said, "You're both free, now."

Raceboy led Super Qwok to the broken Overlord unit. "That was what was controlling you and me." He lifted Knight-in-shining-armor-boy's warhammer. "Here, that was a heck of a shot."

"I've been practicing." Knight-in-shining-armor-boy slid the warhammer into the sling he wore on his back.

Super Qwok looked from Overlord's fallen body to the spaceship still covering the sky above Clifton. "I've never seen a spaceship this big!"

Raceboy wrinkled his nose, "Have you ever seen a spaceship before?"

"Well, no. Now that you mention it. It sure is bigger than I imagined."

Most of the humans had dispersed. Each wobbled his or her uncertain way back home to bed and to the hope that he or she would wake in the morning to an alarm clock and the memory of an unusual dream about standing beneath a spaceship parked above downtown Clifton in the middle of the night. There would be more to remember, but since it would only be a dream anyway, it could safely be forgotten. Right?

The alien creatures, likewise, shuffled their way up the staircase into the craft. Without the Overlord's ability to speak English, there was no real way to communicate with the assortment of creatures. Body language was useless when communicating with disoriented aliens who have just been returned to consciousness after who knows how long while inside space suits on a distant planet with a bunch of other equally confused aliens. Raceboy and Super Qwok had halfway expected that a technology capable of traveling the stars would equip their space suits with universal translators, but it looked like the only one capable of such translation was the Overlord unit lying broken at the foot of the ramp. The rest of the creatures, being less equal than the Overlord, had only deserved to follow orders, not communicate.

There was no organized good-bye. As one of the last aliens returned to the stairs, Raceboy caught its arm. This was a large, long limbed creature with a face like a sloth. Raceboy pointed to the broken shape of the Overlord. The creature acknowledged

Raceboy by kicking the Overlord and screeching.

"I guess that means we'll deal with it ourselves," Raceboy explained.

After the last creature entered the craft, the staircase ascended, then the cylinder slid upwards like an elevator to disappear from view. The circle glowed for a moment before disappearing. The craft hummed. It was a different noise than the rumble of its landing. This was more of a whine. Slowly the spaceship lifted, swiveled, then crept above Clifton until its lights reached the distance. It was as though the ship had race powers and went into Racemode: its lights became a straight line that shrank into the night sky and disappeared in a point of light no bigger than a star.

Raceboy clapped Knight-in-shining-armor-boy on the back of his armor. "Without you we would have all become servants of the Overlord."

"Yea, thanks," Super Qwok said. "That ship was cool and all, but I prefer to make my own choices."

Knight-in-shining-armor-boy said simply, "You're welcome." Then he kicked the broken Overlord. "So what do we choose to do with a broken Overlord?"

THE BUBBLEGUM CAPER

"It's Mr. Mischief," Alex explained to Bryan as the two changed into their superhero costumes. "He's stolen all of the bubble gum from the bubble gum machine at the store. We have to stop him and get that candy back." Alex zipped into his costume and became Raceboy. Bryan took slightly longer, but at last Super Qwok joined his brother.

"Me, too," said Katherine.

"No," explained Raceboy. "You're too young. It's not safe."

"I have an outfit," Katherine said and stomped one foot atop her blanket, which was dragging the ground.

"No," said Super Qwok. "You need more than an outfit to be a superhero."

Zip. Katherine burst into Race-mode and tied her blanket around Super Qwok's mouth.

"Merby fooby," said Super Qwok, which was as close to "Very funny," as he could manage through a pink blanket.

Raceboy untied the blanket and removed it from Super Qwok's face. "We've said, 'No.' You need to listen."

Katherine started to cry.

"Stop crying," Raceboy said. "We're trying to handle an emergency here!"

The boys loaded into the Race-mobile and finally let Katherine

195

get in, also.

"This is ridiculous," mumbled Super Qwok.

"Mommy!" Katherine bellowed as Raceboy turned the car towards the store.

"What's wrong now?" Super Qwok asked.

"I want Mommy." Katherine's eyes were filled with tears.

Raceboy grumbled, "How are you going to be a superhero if you cry the second you leave the house to fight crime?"

The heroes could hear the super-bubble-popping sounds of Mr. Mischief, but they couldn't see him. He wasn't at the store (though the gumball machine was, indeed, empty). He wasn't at the Clifton Public Library. The popping grew louder as the heroes ventured nearer the community park, which was, they knew, one of his favorite places to spread mayhem and cause mischief.

At last the heroes saw Mr. Mischief. He leaned against a tree near the playground equipment chewing a massive wad of gumballs.

Everyone knows that big round gumballs come in a thousand flavors that last for about five minutes, and they make for terrible bubbles. Nonetheless, Mr. Mischief was chonking on his gum and splatting great messy bubbles.

When he saw the heroes, the first thing Mr. Mischief did was blow the biggest bubble he could. Bigger and stickier grew the bubble, until it hung hugely from his mouth nearly as tall as the villain himself. *POP!* The bubble exploded all over Raceboy and Super Qwok. They were totally covered with sticky, gooey, glue-like gum. They couldn't even move.

Mr. Mischief began to guffaw, until a piercing shriek cut him off.

"MOOOOOM!" It was more than a scream. It was a super-powered scream. It was a scream so loud, that Mr. Mischief tried to cover his ears with his hands. He still had the gum in his mouth, but it was forgotten.

"MOOOOM!" Racegirl yelled again. The gum fell from Mr. Mischief's mouth to the ground, and he tumbled forward to step on it. It was so sticky he found himself trapped. "Oh, my ears," he whined. "Oh, the pain." But he was stuck, and couldn't escape.

Super Qwok broke from the bubbly mess and helped Raceboy. Then the boys had an idea.

"Mr. Mischief, you can work off your gum by babysitting Race-girl!"

Since he was stuck in his own bubble gum, he had no choice but to agree.

"Look, Racegirl," said the boys, "we're at the park. Why don't you do some super playing?"

She zipped up the slide and down the slide, on the swings, through the monkey bars, and was back in the time that it took for Mr. Mischief to try to argue for his freedom.

"That's one side-effect of being super-fast," Raceboy explained. "It's easy to get bored."

That's when Racegirl sat in front of Mr. Mischief and simply stared at him. He began to get uncomfortable, shuffling a bit to the left or right. But there was nowhere to go. He was trapped in his own gum.

At last he broke down and began to juggle sticks that he found on the ground.

Racegirl clapped.

Mr. Mischief bowed and did and encore performance. Then he turned his hat upside down and pulled a handkerchief from it, then made the handkerchief disappear into thin air.

Racegirl gasped.

He did a puppet show in which Mr. Mischief escaped from jail and triumphed over the bumbling forces of Raceboy and Super

Qwok, who were neither fast nor strong but only clumsy and dim-witted. "He'd better watch it," Raceboy told Super Qwok.

Racegirl giggled.

Mr. Mischief told dozens of knock-knock jokes, actual funny ones that didn't include either peanut-butter or jelly (which were the only ones Raceboy or Super Qwok ever seemed to come up with).

Only once did Racegirl remember that she missed her mommy, and then she became sad for a moment and shrieked, "MOM!" Mr. Mischief covered his ears and shed tears of his own with the little girl.

After a while Super Qwok unstuck Mr. Mischief from the gum and said, "All right, Mr. Mischief. You've earned your bubble gum."

Mr. Mischief let his eyes snap back and forth between the heroes and freedom. His mouth worked in agitation. He was like a rabbit that is cornered by a predator and is trying to gauge its chances of survival. Suddenly he ran, hand atop his hat to keep it from falling off, racing as though his life depended on his escape.

"Wow. Look at him go," Raceboy said as Mr. Mischief passed the end of the community pool and turned right. "Not quite as fast as me. But pretty fast."

Racegirl frowned and watched her babysitter escape. Her lip quivered. "MR. MISCHIEF!" The sound of her cry echoed down the streets of Clifton.

"Don't worry," said Super Qwok. "We haven't seen the last of him. He always comes back."

THE TIME RACEBOY AND SUPER QWOK'S MOM FOUND OUT THEIR SECRET IDENTITIES PART ONE

THE DRAGON

Once our heroes faced a very different sort of problem. It wasn't a terrible villain. It wasn't a scientific mastermind. It wasn't a perilous monster. Actually, it was all of these things, but it was more than these.

It was worse; it was their mom.

That's right. The Mom of Alex and Bryan found out their secret identities as superheroes. It happened innocently enough. The boys were at home playing when the Race-alarm sounded, and the boys were called out.

A dragon had been spotted rampaging down Main Street of Clifton. This was no ordinary dragon. It was a six-legged dragon, with two little arms right next to its face that it could use to grab food and stuff it into its sharp jaws. It was pink, with blue eyes and purple wings, and it blew fire all around itself and roared down the street like a locomotive. Where it had come from, no one knew. Folks would speculate in the coming days that it had escaped from some mad scientist's laboratory; some even blamed Dr. Devious. Only much later would Raceboy and Super Qwok discover the truth about the dragon.

Alex and Bryan raced to their closet door and opened the secret panel that teleported them to the Qwok Tower, the abandoned grain elevator that was their secret hideout. They changed in an

instant into their crime fighting outfits. Raceboy jumped into the Race-mobile; Super Qwok got onto the Qwok-cycle. They hit the portal that teleported them from the Qwok Tower to a sidestreet in cloaked mode, which means that their vehicles weren't visible to the naked eye. It wasn't until they reached Main Street that they turned off the cloaking devices and their vehicles appeared on the road. And there, in front of them, they saw the dragon.

Each boy said, "Whoa!"

Meanwhile, Alex and Bryan's mom decided she was going to clean their room. Moms have some kind of instinctive programming that makes them appreciate clean rooms, and since Alex and Bryan were outside playing (Mom thought), she decided it would be a good time to clean some of the toys the boys didn't play with and put them in a box to sell during her annual garage sale.

She was planning to go through all the stuffed animals in their closet when she opened the closet door and noticed a thin sliver of darkness, as though there was a second door open within.

Another person would likely have missed such a small switch, but Alex and Bryan's mom was observant. When she flipped the switch, the inside of the closet was replaced with a wide open space: the Qwok Tower. (How, you may ask, can the door lead directly to the Qwok Tower? The switch opened a portal, a direct link that connected the two spaces despite the intervening distance. It was actually an invention of Dr. Devious's that he had tried to use to rob the vault at the First Federal Bank of Clifton. Raceboy and Super Qwok had foiled that plan, then decided to use Devious's invention, since trying to change into superhero costumes in a dormer attic was both dusty and left numerous bumps on their heads. Besides, they were acquiring quite a collection of gizmos and doohickeys and needed a larger space to store everything.)

Mom saw all of the devices of a crime-fighting duo. She realized in that instant that Alex was Raceboy and Bryan was Super Qwok.

And she remembered how, only moments before, she had heard sirens in the distance, which meant that Raceboy and Super Qwok were on the way to danger. "Oh, no! My boys," she gasped, and she knew that she needed to follow and protect them.

Mom raced out of the house, jumped into the van, and drove uptown, looking for signs of trouble. Once she found trouble, she knew she would find Raceboy and Super Qwok.

She didn't need to go or look far before she saw, on Main Street, two superheroes standing beside their vehicles watching down the street as a rampaging dragon raced towards them breathing smoke and brimstone from its mouth. Its coiled tail rolled behind it and whipped with a ferocious crack. The clatter of its claws against the ground was a fearsome sound.

Unaware that Mom was coming, Raceboy said to his brother, "Let's run Maryland," which was superhero lingo for an oft-practiced maneuver requiring teamwork and coordination.

"All right," agreed Super Qwok, who got ready to sling Raceboy high up into the air where he would be able to use his jet-pack and laser-sword for maximum efficiency.

Before they could implement their plan, however, they saw a flash from the corner of their eyes. And there, racing ahead of them, on foot, was their mom.

She yelled over her shoulder, "Don't worry, boys! I'll protect you from the dragon!"

Super Qwok looked at Raceboy, "Do you see what I see?"

Raceboy looked back and forth between his mother and his brother, "Is that—Is that—That's our mom!" He whispered this last because he didn't want anyone to overhear their conversation and realize their secret identities.

"It's all right, boys! I'll take care of it!" Mom yelled.

Super Qwok wrinkled his nose. "Do you think Mom can take care of a fire-breathing dragon with six legs, purple wings, and those little arms that seem perfectly suited for stuffing food into its ravenous jaws?"

Raceboy shook his head. "Uh, eh, uh. We don't have time to hesitate. We better do something about this!"

Yes, mother of superheroes though she was, Mom was not quite a superhero herself. She had a number of supermother powers: she could see dust beneath a doily; she could detect sound waves from crying babies across vast distances; she knew just when to make chocolate chip cookies for an afternoon snack. But she lacked the skills to deal with fire-breathing dragons that have tiny arms beside their mouths.

As Mom intercepted the dragon armed only with a mother's love, the dragon leaned its snaking head at the ground, scooped her up with its extra appendages, opened its long, alligator-like jaw, and tossed her into its mouth.

Super Qwok reacted first; he launched himself with a power leap straight into the dragon's hideous mouth. He landed on the moist tongue beside Mom just as the dragon began to chomp down.

It is a well-known fact that the muscles a crocodile uses to open its jaws are very weak in comparison to the muscles it uses to bite down. In this respect the dragon was no different. It had a powerful bite. Super Qwok had just enough time to put both his hands above his head, brace his feet, and push with all his might against the top of the dragon's mouth as that jaw clamped with the force of a falling mountain.

Rather than a soft, chewy Mom, the dragon discovered its mouth was full of a small, but very unchewy Super Qwok. It began to make gagging noises. It moved its tongue, which danced across Super Qwok's back like the ticklish little terror that it was, then touched his ears with gooey, sticky, dragon saliva.

Super Qwok pushed up with all his might, forcing the dragon's jaws wide, grabbed Mom in a bear-hug and stomped against the bottom of the dragon's mouth. The dragon tried to roar in pain but jetted flames that spurted Super Qwok and Mom to the ground, where Super Qwok rolled and protected Mom as best as he could though the back of his outfit was on fire.

Raceboy raced to put out the fire as fast as possible. He grabbed his mother and said, "You have to leave here, ma'am, for your own protection!"

"Don't worry," replied mom. "Your secret's safe with me. I won't tell anybody that you're my son."

Raceboy grimaced. "Mom! Go back home!"

Meanwhile, the dragon whipped its tale with a ferocious crack and knocked Raceboy to the ground beside Super Qwok.

"Oomph!" Raceboy grunted.

Super Qwok groaned, "Stop, drop, and roll."

The dragon lumbered above Mom and prepared to strike her with a blow from its razor-sharp claw.

Fortunately for Mom, Raceboy was a superhero, and Raceboy was super-fast. As the dragon's claw curled straight at Mom, Raceboy launched himself from the ground and raced like a bolt of lightning. He stood between the claw and Mom, and the claw struck him in the chest, bouncing from him.

Mom gasped, "Ooh, I'll save you! Don't worry, Raceboy!" and she ran around in front of Raceboy and walked right up to that dragon and put her finger in that dragon's face and said, "Now you listen here! I am this boy's mother, and you are *not* going to hurt my boy!"

The dragon paused, wrinkled its reptilian eyes at Mom and went, "Urgh?" because, of course, no mother had ever told the dragon

to mind its own business before. The result was that the dragon decided Mom might taste better cooked rather than raw.

The dragon opened its mouth to suck in air. *WHOO-OH* went the sound of air going into the dragon's mouth. Mom's clothing was ruffled by the powerful inhalation. Both Super Qwok and Raceboy knew exactly what was going to happen to Mom if she didn't get out of the way.

The heroes looked at one another; it was as though they read each other's minds. Raceboy took care of Mom. Super Qwok took care of the dragon.

Racing, Raceboy grabbed Mom and peeled away from the dragon with cheetah speed.

Super Qwok stood right in front of the dragon as it prepared to belch its powerful jet of fire. He timed his reaction precisely, leapt at the dragon's head, reached out to grab the dragon's mouth, and held it shut just before the dragon blew its blast of flames.

As pointed out earlier in this story, the muscles used to open a jaw are significantly weaker than the muscles used to bite down. If the dragon had ever pondered this fact of life, it was much too late now. This experience was just about like trying to blow your nose and having someone pinch your nostrils at the last second. Only, imagine that you were going to shoot your snot about fifty feet before your nose was pinched. And your snot was on fire.

There could be only one result: with a hideous, terrific sound like a mountain collapsing, the dragon exploded into chunks of flaming meat which splattered all over Main Street. The only recognizable piece of the dragon left was its head still clenched tightly in Super Qwok's grip. Nothing else remained except for smelly, stinky, smoky bits.

After the clean-up was complete, Raceboy and Super Qwok donated the dragon head to a museum, where it was stuffed and hung on the wall. Although this seems like the end of the adventure, it's not, because Mom said, "I was so worried about you guys!"

"What are we going to do?" asked Alex later. "Mom knows who we are. We're never going to be able to do anything again without her trying to rescue us."

"I don't know," said Bryan. "This isn't a problem like a monster or a mad scientist, that's for sure. At least those we know how to deal with." Bryan was both right and wrong, as you will see.

THE TIME RACEBOY AND SUPER QWOK'S MOM FOUND OUT THEIR SECRET IDENTITIES PART TWO

NOSE SINCLAIR

Mom said, "Alex, go brush your teeth. It's nearly bedtime. You don't want them to turn green, do you?"

As he stomped up the stairs, Alex grumbled, "Why would I ever want to brush my teeth, anyway. Brushing your teeth takes a lot of time. I'm just gonna go to bed." He didn't believe all that balderdash about green teeth.

Mom must have sensed Alex's intentions. She shouted from the bottom of the stairs. "You know, Alex, superheroes are in the eye of the public, so you need fresh breath and good dental hygiene. Remember, superheroes are emissaries for the public good."

It was true, Alex realized, that as a superhero he was supposed to be an example for people everywhere about how to act, about the choices to make, and about the way to treat others. But the fact that it was his mother reminding him about it—well, that sort of defeated the point. Life is all about making choices, good choices, the best choices you can based on what you know and what is fair to everyone involved. But when a mother reminds her son about why he should make choices, well, that's really changing the way the choice is made; it's skewing the choice so it's not really a choice, it's coercion. At least, that's how Alex saw things. It's not heroic to be heroic because your mom makes you. True heroism is a choice that comes from inside. And this was what really bugged Alex the

most about Mom reminding him to brush his teeth. "Gah! Why does being a superhero have to be so difficult!" he grumbled as he spread toothpaste on his toothbrush.

Mom yelled up the stairs, "Alex! I need to run to the store to grab some chocolate chips. I'll be back in a couple of minutes. Make sure your brother brushes!"

Little did Mom know that there was a new villain in town, a villain who had heard all about Raceboy and Super Qwok, a villain who wanted to discover their secret identities.

This villain had a distinctive triangular shape. In fact, he was a giant nose, a walking nose, a nose with feet and arms. He had no head because his entire body and head was a nose. He had no teeth because he was a nose. He had no hair (well, outside, anyway) because he was a nose. This villain's name was Nose Sinclair.

Nose Sinclair's problem was that he was nosy. He wanted to know everybody's business. He was always trying to find out what was going on in everybody's life. "Nobody knows like Nose Sinclair," he always said. It was his motto, though sometimes he simply shortened it to, "Nose knows."

Nose Sinclair had been very successful nosing his way into information that people would pay lots of money to learn, and right now he had a big hunch that a couple of nefarious types would be willing to shell out some serious scratch to get the real identities of the boy heroes. That was why he was in Clifton, and that was why he thought it made sense to grab the first lady he saw on the street and ask, "How do I find Raceboy and Super Qwok?"

If she was surprised to discover that she was talking to a walking (and talking!) nose, Mom was too polite to show it. Instead she answered, "Wherever there's trouble, that's where you'll find Raceboy and Super Qwok."

This gave Nose Sinclair an idea. He grabbed Mom's arm and

said, "Good. You can be my hostage. They'll have to show up now!"

Mom looked at him reprovingly. "Surely you must be kidding!"

Nose Sinclair snorted in her direction. "Look," he explained, "if you don't come with me, I'm gonna run all over you."

Mom glared. "I'm warning you. I know Raceboy and Super Qwok, and they will rescue me. See if they don't!"

The walking nose huffed and puffed with laugher. "I'm a nose, lady! I can't see anything!"

"Then how do you know what's going on?"

"I sniff. It's like sonar. You know, what bats use."

Mom wrinkled her own nose. "I thought sonar was sound."

"Same thing. To a nose."

Then he grabbed her and started pulling her down the street.

Once upon a time Raceboy and Super Qwok had given Mom a heart-shaped patch to activate if ever she needed help. Only since she discovered the boys' secret identities did Mom truly understand why the superheroes had given it to her, and at this moment she was especially thankful to be able to reach up and tap the transmitter that would send a homing beacon to her boys, her own superheroes...

The Race-alarm went off just before Bryan stuck his own toothbrush in his mouth.

"C'mon!" said Alex, tugging on Bryan's arm. Bryan set his still-full toothbrush in the cabinet where it wouldn't be too obvious, then followed Alex into the portal to the Qwok Tower. "It's Mom!" Alex said. "She's in trouble."

The boys blazed across Main Street in their super vehicles towards Mom's signal. Then they saw their mother. It was a difficult scene to miss, actually: their mom screaming and swinging a purse at a giant nose with legs and arms.

This must be a dream! thought Super Qwok as he leapt from the Qwok-cycle.

Raceboy zipped out of the Race-mobile. *I've never seen anything like that,* he thought.

Both Raceboy and Super Qwok closed in on Nose Sinclair. The giant nose did something that no one would have expected, except maybe four-year-old boys like Super Qwok, and six-year-old boys like Raceboy. Nose Sinclair leaned backward, put one hand against a nostril, and fired a snot rocket straight from the other nostril at the boys. Both boys dodged out of the way as the big, green, gooey, splattery booger fell on the ground.

"Eeew," cried people on the street.

Nose Sinclair blocked his other nostril and prepared for another shot. With a terribly gross sound, the booger bullet blasted from the schnozolla that was Nose Sinclair.

Splat, it also hit the ground.

Raceboy and Super Qwok looked at one another. Both boys had blown their noses before, and both boys could count to two, which was the total number of nostrils in Nose Sinclair's arsenal. Surely Nose Sinclair must have used up all his ammunition.

Raceboy zipped towards him; hot on his heels came Super Qwok.

Nose Sinclair, still leaning back, blew with all of his nasal power and created a strong pulse of wind that pushed Raceboy back, but it didn't quite have enough force to stop Super Qwok. With his strong steps, Super Qwok pulled up close to the giant nose and yelled, "That's it, Nose Man! You're done for!"

Even a giant nose needs to breathe in. Nose Sinclair had breathed out to his limit, and just as Super Qwok got to telling him, "That's it," Nose Sinclair was forced to inhale.

He gasped. It was as though his breath had been taken away, and he couldn't breathe.

Super Qwok asked, "What's wrong? I haven't even touched you, yet. I'm about to slam you with my super strength."

Nose Sinclair gasped and whuffled as he tried to breathe.

Mom looked back and forth from Super Qwok to Nose Sinclair. She had one eye wrinkled as though trying to figure out a puzzle. "Did your brother make you brush?" she asked severely.

"Well, he was supposed to, but then we got the alert—"

Nose Sinclair tried to breathe in again and choked.

Super Qwok blew straight into one of the nostrils. "Does that smell bad, Nose Man?" He blew again.

The giant nose wheezed and began to turn blue.

"Phoo," Super Qwok blew in the other nostril.

Nose Sinclair fell over in a faint, and Super Qwok had not even touched him.

After the Police Captain arrested Nose Sinclair for attempted kidnapping and took him to the Clifton Jail, Mom took Raceboy aside and whispered, "I can't believe you didn't make him brush his teeth! You two get those super vehicles back to your super garage or whatever you call it and the first thing you do is—" Mom noticed people were looking at her curiously. She frowned, then said very loudly, "Oh, Super Qwok! Thank you so much for saving me from that hideous nose!"

This gave the boys time to get away.

"You're welcome, Ma'am. Just doing our civic duty," explained Super Qwok to Mom and any nearby people within earshot. With one final Mom-look at her boys, she turned and strode off toward the store and the chocolate chips she needed.

The boys watched her walk away for a moment before returning to their vehicles and driving back to the Qwok Tower. Once inside they changed back into their pajamas and took the portal back to their room.

"I better get brushing," Bryan said, "before Mom gets home." He found the toothbrush right where he'd stashed it in the cabinet, but reflected on how such a small thing as a tooth brush could change the outcome of a day.

THE TIME RACEBOY AND SUPER QWOK'S MOM
FOUND OUT THEIR SECRET IDENTITIES PART THREE
TROLL TROUBLE

With Nose Sinclair out of the way, Alex and Bryan felt that they deserved some time to relax. They were both stressed out about Mom knowing their superhero identities. At dinner time she would make comments like, "For my little superheroes," as she spooned them double-helpings of beans. Or at bedtime, after she'd read stories, she would tuck them in and say, "Now you say an extra prayer that there are no dangerous situations. I'm always so worried about you when you have to go out into dangerous situations."

Alex and Bryan lounged in their room for a moment's peace. Alex said, "We've got to figure out a way so that Mom won't worry about us anymore."

"I know," agreed Bryan. "But what can we do?"

"There has to be a way to make Mom forget about knowing that we are superheroes."

Bryan thought about this for a moment. "We could try to hypnotize her," he suggested.

"Yeah, but how are we going to do that? I read a book about hypnosis, and when I tried it on Maddie she just walked away."

"You tried to hypnotize the dog?"

Alex said, "Well, sure. I wanted to hypnotize her so she wouldn't eat food from the table."

"Maybe we could find an amazing hypno-ring. I've heard they

sell those kinds of things sometimes."

"But where will we get a hypno-ring from?" Alex asked.

"I don't know. Maybe we can just keep our eyes open for it."

It wasn't much of a solution, they knew. But they decided it was the best plan they could think of and would have to do for now.

When the Race-alarm went off one Friday evening, both boys sped to downtown Clifton in their super vehicles to confront a towering shape. From a distance it looked like a walking toddler, only it was the size of a two story house.

"What is that?" Raceboy wondered in the Race-mobile.

Super Qwok didn't ask, as he pulled up on the Qwok-cycle. His first thought was, *That's a troll!* And he was right.

The troll had feet the size of automobiles. Its arms hung to its knees as it swung them left and right. The one part of its body that didn't seem to be sized proportionally was its head: huge feet, huge legs, huge belly, huge arms, and teensy-weensy little head.

"You know what that means?" asked Super Qwok as both boys leapt from their vehicles and raced toward the creature.

"What?" Raceboy replied.

"It's got a little brain."

At that moment the troll opened its mouth and roared, "Raaah!"

"Its mouth is bigger than I would have guessed," Raceboy said.

Super Qwok nodded. "I think that's because it has no neck, and its mouth runs all the way to its chest."

The troll grabbed the trunk of a crabapple tree and pulled it straight from the ground, roots and all. It began to swing the tree back and forth at the boys like a golf club.

Raceboy and Super Qwok jumped out of the way as the troll swept the ground and left a trail of green leaves. Raceboy drew his laser-sword and switched it on. As the tree came down, he cut branches from it and began to shear away the limbs.

Super Qwok punched branches, and they cracked or snapped off.

The more the troll swung the tree at Raceboy and Super Qwok, the smaller the tree became. First it lost branches. Then it became a small tree. Next it was nothing more than a bush. And at last the troll had nothing more than a teensy-weensy troll-sized toothpick in his hand. The creature looked at it and began to cry.

Big tears fell from his little-brained head to plop against the ground. The troll stomped his boat-sized feet, causing both boys to shimmy and shake and lose their balance. The troll was having a troll tantrum right above their heads.

Super Qwok had an idea. "Give me your hands!" he told Raceboy.

"What are you going to do?" Raceboy asked, bewildered. He was trying to figure out how hand-holding was going to distract a tantrum-throwing troll.

The second Super Qwok took Raceboy's hands he began to jump and sing. It wasn't a recognizable song; instead it was a sort of wordless, happy song. It had lots of hopping and head-bobbing and fun. "Das das das da dat," sang Super Qwok.

It took Raceboy less than a split second to understand what his brother was doing. He thought Super Qwok was either playing the deadliest game in the world, or demonstrating himself a genius of troll psychology. Raceboy sang along. "Das das das da dat!"

The troll stopped its tantrum as it watched the boys spin and twirl and sing. Those boys were dancing and jumping, and it looked like an awful lot of fun. Its tears quickly dried as it jumped up and down. This was hard on the nearby houses, but at least the troll wasn't trying to kick the boys.

When at last the boys stopped their singing dance, the troll looked down and stopped its own growly singing also.

"Uh-oh," said Raceboy.

"What?" asked Super Qwok.

"I think we've made a new friend."

The troll smiled and said, "Ma-ma. Da-da."

Now Raceboy and Super Qwok had double trouble: their mom knew she was their mom, and a baby troll thought they were his mommy and daddy!

"Why don't we lead it somewhere safe?" Super Qwok asked Raceboy.

"Where is a safe place for a troll?"

"Troll City?" Super Qwok offered.

Raceboy wrinkled his lip. "Where in the world is that?"

"I don't know. I thought you might know! Well, the only other place I can think of is maybe that old, abandoned barn where we stopped Professor Solaris."

"Good idea," Raceboy agreed. "We can bring him out of town to the country and radio the Police Captain. Maybe he can get the military here or scientists who study trolls." He yelled up to the troll, "C'mon, big guy! Come with us!"

Raceboy and Super Qwok started to walk down Main Street toward the north-most railroad crossing.

"Ma-ma," said the troll as it followed. "Da-da."

As the boys led the troll northwest out of town, a furious debate broke out. "I'm its dad," Super Qwok said.

"No, I'm the dad!" Raceboy declared.

"No, you're its mom," Super Qwok said.

"Speaking of Mom," said Raceboy, "it was nice that she let us take this one on our own."

"Oh, I doubt she did that on purpose. She was probably doing something and didn't notice the Race-alarm. She'll probably show up any minute now." Super Qwok was nearly right. Mom had been in the basement putting groceries away and had not noticed that the boys had taken off.

The abandoned farmhouse looked unchanged from the night the boys had defeated Professor Solaris and saved the world from his plan to destroy all electronics with his solar flare generator. They slid the door to the barn open, and the troll was just able to crawl into the barn on its hands and knees.

"It's a tight fit," Super Qwok said. "Now what are we doing to do?"

"At least he can't do any more damage to Clifton if we're here in the country. At least we've got that going for us."

Raceboy and Super Qwok slid the doors shut.

"Troll," said Super Qwok. "You need to go night-night."

"Night-night?" repeated the troll. It was confused and looked at them with blank yellow eyes. "'Night-night?"

Super Qwok tried to explain. "Daddy," he pointed to himself, "and Mommy," he pointed to Raceboy, who swatted his hand with super speed so that it flipped away, "want you to go night-night."

"No night-night," said the troll.

Raceboy tried. He pointed to himself, "Daddy says go night-night. And Mommy, too." He pointed at his brother.

"No!" The troll punched a hole in the wall of the barn.

Even if the boys had known a little something of troll customs, their plan would probably not have worked the way they imagined it. For one thing, troll mothers never tell their children what to do. They usually roar and spit all over them first, then add a healthy dose of troll smacking. Second, trolls are nocturnal. They stay awake during the night and sleep during the day. Therefore telling a troll to go night-night didn't make any sense to such a small-brained creature. The troll would maybe have understood if the boys had said, "Day-day," but since it was actually turning dark outside, these two thoughts would have confused its already confused brain, and the result would likely have been the same as what happened next.

Super Qwok shook a finger at the troll and used very human logic, "You must listen to Daddy and Mommy because we give you good advice. Very important. Daddy and Mommy keep you safe."

The troll shook its head. "No night-night. No Da-da. No Mama. You bad-bad." With that the troll kicked and shattered the door, knocking it off its hinges.

"Uh-oh," said Raceboy. "I don't think it thinks we're its mommy and daddy anymore."

The troll worked its way back out of the barn, picked up the door, and threw it at Raceboy and Super Qwok. They ducked as the door spun over their heads and crashed against the door on the opposite end of the barn, blasting the other side open.

The troll reached for a tree, ripped it from the ground, and began to beat the barn with it.

Raceboy and Super Qwok heard the barn groan and clang. It began to collapse. As lumber fell all around them, Raceboy kicked into Speed-mode, hefted Super Qwok and escaped just as the barn crumbled in an explosion of dust.

The troll took no notice of the boys. The moon had risen; the troll had no desire to go day-day; its slurping, growling shape lumbered toward the lights of Main Street.

"C'mon," said Raceboy, let's get back to town. He took off in Speed-mode, and Super Qwok tramped along at his own normal pace. In a moment Raceboy burst back and said, "Hurry up! I've already been to town and back. You've only gotten to the end of the drive!"

"Race Qwok time," said Super Qwok, and he leapt on Raceboy's back.

"Oomph," said Raceboy. "You could have warned me."

"Giddyap!" Super Qwok kicked his heels.

"You're lucky I don't drop you and leave you to your own speed," grumbled Raceboy, but zip, he kicked into Race-mode and zinged over the country roads in an instant, catching up with the troll just as it made its way back into Clifton. As though it had never left off, the troll uprooted another tree on Main Street and began sweeping it against cars and even the supports holding the awning over the Main Street Diner.

"I'm having déjà vu," Raceboy said.

"Oh, no," said Super Qwok. And with good reason. From the west side of the tracks a van moved closer and closer to the troll, the female driver looking left and right as though searching for two young superheroes. "Mom!" said Super Qwok. "She must have discovered we were gone!"

Mom parked the van and ran up to the two-story shape of the troll. "You terrible…" Mom was at a loss for words, unable to fit the creature into any recognizable kingdom, phylum, class, order, family, genus, or species. At last she said, "…monster."

The troll cocked its head at her momentarily, like a dog that has just witnessed a human behaving badly. Except that this human was chastising a two-story troll with very little brain. "Now you stop destroying the town!"

Mom turned her attention to the boys. "Boys, you step back. Don't worry, I'll take care of this." Mom pushed on the troll's toe. The troll wiggled its toe, and Mom tipped over, nearly falling to the ground. She would have struck the ground, too, except for Raceboy. He burst into Speed-mode and caught her by the shoulders and set her gently on the ground.

The troll lifted its foot and brought it down right on Raceboy and Mom. Raceboy raced in circles with his arms up, tickling the underside of the troll's foot at super speed. This unexpected tickle-torture caught the troll off-guard, and a loud guffaw broke from its lips. The troll kicked its leg up and away from Raceboy, losing its balance to tip over and crash against the pavement.

Super Qwok took advantage of the prone creature and dealt it a very precise blow to the troll's forehead. The troll's eyes rolled back in its head and its breath gurgled peacefully. It was knocked out.

The Police Captain arranged for a flatbed truck. Super Qwok loaded the unconscious troll onto the flatbed while Raceboy attached the cables to secure it. The driver took the troll on a road trip to a university to be studied, and where, presumably, it lived out the remainder of its life in a natural troll habitat.

Mom took the van home while Raceboy and Super Qwok breathed yet another sigh of relief that their identities were intact, their mother hadn't been damaged, and the town was still safe.

This would have been all well and good if the troll had been the only troll. Unfortunately, it wasn't the only troll. In fact, it was a baby troll, and baby trolls usually have mommy trolls.

Trolls aren't like people. First, they're big. Second, they have the brain capacity of a mosquito. Third, they are mean. Nothing makes a momma troll mean like losing her darling baby troll. After all, without the baby troll, there's no one to fetch her a water tower to drink, or to hand her the troll remote when she wants to change the troll-vision channel, or to grunt, "Ook, ick, ug," which I've been told means "pretty ugly" in Trollish (The linguist, John Hanson, in his doctoral thesis, explains that this is not an oxymoron...at least, not to trolls). Momma trolls depend on their baby trolls to do all the things momma trolls don't feel like doing themselves. And when momma trolls have to pull themselves out of the recliner and come looking for their troll-spawn? Watch out, superheroes!

The momma troll that stomped her way into Clifton hot on the scent of her baby troll was mean and meaner. If you think the baby troll with the small head and small brain was bad, you should see its mom. Its mom was twice as tall as the baby troll, though, to be honest, her brain wasn't a whole lot bigger—she had just had it longer. This isn't to say she was very smart, because trolls aren't broke out in brains, as they say.

The troll momma came into Clifton swinging telephone poles like a ninja with ninja swords. Left and right she swung the poles, smashing the lights along Main Street, street signs, buildings, and automobiles.

It was only a moment before the Race-alarm summoned both Raceboy and Super Qwok, and they found themselves confronting an even bigger, badder, version of their previous night's problem. The image of the troll momma before them caught them off guard. It wasn't simply that she was monstrously huge, or terribly ugly; it was that she was wearing a blond wig with long, cascading tresses that fell past her lumpy shoulders. The blood-red of her lipsticked lips stretched across her face like an open wound. She wore a skirt and a blouse, or perhaps they were the draperies from a Vegas magic show. Clearly this troll had a half-baked awareness of human beauty, and just as clearly the creature had mimicked human beauty as best as it could.

Mom left black skid marks on the road as she stopped the family van between Raceboy, Super Qwok, and the towering troll. Raceboy and Super Qwok had begun to call the van "the Mommobile" because as soon as there was an emergency Mom would drive up, run out, and ...

"No, no, no, no! You boys! I refuse to let you attack this giant troll creature..." she hesitated. "...Person. It's too dangerous. You could get hurt. I can't let you go— You know, I'll take care of it! You guys just sit there on the curb. I'm going to take care of this."

"Mom!" said Super Qwok. "We're superheroes."

"Mom!" said Raceboy. "We're gonna handle it!"

"No, dears. You sit there on the curb. Don't move! I will take care of this." She turned from the boys, strode straight up to the four-story troll and yelled, "Listen here, you bossy troll, you!"

Raceboy asked, "Didn't this just happen yesterday?"

"Yes," answered Super Qwok.

"Do you think it's going to end any different?" asked Raceboy.

"Does it ever?"

Mom yelled, "You listen here! I don't appreciate you beating around our town and breaking things."

The troll reached down, picked Mom up, and popped her straight into its lipsticked mouth.

Raceboy inhaled sharply and faster than you can say, "Pretty ugly!" burst at full speed, grabbing Super Qwok and dashing behind the troll, where he threw his brother down and leapt into his arms. "Throw!" he ordered.

Super Qwok aimed Raceboy at the back of the momma troll's head and hurled him. Raceboy added a burst from his jet-pack and slammed into the troll's flowing wig. The troll coughed Mom out.

Below, Super Qwok ran through the troll's legs and saw his mother plummeting toward him. He grabbed her mid-stride and gently placed her on the ground alongside Main Street.

"Mom, will you please sit on the curb while we take care of this troll?" he asked politely.

Mom, who had never before been coated with troll slime, sat on the curb, puzzled. She didn't answer, and Super Qwok took her silence as an agreement that she would stay out of the way.

Raceboy steered his jet-pack to set him beside Super Qwok. "Plan A. Same as yesterday. Get it on the ground, then knock it out with a power punch."

Super Qwok said, "Sure."

Raceboy sped around the momma troll's big feet, uncoiling a rope from his utility belt as he did so and tightening it around her ankles. She began to teeter, but unlike the baby troll the day before, she did not fall. Instead she tugged and Raceboy's rope snapped. It fell in shreds to the ground. Raceboy stopped beside Super Qwok and said, "I guess that didn't work."

He paused too long. In the time it took him to say those five simple words, the momma troll swung one long arm down and swept him up in her thick troll fingers. She looked at him. Raceboy had enough time to notice that she didn't have whites in her eyes; instead, she had a moldy yellow. And her irises were the same green as unhealthy snot. The troll momma was looking at him as though she thought he was a very tasty sausage that she was going to chomp down on.

Super Qwok drew his laser-sword. Most people would have used the sword to cut the troll momma, but not Super Qwok. He did something that no person, not even a troll momma, wants. He ran straight at the troll momma and leapt. His jump contained all of his power and carried him higher than a building, higher than a two-story building, high enough to use his laser-sword to chop straight through the belt holding up the momma troll's skirt.

Her skirt fell to the pavement.

That momma troll was so embarrassed she tossed Raceboy and tried to cover-up her troll underwear.

Raceboy fluttered through the air like a discarded tissue, twisted his body, fired his jet-pack, and directed himself straight back at the troll momma's head. He wrenched her long, flowing wig and carried it with him out of her reach. He dropped it on the west side of the tracks where it flopped atop a grain elevator.

The momma troll shrieked after her flying wig, realized she had left her skirt behind on Main Street, did an abrupt about-face and reached the skirt. She attempted to cover herself with the skirt as she howled from the town, clomping into the distance, never to be seen again.

Raceboy and Super Qwok brought their mom back home. After they changed back into Alex and Bryan, the two boys hosed Mom off with the garden hose, and scrubbed her with a scrub brush. Troll slobber, it turns out, is very gooey and sticky.

You might think that since this was the end of the trolls, that it was the end of the problems. But Bryan said, "You realize we've had how many monsters now in Clifton all in a row?" It hadn't really started as a question, but that's the direction it ended.

Alex used an old toothbrush to scrub behind one of Mom's ears. "There was the dragon. Then after the dragon, the baby troll. Then the mother troll..."

"Don't you think it's mysterious that all of these fantasy creatures have attacked, and they've done nothing except destroy?"

Alex hmmmed. "Now that you mention it, it is mysterious that these fantasy creatures, these magical creatures, seem to be attacking, but the only thing they want is destruction."

"That's right," said Bryan. "I think there's something behind this. Someone or something that's controlling all of these creatures. Something that's using some sort of a power to—"

Before Bryan could say the rest of that sentence there was a terrible crash from Main Street.

"What was that?" asked Alex.

"I don't know," said their wet mother, "but you're not going to go and investigate. You boys need to stay here where it's safe."

"Mom," explained Bryan, "if we stay here where it's safe, then the rest of the town will be destroyed, and then this won't be safe any more. We are what makes Clifton safe! Superheroes have to protect other people! We have a responsibility!"

Mom shook her head wearily. "No. I'm putting my foot down right now. You cannot go to that monster!" Both Alex and Bryan knew, because they were good boys, that they had to listen to their mom. They hung their heads.

BOOM! Another crash came from uptown. People screamed in the distance. "Help! Help!" could be heard. Another voice yelled, "Where's Super Qwok?" and, "Where's Raceboy? Where are they?"

Alex and Bryan looked at one another, then at their mother. "Mom! You've got to let us go!"

Mom looked into their eyes and as she did, she heard again the cries, "Super Qwok! Raceboy! Where are you?" She knew she had to let them go.

"All right," she said. "But I'm coming with you!" She grabbed a ski mask from the closet and pulled it over her still-wet head.

"Oh, no!" said Bryan.

THE TIME RACEBOY AND SUPER QWOK'S MOM FOUND OUT THEIR SECRET IDENTITIES PART FOUR
ATTACK OF THE WYRM

Mom followed the boys through the portal into the Qwok Tower. She adjusted her ski mask so she could see.

Raceboy and Mom took the Race-mobile; Super Qwok rode on the Qwok-cycle.

Main Street was already ravaged from the monster attacks of the previous few days. It wasn't very surprising for the boys to see that again a giant creature was attacking the town. What was different, however, was that neither the boys nor Mom knew what to call the creature.

It looked like a spaghetti noodle.

You may be under the impression that on the scale of dangerous things in the universe, a noodle would fall somewhere between stuffed orangutan and potted daffodil. But imagine a noodle that's as long a city block, as big around as a car, and with a giant circular mouth that doesn't just have teeth at the top and the bottom; no, instead it has teeth all the way around its mouth in a circle, and that mouth squeezes closed and opens up like puckering lips. That's the kind of noodle we're talking about here: a giant worm, but with teeth.

It had already rolled atop numerous cars, flattening them like a steamroller. It had broken down the awnings on three store-fronts with its tail. The town sign that had formerly read, "Bake Sale

Saturday," was scattered in thousands of glass fragments and plastic letters across a parking lot.

"It looks like a giant worm!" said Super Qwok.

Raceboy said, "Wyrm with a 'y,' like a kind of wingless dragon. I've read about them."

"Well, we've got to face it either way, worm or wyrm. What do you suppose we should do?"

"Stop it, I guess." Raceboy flipped his laser-sword from his utility belt and it sizzled blue. He burst toward the creature and swung the energy blade. *ZZZZ-CRASH!* The laser-sword struck the scales of the creature, the giant rings that surrounded it, and Raceboy realized that the rings were actually armor. They protected the wyrm from weapons as powerful as laser-swords. He turned off the laser-sword, knowing he would need to find another way to stop the monster.

Super Qwok, meanwhile, had run forward and grabbed the wyrm's tail. The creature twisted and flung Super Qwok high into the sky. He barely landed on his feet, then raced forward again, fist raised.

"Wait!" shouted Raceboy, but it was too late. Super Qwok punched the wyrm. The clang of his punch was the sound of a church bell or distant chimes. The echo of it reverberated. Super Qwok shook his hand. That hurt! Above him the vibrating bulk of the creature roared.

The wyrm was a powerful creature indeed. It wasn't able to be bent. It wasn't able to be punched. It wasn't able to be cut with a laser-sword. How in the world were the two superheroes going to do anything about it?

"How does it see?" Raceboy asked.

"How does it smell?" Super Qwok answered.

The wyrm rose above them like powerful pasta and roared. The

sound echoed terribly through the town.

Mom decided it was her turn to use her normal powers. She raced in front of the wyrm in her ski mask and lectured it. "Now you listen here! You go right back to whatever hole in the ground you slithered out of and stay there."

The wyrm bellowed again, its head twirling high above in the sky. Without real super powers or weapons, Mom resorted to her only option: her purse. She twirled it over her head. Around and around she twirled the purse, like a ski-masked David facing a noodle-shaped Goliath. The wyrm opened its mouth and lunged. Mom threw. The purse sped right into the monster's mouth. The wrym chomped down on Mom's purse. It was filled with things like make-up, nail polish, credit cards, and keys.

While it was not a very good idea to throw keys or a driver's license into a monster's mouth, she had thrown credit cards, which are notoriously evil, and make-up, which is notoriously bad tasting. The monster took one bite and started coughing as only a giant, city-block-long wyrm can: *BLEH-BLEH*. The sound of that cough gave Raceboy his super idea. He pulled a Race-grenade from his belt and said, "Super Qwok, knock it again!"

Super Qwok did. The monster rolled and bellowed. Raceboy tossed a Race-grenade into the monster's open mouth. The circular jaws chomped and swallowed. There was an instant's silence as the monster sat still. As both boys watched the wyrm, they heard the sound of thunder from miles away.

"What was that?" asked Mom.

Raceboy said, "I think that was the end of the wyrm."

Indeed, the wyrm wavered like a piece of grass in a windstorm, then fell to the road with a loud clang.

Super Qwok moved closer, kicking the edges of the creature's armored rings. "I think you got it, Raceboy."

Raceboy thought so, too. He walked up and pushed on the solid armor. "Yup, I got it."

Mom appeared beside them. "Oh, I'm so glad that my purse did the job."

"Sure, Mom," agreed Raceboy. "Except, didn't you have things like your driver's license in there?"

"Oh, no!" exclaimed Mom.

Super Qwok said, "We'll try to open the wyrm's mouth and find your stuff. C'mon, Raceboy." Both boys moved to the unmoving mouth and tried to pry the sharp teeth away from one another. They were tugging at either side of the thick jaw when something happened that they didn't expect: the backside of the wyrm rose skyward and turned to them. The wyrm didn't have one head: it had two! Each end was a head! The new mouth opened above them and cried a shrill, "Raaaaah!" And the mouth plunged straight at Mom. Super Qwok was closest, and he pushed Mom out of the way just in time so that it didn't take a bite out of her. What it did bite was Super Qwok.

The wyrm lifted Super Qwok in its teeth. It prepared to toss him into the air and to open its circular mouth and swallow him whole in one giant gulp.

From below, Raceboy saw the wyrm's neck curl and flick and he fired his jet-pack as Super Qwok spun away from the monster's teeth for a split second to hang above its widening maw. As gravity began to pull Super Qwok back into the wyrm's mouth, Raceboy latched on to his brother. The ring of teeth clamped on empty air while Raceboy carried Super Qwok into the sky. The creature howled and writhed.

Super Qwok said, "I was ready! I was going to handle it!"

"You were not!" Raceboy argued.

"Watch this!" Super Qwok lit his own laser-sword. It was red.

"Oh," Raceboy said. "I think I'm thinking what you're thinking now."

"It will be a little bit drooly."

The wyrm had stopped looking for the absent Super Qwok and had re-targeted Mom. Its snaking neck was shifting and trying to get into position to snap her up.

Super Qwok said, "We need to distract it."

"Drop another of my Race-grenades. Here, they're on my utility belt."

Super Qwok pulled the pin on the grenade and slung it straight at the monster's side opposite from where his mother stood. It activated with an explosion that rattled the street.

"Aim for the mouth," ordered Super Qwok.

"Will do." Raceboy shifted Super Qwok, holding him in a hug with his left arm. He lit his laser-sword and held it at the ready in his right hand. The boys together jetted straight at the wyrm's mouth with two energy blades held out; they streaked like a falling angel with neon red and blue wings.

The wyrm opened its mouth to howl at the sky. Raceboy gunned the jet-pack, and the two disappeared straight into the wyrm's mouth.

Mom screamed. "My boys!"

Above, the monster's mouth closed. In that instant she knew she would never see her boys again.

Except...there was a sudden flash of red-and-blue fireworks and the wyrm began to tremble violently, to convulse, and its head began to unfold. As Mom looked up, she no longer saw the wyrm's head, but only Raceboy and Super Qwok standing at one end of the noodle-shaped body, their laser-swords aglow. They rode the trunk of the wyrm's body as it fell like a vast sequoia felled by Paul Bunyan. Arm in arm, side by side, like a pair of synchronized divers, they descended with the falling body, and at the last instant, as the body struck the street, each boy stepped lightly on the ground, and at that same moment each clicked his laser-sword off. The dust from the falling creature flowed around their feet as they stood before their mother.

"See, Mom," said Raceboy.

Super Qwok finished, "We had it all under control."

Mom gasped and reached to hug them.

Raceboy said, "Mom, don't hug us! We're supposed to be superheroes. C'mon, we've got to talk to the Police Captain. Is your mask straight?"

Mom fidgeted with her ski mask to make certain her real identity was protected.

"Just hang back and act normal," Super Qwok cautioned. "Actually, you'd better let us do the talking."

The Police Captain approached. "Thank you, Super Qwok and

Raceboy! Without you I don't know what would have happened to Clifton."

Super Qwok said, "You're welcome, sir, but we don't think this is over."

"What do you mean?" asked the Police Captain.

Raceboy said, "We think something is going on that's bigger than these monsters."

"I don't understand," the Police Captain shook his head. "What could be bigger than the monsters that have attacked Clifton in the last week? Dragons, trolls, even large—" the Police Captain motioned at the still shape of the wyrm, "—something-or-others."

"Exactly," said Raceboy. "That's what we mean, sir. It seems that some person or persons are trying to destroy Clifton using every means they have at their disposal. Someone or something with access to monsters. Someone or something that can send them, or direct them, or maybe even control them."

The Police Captain gasped. "Like an arch-villain? What a hideous thought."

"Exactly," said Raceboy.

Super Qwok said, "We think this villain will be here sooner or later. And we think, based on the frequency of these attacks, that it's going to be sooner."

Police Captain nodded at Mom. "Who is your new assistant?"

Raceboy thought quickly. "This is Mom-lady," he explained. "She helps us sometimes."

"Mom-lady," said the Police Captain, "thanks for your assistance. Any friend of Raceboy and Super Qwok is certainly a friend to Clifton."

As they walked back to the wyrm's still body to look for Mom's purse, Mom said, "Mom-lady? Couldn't you think of anything more creative than that?"

"He put me on the spot! You want something different? What about Super Mom. Power Mom. Mom-girl."

Mom said, "I was thinking something cooler like 'The Masked Avenger.'"

The boys stood side by side and looked at one another hesitantly. Raceboy said, "The Masked Avenger? Okay, then Masked Avenger. This is the part of being a superhero that no one likes to talk about. This is the part where we dig through the remains of a giant monster to locate your driver's license so we can protect your secret identity."

"Yuck," said Super Qwok. "It looks like spaghetti."

"Spaghetti on the outside, spaghetti on the inside," shrugged Raceboy. "Oh, Masked Avenger, what are we going to have for dinner?"

"Salads," said Mom.

Both boys groaned, but they did agree: anything was better than spaghetti.

THE TIME RACEBOY AND SUPER QWOK'S MOM FOUND OUT THEIR SECRET IDENTITIES PART FIVE

MASTERMIND'S MYTHIC MONSTER MASH-UP

Who or what motive force was directing powerful, fantastic monsters against the Village of Clifton? Why were these attacks focused solely on Clifton? Could Raceboy and Super Qwok stop the next monster attack, defeat the unknown villain, save Clifton, and most importantly, figure out a way to stop Mom from following them on every dangerous mission? All these questions will now be answered.

When the Race-alarm sounded, Alex said, "Another monster."

Bryan nodded.

And though Alex was right, as he turned from Main Street onto Fourth Avenue, the boys and Mom discovered that he was only twenty-five percent right.

It looked as though someone had opened a book of mythological creatures and shook it upside-down, dislodging from its illustrations the very monsters that populated the legends of long ago. Not one, but four terrible monsters of yore prowled the street.

The first was a griffin, with the body of a lion and front legs, head, and wings of an eagle. It had intense eyes, and its head moved in rapid jerks, flicking back and forth; its piercing cry was part shrieking eagle, part laser cannon.

The second was a manticore. It had the body of a lion, the tail of a scorpion, and the face of a man. The face, though apparently human-like, did not appear to be intelligent in the "Let's have a cup of tea and discuss what you thought about that last Raceboy and Super Qwok Adventure" sense of the word. Rather it was a more stomach-driven intelligence, barely past "I chew superheroes for lunch," and not quite to "I should use this leftover cape as a napkin to wipe my lips."

The third was a sphinx. It had the body of a lion and the head of a human. Although it shared two of the three beast bodies with the manticore, it gave off an entirely different feel than its amalgamated cousin. The sphinx's face seemed serene, though its eyes appeared methodical and penetrating. While the manticore prowled with raw energy and aggression, the sphinx slid over the pavement in a calculated crawl, purposeful and precise.

The fourth was a giant three-headed dog: one head was on the left, one on the right, and the last in the middle. Of course the most famous three headed dog was named Cerberus, and while it was unlikely that the real Cerberus had abandoned his mythic post at the gates of the underworld, it was likely that the two must certainly be close relatives.

The four monsters prowled Fourth Avenue, heading toward Main Street. They were only a block away.

"Four monsters," Raceboy said.

"And only two of us," Super Qwok agreed.

"Three," said Mom, adjusting her ski mask.

"Two of us with super powers, I mean," Super Qwok corrected, looking at Mom's wooden spoons. She had traded in her wallet and purse for a pair of dollar-store wooden spoons which she held like daggers.

Raceboy said, "This looks like a job for Knight-in-shining-armor-boy and Racegirl."

Mom stiffened and turned to wag one of the wooden spoons in

his direction. "Oh, no you don't! Your little sister is too little to go saving the world with super powers. I won't have her facing any watchamacallits—"

"We need Racegirl," Super Qwok said.

"Don't you even think about it! It's bad enough that you two are out here facing monsters and noses, but your little sister is off-limits!"

The griffin shrieked; its cry echoed across the town. One of Cerberus's heads howled a mournful, echoing wail. Another snarled. The last barked angrily.

"Mom, we need her!" Raceboy said. "I'm sending a message to Knight-in-shining-armor-boy, and I'm calling Racegirl." He activated a homing beacon, sending the message to Knight-in-shining-armor-boy and also home to his two-year-old sister, Katherine.

Mom glared. "I'm putting a stop to this right now! And I'm taking care of you later, mister. Just wait till you're out of that uniform!" She turned and went into attack mode, slinging a wooden spoon straight at the griffin's feathered head. "Hi-ya!" The wooden spoon clanked on the griffin's beak. With a glare the griffin chomped the wooden spoon in two and cried, "Screee!"

Super Qwok faced off against the Manticore. It smiled and licked its lips hungrily. Its scorpion tail lashed out. Super Qwok dodged left, and the scorpion tale struck the ground.

Raceboy swept Mom out of the way as the griffin took to the air. The winged creature began swooping, its claws reaching for Mom and Raceboy, who had to keep dodging.

Scant moments later a robotic horse clattered down the block. On its back was Knight-in-shining-armor-boy along with Racegirl. She bounded from the horse's back in a blur and blasted straight into the sphinx. The monster rolled backwards.

Knight-in-shining-armor-boy charged Cerberus; the large dog

reared and snapped at his hands as he wielded his warhammer.

Raceboy tried to move back and forth in the fray, giving the advantage to everyone as he could. He knocked the Manticore's tail just as it was about to skewer Super Qwok with its nasty, poisonous barb. He tripped the sphinx so it fell in front of Racegirl. He pulled Cerberus by the tail so that all three of its heads reared back and howled with pain.

Just as he popped the griffin on the underside of its beak there was a scream, and it didn't come from any monster.

Raceboy, Super Qwok, Racegirl, and Knight-in-shining-armor-boy turned. Mom was trapped, struggling in the grip of . . . Dr. Brick? No. Dr. Devious? Uh-uh. Mr. Mischief? Not even close. Whoever this new villain was, the heroes had never before seen his like. His head—his skull, actually—was oversized, almost as though he wore a skull-shaped helmet. Except that the skull-case was a transparent green, like the kind of green glass that still lingers in broken chunks in alleys and forgotten places. Within the curved sphere of the brain-case bubbled a gray-green ball of gelatin: his living brain.

Although the man who clutched Mom spoke in a high-pitched voice, the sound was a sweet song that slid through their thoughts straight into their own brains. "Leave my beasts alone if you value her life," he ordered. Then he laughed a long, diabolical—yet musical—laugh.

"Your creatures?" Raceboy swatted at the griffin again, evading another dive-bomb attack from the winged, taloned beast.

"Of course!" gloated the villain. "I am Mastermind! All creatures are mine, to be used."

Raceboy found his thoughts wandering down a new path. He wondered at the music in Mastermind's voice, the melody as his words bounced. And he wondered if the next words Mastermind

239

spoke were present in his ears, or if they had simply popped like tiny thought bubbles, into his mind: "And to be discarded when their purpose is done." He felt that there was a meaning to them, but try as he might, his thoughts could not wrap themselves around that meaning, or make sense of it. It was only a song that—

Raceboy found himself rolling across the ground, talons digging into his shoulders, a sharp beak wrenching at the back of his neck. How did I get here? He wondered as he yanked a griffin claw and spun the creature at Mastermind. The villain reached and petted the head of the griffin; when he cooed it looked to him with the supreme trust of a dog for its master.

Super Qwok saw Raceboy fall and ran at Mastermind, his fists balled for the attack. The griffin snarled and bounded in the way. Super Qwok batted it aside and took a swing at the glass-like skull. But Mastermind's eyes were so sad and trusting, he found that the muscles of his fingers simply could not clench, not in anger, not in violence. Those eyes were peaceful, and his hands were peaceful; they were tools to help Mastermind take care of his animals, never harm Mastermind…

Next thing Super Qwok knew, he was lying on the ground, looking at the sky, saying, "What just happened?"

Raceboy helped him to his feet. "Don't look into his eyes! Don't listen to his voice! He has powers—"

Indeed, Mom herself was no longer squirming in Mastermind's grip. Her eyes behind the ski mask were not filled with either anger or loathing. Her eyes seemed peaceful and content…and distant. She no longer appeared to be controlling herself; it was as if Mastermind was controlling her remotely. He said, "Go, now, and attack them!" and though he spoke it, his voice was a song, a victory march.

Mom wielded her one remaining wooden spoon and charged

Racegirl. If the boys needed any proof that Mom was fully under Mastermind's control, it was that she chose, of all the present heroes, Racegirl as the target of her attack.

Racegirl had the least experience fighting criminals or monsters, but with her super speed she was able to evade both the sphinx, who she had been fighting, and Mom's vicious wooden spoon attack. Racegirl ducked. The sphinx did not. *CRANK!* The spoon slammed right into the side of the sphinx's head and snapped in half. The sphinx howled, its cry an odd combination of growl and "Ow!"

The sphinx leapt to the attack. Racegirl burst into Speed-mode and stayed one step ahead of the angry creature. She led the sphinx in circles around Mom. Around and around and around and around in a circle Racegirl led the sphinx, which appeared to be chasing its own tail, before it finally collapsed in total dizziness. Giggling, Racegirl again ducked under Mom's outstretched arms and in a flash of superhero-tights zipped over to Raceboy, Super Qwok, and Knight-in-shining-armor-boy.

The sphinx wobbled to its feet, then stood facing the heroes. Mom lined up with the monsters and Mastermind.

The two forces stared at one another. Raceboy said, "What do you want?" He knew he didn't want to hear the Mastermind's so-slippery-sweet voice, but he needed to know the answer. "Why do you send your creatures against Clifton? There is no reason for you to attack us!"

"There are a number of reasons why I should like to see Clifton destroyed, and thankfully, they are all here before me."

"Us?" Super Qwok asked.

"Only the most powerful heroes in the land. I already have the power to control an army of creatures. What better way to gain fame than to destroy you? And with you out of the way, there is nothing to stop me from taking over the world!"

Raceboy pointed out, "Except we've stopped your creatures."

For that split second Mastermind wavered, "Eh, well, that's true, but now I've come to finish you myself." His voice gained momentum and force, almost like an attack. He cried, "There is nothing that can stand in my way!" As if to punctuate his exclamation, all four creatures, and Mom, and Mastermind, attacked.

Chaos ensued exactly like a square dance except without the music, the dancing, the square, the partners, or anyone to call the steps. Actually, it wasn't so much a square dance as a melee. The word melee (pronounced "mey-ley") is a disorganized battle between a group of people, or a confusing jumble; put the two definitions together and you have a fight that includes amalgamated animals, pre-teen superheroes, a mother attacking her own children, and a villain showcasing a transparent brain-case. To top it all off, Mastermind began to fire an attack-ray from his eyes. The beams of red light shone like a laser. He tried to aim the beams straight at any of the heroes, but especially toward their eyes.

Knight-in-shining-armor-boy ducked the first blast, then raised his mirrored shield. He blocked the attack-ray, rebounding it straight at the griffin. The creature had been screeching, "Scree—" and then the blast struck its eyes and it grew still and dazed.

Raceboy dodged through the manticore's striking tail, and yelled at Super Qwok, "Get Mastermind! Get Mastermind!"

Super Qwok rolled his own eyes. He was, at that moment, beneath Cerberus engaged in an all-out wrestling match; one of the dog heads clamped Super Qwok's wrist while he yanked the jaws of a second. But the griffin shook its head confusedly. It turned its eyes to Raceboy, then stared at Mastermind for a moment before it spread its eagle's wings and launched its lion's body into the air. With a ferocious cry it swooped toward Mastermind.

The green-skulled villain howled, "No, my pretty griffin! You cannot turn on me!"

The griffin hesitated, torn between a desire to listen to Mastermind, and a desire to listen to Raceboy.

"It's a mind-control ray!" Raceboy declared, amazed. "Anything struck by it can be controlled!"

Mastermind re-zapped the griffin with his attack-ray and yelled, "Attack Raceboy and Super Qwok!" Shaking its head again, the griffin turned and lunged at Knight-in-shining-armor-boy, who batted its beak with the handle of his warhammer.

For the four superheroes, Mom was a huge concern. She wasn't a threat to them with her attacks, but she was a threat to herself. Without super powers she could be hurt. Statistically speaking, with all of the fast moving heroes, talons, fists, monsters, tails, teeth, and Knight-in-shining-armor-boy's warhammer, it was only a matter of time before something would strike her.

Racegirl did a good job using her speed power to keep Mom away from the heavy wrestling that was going on between creatures and heroes. She lured Mom away from the snapping tail of the manticore and the shining warhammer of Knight-in-shining-armor-boy. Mom showed no emotion or awareness as she tried to kick and swing punches at her tiny daughter. She watched blankly as Racegirl zipped under the punches, twisted around the kicks. Then Racegirl would use her super speed and blast behind Mom, where she would tap Mom's back. Mom would spin to find a target that continued to lead her out of brawling bodies of heroes and monsters.

Raceboy used his own speed to help Knight-in-shining-armor-boy and Super Qwok to evade Mastermind's attack-ray. As red laser blasts struck nearby, he would nudge and sometimes shove his brother or his friend out of the way, or push the monsters in the way. Knight-in-shining-armor-boy was also able to use his shield to block the rays, or if he was very skillful, bounce them straight at one of the creatures. Each time one of the creatures was struck it would hesitate in confusion until one of the heroes ordered it to attack Mastermind. In this way, at one time or another, each of the monsters was attacking Mastermind until he could blast it with his mind-control ray and re-order it to attack the heroes.

After Cerberus began to attack Mastermind (again), Super Qwok punched the sphinx right in the nose. Knight-in-shining-armor-boy deflected one of Mastermind's attack-rays, and Racegirl pulled Mom straight into the beam so that she stood stone still. Super Qwok backed into Mom, pointed and said, "Mom, go sit on that park bench!" She followed his finger to see a bench near the sidewalk.

Very quietly Mom walked to the bench and sat out of the way. Mastermind did not seem to notice, but then, he was intent on zapping Cerberus. He was getting very frustrated. He knew that if he could just strike one of the four heroes with his attack-ray the tide of the battle would turn, but they were always jumping out of the way of his beams! Or back-flipping out of the way. Or tricking him into firing just in time so that they jumped out of the way as he zapped the sphinx or Cerberus or the manticore or the griffin.

By this time the poor animals were so confused, having been zapped so many times, that they were starting to get dizzy. To the creatures it must have seemed that someone had pulled the rug out from under their memories, not once, but again, and again, and again. And a memory can only fall flat on its face so many times before it finally says, "Enough!"

Finally the four creatures simply sat on the ground beside one another, put their paws (or talons) over their heads and waited for it all to get over.

Mastermind yelled, "What? I command you to attack!"

Raceboy said, "Looks to me like your creatures are too worn out from all the commands you've been giving them to attack any-body." As if to punctuate this statement one of Cerberus's heads whined.

Mastermind roared, "I am the Mastermind! I will be the World Controller! I will destroy you, and afterward the time of the World Controllers will begin!"

Super Qwok said, "Oh, really?" The four heroes looked from Mastermind to one another. They looked at Knight-in-shining-armor-boy's shield. Knight-in-shining-armor-boy nodded ever-so-slightly. Carefully the four crept nearer to one another.

"He's not very nice," Racegirl said.

"No," Raceboy agreed. "I don't think he could control a Mexi-can jumping bean."

Knight-in-shining-armor-boy said, "Or one of those invisible dog leashes. I don't think he could even—"

The shield swooped up at the same instant Mastermind fired the beam of his attack-ray. Into the reflective face of the shield the beam struck and rebounded, striking Mastermind in his green-glass skull-case. Now it was the Mastermind who stopped and stood still, looking dazed.

Raceboy burst into Race-mode, put a hand on the confused vil-lain's shoulder and said, "Mastermind, you're a nice person now. You don't want to take over the world." He patted Mastermind's shoulder. Mastermind just looked at Raceboy's lips, and moved his own lips, as if trying to follow the meaning of the words through mimicry.

"I'm a nice person now," Mastermind murmured. "I don't want to take over the world."

Super Qwok approached. "You like all creatures and want to be their friends. You don't want to control them."

"I don't want to control creatures," agreed Mastermind. "I like all creatures and want to be their friend."

Racegirl said, "From now on you want to help people with your powers."

As though the idea seemed to taste good, a soft smile crept across Mastermind's face. "I do want to help people with my powers."

And Knight-in-shining-armor-boy said, "You don't want to hurt anybody because that would make you feel bad."

Now Mastermind's face fell, and he spoke sadly. "Hurting people would make me feel bad."

The four heroes paused. "You've hypnotized the dog before," Super Qwok prompted Raceboy.

"Yeah, but it didn't work!"

Knight-in-shining-armor-boy said, "Try it anyway."

Raceboy shrugged. "Okay." He addressed Mastermind. "When I snap my fingers three times you will wake up and you will have forgotten that we ever had this conversation."

Raceboy's fingers snapped once, twice, three times.

Mastermind said, "Why, what just happened?" He looked around at Clifton, and saw the four creatures

hiding beneath their assorted limbs. "These poor creatures!" He raced over and began to pet them gently. "Look how sad they are! Poor creatures, come here, my poor creatures."

The griffin, manticore, sphinx and Cerberus must have noticed a difference in Mastermind. They raised their heads and responded to his touch.

"I should take these creatures home. They don't seem well." He turned to the heroes. "I don't think we were introduced. I'm Mastermind. What were your names?"

"Raceboy," said Raceboy with a nod.

"Super Qwok," Super Qwok grinned.

"Racegirl," Racegirl curtsied.

"Knight-in-shining-armor-boy," said Knight-in-shining-armor-boy from beneath his visor.

Mastermind said, "I can't for the life of me think why, but I'm certain I owe you my thanks." He seemed momentarily disappointed, then shrugged it off. "Ah, well, my memory's not what it used to be, I suppose! Come on, my pets!" The four creatures rose. Mastermind climbed on the griffin's back and the four beasts trotted away from Clifton.

As they rode away, Racegirl called, "Good-bye, Mastermind!"

The green-skull turned, and Mastermind lifted a hand in a final farewell.

"Now," Raceboy said with a knowing look at Super Qwok, "we have some business to take care of with Mom."

The four heroes approached Mom, who lounged peacefully on the park bench.

"Mom?" asked Super Qwok.

"Yes," smiled Mom.

Raceboy said, "It's very important to protect our secret identities. So we have to tell you this: you are going to forget the identities of Super Qwok and Raceboy and Racegirl and Knight-in-shining-armor-boy."

Mom agreed, "I am going to forget…"

"All you know about Raceboy, Super Qwok, Racegirl, and Knight-in-shining-armor-boy is that they are costumed heroes who save Clifton."

"Yes, I know that they save Clifton…"

Super Qwok said, "Alex and Bryan and Logan are little boys. Katherine is a little girl. None of them are superheroes."

Mom seemed perplexed by this comment. "Of course they aren't superheroes. They're just children…"

"When I snap my fingers three times," added Raceboy, "you will wake up. You will not remember this conversation."

Raceboy snapped once, twice, three times.

"Oh, for heaven's sakes," gasped Mom. "Why am I wearing this ski mask? It's practically summer!?"

"Don't worry, Ma'am," said Knight-in-shining-armor-boy. "We'll get you back home safe and sound. You were caught by a villain named Mastermind, and he tried to hypnotize you."

"Oh, he didn't though, did he?"

"We stopped him," said Super Qwok. "And now things can finally return to normal."

Raceboy sighed, "Thank goodness."

And so the world was once more saved by Raceboy and Super Qwok, with help from Racegirl and Knight-in-shining-armor-boy. The side-effect of this world-saving was that Mom no longer remembered their secret identities.

Later, as they lay in their beds, Bryan said, "I think I'm going to miss the Mom-mobile."

Alex snorted, "You can't be serious!"

Bryan laughed.

How Super Qwok's Silly Pants Saved the Day!

Bryan had a problem. His normal superhero pants weren't clean, and the only other pants he could find to wear looked silly.

"You can't go out like that," Alex told him through giggles. "You look silly!"

"But I need to fight crime!" protested Bryan.

Katherine agreed with Alex. "Bryan, no one will be able to take you seriously if you wear those pants in public!"

Bryan didn't have a chance to reply because as he opened his mouth the Race-alarm sounded.

"It's the Wicked Witch," Alex reported after speed-reading the printout on the Race-computer. "She's stealing candy from little children. Let's go!"

Brief moments passed, and the three heroes sped off in the Race-mobile to find the Wicked Witch.

As the Race-mobile vroomed down the streets, Super Qwok looked down at his pants. "Maybe I will sit this one out, if you don't mind," he said.

Raceboy shrugged. "Suit yourself," he said, which he thought he was pretty clever.

In the distance she appeared: a black robed figure with a broom and a bag full of candy. Raceboy braked, put the car in park, and exited the car in a flash. He ordered, "Stop, Witch!" as he swept past her, lifting the bag of goodies straight out of her hand.

The Wicked Witch looked down at her now empty hand and shrieked. She lifted her broom and began sweeping the dirt all around her. It rose, formed a cloud, and hid her from the heroes. Within the cloud she cackled and giggled with mirth.

Raceboy tried to race through the cloud and knock her out of the dust, but each time he passed clean by her. The sound of his racing feet over the ground wasn't like a pitter-patter; his footsteps ran together to form a *WHOOSH, WHOOSH, WHOOSH* like a giant puffing out, out, out.

The Witch's laughter within the cloud infuriated Raceboy.

Racegirl said, "Let's huff and puff and blow this Witch down!"

Both heroes inhaled then blew with all their might. The dust swirled, bent, and scattered beneath the force of their combined breath.

Angrily, the Wicked Witch raised her broom, and *KA-ZING*, a bolt of lightning sizzled straight into Racegirl. She didn't have a chance to dodge; she was frozen like a statue. She wobbled, then tipped over and fell to the ground without a sound.

Raceboy yelled and charged the Wicked Witch. She said a single magic word and immediately Raceboy's body turned limp, his feet stumbled, his arms splayed, and he fell chin first onto the ground at the Witch's feet. He began snoring peacefully, his breath fluttering like tiny beating bird wings as he inhaled and exhaled.

Super Qwok sighed. There was no

one else to stop the Wicked Witch.

He moved from behind the Race-mobile. He didn't race, and he didn't charge. In fact, he moved in such an un-heroic manner that the Wicked Witch didn't see him until he stood right before her above his sleeping brother.

"What do you want?" snapped the Wicked Witch, her lip curled in a snarl. She looked at Super Qwok's masked face; her beady eyes traveled down to the SQ emblazoned on his chest, then down still more until they gazed upon his pants. Her lip quivered briefly and a short giggle of laughter broke free from her mouth. Then like a volcano, the giggle erupted in gales and guffaws. She bent over. Tears dripped from her eyes, ran off her cheeks, and dropped to the ground.

With a shrug, Super Qwok snapped the Qwok-cuffs on the Wicked Witch. She didn't seem to notice; her sides quaked with laughter.

He reached down

and touched Raceboy, who woke up mid-snore with a grumble. He touched Racegirl, who snapped out of the spell and blinked dazedly.

When the Police Captain arrived, the three heroes loaded the Wicked Witch into the back seat of the police cruiser. Super Qwok asked, "Are my pants really that silly?"

The Police Captain could only laugh as he drove away.

"You should wear them every time the Race-alarm goes off," Raceboy said, but Super Qwok made sure he never wore his silly pants again.

SHOOTING STARS

Dr. Devious had come up with yet another diabolical plan to enhance his powers, to defeat Raceboy and Super Qwok, and conquer the world. To do this he needed an advantage outside of this world. To do this, he turned to the stars.

Every year in August, the Earth passes through the tail of the comet Swift-Tuttle. Tiny pieces of comet dust fall into the Earth's atmosphere, creating the shooting star showers called the Perseids.

Dr. Devious had formulated a theory that if he could harness the power of the shooting stars he would be able to use the energy to take over the world. On August 12th, Dr. Devious stood on the top of one of Clifton's grain elevators, looking at the sky above, watching for the first signs of the Perseids.

It was a new moon, which meant that there was no moon in the sky, or to be more accurate, the moon was totally covered by the shadow of the Earth. This left the shooting stars bright as they fell against the inky blackness of the night.

First a tiny star fell, then a bigger star. But Dr. Devious waited. He watched for a perfect star. Over his shoulder he carried an invention. It looked something like a bazooka with a giant metal hand sticking out of the barrel. He called it, "The Star Catcher 1000."

Still watching, Dr. Devious saw another star. He pulled the

trigger on the Star Catcher 1000. The metal hand shot from the bazooka in a blaze of hissing orange flames and smoke. Although the night was too dark and the distance too great to see, Dr. Devious had designed the Star Catcher 1000 to reach out and grab the delicate shooting star before it could either disintegrate or strike the Earth. It would then descend on a cushion of air (another of his own inventions, although he had originally designed it for Mr. Mischief, who was trying to steal the crown from the Statue of Liberty) and land in his outstretched hands.

Alex and Bryan had just spread the blanket on the ground of their back yard. The grass was moist with dew; the night air was just cool enough for a sweatshirt or a jacket. The chirping noises of crickets surrounded them. And there were no clouds to block the view of the Perseid meteor shower.

Mom and Dad were still banging around by the deck trying to lug some of the folding chairs out to the backyard when a flash like a firework shot from the top of a nearby grain elevator.

"Meet me," Alex said to Bryan. Then there was a blur, and Raceboy ran toward the grain elevator.

Bryan rolled his eyes and changed in the garage before he took off after his brother.

Atop the grain elevator, Dr. Devious chuckled with anticipation as the mitt of the Star Catcher 1000 hummed its way toward him. It blinked; he had added a blinking LED to the unit's base to make it easier to see.

"Dr. Devious," said a voice that was all-too-familiar to Dr. Devious. "You are not going to succeed in your plans!" It was Raceboy. He stood beside Dr. Devious, hands on his hips.

Dr. Devious growled, "That's the last time you'll sneak up on me!" He pressed a button on his belt.

Despite Raceboy's super-fast reactions, he found himself jetted away from Dr. Devious on a stream of air that carried him sideways over the edge of the grain elevator. Where did it come from? He wasn't sure. But it had come from Dr. Devious as he pressed the button on his belt.

Anyone who has ever taken a tumble down stairs or off a ladder can tell you about the moment when you are no longer in control of your body in relation to the Earth. Yes, you can control your limbs. You can curl up into a ball, or try to shift your body and twist to land on your feet. But without that familiar connection to the Earth, you discover very quickly that you have nothing to push off from. And since you probably didn't plan on plummeting from the top of a staircase or the top of a ladder or the top of a grain elevator, you don't actually begin from a convenient position for falling. You tend to be upside down, sideways, twisting while the familiar control you have always used to move across the Earth has abandoned you. And, in a fraction of a second, that connection to the Earth is going to be renewed in a very abrupt way.

This is what Raceboy felt as his body fell. He was fast—super fast—but while he was in free-fall, he was helpless. The ability to flap his arms in super speed didn't turn him into a bird; super speed just made reality feel like it lasted longer as he fell 9.8 meters per second squared straight at the grass and gravel and ground.

Dr. Devious chuckled. He leaned over the edge of the grain elevator to watch expectantly. His face changed from smile to grimace, and he cursed. "No!"

Raceboy landed in Super Qwok's outstretched arms.

"You arrived just in time," Raceboy said. "I thought I was a goner."

Super Qwok said, "I don't think I'll apologize for not getting here sooner."

Dr. Devious turned to the Star Catcher 1000 as it wafted above his head. He grabbed, retrieved the robotic hand, and opened the fingers. In the palm of the metal hand was a single glowing piece of meteor the size of a baseball.

"Ah ha!" said Dr. Devious, forgetting momentarily about Raceboy and Super Qwok. "My theory was accurate. Falling stars are not dead lumps of rock but a living source of pure power!" And he lifted the fallen star from the robotic palm, holding it between his hands where it blazed like a beacon, a lighthouse. The glow lit his face unevenly, a flame from a campfire. He held the fallen star close between cupped hands as though praying, embracing, absorbing the star.

The boys on the ground below could see his glowing shape. Raceboy said, "I have a bad feeling about this."

Dr. Devious directed the star energy in a tight beam, sending it shooting straight at Raceboy and Super Qwok. The blazing star-powered beam burned a sizzling spot at their feet.

"Yikes," said Super Qwok.

Raceboy said, "Super Qwok, we have to stop him. If he uses that star energy, he might be unstoppable."

"What goes down can go up," Super Qwok said.

"Like a yo-yo?" Raceboy asked.

"Step up," Super Qwok directed Raceboy, linking his fingers together and holding them out like a stirrup. Raceboy stepped into Super Qwok's fingers, pulled himself up by Super Qwok's shoulders. "Try to land on your feet this time. And have a hand on your Race-chute. Just in case."

Super Qwok hefted with all of his might, aiming Raceboy at Dr. Devious atop the grain elevator. Raceboy was launched like a catapult's charge, like a bottle-rocket, into the air. He put his arms straight above his head; he held his legs straight, with the toes pointed; he was an arrow flying at Dr. Devious.

There was no time for Dr. Devious to avoid Raceboy; the hero struck him in the chest. The glowing star slipped from his grip, rolled across the sloping surface of the grain elevator, along its curving edge, then fell.

Super Qwok saw the glow flip over the edge and plummet toward him. He caught it before it could hit the ground.

Raceboy lifted Dr. Devious, who, in broken voice wailed, "No! You can't defeat me!"

"What about this?" Raceboy began twirling the doctor, like one of dad's dowel rods, or a baton, or a fake plastic sword. *WHE-WHE-WHE-WHE-WHE-WHE.* He spun Dr. Devious so fast that Dr. Devious couldn't talk. He could only say, "Uhb-uhb-uhb-uhb-uhb-uhb."

When Raceboy finally stopped spinning him, Dr. Devious whimpered, "Oh, I think I'm going to be sick."

"Serves you right," Raceboy said.

Super Qwok peered into the glowing stardust. He could feel the power. Although it had faded now, no longer a baseball , but something closer to a bouncy ball, it still oozed with energy. Energy that Dr. Devious would turn to his own vile ends. Super Qwok wound up and with all his might hurled the fallen star back across the sky. It streaked brightly over the trees and faded, disintegrated in its descent. All of the powers dissipated. Dr. Devious could no longer use its power.

"Incoming!" Raceboy called. Super Qwok looked up and saw the white lab coat ripple as Dr. Devious discovered what it felt like to plummet in free-fall straight at the ground. Judging by the way Dr. Devious screamed, Super Qwok figured he didn't think much of the experience.

Super Qwok caught him gently and set him down. "See, Dr. Devious. Aren't you glad Raceboy made sure I was here before he threw you down? Too bad we can't say the same for how you treated him."

Dr. Devious wobbled and groaned.

After they led Dr. Devious to the police station, the Police Captain said, "Raceboy and Super Qwok, I can't keep Dr. Devious in jail."

Raceboy argued, "But do you realize what he could have done with the stardust and the power from the falling star?"

"We don't know that. Everything I know about shooting stars says that they're space rocks, maybe with some minerals, but essentially free for the taking. We have no proof that catching a star would have allowed Dr. Devious to take over the world."

The boys stared silently at Dr. Devious.

"He did trespass," said the Police Captain, "but we usually give warnings for that. Really, we have to let him go."

Dr. Devious allowed the slightest hint of a smile to cross his lips.

"No," argued Super Qwok. "He'll come up with another plan to take over the world."

The Police Captain shrugged, "It's the law. We can't hold him for what he may do, only what he has done. There's no law against catching a shooting star. They're not of this world. Our laws are for this world."

He took the Race-cuffs from Dr. Devious's wrists. Dr. Devious peered through his glasses at the two heroes, then wrinkled his nose as though to deliver a lecture. He must have thought better of it, however, because he turned and walked from the police station without a word.

Back at home, Alex and Bryan joined their parents on blankets and lawn chairs in the back yard. Katherine and Anna oohed and aahed with each new shooting star. Dad said, "Where did you two go? You missed a great shooting star a while ago."

"Yeah," said Mom. "It flew right over our heads."

The boys tried to act excited, to enjoy this peaceful time spent watching falling stars with their family, but each falling ball of light was a reminder that somewhere, Dr. Devious was free, maybe even watching the same falling star, with his mind bent on formulating a diabolical plan to destroy Raceboy and Super Qwok and to take over the world.

Vorlox Rising

It had been a long day…First, Mom had taken them to garage sales. Sale after sale in the hot sun, and neither Alex nor Bryan had anything to show for it. Mom had bought Katherine some trinkets, and Anna had come across an Elmo book, but all the superhero toys had turned out to be duds.

Worse, after garage-saling all day, Mom had brought the kids to Sears. The boys shared a chair outside the dressing room. Mom was inside, helping Katherine try on new jeans for her first day of preschool. Anna, meanwhile, was helping out by crawling under the dressing room door.

"Anna!" ranted Mom for the umpteenth time. "Oh, if only your dad didn't have to work…" A hand reached under the door and grabbed Anna's two-year-old leg.

"Thank goodness Anna doesn't have super powers," Bryan whispered.

Mom caught Anna's ankle and pulled her under the door. Anna grinned at her waiting brothers as she disappeared into the dressing room with a happy giggle.

"Yeah. Can you imagine it?" Alex wondered.

Mom lectured, "Anna, will you sit still—" when an explosion of breaking glass interrupted her. The main store entrance was gone; in its place was smoke-filled daylight.

Alex and Bryan's eyes met; they dashed beneath a nearby clearance rack.

A giant contraption crunched through the wreckage of the door, over the dust and smoke and broken glass. It was man-shaped, though taller than a man. Cylindrical arms pointed straight down. It walked on wide, squat legs that were jointed like a dog's hind legs.

"It's some kind of robot drone," Alex said.

"Mr. Mischief?" Bryan asked.

"No telling, but it's time for action."

The contraption plowed through clothing racks. Metal crunched. Fabric stuck to its thick metal toes as it hissed and wheezed straight toward the dressing room.

That was as far as it got. Suddenly it was no longer walking on the ground. Instead, it was held aloft by a six-year-old superhero: Super Qwok. He stood in the middle of the department store,

suited in his gray costume with red mask and gloves.

The robot's humming grew louder. A bright eruption of light zapped from the end of one of its cylinder arms. The blast struck the ground, leaving only a crater. The robot drone clattered awkwardly on its mechanical legs. But where was Super Qwok?

Super Qwok waved at the drone casually beside the crater-from the safety of Raceboy's arms. "Good thing you weren't any slower," he said. "I'd have been vaporized."

"Something's not playing nice," Raceboy said.

"How about a little Race-ball?"

The robot adjusted its upper torso. Servos within the machine-whined, and it directed a mirrored view plate at the two heroes.

"You pitching?" Raceboy asked as he set Super Qwok down.

One of the cylinder arms pivoted. The blaster was taking aim for a finishing shot.

"Sure am," Super Qwok smiled and lifted Raceboy. Super Qwok wound up as the cylinder neared position to point at the heroes. He pitched Raceboy straight at the robot.

Raceboy held his legs against his chest as he spun; the instant before he struck the machine there was a click and bright blue beam of light: Raceboy's laser-sword. It snicked on and swiped, cutting through the robot arm, separating it from the metal trunk. Raceboy extended his legs, opened his body as he landed on the opposite side of the crater. Then he used the forward momentum to crouch and rebound in a backflip. He landed squarely on the robot's shoulders.

"Hey! Save some for me!" Super Qwok yelled.

But it was too late. Raceboy plunged his laser-sword in the middle of the robot's view plate. A hiss, a crackle, and a final wheeze came from the machine as it buckled forward. With practiced precision, Raceboy stepped from the falling shoulders onto the ground as it hit, landing beside Super Qwok as easily as if he'd stepped from an escalator.

"Humph," said Super Qwok. "I don't even get leftovers."

The dust in the store cleared. The tips of people's heads peeked from behind shoe racks and cash registers and baby cribs.

Super Qwok studied the machine. "These aren't any kind of letters I've ever seen," he said, as the first mall security officer approached the boys, one hand holding his hat, the other his belt.

"Except," said Raceboy, "you're only going into first grade, so you're just learning to read. Here, let me look." He leaned over the panel. Super Qwok was right; the characters were not letters. They looked more like hieroglyphics stamped onto the machine's side.

"Nope, doesn't look familiar to me, either."

"Take a picture with the Race-camera," Super Qwok suggested.

"Good idea. Then we'll feed the image into the Race-computer, and see if it can find a positive match."

Raceboy snapped images with the hi-res camera in his wrist band, and Super Qwok handled the mall security. He ensured that they had followed protocol to notify local authorities about the emergency, especially experts to analyze the wreckage and clean up the mess. He thanked them for their prompt response to the emergency. Of course, no introductions were necessary; everyone knew Super Qwok and Raceboy from their numerous front page newspaper articles and ten o'clock news stories.

When Super Qwok turned around, he saw Mom. She put a hand on his shoulder. "Thank you, Super Qwok, for saving my little girls and me." Anna bopped out from behind Mom's leg and grinned. Katherine rolled her eyes. It always annoyed her when the boys got to use their super powers and she didn't. "But," Mom continued, "I can't find my boys!" Her voice held a note of hysteria. "They disappeared when that thing burst into the store!"

Super Qwok glanced at Raceboy; their eyes met; Raceboy nodded. His look explained, "I'll take care of this so you have time to change." Super Qwok nodded.

Raceboy approached Mom with his arms open at his side, pulling himself into the conversation, and the attention away from Super Qwok.

"Don't worry, Ma'am. It's all under control. Super Qwok, do you think you can locate either boy while I wrap-up with mall security?"

"Will do," Super Qwok said truthfully as he disappeared behind a row of clothing racks.

Raceboy turned to the mall officer and compared notes briefly about the machine. Soon he approached Mom, "Ma'am, is this one of your boys?" Behind him, Bryan gave Mom his sheepish smile.

"Mom!" he exclaimed and raced up to hug her.

Mom wrapped Bryan in her arms and buried her face in his shoulder. When she looked up, Alex stood beside them. "Mom, that was scary." He thought the way his voice broke on the last word was particularly convincing. Mom reached an arm and pulled Alex into her hug too.

"I'm okay, Mom," Alex said. "Really," he grunted as Mom squeezed the boys even harder and began to cry relieved tears.

At last Mom said, "Where's Raceboy?"

Alex looked around. "He was just here. Huh. I wonder where he went." He turned to Bryan and said, "Wasn't it cool to see Raceboy and Super Qwok! I mean, didn't they look so cool when they were fighting that thing, that whatever it was?"

"Yeah," Bryan agreed. "They sure were tough."

The mall security guard asked Mom for some information to complete an accident report. Alex continued, "Raceboy was awesome. Did you see what he did? Like the way he flew at the robot! And those moves when he turned on his laser-sword." He mimicked the laser-sword, make humming sounds as he waved a pretend energy blade around, simulating the battle. "Slam, wham. He totally took out that robot like something in an action movie. I mean—" Alex grunted, looked down to discover Bryan's elbow in his side.

Bryan whispered, "Lay off. You're overdoing it."

"What?" Alex asked innocently. "I'm Raceboy's biggest fan."

"And I'm Super Qwok's," agreed Bryan. "It looked to me like Raceboy hogged the robot so Super Qwok didn't get a chance to get in on the action."

Katherine wrinkled her nose and said, "Looked to me like no one even let Racegirl help. I'll bet she is mad."

Alex ignored her. "Looked to me like it was Super Qwok's idea to play Race-ball."

"Humph. Probably be the last time he has that bright idea. Ball hog."

Silence fell uneasily except for Mom and the security guard as they completed all of the required fields on the form, and Anna, who was trying to swing from bathrobes, "Whee!"

As Mom loaded the kids into the family van, she said, "Why don't we stop and get a bite to eat on our way home? There's nothing like a brush with death to make you feel like dropping a couple of dollars on food."

"Where are we going?" Alex asked.

"Where else?" Mom tossed back.

"Taco Bell," groaned Alex, Bryan, and Katherine. Anna giggled and sang, "Taco Bell Bell Bell, Taco Bell Bell Bell."

Mom normally used the drive-thru, and everyone was stuck eating in their various models of child safety seat for the twenty-five minute drive home. Tonight, however, she surprised everyone when she said, "Let's go in and sit down for a change. I could use a breather. And your dad won't be home from the library for another hour, anyway, so we have time."

It was after Bryan cleaned up on his second cheese roll that his eyes got big, and he grabbed Alex's arm. To Mom, Bryan said, "Bathroom break. It's an emergency!" Without waiting for a reply, Bryan drug Alex to the bathroom.

They could hear Katherine behind them: "Me too! I've got to go, too!" and Mom hushing her, saying, "Just a minute—"

"What in the world?" Alex asked as the bathroom door thumped shut behind him.

Bryan took stock of the bathroom—they were alone—and began reversing his clothes, revealing his gray Super Qwok costume. "No time. Get changed." Before he had finished the words, Raceboy stood before him fully garbed in gray and blue. "Speed sure is handy," Bryan grumbled as he pulled on his mask. That was the instant when the world outside the bathroom erupted like Mount St. Helens. The bathroom walls shook. "Go!" Super Qwok yelled as he shattered the door with a powerful punch.

The restaurant, or more accurately, what was left of it, no longer had a roof. Standing above, looming over the Taco Bell like the giant come down from the beanstalk, stood a second, larger robot drone. It was obvious to anyone who had seen the first robot that this machine was from the same mechanical family. It had more appendages: tiny arms and pinchers that twirled and reached, but the view plate was the same flat plate of mirrored glass.

Super Qwok took stock again. He found Mom beneath the table they had been seated at, her body covering the girls protectively.

"This looks like a job for Super Qwok!" he said as he leapt onto the garbage can and catapulted himself at the robot. As he soared closer to the robot, he was not entirely surprised to see that Raceboy had beaten him to the punch. Racing up the leg, a blur of motion nearly invisible in the evening sun, slid the blue glow of a laser-sword.

Super Qwok, already in motion and airborne, continued his power punch. He brought his right fist around to collide with the chest area of the robot as he reached it. The metal clanged. He felt the punch reverberate up his forearm to his shoulder. For every action there is an equal and opposite reaction, he knew, though he

would not have been able to identify it as Newton's Third Law of Motion. It was more of an intuitive understanding from his body as it was propelled away from the giant robot. He turned a back-flip, braced his legs. Landing, he watched the panel he had struck fall from the rest of the machine; but also, he saw the blue streaks of the laser-sword continuing to slide around and around the machine, like a blue sparkler on the Fourth of July. Except this was no hissing sparkler in the hands of a regular eight-year-old trying to write his name in cursive. This was a laser-sword in the hands of Raceboy.

Pieces of the machine rained on the Taco Bell parking lot. Raceboy continued to hop, leap, twist, and flip all around the machine, swinging from an arm, leaping onto a metal shoulder. He was a blur, and behind him the machine slid apart in a landslide of severed metal.

After carving the upper torso of the machine into refuse, the two legs stood motionless in the parking lot. Raceboy landed, looked between them to Super Qwok, and gave him the thumbs up sign before he pushed the robot leg. It, along with its twin, and what was left of the waist, fell over and crushed the drive-thru ordering price list flatter than a tortilla shell.

Raceboy disappeared. Super Qwok took the hint, and using the dust and noise and distraction, slid back into the bathroom, where he returned to his normal jeans and t-shirt. Thinking fast, he rolled around in some dirt to make sure he looked the part before coming back into the restaurant.

Alex was already at the table helping Mom up. Of course he was already in his regular clothes. "Are you alright?" he asked.

Far away, sirens wailed. They increased in volume. For the second time in one day, the boys, girls, and Mom discovered themselves part of the wreckage of an attack from a mysterious machine. As the clouds of dust cleared, people began pulling themselves out from under tables, or behind counters, or (in the case of one poor woman who smelled like nacho cheese and hot sauce) out of the garbage can. The restaurant manager, her Taco Bell hat replaced with a mound of meat and rice, yelled, "Is anyone hurt? Is everyone okay?"

"We're going home!" Mom declared. Her lips wrapped around

the words slowly, and her voice was hollow, as though she was being powered by remote control. She did not sound like she was going to cry; instead she sounded past crying, like a person who has already cried too much and has gone on to the next level. What that next level might be, neither Alex nor Bryan knew, but from the tone they knew it was something even more dangerous to ignore.

"Mom, you're cut!" Bryan said, putting a finger against a bloody streak in her hair.

"It's nothing," Mom said.

Alex helped Katherine and Anna out from beneath Mom. Katherine wrinkled her nose at Alex, which was as close to saying, "Racegirl wants to help," as she could come with Mom around. As he pulled Katherine to her feet, he caught the glint of a metal amulet he had never seen before.

"What's that?" he asked.

Katherine smiled. "Do you like it? I got it at one of the garage sales."

"It's neat," Alex said.

"Mom said I could wear it if I was good, and I was good." She touched the charm with her four-year-old fingers. "You should see the box it was in. I'm going to put my princesses in it. It's big enough."

A police car pulled up outside the restaurant. A fire engine rolled to a stop, followed closely by an ambulance. Police, fire, and other emergency personnel invaded. Mom may have wanted to go home, but there was no going home when the police officer took her by the arm and led her and the kids from the restaurant to be checked over by waiting paramedics. When they discovered the cut on her head, the paramedic told her, "You've won a ride in the ambulance."

"All right!" Alex and Bryan said together.

Anna asked, "Can I win, too?"

"You can all go with your mom," the paramedic told her, patting her head.

The area outside the restaurant was quickly organized. The police officers cordoned off the restaurant, some firefighters worked on making sure the building wasn't burning, others led or helped people from the wreckage, and the paramedics checked people over. Although Raceboy and Super Qwok had stopped the robot's attack, many other heroes had to work very hard to take care of the aftermath of the battle. Alex and Bryan watched the activity in awe, impressed with the discipline and earnestness displayed by these everyday heroes. Alex even felt a little bad about the drive-thru kiosk when he watched a blue-suited policeman look at the tumbled down legs and scratch his head with his police hat.

Time passed, and soon the family was off to the hospital in the ambulance. Mom said that Dad would be meeting them there. At the hospital, a doctor checked Mom's head and declared that she would, indeed, be needing staples. Dad arrived in a panic, hugged Mom and the little girls before grabbing both boys in a hug as well.

*   *   *

The doctor pressed the stapler to Mom's head and hit the trigger: the stapler clicked and the walls shook. He wrinkled his eyebrows, looked at the stapler in his hand as though wondering, "Did I do that?"

Bryan whispered, "I think we should go check that out."

A second rumble of walls echoed. This one seemed to be closer, and it was definitely not from the doctor's stapler.

Alex nodded, and when the doctor said, "Just a minute. I'm going to figure out what's going on out there," Alex and Bryan followed him to the door.

"Me, too!" said a little voice as a four-year-old's hand grabbed Alex's arm. Except, the voice spoke in Race-mode, so it was too fast for the normal human ear to make out.

"Katherine, you stay with Mom," Alex said, equally fast.

"I want to help."

"You are helping when you stay with Mom!"

"No, I'm not. You just don't appreciate my powers. You just don't want my help." She folded her arms.

"That's not true," Alex argued. "Super Qwok and I can handle this. If we all disappear at once it will be too suspicious. We need you to help us by covering for us. And protecting Mom. Just in case."

There was no mistaking the anger in Katherine's frown, but she did zip back to Mom and let Alex get out the door. Since the entire exchange had taken place in super speed, only a fraction of a second had passed in regular time.

The hospital had a great many doors. The boys opened one and found an empty medical records office. When the door reopened, Raceboy and Super Qwok stepped into the hall.

"This way," Super Qwok said, but Raceboy had already left him in the dust. The blur that was Raceboy sped ahead. "Not again," Super Qwok sighed.

By the time Super Qwok caught up with Raceboy, he was at the door they had left Mom, Dad, and the girls within. And instead of the door, there was a gaping hole filled with a much smaller and rounder robot than either of the previous drones.

This one was covered with arms and tentacle-like hoses. It had three legs with three joints each. The arms were attached to different rings, each of which appeared to spin separate of the others. It did not have a view plate.

As Super Qwok neared, he saw Raceboy throw punch after

punch, but each was deflected by one of the many arms spinning from the different sides of the machine. Snicker-snack. Raceboy lit his laser-sword and swung it in a lightning fast combo. Super Qwok was surprised to see the sword bounce — not from the machine itself, but from some sort of energy shield. The contact of the sword with the shield caused a violent explosion, sending Raceboy hurtling backwards against the wall, where he slid, stunned, to the ground.

Now, it's finally a job for Super Qwok, he thought with a mental cracking of knuckles. He didn't really crack his knuckles, because there was no time. Instead he dashed toward the spinning arms of the machine, which had moved further into the room. There, beyond the machine, Super Qwok could see Mom and Dad huddled together over the girls, while the machine peeled off each adult with long, snake-like grippers, and reached for — Katherine? What could the machine want with Katherine?

The look on Katherine's face told the entire story: *Why me?* she was asking. *I'm not in a superhero costume. As far as anyone knows, I'm a four-year-old girl. Why would a machine want me?*

Super Qwok didn't worry about the why's. He grabbed one of the arms and wrenched it from the machine, then clobbered the machine with its own arm. Removing the arm exposed an opening which Super Qwok punched straight through. He clenched whatever electronics he could from deep inside the device. With a yank he pulled out a handful of mechanical guts and threw them to the floor. Some of the hands ceased their reaching and rotating. Super Qwok repeated the process, this time moving his arm all around the interior of the robot. With each motion other arms and pinchers quit their rhythmic motion, until at last Katherine fell from lifeless robot grippers to the floor, where Mom and Dad scooped her up. She hadn't cried the whole time, but her face was pale, and her eyes were as big as half dollars. Despite her super powers, the whole experience had caught her off-guard. She wasn't used to being grabbed by robots, especially not in her regular clothes. When she finally had a chance to breath, her crying shriek echoed to the high heavens.

The machine gave a mechanical burp, or wheeze, and tipped to one side.

Raceboy, recovered somewhat, leaned against Bryan and pointed to the writing on the machine. It was the same as the first machine they had photographed.

Super Qwok pulled the broken drone from the room, and Raceboy came with him. "What are you doing with it?" he asked.

"I'm going to get it out of here. I think Mom's going to have a breakdown if she looks at another of these machines. Besides, one of us needs to get back in there and cover for the other so that she won't start to suspect anything.

"Good idea," Raceboy said. He jumped and changed at super speed. Even directly in front of Super Qwok it was an impressive feat: to jump up in full superhero costume and land in regular clothes. Super Qwok lugged the machine back through the broken doors and wreckage that indicated the path of the robot's entrance to the building.

Returning to the room, Alex acted as though he'd been present for the whole thing. He was relieved to discover that no one had really noted his absence, and that Katherine's attempted…kidnapping? was the main concern. Mom's doctor, and a variety of techs were present, plus three hospital security guards. They were all trying to calm Mom down. She was hyperventilating, saying, "Raceboy and Super Qwok. Three times. Raceboy. Super Qwok. Saved us." Her voice continued to trail off as she spoke in sentence fragments.

In a moment Bryan also appeared beside Alex, and the two sat quietly, out of range of the adults, conspiring.

"Where's it at?" Alex asked.

"Threw it into the Kankakee river," Bryan murmured. "It was weird. Just before I threw it, I could swear there was this shadow, this snaky mist that floated out of it."

"Smoke?"

"Nah, it was almost a smoky eel. Weird." Bryan grimaced.

"We've got to ditch Mom so we can trace these things to the source."

"It's hard to do when she's always around when they attack."

"And what about that last one? Looked like it was going for Katherine," Alex said.

"It was. I don't know that it was interested in hurting her, but it most definitely wanted Katherine."

"Why in the world would robots attack three times to try to get Katherine?"

Silence from the boys.

Bryan said, "Maybe they're sent from the future to destroy Katherine because she's going to grow up to start a rebellion or something?"

"You've been watching too much science fiction. I think it's her necklace."

"What, robots love jewelry?"

Alex said, "No, that's the thing. I don't think that pendant is jewelry. I think it's something else."

"A homing beacon for psycho robots?"

"You got any better ideas?" Alex asked.

Bryan shrugged. "Seems like a stretch. You could blame Anna's book from the garage sales for that matter? Maybe the robots like Elmo."

Alex glared. "If you had looked at it, maybe you wouldn't be such a smarty pants."

Byran opened his mouth to say something really smarty pantsy, but seeing that Alex was being serious, he said, "Fine. We'll look into it. If we ever get back to the Qwok Tower."

"Yeah, at this rate Raceboy and Super Qwok are going to have to take Mom, or Katherine, home!"

It wasn't Raceboy and Super Qwok who accompanied Mom home. It was a task force of National Guardsmen. After involvement in three separate attacks from three separate robots, a group of Guardsmen in Humvees drove Mom, Dad, Alex, Bryan, and the girls back to Clifton. They then set up surveillance around the house. "It's only for the next couple of days," explained the sergeant to Dad. "Just to make sure something else doesn't happen. Your wife and children are the only victims to be present at all three of the attacks, and we don't want to take any more chances than necessary."

Inside, Mom said, "It's bed time. I don't care about baths. I don't care about bedtime stories. I don't care about midnight snacks. I want all Winkel children into their beds in ten minutes. If your teeth aren't brushed in that time, tough."

It didn't take Alex ten minutes to brush his teeth, even without the use of his super powers. Bryan, on the other hand, dawdled. He raced around in his underwear for nine and a half minutes, and only when reminded that he was on a time limit did he skid frantically into the bathroom. Two swipes with a wet toothbrush were all he had time for.

Once Mom was safely downstairs, Bryan and Alex met at Katherine's bed. Each boy stood at her side and looked at the amulet, which was still around her neck.

"Katherine," Alex whispered, shaking her shoulder. She moaned and turned to her left. "Katherine!" he shook harder.

"Never mind," Bryan said. "It was a long day. She is only four. We'll have to tell her about it tomorrow."

Alex carefully slid the necklace up the back of her neck then off her hair. He held it out to Bryan. Grabbing the chain, Bryan looked into the jeweled surface of the pendant and wrinkled his brow.

Katherine sighed in her sleep and rolled over. Both boys returned to their closet door. Bryan struck the hidden switch, and instantly the portal connecting the inside of the closet with the nearby Qwok Tower opened. He stepped inside, and Alex followed. The portal closed behind the two.

"Whew," Alex exhaled. "I thought we were never going to get back here!" The Qwok Tower was housed within a nearby abandoned grain elevator. Its open interior, once upon a time filled with dried corn, spread above the worktables and computers like the ceiling of a medieval cathedral, but without the elegant artwork. Although unused for a long time, the Qwok Tower still smelled like rotted, stinky corn. As Alex liked to say, it was the perfect defense to keep intruders away from the Qwok Tower; well, any intruders with noses, anyway.

Alex moved immediately to a workstation and booted the Race-computer. He began punching keys, plugging in the Race-camera to upload the shots he had taken of the first drone from the mall.

Bryan, meanwhile, still had the amulet, and was holding it out at arm's length, letting it twist back and forth. "It is unusual," he admitted.

"As we suspected," Alex said after a while, "There are no matches for the language written on those machines."

"Alien, then," Bryan said.

An unexpected voice crackled to life. "You are in grave danger," it said. The voice came from the Race-computer's speakers. The voice sounded awkward, as though it was trying to wrap its mouth around the unfamiliar shape of the English language.

For a moment both boys looked at one another. Finally, Bryan asked Alex, "Did the computer just talk to us?"

"Dang it!" Alex said, swinging his fist. "If you heard it, then I wasn't imagining it!"

Both boys looked back to the computer screen, which had not changed.

"This is one of your ridiculous practical jokes, isn't it?" Bryan accused. "You recorded yourself on the computer and then —"

"Humans," the computer interrupted, its voice gaining strength and familiarity with the language. "You are in grave danger. While I am in your presence you are not safe."

"Guess we need a new Race-computer," Bryan sighed.

"I am not the computer, as you well know in the intuitive centers of your brain. I am what you think of as the 'amulet.'"

"Bad enough when I thought the computer was talking," Bryan mumbled, "but now the computer is telling me it's really a talking necklace. This just gets better and better."

The computer continued, "Jest not, Bryan human. There is much you cannot understand, but this you can. I have found a vehicle to communicate with you in your language, and I bring you warning. While I am unprotected in your presence you are in danger."

"So what do we do?" Alex asked.

"I must be locked in a lined chamber, like the container I have been inside for many years. I must only be removed for short periods of time; otherwise I will be followed, located, and destroyed."

Bryan, for all his jokes, was faster than Alex. Not Raceboy fast, but the fastest to realize that the chamber the voice referred to was the case it had been inside at the garage sale. He returned to the house and retrieved it. Katherine had, indeed, stored her princesses in the canister. He left them in a pile on the ground.

Back in the Qwok Tower, Bryan held the container out and Alex prepared to lower the necklace into it.

"I will not be able to communicate with you while inside this chamber," the computer voice explained.

"How often can we open the container?" Alex asked.

"You must wait seven days," the voice said. "But hurry, otherwise I fear it may be too late for this place."

Snap, Bryan closed the lid.

"Now what do we do?" Alex asked.

"Wait a week," Bryan said. He held the container while looking down at it. It reminded him of a jewelry box, but bigger, and made of plain metal. It was very heavy, he realized, for a box this size.

*   *   *

The next day Katherine had a giant eruption of her own when she discovered that both her new necklace and her new princess container were missing. Mom stood at the door to the girls' bedroom with her hands on her hips. Both boys shook their heads and shrugged their shoulders, then tried using body language to let Katherine know they would fill her in later. It didn't work. She cried hysterically.

"We'll help you look," the boys offered, but Mom followed them through the house distrustfully, as though wary of whatever joke the mean older brothers were playing on their vulnerable little sister. Finally, Anna defused the situation by convincing Katherine she was the culprit when she didn't deny anything. A couple of leading questions later, and Katherine had convinced herself that Anna had flushed the necklace down the toilet, then lost the princess container, possibly in the toy room where it was unlikely to be found until an archeological dig broke through layers of strata to uncover it.

Anna, pleased with the attention, continued to smile and agree with Katherine. She would have agreed that she had given the necklace to a dolphin bound for Atlantis if Katherine had asked. Never mind that Anna had been asleep the second her head hit the pillow, and she hadn't gotten up until Katherine did. That sort of logic never crossed Katherine's mind.

Only later, when Mom was out of ear-shot, were the boys able to take Katherine to the Qwok Tower and explain the story to her. She was less interested in the mystery surrounding the voice than she was in glaring at them for taking her necklace and the box.

Bryan looked heavenward, exasperated. "We tried to wake you up!"

A week is a very short period of time when you are looking back over it, but a very long period of time when you are looking forward through it. The television news and newspapers showcased stories about mysterious robberies of equipment manufacturers and electronics warehouses, but those stories tapered out over the course of the week. Each night the boys speculated in whispers after bedtime about the nature of the amulet, and each night Bryan finally said, "Forget it. I'm not thinking about it anymore. It's making my brain hurt." At which point he would drift into a dreamy slumber and snore peacefully for the rest of the night.

Alex's brain, meanwhile, continued racing. He would wonder about the amulet until his mind got mixed up and he began to confuse his dreams with the amulet. *What if the amulet was really some crystalline alien technology?* he would ask. And then these thoughts would jumble up with other day events, and he would think, *What if the amulet is really a French toast stick trapped in a crystal alien?* Really, it made sense before he fell asleep, but when he woke up the next morning he would shake his head ...

After three days, the contingent of National Guardsmen returned to base and left the Winkel house unguarded. Things seemed to have returned to normal. Mom hadn't been involved in any mysterious attacks. Katherine had finally stopped glaring, sort of. At last the seventh day arrived. Alex, Bryan and Katherine left Anna quietly playing with dolls in the toyroom.

"You think she's okay?" Bryan asked.

"Of course she is," Alex said. "Just don't say anything to her, and she won't notice we've gone."

They returned through the closet to the Qwok Tower with the closed container. Alex readied the Race-computer and adjusted the volume. Katherine sat near him. Bryan set the canister down on the table and motioned to Alex.

"Remember," Alex said, "I'll ask the questions. You just be ready—"

"I know, I know!" Bryan said.

Alex clicked the stopwatch button on his wrist watch, and Bryan flicked open the canister.

"Prompt," said the voice. "I like that." The voice, like the last time, came from the speakers of the Race-computer.

"How much time do we have?" Alex read from the questions the boys had prepared.

The voice answered, "Fifteen minutes is a safe amount of time. I won't be traceable for fifteen minutes."

"Who are you?" Alex asked, keeping an eye on his watch. He looked at Bryan, who had one hand on the lid of the container.

"You may call me Vorlox. It is not precisely my name, but it is close enough for your human brains."

"What are you?" Alex read from his script.

"Think of me as a seed, or a caterpillar. I am not the finished form of what I will be—if I survive to the next stage."

"Oh, like evolutions in Pokémon," Alex said. Katherine rolled her eyes and stuck out her tongue.

The voice did not answer immediately. At last it said, "I am unfamiliar with this Pokémon, but evolution is along the lines of what I mean. In the proper circumstances I will evolve into the next stage of my existence."

"What is the next stage of your existence?" Now Alex was totally off the script. Bryan frowned at him from where he held the box lid.

"My form will resemble one of your Earth trees, or perhaps more accurately, a neuron, or brain cell."

"What will happen if you stay out of the box for more than fifteen minutes?" Bryan asked, trying to get Alex back on track with his questions.

"The Proteans may be able to lock into my thought patterns and target me."

"Proteans?" both Alex and Bryan asked together, which was definitely not on the script.

"They wish to ingest my thought patterns, as they have been doing to you humans for seven hundred years."

"Whoa," said Alex, who tossed his remaining questions into a nearby garbage can. "What do you mean? Give us a history lesson here!"

Vorlox explained, "Since the universe began, the survival of my people and the Proteans have been entwined in a cycle. My people spread seeds throughout the galaxy. The Proteans feed on these helpless seeds that float through space like—"

"Space dandelions," Katherine interrupted.

"Similar, yes," Vorlox agreed, "But then, we are dangerous to Proteans as well, because once evolved, it is we who become the hunters, and we seek out the Proteans for nourishment.

"Approximately seven hundred Earth years ago, I fell to this planet, your Earth. I should never have been here; I should live my life—including my evolutions—in deep space, far from any inhabited world. But I was pursued by three Proteans, and before I could evolve, I directed myself to the only planet near enough with life. I crashed on Earth. The Proteans who followed me had exhausted themselves traveling through deep space. They are a shadow race, a people that feeds on thoughts the way you feed on food. My thoughts are especially rich for them, and would power them to escape this world, to travel far in the universe. Earthling thoughts are infinitesimally less nourishing to them, and though they can survive on this world, they are trapped until either they find a way to be physically carried into space, or they find me and feed on my essence."

"You're only the size of a nickel—how can your essence be any more filling than a human's?" Alex asked.

"You are making judgments from your experiences; I am outside the experience of anything on this Earth, as are the Proteans. You can imagine a part of you that has no physical substance: a soul, or a mind, or a spirit, yes?"

Both boys nodded. Katherine wrinkled her forehead.

"Imagine such a spiritual essence as it passes through time. It doesn't grow in size, but it accumulates experiences. We Vorlox—yes, I gave you a name for my people rather than a name for myself, because such an individual name is illogical for us—pass on our experiences and memories to the new seeds that we hatch. Thus I have accumulated centuries and millennia and eons of experiences. These experiences feed Proteans. You humans have only short amount of time to accumulate energy of this sort, and to the Proteans you can but keep them alive only barely."

"They didn't look barely alive to me. I mean, they had those giant robot forms, and it looked like they evolved to counter my skills," Alex pointed out.

"You aren't seeing the Proteans as they really are," Vorlox explained. "They are mere shadows that take control of machines. Their skill in mechanics has had a very negative effect on your Earth, I am afraid. They have used their influence much as I have mine, but whereas I have used my influence to hide, they have used theirs to help humans invent ideas. It has been slow for them, but they have finally increased human knowledge to the point where you have nearly given them the stars. They have but a few short centuries of development ahead before humanity will send them into far space without even knowing what you have done."

"All technology has been developed because of Proteans?" Bryan asked.

"Well, not all. But the motive force was their need to depart the earth, and your human ingenuity was the tool they could affect to get them closer to their goal. The machines you fought, for example, were constructs that they built and controlled. While they don't have the ability to construct the parts—that's what they use you humans for—they can take existing parts and put them into new shapes. Give them a factory, and they will shape a new construct from the available pieces. They then take over that shape and control it until it is destroyed. Disembodied, they are confused for a time, until they gather their wits and can take over another machine.

"They are shadows, but they do have substance. It's hard for humans to make out—especially hard now that they are much weaker from the centuries spent without nutrition here on Earth. But they can be caught if you have a prison that can contain them."

"I'll bet that was the strange shape I saw," Bryan mused, remembering the squiggling, smoke-like like eel he had seen after the last robot attack.

"What could hold a Protean?" Alex asked.

"While they are in their natural state they are very weak; a glass jar would be enough."

"I don't get it," Bryan said. "Technology isn't bad. You couldn't have talked to us without technology—you needed the Race-computer. If the Proteans have taught humans about technology, then they must be good!"

"There are a lot of good technologies," Alex agreed. "There are satellites and space stations and electricity…and video games."

"And princess cartoons on DVD," Katherine added.

"You speak honestly from your frame of reference. This is the system you have always known. But think: what good comes from these technologies? What bad? Every action has a reaction; every positive has a negative. Technology should not ignore long-term negative consequences for short-term positive results.

"Yes, technological advancement is the natural evolution of sentient beings. Humans were advancing prior to my coming to Earth, but the Proteans changed that advancement; they hastened your planet's evolution, producing damaging side-effects. Think of combustion engines; they are quintessential Protean technology. They use a finite energy source for short term gain. There are numerous other energy sources available, but the Proteans needed the fastest way to reach space and escape Earth. What other trade-offs have been brought about by this meddling? Landfills of waste? Products designed to break and be replaced rather than repaired? Disposable everything? Super viruses? How much better off would human technology be without the influence of the Proteans? Look into your hearts and tell me that my words are not true."

For a moment the room was silent. The boys understood the gist of Vorlox's explanation; even Katherine had an inkling.

Alex asked, "So what would happen if the Proteans left Earth? What would Earth technology be like?"

"It would take Earth years for the damage to be undone, but human ingenuity would win out. You would see better cause and effect, less waste, less pollution, less damage to your Earth."

"I think everyone would cheer for less pollution," Bryan said.

Alex asked, "So, you've been here on Earth for seven hundred years, always about to be eaten by these Proteans?"

"Always in danger of being eaten. But although I could never find a vehicle to communicate with you humans, I was often able to influence your decisions. Through intuitions or desires I was able to be protected in certain ways that hid my essence from the Proteans. I was protected on an altar as a relic of St. Peter's kidney stone, have spent time in the furnace of a smithy in New England, and have been a rare, expensive amulet passed down through a noble family. I have also spent a number of lifetimes hiding in the stomach of various individuals whose life energy was sufficient to mask my own from the Proteans. And now I have, through fate or fortune, been placed in your hands. If I've ever hoped, in the seven hundred years that I've been on this planet, that there could be a way to free me from this world, I hadn't found it until I met the three of you."

Each child thought about these words as Vorlox continued, "You have the ability to fight off the Proteans in ways that many humans do not. And you have the creativity to think of a solution to my problem. You also have the attitude of getting things done despite hardship. I can tell that you have faced difficult odds and have come out on top."

"I'm thinking of a solution right now," Alex mused.

"Me too," said Bryan. "And it *doesn't* involve Race-ball."

"But I bet it does involve some catch."

Unexpectedly, the interior of the Qwok Tower was illuminated by a bright flash of bluish-white light that faded as quickly as it had begun.

"What—" Alex said.

"Oh!" Katherine shouted.

Bryan said, "I've seen light like that before."

"Twice," Alex agreed.

The three looked at one another, stunned.

Alex asked, "You did shut the door, didn't you?"

Bryan shrugged. "I dunno? I thought so—"

Through the Race-computer speakers, Vorlox spoke, "There are four of you, now."

"Four?" asked Alex, Bryan and Katherine together.

"I'm afraid," Vorlox said, "that we are nearing the end of our safe fifteen minutes."

"That's okay, Vorlox," said Bryan distractedly. "The next time we see you, we will have something ready. We'll rid the world of the Proteans once and for all."

He closed the lid with a clap, set the container on a desk, and followed Katherine and Alex to a rack of artifacts from past adventures that were stored on shelves. A single, silver meteorite sat on the bottom shelf, and in front of it, sleeping with a smile, lay Anna.

"Oh, no," said Bryan. "This will not be good."

"Anna, wake up," Katherine said, gently shaking her shoulder. "You're a superhero now."

*   *   *

"But I'm not a babysitter!" Katherine argued.

Alex exhaled. "Just stay with her. We don't know anything about her powers. This is really dangerous. I mean, the future of our world hinges on the outcome of this battle."

Anna blinked sleepily and rubbed her eyes.

Katherine stood straighter. "You need all the help you can get."

Bryan shook his head, "We can handle it. You and Anna will just be in the way."

Alex covered his head and shook it back and forth.

Bryan's mouth hung open; he tried to grab his words and shove them back down his throat. None of the laws of motion he was familiar with included taking back words you shouldn't have said.

"In the way!" Katherine shrieked. The entire interior of the Qwok Tower echoed with her cry. "That's what you think of me? That I'm in the way?" Tears began to drip from her eyes.

Anna puckered her lips and crossed her arms and glared at her brothers.

"No, no, I didn't mean that," Bryan tried.

"Go," Katherine told him. "Do it right now. Forget Racegirl. I'm done with her. I'm not living in your shadows anymore. C'mon, Anna." Katherine put her arm around Anna and the two disappeared into the portal back to the closet and the boys' bedroom.

"Wow. That could have gone better," Alex said.

"I didn't mean it like that!"

"Let's just get this done with. She'll calm down. You can explain what you meant when we get back." Alex paused. "You can explain it, can't you?"

Bryan said, "I just meant that it's easier when we don't have to worry about her—"

Alex shook his head. "I hope you can do better than that."

$*$ $*$ $*$

"Tell me again why we picked soybeans?" Super Qwok asked.

"It was in the newspaper last week: due to increasing energy costs soybean farmers are going to lose fifteen dollars per acre. If they're going to lose money anyway, then it won't matter if we wreck their fields. Maybe crop insurance will even make things better for them." Raceboy kicked some dirt from his superhero boots.

Super Qwok pondered the plight of farmers for a moment, thankful he was only a superhero.

The boys stood in the center of a one-mile field. They had plotted an area equally distant from Clifton, Ashkum, Kempton and Fairbury. Raceboy had cleared a circle twenty feet in diameter of soybeans and set the case in the precise center. Although the case was closed, Vorlox sat atop it, glistening in the noonday sun.

Without aid of computer speakers, the amulet was silent. Raceboy and Super Qwok both wondered what the mysterious creature was thinking. *After all,* thought Raceboy, *we are using it for bait…and we didn't give it much choice in the matter…*

"Tell me again what our plan is?" Super Qwok asked.

"Win," said Raceboy, pointing to a shape in the sky, then a second.

Super Qwok caught motion from a third shape and pointed. "Right on time," he said.

"How long can you hold your breath?" Raceboy asked.

"Long enough. First we have to get those Proteans out of their drones!"

Although the machines had always attacked before, they landed on three sides and stood silently, letting their towering size block large portions of the blue sky.

"Parley," one of the machines declared. Its voice echoed from within its large body. It was slightly bigger than the others, triangular in shape. It actually looked like an iron giant in a ball gown, or an overgrown Christmas tree. It had no obvious appendages, but instead was covered with multicolored dots, which only enhanced its Christmas flair. Atop its peak it had a single, spinning eye that turned like a high-speed light house or a disco ball.

Raceboy motioned to Super Qwok: you or me? Super Qwok shrugged, and cleared his throat. "What do you want?" he yelled at the Christmas tree shaped robot.

"We will take..." said the first robot.

"The seed..." continued the second robot. It looked like a giant letter T, with long whip-like tentacles hanging from the ends of its cross braces and a single, giant beak like the mouth of a squid at its center. It had no eyes to speak of, or any kind of view plate.

The third robot finished, "That you are protecting." This last was the shortest of the three, round like an enormous beach ball, covered with stripes. It added, "We will destroy you…"

"If you don't…" said Christmas Tree.

"Give us the seed," finished Letter T.

"Now," demanded Beach Ball.

"Wait a minute," Raceboy said, speaking up for the first time. "No one invited you here. You have no right to show up and try to take something that doesn't belong to you. Besides, this amulet wouldn't go with your outfits."

"If you really want it, you'll have to catch!" Super Qwok yelled, and he ran forward, grabbed up Vorlox, and with a twisting throw hurled the amulet high over the Christmas tree shaped robot. If any of the robots would have been constructed with heads, they would have tilted them to follow the arc of the flying object into the distance.

"Oldest trick in the book," Super Qwok murmured as he threw a powerful punch into the base of Letter T. The blow resonated within Letter T. Super Qwok expected to see the tower topple, but instead the whip-like arms snicker-snacked, and reached for him. He jumped forward and they brushed the spot where he had just stood. They were not single strands; rather, they were braids, like electrical cabling or twining hair. He jumped back and avoided the second reaching coils.

Raceboy, meanwhile, ran toward Christmas Tree. All at once the colored dots across its shape activated, and he discovered that they were really lasers. It took all of his speed to dive and cartwheel through the array of lasers flashing wildly around him. He tucked his knees up to begin a somersault in midair, and rolled to the ground, hopping straight up to cartwheel to the left. Around him soybeans hissed as lasers scorched green leaves. The smell of burning greenery assaulted his nose. "Not good," he muttered.

Behind him Beach Ball opened from the bottom, its sides exposing legs like slices of an orange. Over the ground Beach Ball raced, and two of the eight slices rotated to reveal twin faces without eyes but with a long alligator snouts filled with sharp metal teeth. The machine looked like a two-headed beetle.

Super Qwok darted into the base of Letter T and delivered another power punch. The giant shape quaked but did not fall.

Raceboy raced up the side of Christmas Tree, through the lasers, to the spinning eye at the top. He jumped while snapping on his laser-sword. Spinning and stabbing straight at the machine's eye, he readied his grip for the impact. But there was a hiss and a pop, and he saw the eye suck the energy straight out of the laser-sword. It was as dead as the triple-A batteries in Bryan's remote control tarantula. Clang, went the now useless handle of the laser-sword against the eye. For a hideous moment, the eye stared straight at him and flickered.

"Things could be worse," yelled Super Qwok below him, dancing between the swishing strands of Letter T. That was the instant one of the two heads of Beach Ball decided to snap at Super Qwok. The hero ducked in time to save his head, but not the tips of his hair. "If I were any taller," he muttered, "I'd be a lot shorter!"

Atop Christmas Tree, Raceboy would have answered that things were, in fact, worse, but he couldn't. The eye was more than an eye. He couldn't tear his gaze away from it. Housed in the center of the cone at the apex of the machine, it spun with an internal fire. It flickered blue, then green, and orange; it was as though the eye of the machine were staring into him, fixing him in place like a Certificate of Completion for the local summer reading program tacked, fixed, stuck to the bulletin board of the toy room. He stood still, a statue, as un-raced as he had ever been before, then began to slide down the sloping side of the towering machine.

Super Qwok managed to shift to the base of Christmas Tree in time to catch the rolling figure of his brother. "Raceboy!" he yelled at Raceboy's distant eyes, which remained unfocused and hazy. "C'mon, buddy, snap out of it!"

A laser beam snipped awfully close to his shoulder. He turned and glared at the Christmas tree shaped robot. "You really don't know who you're dealing with, do you!" he yelled. Then he moved with the finesse of a martial arts master, set Raceboy to the ground, and rolled toward Christmas Tree. He neared it. Lasers zapped.

Super Qwok was not Raceboy. He did not zip about at lightning speed. He did not zoom up the side of the robot. He did not dance around in carefully contrived contortions. Instead, he put his hands beneath the base of the machine and lifted.

To you or me, regular humans without the benefit of augmented strength, this would have been as ridiculous as trying to shoulder an elephant, roll a beached blue whale, or even tip an old fashioned safe: you know, the kind that drops on cartoon characters and leaves a crater in the ground with a waving white flag? Those things are heavy! If you cloned yourself with Dr. Devious's cloning machine and asked all of your clones to help you lift this giant robot, it still wouldn't work. This thing was that tall, and it was that heavy.

But we're talking about Super Qwok. And he was mad. Not just a little bit mad, either. He was wroth, an old word that means frothing at the mouth, writhing in anger. He had discovered that this anger did something to his strength. Like a balloon that blows up, his anger had puffed up his strength so that when Super Qwok lifted things, things began to happen.

First, his feet began to sink into the dirt, which couldn't support such enormous weight focused atop such a small body. Second, the Christmas Tree began to rise up. Lasers tried to spin about at him, but they were designed for a fast moving, zippy assailant above its base, not a stationary powerhouse like a six-year-old forklift beneath it.

As Super Qwok leaned back, the Christmas Tree robot rose higher and higher, until he had achieved a perfect balance, that point where the weight was equally distributed above him and he could move. Except, he couldn't move much, because he had sunk so far into the rich black soil of the field. So he did the next best thing: he threw it...right at Beach Ball.

If there was one thing Beach Ball was not designed to fight off, it was the massive, circular base of a Christmas Tree landing atop it. The ground quaked, and when the dust cleared, Beach Ball was nowhere to be seen. At least, no recognizable parts of Beach Ball were anywhere to be seen. And Christmas Tree was on its side, the spinning eye at its tip as still as the star over Bethlehem which the wise men followed to find their way to the savior's birth.

A sudden coiled tentacle wrapped itself around Super Qwok's waist and lifted him high into the air. It was like being lifted by the branches of a willow tree. Super Qwok felt the wind whipping past his cheeks, and he knew without having to look that the Letter T had gotten a hold of him with a tentacled arm, and was probably going to—

Visions of what the Letter T could do raced through his head. He began to peel the fibers of tentacle away from his body, but more of the fine fibers of metal wrapped around him. It was like being caught in robotic hair. He looked around for Raceboy, but his brother was no longer on the ground where he'd left him. Had he woken up? Was he even now Racing with his laser-sword to sever the tendrils trapping Super Qwok?

No. Looking again, Super Qwok saw Raceboy, still senseless, wrapped in Letter T's other tentacles. Both boys were trapped.

Letter T lifted Super Qwok, now more wrapped in the coiled tentacles than ever, towards its parrot-beak mouth. "This is ridiculous!" said Super Qwok, looking at the sharp steel beak. As he neared it, the beak opened, revealing a wide, dark emptiness filled with tiny spinning drill bits.

"If you're not too high and mighty to accept," said Katherine's voice below them, "we thought we might offer to help you."

Super Qwok did a double take. Katherine stood at the base of Letter T wearing a superhero uniform he'd never seen before. It was pink, and she had a flower on her chest. Beside her, a very un-heroically costumed Anna strutted in toddler blue jeans and a purple shirt with butterflies. The only indication that she was a superhero was her purple mask.

"Racegirl!" Super Qwok yelled.

Katherine put her nose in the air. "No, I am Flowergirl. Racegirl quit, remember? And this is Dr. Destructo."

"Doctor what?" Super Qwok yelled.

"Do you want help or what?" Flowergirl shouted. "I don't think you have much time."

Super Qwok looked back and forth between his sister and the grinding drill bits in the parrot beak. "Yes! Yes!" he shouted. "Help would be very helpful right now."

Racegirl, no, *Flowergirl* seemed to concentrate for an instant, then suddenly the soybeans in the field around them matured a month in a moment. Super Qwok stared.

"That's it? That's my help?" He yelled. He could hear the revving of the bits as the coiled arms lowered him into the beak. He struggled against the strands.

"I'm still learning," Flowergirl shouted.

Letter T's coils released Super Qwok and Raceboy at the same time. Super Qwok covered his face with his hands, could feel the heat of a foundry's furnace blasting from those spinning bits, when something grabbed his foot just before he struck. He looked up and saw an entirely different type of coiling tendril holding him; strands of plant root wrapped around his ankle. He looked for Raceboy; he, too, dangled from finger-like plant roots. Then Raceboy's eyes blinked, and he shouted. "Ahh! What is that?" He pointed at the spinning drill-bits just beyond the tip of his finger.

The plant roots moved, lifting both heroes away from the grinding bits and the sharp metal beak.

Letter T roared and reached.

Anna—Dr. Destructo?—yelled, "Hey, guys, watch what I can do!" She lifted her arms above her head. A purple glow formed around her hands, became two glowing balls. She brought her hands together in a clap, and the glowing energy blasted from her fingertips. It arced right through the beak of Letter T and blasted out the other side, fizzling like a Roman Candle. Immediately the coiled arms dropped, dangled lifelessly. Letter T toppled like a tower of blocks after meeting Anna for the first (and last) time.

The waving plant roots set Raceboy and Super Qwok on the ground.

"What?" asked Raceboy, one hand on his head. "What happened?"

"Morning glory vine," Flowergirl explained. "Mom says it's a weed, but it has a very aggressive root structure. It's easier to work with."

Above, rising like purple fog from the three broken machines, three wraith-like shapes rose in the sky and whirled with one another.

Raceboy shook his head. "No, just tell me later. Super Qwok! Time for Operation Vacuum Pack! Where's Vorlox?"

Super Qwok pulled the amulet from his utility belt and smiled.

"You didn't think I'd throw it, did you?"

"No time!" Raceboy yelled, keeping his eye on the sky shapes. The Proteans, in their natural form, were homing in on Vorlox.

Like eels of shadow, the three slippery, salamandrine shapes swam through the air straight at Super Qwok. They flowed in slow motion like water streaming over rocks.

Super Qwok clenched Vorlox close to his chest as though praying. He looked to the sky with his eyes closed and took one final, long gulp of fresh air. He stood above the closed case that had once been Vorlox's home for fifty odd years.

The shapes of the Proteans were nearly to Super Qwok's clenched hands.

Raceboy blasted past at full speed, his legs pumping faster than the fastest engine, his arms cranking his body forward, a blur of spokes rattling around the hub that was Super Qwok. Around and around, faster and faster, steps drumming faster than a pattern, but a hum of footfalls revving like the whine of car pistons singing speed. He blazed a circle around Super Qwok, who stood still within, and the air around him became trapped in the spinning figure of Raceboy.

Dust from the trampled field mingled in a whirling dust devil, caught within the vortex created by Raceboy's circling. Caught, too, were the three Proteans, their insubstantial bodies buffeted in the mix of spiraling dirt. They spun like wet leaves in a whirlpool.

Within the whirlwind, Super Qwok bent, opened the case, and removed a Dustbuster. He turned it on. *VRRRRRRUUMMMM-MMM* whined the small hand-held vacuum.

Looking through his mask, left hand still holding Vorlox tightly, he aimed the end of the Dustbuster at each of the swirling shapes. The first one disappeared like a gummy worm or a spaghetti noodle into a robot alligator's mouth. Then the second. The third tried frantic rolls to the left and the right, but it, too, was too slow and weak to fight the Dustbuster. Super Qwok left the machine running to hold tight to the Proteans and placed it into the case. Raceboy began slowing. Super Qwok exhaled, prepared to take a fresh breath, and latched the case.

"Now to get Vorlox into space," Raceboy said as he came to a stop at Super Qwok's side.

Super Qwok pointed at a motor cycle parked on the nearby gravel road. "What is that?"

"It's the Flower-cycle," Flowergirl answered.

Super Qwok growled, "It looks like the Qwok-cycle with a flower sticker on the gas tank. And it's painted pink!"

Flowergirl said, "Oh, it's not the Qwok-cycle anymore. Dr. Destructo and I painted it with some spray paint from the basement. Careful, though. Don't touch it. I think it's still wet."

Super Qwok leaked air like a punctured Qwok-cycle tire. "You painted my superhero vehicle?"

"Correction, my superhero vehicle," Flowergirl said. "You have to ride with Raceboy in the Race-mobile. I can ride a two-wheeler now. Without training wheels."

"But—" Super Qwok tripped over a mental speed bump. "But— But—" Actually, three mental speed bumps.

"What happened?" Raceboy asked. "You've always been Racegirl?"

She shrugged. "I don't know.

I'm different, now. I think maybe when I was little, I was one thing, sort of had powers like you. But now that I'm getting older, I'm becoming more and more me."

"You've always been you," Raceboy said.

"Not so much," she countered. "When I was little, when I was just two, and had just touched the meteorite, I think I was what you boys needed me to be. Now I'm what I need me to be."

Super Qwok asked, "But what about Anna? Is she what she wants to be?"

Flowergirl shook her head. "Mmm, I don't think so. I think she's still working on it."

"I think I can make a bigger pow than that," Dr. Destructo explained. She held her arms out and the purple glow began again.

Raceboy put a hand on her shoulder. "That's enough, Dr. Destructo. Good job." The glow faded.

Super Qwok asked, "Who came up with the name 'Dr. Destructo,' anyhow?"

"Oh, Dad did," said Flowergirl. "He always calls Anna that when she gets into things. She's still in the terrible two's, you know."

"We know," agreed both boys.

"So can you still use Race-mode?" Raceboy asked.

Flowergirl shook her head. "Yes, but I think it's going away. I can still use something like Race-mode for plants, like how I could make

the morning glory vines grow so fast. I can also sense things from animals. I noticed it a while ago, when we faced Mastermind. But I wasn't sure what was happening. I don't think I can control animals because that would be the wrong way to get their help, not like Mastermind, but I might be able to ask animals for help. And plants, of course. That's why I'm Flowergirl."

"Flowergirl and Dr. Destructo," Raceboy mused.

"Flower-cycle," Super Qwok moaned.

*   *   *

Later that night, the news was astir with stories of mass break-ins at certain electronic and machine factories throughout Kankakee-land. Even the Chicago news was covering the story. Alex and Bryan lingered in the living room with action figures, acting disinterested. They heard that additional reporters had been sent west of rural Clifton, where the rubble of three giant collections of machinery appeared to have been detonated for reasons that could only be speculated. One commentator thought it was terrorists. Another thought it was a mass hoax by a local group of activists. Dr. Brick managed to get interviewed in the Clifton Asylum for the Criminally Insane. He explained that Raceboy and Super Qwok were behind the wrecks as part of their villainous plan to take over the world. "Can't please everyone," Alex had one of his action figure robots growl.

"Especially not insane mad scientists," Bryan's action figure barked back.

It was just after dinner, while putting away his dirty dishes that Mom looked over at Bryan and said, "Did you cut your hair?"

"No!" Bryan said, running a hand over his head. Then he remembered the close call with the Beach Ball machine's snapping jaws.

"Yes, he did," Alex said.

Bryan's look could have been bottled into a laser gun and used to attack giant alien robots.

Mom's hand clenched a dishtowel and trembled dangerously. "Go to your room right now!" She said. "You know better than that, young man! No snack for you tonight!"

Alex looked back and forth between Mom and Bryan before he spoke carefully. "All right, I cut it for him. I thought I could make it look cool."

"What!" exploded Mom. "If any of my children know better, it's you, Alexander. You have just grounded yourself from video games for the rest of your childhood! Now go to your room, too."

Bryan sighed his way out of the kitchen. Alex followed sheepishly.

"That's what we get for saving the world," Alex mumbled as they climbed the stairs.

"Yup, no respect," Bryan agreed.

In the kitchen, Dad finished chewing his piece of pizza and said, "At least it doesn't look too bad."

"I only cut paper," Katherine explained matter-of-factly. "Anna cuts everything."

Anna giggled and gulped a piece of pepperoni.

"Do we still get snacks?" Katherine asked.

*   *   *

"A favor?" asked Dr. Kensington. He spoke from his offices at Cape Canaveral. He could see Super Qwok and Raceboy in the view screen of his computer from the Qwok Tower, where they stood before the camera of the Race-computer.

"Yes," explained Raceboy. "We have two things that need to be placed in space."

Dr. Kensington frowned briefly. "Ah, well," he hesitated.

"It's a matter of global security," Super Qwok offered.

303

"How big of items did you say they are?"

"Oh, about the size of an acorn and a dustbuster...in a jewelry box," Super Qwok said.

The good doctor rubbed his pointed gray beard. "Hmm. That's not too bad, I suppose. At least it's not something the size of a Volkswagen. Well, I suppose we could delay the experiment on the effects of global warming on dandelions...Anything you boys can let an old scientist in on?" he asked hopefully.

"Sorry, sir," said Raceboy. "Suffice it to say that the two need to be jettisoned away from Earth together. Other than that we can't say anything else."

"Well, after all your help with Professor Solaris, I suppose it's the least we can do to express our thanks. You probably already knew that Atlantis is scheduled for launch in six days, didn't you?"

Raceboy and Super Qwok nodded. "Of course," Raceboy agreed.

"Then we'll make arrangements and see to it that your packages are delivered."

Six days later, the shuttle launch went off without a hitch. Alex and Bryan were in school, and didn't see it live, but were able to convince Dad to pull it up on the internet at the official NASA webpage, Nasa.com.

"There you go, Vorlox," Bryan said under his breath as the shuttle pushed its way against the Earth's atmosphere and raced towards space.

"What's that?" Dad asked.

"Nothing," Bryan said.

"You said, 'chicken pox,'" Dad said. "I heard you. What are you talking about?"

"Seriously, Dad. It's nothing," Bryan said.

*   *   *

Alex and Bryan stood over the small hole. Katherine leaned

304

against Bryan, and he put an arm around her shoulders. Anna danced around singing, then fell over and started crying, "Owie! I need a Band-Aid!"

Alex helped her to her feet and said, "Look, Anna, we're going to plant a tree."

In a moment she had forgotten all about her owie, and was happily pulling handfuls of dark moist dirt from the pile beside the hole.

"Not yet," Alex said. Bryan let go of Katherine and bent down to hold the oak sapling that Dad had brought back from Grandma and Grandpa's river bank. Alex began scooping the loose dirt around the young tree. Anna helped, though a couple of thrown handfuls did wind up in Alex's hair.

"You get to water it, Katherine," Bryan said, and when the tree was surrounded by fresh dirt, he helped Katherine tip the green watering can to sprinkle water on the roots. Long before the water had all soaked into the soil, she was distracted by Anna leaping after a Monarch butterfly. Bryan finished the watering and said, "I'll think of Vorlox whenever I look at this tree."

"Me, too," Alex said. "It's good to know that Vorlox is up there, somewhere, taking root in space."

"And that it's protecting Earth from Proteans so that they never feed on our thoughts again."

The boys stood together and looked at the newly planted tree. Katherine stopped long enough to say, "The roots are fine. I've given them a boost. But not too much; if you try to rush nature too much, the fibers will be weak."

"Oh, like for every action there is a reaction?" Bryan asked.

From the sliding door a voice called, "Where's my Dustbuster?" It was Mom, and she didn't sound happy.

Alex said, "You want to explain it?"

"What, that we sucked up three alien life forms with it, then dropped it in that garage sale box of Katherine's whose disappearance we claimed to know nothing about? And then we launched it into space on the space shuttle with a seedling from an ancient, intelligent star tree? No way. You tell her."

"All right," he said. Then he yelled, "I don't know, Mom!"

"Well," Bryan said, "it's not like you're lying. We really don't know where the Dustbuster is."

And the two boys looked to the sky again, and wondered. How long would it take for the seed to grow, to evolve? For its roots to shift the latch on the box? For the box to open? And for the Proteans to escape... right into Vorlox's waiting fingers?

All Hallow's Eve

"What should we be for Halloween?" Bryan asked.

"I was thinking it would be fun to dress up like my favorite superhero," Alex answered. He continued drawing the cartoon strip he had been working on. It was called, "Raceboy Defeats Dr. Devious...Again!"

"You want to dress up as Super Qwok?" Bryan asked.

Alex held up the cover of his newest comic. "Of course not. You know I meant Raceboy. He's my favorite."

"You're pathetic. It would be way funnier if you dressed up as Super Qwok and I dressed up as Raceboy, especially since you are Raceboy and I am Super Qwok."

After a moment's silence, Alex said, "You know, I think we should do something wacky. More mischievous." He paused. "More devious."

The play on words struck Bryan like a light bulb. His smile grew wide, "You mean..."

"I think it would be funny."

"We'll probably get arrested," Bryan said.

"Nah," Alex replied. "You and I, dressed up like Mr. Mischief and Dr. Devious. I think this could be the best Halloween ever! That is, if Mom lets us. She's hasn't been able to even stand hearing Dr. Devious's name since that time he hypnotized her and

307

convinced her to give him all her valuables..."

Meanwhile, in another part of Clifton, the self-same diabolical criminal masterminds were involved in their own Halloween discussion.

"We need," said Dr. Devious, "diabolical criminal mastermind costumes. We need costumes that scream evil villain!" He had a nasal voice with overly dramatic emphasis on his words. In fact, he sounded very much like an actor portraying a mad scientist in a movie.

"You could just go dressed up as yourself," Mr. Mischief pointed out. "Nothing screams evil villain like Dr. Devious." His voice, in contrast, was friendly and bumbling. If anything, it screamed, "Trust me!" which probably explained why he was able to cause so much mischief.

"Hmm," Devious rubbed his chin. "But Halloween is about dressing up! I'm not really dressing up if I dress up as myself. That's just what I do after showering. I know, how about I dress up as you, and you can dress up as me! That would still scream diabolical criminal mastermind."

Mr. Mischief hesitated. "Well," he said, and did not commit. "I think maybe we could do something a little more diabolical."

"Like what? What could be more diabolical than dressing up as Dr. Devious and Mr. Mischief?"

"I think you can dress up as Raceboy and I could dress up as the other one."

"Super Qwok?"

"Yea, the strong one. And then we can really have some fun as we cause mischief and havoc through Clifton!"

There was a moment of silence. Devious pushed his glasses up on his nose. He frowned. He rubbed his hair with a hand. He hmmed and hmmmmed. At last he said, "It's so brilliant I'm surprised I didn't think of it myself!" He began rubbing his hands together, his voice gaining energy as he spoke. "Yes, we can dress up like those costumed superheroes, and then when we perpetrate crimes and behave like absolute villains, none of the townspeople, including that good-for-nothing Police Captain, will know who the good guys really are! And once we have earned his trust with our duplicity, we will have the run of the town. And when the good guys do finally show up, we can doubly confuse them by being their doubles! Excellent, excellent. Now that is diabolical, criminal, mastermindful!"

Meanwhile, in yet another part of Clifton, the Wicked Witch swatted one of her pet monkeys with a broom. She wasn't sure if it was Seamus, Remus, or Amos, but the monkey sure skedaddled. "So, boys," she said to the monkeys. "It'll be Halloween soon. And you know what that means?"

Seamus, Remus, and Amos all nodded.

"That's right," agreed the Wicked Witch. "Loads of filthy children gallivanting about town in witch costumes, cackling over candy. It's enough to drive an old woman to bathe in her own cauldron—if it hadn't been stolen and ruined by those sniveling super pipsqueaks." For a moment she babbled, her anger bubbling over like boiling spellsoup in the very same cauldron she was missing. Seamus (or Remus or Amos—nobody ever really could tell those monkeys apart) padded over and patted her arm. This reassuring gesture broke the witch from her trance and she snapped the monkey with her broom. "Of course," the Wicked Witch agreed, "I have a plan. A little something this year to get back at those goody-two-shoes. I think it could be my masterpiece."

The Wicked Witch spun around three times, raised her arms (broom and all), and said a magic word that sounded like six syllables without a single vowel. *POOF!* Smoke appeared around her in a cloud, and when it cleared, the Police Captain stood in her place. "Ha, ha, ha ha!" the Witch's voice laughed from the mouth of the Police Captain. "And there's more, my pretties, but I'm saving it for All Hallow's Eve. Rest assured, I will create chaos in the streets, and those heroes will never know what hit them!"

*   *   *

Alex had tried to explain to Mom why dressing up as an evil villain would be a good idea.

"I don't know," she said. "It seems like idolizing a villain sends the wrong message to people."

Alex wrinkled his nose, "Are you kidding? What about wicked witches, bloody zombies, axe murderers, and psycho surgeons? Do those send a positive message?"

Mom stared at him, "Your tone, young man, doesn't send a positive message."

Alex shut his mouth. With all his super powers, his speed, and his skill at fighting criminals, his greatest challenge continued to be watching what he said and how he said it.

The front door creaked open, and Dad stumbled in, arms full of briefcase and coffee thermos and coffee cup. He kicked his shoes off and greeted Katherine and Anna, the two howling girls who clattered down the hallway in high-heeled dress-up shoes shouting, "Dadd-eeeeeee!"

"Just a minute girls—let me set this stuff down," he said as he knelt to get rid of his armfuls of work junk. Then he scooped both girls up and walked into the living room.

"Alex seems to think he should dress up as Dr. Devious for Halloween," Mom said by way of greeting. "And Bryan wants to be Mr. Mischief," This was spoken in Mom's "I'm not happy about this" voice.

Dad frowned, rubbed his chin, then shrugged and said, "And?"

Mom stared, "Don't you think it sends a bad message to allow them to dress up as villains?"

Dad's voice sounded hesitant, "As though dressing up as blood covered surgeons doesn't? Lots of kids dress up in grisly, gruesome, gory, ghastly costumes. These two have dressed up as Super Qwok and Raceboy for, oh, three years now. It's kind-of funny to see them switch sides, dress up as villains. Besides, Dr. Devious and Mr. Mischief costumes have got to be cheaper than Raceboy and Super Qwok costumes. We just have to find a bowler hat."

Mom harumphed, a sound that said she didn't agree but wouldn't push the point. Mom didn't have a super power, but if she did it would have been communicating clearly through body language and non-verbal cues. She was masterly at conveying her dissatisfaction with something as simple as a harumph or the way she closed a cupboard. From anywhere in the house it was possible to tell Mom's mood.

"What's wrong, Mom?" Bryan asked, coming into the room. "I heard you do that thing you do that sounds like you're upset about something."

Mom asked, "Bryan, are you really going to dress up as Mr. Mischief?"

"Are you going to let us?" His voice couldn't contain his excitement.

"Your father doesn't seem to have a problem with it," she replied, which, both Alex and Bryan realized, answered the question by pushing responsibility for such a bad choice onto Dad.

"Yes!" both boys said together. "Let's get our costumes ready!"

*   *   *

Halloween fell on a Saturday. As usual, trick-or-treat hours were between 4:00 PM and 7:00 PM. Alex stepped out of the house clad in a white lab coat complete with wacky mad-scientist hair and a pair of oversized glasses. Bryan wore a bowler hat and striped shirt and strutted with an amiable air down the front stairs.

"And don't you two get into trouble!" Mom finished her warning with a finger wag. She had the girls loaded into the van to take them trick-or-treating. The boys, as a final triumph of Halloween autonomy, had convinced their parents to let them trick-or-treat on their own.

"We won't, Mom," said Alex with a wave.

Bryan tipped his hat to Mom with a wide smile as he and Alex began walking down the sidewalk to the east side of town. Mom buckled the girls into their car seats and said, "I have a bad feeling about this."

Anna smiled, but Katherine said, "Oh, Mom, I forgot my purse!"

"You don't need a purse," Mom replied. "We're going trick-or-treating, remember?"

Katherine's blue eyes grew wide, and her voice squeaked, nearly a whine, "Mom, I have to carry my new purse!"

Mom frowned. "Katherine, you are a fairy. Fairies don't have purses."

"It's green," Katherine explained.

It has generally been accepted that there are some battles worth fighting. Conversely, there are some battles better avoided. Mom took one look at Katherine's quivering lip and said, "Hurry inside. You're wasting trick-or-treat time."

Katherine unbuckled, dashed out of the van, up the front steps, and into the door, where she passed her dad who was holding the candy bowl. "Where are you going?" he asked.

"I need my purse!" she declared, as though it made perfect sense.

"What do you need a purse for?" Dad called after her. "You're a fairy!"

Dad turned back around as the door opened and closed for a

black robed witch. "Hi, Dad. I need a purse, too!"

Dad said, "Witches don't carry purses."

Anna giggled. "You're funny, Dad!" She followed Katherine into the toy room. Both girls returned carrying purses. Katherine had a green purse with pink flowers; Anna's was pink plaid with sequins. The purse definitely did not match the fake black crow Dad had wired to Anna's pointy witch's hat.

Dad shook his head and dropped a candy bar in each girl's purse as they passed, kissing Katherine on the forehead then twisting his face sideways to duck under the brim of Anna's witch hat and kiss her cheek. He followed both girls out onto the front porch as they loaded back into the van. Mom started the van and carefully backed out of the driveway.

A group of teenagers walked up to the front door. Dad waved at the van while tossing some candy into the bags of a red faced devil, a storm trooper, and a couple of kids too lazy to dress up but energetic enough to walk around and growl, "Trick-or-treat."

*　　*　　*

When Alex and Bryan got to Main Street, Bryan looked both ways and said, "Let's go to St. Bartholomew's. I hear they give full size candy bars there on Halloween."

"Are you kidding? We're not going to trick-or-treat in a bar!" Alex said. "Mom and Dad would definitely kill us — twice!"

"How're they going to know?" Bryan asked. "We're dressed up, remember?"

"No," Alex said firmly. "Dad says it's how you act when no one's watching that proves what kind of person you are."

"I'm a candy-hungry person!"

"Candy-hungry enough to act like a villain? That's how villains convince themselves that what they're doing is right. That's how Dr. Devious can do the things he does."

Bryan harrumphed. "Well, you *are* Dr. Devious," but he didn't argue the point about St. Bartholomew's Pub as the boys passed its screen door. He also couldn't help but notice how dark it appeared inside the bar, and the smell of stale smoke that crept from its door like the fog in a haunted cemetery.

"Let's try the store," Alex offered. "Since they sell candy bars, maybe they'll have big ones for us."

The Clifton grocery store had power doors that opened (sometimes) or had to be pushed (the rest of the time). Today they opened with a clank, and into the store strode Dr. Devious and Mr. Mischief.

The cashier took one look at the boys and her lips began to tremble. She looked at the poster taped beside the cash register.

It contained the portraits of two men: one a bespectacled scientist with crazy hair and a white lab coat, the other pleasant faced with a striped shirt and a bowler hat. Above the pictures it proclaimed, "WANTED!" Below the pictures it read, "DANGEROUS!"

She looked back and forth between Alex (a.k.a. Dr. Devious) and Bryan (a.k.a. Mr. Mischief) before she pushed a red button on the store telephone.

Immediately a red light began flashing above the phone, and a piercing alarm began its clamoring wail.

"Oh, no!" said Alex. "What did you do that for?"

The cashier waved her hands. "Don't hurt me!" she gasped, and then without warning she hit a button on the cash register and removed her entire drawer. "Here," she said, turning the drawer upside down so that the contents spilled (mostly) into Alex's candy bag. "Take it." She opened the other drawer from the other cash register and dumped it in Bryan's bag. "Just take it and go!"

"Uh," said Alex.

"Trick or treat?" Bryan added.

A voice behind them ordered, "Freeze! Stop right there. Drop whatever you've got in your hands and turn around!"

Alex and Bryan's eyes met, and simultaneously they dropped their candy bags. Except neither bag was a candy bag now: instead they were both full of the store's money. Alex said, "This can't be good."

Arms outstretched, Alex and Bryan began to turn to face a voice they knew all too well: the Police Captain. The Captain nodded in the direction of the cashier. "You can go ahead and get rid of the alarm, Phyllis." The relieved cashier typed some numbers into the phone's touch pad; the alarm stopped and the red flashing light ceased its spinning.

"This isn't how it looks, Captain," Alex said. He was suddenly aware of the music playing on the store's speakers: some 1990s rock ballad about lost love.

The Police Captain snorted. "It never is with you, is it, Devious? One excuse after another. What do you have to say for yourself this time: did she just pour the money in your bag?"

"Well, actually," Alex said, "yes. That's pretty much it."

The Police Captain snorted. "What, you're too lazy to make up your own excuses this time?"

"No, no, it's not that," Alex said, "We came in to trick or treat and she hit the alarm and dumped all the money in our bags. Honestly. And I'm not really Dr. Devious. This is just a costume."

The Police Captain snorted. "Like I haven't heard that one before. You should know better than to tell me stories, Devious. You've escaped from my jail one too many times for me to trust anything you say."

"Can we be of assistance, Captain?" asked another voice. The door closed behind a sloppily suited Raceboy accompanied by a frumpy Super Qwok.

Alex and Bryan stared at the costumed superheroes with feelings that blended between shock, horror, and disbelief. This Raceboy was, first off, not a boy. He was too tall and had some scraggly whiskers on his chin. Under his mask he wore a pair of large glasses. His hair, also, was wildly sticking out in ways that Raceboy's hair never had. The costume fit tightly—too tightly, revealing a distended belly that either indicated third world starvation or first world middle age.

Super Qwok was no better. He had an amiable smile, sure enough, but his head was nearly bald. And the way he was wearing his costume made him look like he had just returned from the gym; except he wore this costume like a man who wondered what it was like to dress up like a man who worked out.

"Who are you?" asked the Police Captain.

The fake Raceboy pursed his lips and made a great show of putting his hands on his hips and pushing his chest out. "I thought it was obvious that I am Raceboy, and I am here with my compatriot Mr. Mi—" He stopped, cleared his throat, wrinkled his lips in a brief snarl and continued: "Super Qwok."

For a full minute the Police Captain stared at them. At last he said, "This is like a joke, right? Halloween and all that? Trick or Treat, but I get the Trick?"

"I told you it would come to this," Fake Raceboy explained to Fake Super Qwok. "Observe," he commanded the Police Captain. Then taking the pose of a speed sprinter, Fake Raceboy reached down to his utility belt and flipped a switch. A sudden crack like a localized sonic boom split the air, knocking the Police Captain's hat off of his head. He bent to pick it up. When he looked up, the fake Raceboy stood before him, hands outstretched. "See?" he asked.

"See what?" asked the Police Captain.

Fake Raceboy sputtered. "I just ran around the store!"

"No you didn't," said the Police Captain. "I was watching. You just stood there and flipped some sound device on your waist, and then told me you raced around the store. I'm not falling for that old gag."

Fake Super Qwok said, "You blinked. That's why you didn't see it."

Fake Raceboy inhaled stiffly and pulled his lips into a frown. "I shall repeat the demonstration. This time I shall bring a gallon of milk to you. Observe!"

Once again he took his mark. Once again he flipped a switch at his belt. And once again a sonic boom knocked the Police Captain's hat from his head.

This time when the Police Captain looked up, it was to see Fake Raceboy holding a gallon of milk. "You see," explained Fake Raceboy, "I just raced to the back of the store and brought you a gallon of milk."

"Huh," said the Police Captain. "I guess you could be Raceboy. But what happened to your hair? And you're wearing glasses. You never used to wear glasses."

Frowning, Fake Raceboy explained, "Let's just say it's all Dr. Devious's fault. And I prefer not to talk about it." The tone of his voice was both sulky and pouty.

"What about him?" asked the Police Captain pointing at Fake Super Qwok. "He doesn't look anything like Super Qwok. I suppose that's Dr. Devious's fault, too?"

"It would be more accurate to blame Mr. Mischief," Fake Raceboy explained with a wave of the hand. He leaned closer to the Police Captain and whispered, "And I wouldn't bring it up if I were you ... he's very sensitive about his hair."

The Police Captain nodded. "All right, Raceboy. Well, you'll be glad to observe who I have here. We have a robbery in progress stopped by my timely intervention and this quick-thinking cashier's—" he paused and nodded to the cashier, "uh, quick thinking. Our culprits are none other than Dr. Devious and Mr. Mischief."

"I'm not Dr. Devious," Alex explained. "That's," he pointed at Fake Raceboy, "the real Dr. Devious!"

"Absurd!" exclaimed Fake Raceboy. "I have already demonstrated my curriculum vitae with observable velocity. You, on the other hand, have demonstrated your guilt with observable sacks of money. Actions speak louder than words, as I have so often heard Raceboy say."

"But you said you are Raceboy!" Alex pointed out.

"Indeed," Fake Raceboy corrected, "I tend to speak in third person from time to time. It is a disappointing habit, I'm afraid, brought on by my fame going to my head."

Alex could feel his anger building.

"When do I get a turn?" asked Fake Super Qwok out of the blue.

"Huh?" asked the Police Captain.

"Well, you got to use your super powers," he told Fake Raceboy pointedly. "When do I get to use mine?"

Fake Raceboy told the Police Captain, "He wishes to make a show of his super powers for your benefit, if you don't mind. He always gets so jealous when I get to use my powers, and he doesn't. Juvenile, I know, but there it is. His talents really are more physical, if you know what I mean. Not much by way of—" Here Fake Raceboy tapped his forehead.

Now it was Bryan's turn to feel his anger surge.

Fake Raceboy continued, "Do you have an automobile to be moved or a building to be demolished, perhaps? He is quite capable."

"That's all right," the Police Captain told them. "I think it's better if we hold you in reserve, Super Qwok. Save your powers for when we really need them. Actually, I think I have everything here pretty much under control. If the two of you want to help me get these criminals into the police cruiser so I can get them back to the jail that would be most helpful. Here Phyllis, why don't you take the money and make sure it's all there?" He handed the half full bags of money to the cashier, who dumped the piles on the checkout belt. Fake Raceboy took hold of Alex while Fake Super Qwok grabbed Bryan.

"Your hair's too neat," said Fake Raceboy to Alex, the Fake Dr. Devious.

"You have too much hair," said Fake Super Qwok to Bryan, the

Fake Mr. Mischief.

Both boys held their tongues. They couldn't talk too much or risk revealing their secret identities.

Alex and Bryan found themselves handcuffed and stood waiting beside the Police Captain's squad car.

"That could have gone better," Alex said.

*   *   *

With bags half-full of trick-or-treat candy, Katherine and Anna strode purposefully up to a white Victorian house.

"Oh, what a darling purse!" the gray-haired woman on the front porch declared.

"Thank you," said Katherine. "Trick-or-treat," she added, feeling very proud of her green purse with the pink flowers.

The woman turned to Anna. "And you have such fashion sense, for a witch!"

Anna giggled and looked down at her own pink purse. "Trick-or-treat,' she said.

"Here you go!" the woman said as she plopped some big zip-lock bags into the girls' trick-or-treat candy.

As the girls walked back down the block, Mom asked, "What did you get?"

Katherine and Anna looked into their bags. Katherine frowned. "A homemade popcorn ball," she said.

"Oh," Mom replied. "I didn't know anyone still gave those. We'll just have to feed the birds with them or something."

"Why?" Anna asked.

"Well, honey, it's not a good idea to eat anything that's home-made if you don't know who made it. They could put something in it. Oof," Mom said as she was pushed aside. She looked up to see that the Police Captain had just shouldered her off the side-walk. "Well!" she exclaimed.

Katherine and Anna watched the Police Captain walk up to the door and say, "Trick-or-treat!" When the elderly lady tried to give him one popcorn ball, he took her entire bowl and dumped it into his bag. The woman began to howl, but he pushed her back into the house before skipping down the stairs. As he disappeared down the block, three slouching, wobbling shapes joined him to exult over the popcorn balls.

"That," said Mom, "may be the oddest thing I've seen in my life."

*   *   *

The Police Captain turned to Fake Raceboy and Fake Super Qwok. "Aren't you two going to disappear into the sunset, or whatever you do whenever the paperwork begins?"

"There's paperwork?" inquired Fake Raceboy. "Does it include mathematics?"

"Well, sometimes we do have to calculate certain things—skid marks and such."

"Excellent! Would you like help with your calculations? I have been practicing my calculation skills just recently and am quite proficient at logarithms, exponents, and scientific notation."

"No, Raceboy, Phyllis will be doing all the complicated math. All we need to know is whether they had over $250 in the bag. Besides, you usually do the apprehending, and I write up the report. Right about now you race off."

"Perhaps you could show us this report of which you speak?" Fake Raceboy inquired.

"Um." The Police Captain seemed at a loss for words.

Fake Super Qwok said, "We were thinking we'd come back with you to the jail. Perhaps we can help a little more."

"Oh," said the surprised Police Captain. "It would be nice to make certain these dastardly criminals are locked safely away." He opened the door and the two fake superheroes assisted the fake villains into the back seat.

After the door was shut, Bryan told Alex, "I could break these handcuffs with a squeeze of my forearm."

"Just wait," Alex said. "We can escape at any time."

"Are you kidding? Sit here and let those two buffoons make laughingstocks out of us? I can't stand it! Did you see that hair!"

"Look, I know you're not bald, and you know you're not bald. The fact that the Police Captain fell for it, well, let's just chalk that up to a failure on the part of the American educational system."

"It could be his genes."

"Sure, it could be. Nature or nurture, we could argue it all day. Point is, he thinks they're us. And he thinks we're them. What are we going to do about it?"

"I could break out of these handcuffs with a squeeze of my forearm," Bryan said.

The front passenger door opened. "I'll just sit here," said Fake Raceboy. "You get in the back with the prisoners, Mr. uh, I mean Qwok."

Fake Super Qwok opened the door beside Bryan and growled, "Scootch. I'm stuck back here with you."

"I'm already buckled!" Bryan exclaimed. "And besides, I'm handcuffed."

"Stop whining and scootch." He looked around to see where the Police Captain was at. The Police Captain was still walking around the outside edge of the vehicle, so Fake Super Qwok leaned in, "Look, buddy, I don't know who you are, but you've got some nerve dressing up like Mr. Mischief. I'm liable to make you sorry you ever messed with Super Quad."

"Qwok," Bryan said.

"What?"

"Your name is supposed to be Super Qwok."

"That's what I said."

"No it isn't. You said Quad."

"Quad, Qwok. Whatever." Fake Super Qwok unbuckled Bryan's seat belt and shoved him to the middle of the back seat, then squeezed his own butt cheeks onto the car seat.

"He's right, you did say Quad," Fake Raceboy pointed out. "It was probably just a slip of the tongue since there are currently four of us in this car and quad is a prefix that indicates 'four' as in 'quadrilateral' or 'quadrangle.'"

The Police Captain opened his door and slid into the driver's seat. "It's awfully nice of Raceboy and Super Qwok to come back to the jail with us and make sure we tuck you two villains in bed for the night, don't you think?"

"Awful describes it," Alex agreed.

"I'm not buckled," Bryan pointed out.

"Whoops, Super Qwok, can you see about buckling Mr. Mischief back there? I don't want to pay for a ticket if we get pulled over." The Police Captain proceeded to snort in laughter at his police humor.

"Ow, he pinched me!" Bryan exclaimed.

"Who, me?" asked Fake Super Qwok. "Whoops, I'm so sorry, Mr. Mischief."

"Ow, you did it again!"

Finally Fake Super Qwok finished buckling (and pinching) Bryan into the middle seat of the squad car.

"Aren't you going to buckle up?" Alex asked Fake Super Qwok.

"Nah, superheroes don't need to buckle up. We're, like, specialer than other people."

"That's not true!" Bryan said.

The Police Captain interrupted, waving a finger. "Now, now,

for once I have to agree with Mr. Mischief. Super Qwok, it's important to set an example and always wear a seat belt, even if you have extraordinary powers of super strength. Besides, it's the law!"

Fake Super Qwok grumbled under his breath and buckled himself. The words sounded something like, "Just wait till we get you back to your jail, cream puff," though neither Bryan or Alex could be certain of anything except the extremely unpleasant grumbling.

At last the Police Captain started the car and put it in gear. "You know, Raceboy, I can't think of the last time you two rode with me in the squad car. Where's the Race-mobile and the Qwok-cycle?"

Fake Raceboy waved a hand, "Preventative maintenance. Oil change, tire pressure. Those sorts of things."

Alex had tried, but he couldn't stand it any longer. He squeaked just one little smidgeon of reality at Fake Raceboy, using something Dr. Devious could likely say: "I always heard that the Race-mobile used a fusion engine."

Fake Raceboy turned to look over his headrest. His voice dripped, "And what makes you such an expert on the Race-mobile?"

In his haughtiest tone, Alex replied, "I have made a careful study of the Race-mobile. From a distance, of course, since you always defeat me so easily. I have even attempted to diagram the Race-mobile on construction paper. With crayons, since I don't dare use anything with sharper points for fear of hurting myself."

Now it was Fake Raceboy's turn to steam. His eyes were like burning lasers as he glared at Alex in the Dr. Devious outfit.

"Well, here we are," the very chipper voice of the Police Captain said to his carload of impostors. "Super Qwok and Raceboy, if you would help me with these super villains..."

The station was a simple square building constructed from brick and cement. The only windows were at the front near the main entrance. Both "heroes" led both "villains" from the car into the main entrance, down a hall, and around a bend to the jail entrance.

As a small local jail, the facility was only meant to hold prisoners until they could be transferred to the county jail or another larger facility. There were six cells, which were small, hardly larger than a king-size bed. Each had three walls of solid blocks with a fourth wall that was half reinforced rebar steel and half solid steel door. The Police Captain led Alex and Bryan in the company of Fake Raceboy and Fake Super Qwok to the cells, where he directed Alex into the first cell and Bryan into the next. The doors closed.

"What's that in the back corner of that cell?" Fake Super Qwok asked, pointing to the rear of a third jail cell.

"Huh?" asked the Police Captain. "Where?"

"Over there," Fake Super Qwok pointed toward the back of the cell.

The Police Captain stepped inside the cell, his eyes narrowing as he scanned to find the mystery something. Which didn't exist. The cell door clanged behind him and Fake Raceboy declared, "That was more easily managed than I expected, Mr., Uh, Qwok."

"Like taking babies from their candy," agreed Fake Super Qwok.

By this time the Police Captain had found a way to make his voice work, and he said, "What's going on? Super Qwok, Raceboy, let me out of this cell right now!"

But both of the fake superheroes were snickering in a most unheroic way as they gloated. Fake Raceboy exclaimed, "Now that you are out of the way, we superheroes must make the rounds stealing from all of the local businesses. And we will start with that ridiculous store!"

"But why?" asked the Police Captain. His voice broke in disappointment.

Fake Super Qwok pointed at the other cell, the one with Alex in his Dr. Devious outfit. "Just ask that mad scientist," he exclaimed.

"Ask him what he did to us to turn us to evil."

Fake Raceboy smacked him with the back of his hand, "Why did you tell him that, you dolt!"

"Because it's funny! Get them," he motioned vaguely in the direction of Bryan and Alex's cells, "in trouble."

"Yes, but it was much more diabolical to let the authorities believe that our actions, that is, Raceboy and Super Qwok's actions, are our own. Not the result of Dr. Devious. It's an issue of volition."

"Oh, right. Volition." Fake Super Qwok thought about this for a moment, rattled the Police Captain's bars. "Well, never mind what I said about the mad scientist thing. I was just joking. Really we just decided to be evil because there's more money in it. And if you catch us, you should send us to jail for a long, long time. Super Qwok and Raceboy, I mean." He laughed a mean, deep throated laugh that sounded completely unlike any laugh laughed by Super Qwok. Then they were gone. The police station was empty except for its prisoners.

*   *   *

Meanwhile, in another part of Clifton, the closest thing to villainy were the stale homemade popcorn balls being passed out by elderly women in Victorian houses. Mom said, "Are you two ready to be done for the night? It's getting late."

"What time is it?" Katherine asked.

"Six-thirty," Mom said.

"I can fit more," Anna said, looking in her bag which she had already dumped all over the floor of the van.

"Of course you can, dear. You've emptied it twice. The point is, should we be done for the night? I'm wondering how Alex and Bryan are."

"They're fine, Mom," Katherine said.

"What makes you so sure?" Mom asked.

Katherine shrugged and didn't answer. She meant to explain that she thought the boys could take care of themselves, but she didn't because she noticed something strange. Instead of fewer trick-or-treaters on the streets, there now appeared to be more. The sun had gone down and the air was cold. Something about these new trick-or-treaters was also cold. Their costumes seemed oddly consistent, like they had all dressed up to match one another in dirty, worn out clothing. Katherine was still young; she couldn't think what they reminded her of, because they didn't remind her of anything she had ever seen before. *They are odd, though,* she thought. *Very odd.*

*   *   *

Alex's thoughts raced: The Police Captain thinks we are the bad guys. And he thinks the real bad guys are the good guys. Who've gone bad. And since everyone thinks we're bad anyway, no one will be surprised when we make a bad guy escape...except we can't use our powers! Unless I pretend to be Dr. Devious to the extreme...

"Captain!" he shouted. "I have two things to tell you that you need to know."

"What?" asked the dismayed Captain from his own cell. After being locked up in a cell in his own jail, he wasn't really interested in hearing from Dr. Devious, even if the Dr. Devious was a fake one.

Alex took a breath and tried to talk in the same manner as Dr. Devious. "First, I have prepared for the eventuality of our imprisonment by augmenting my good friend Mr. Mischief to become an escape artist. Well, not really an escape artist. He is currently augmented to be more like a walking wrecking ball."

"And what's the other thing?" asked the Police Captain in a voice that declared that things couldn't get worse.

"Just this: I don't believe those two costumed buffoons were the real Raceboy or Super Qwok. In short, I believe they were imposters."

"But why would anyone dress up as Raceboy and Super Qwok?" His voice held a plaintive note.

"Aside from the fact that it's Halloween?" asked Bryan.

"Point taken," agreed the Captain.

"Break us out, Mr. Mischief," Alex said. "We have some imposters to catch."

Bryan put both hands around the bars of his cell and yanked. The bars bent, stretched, and distorted until he could step through the opening. He walked over to Alex's cell and was about the repeat the process when the Captain begged, "Can you just get the extra set of keys from my desk? I don't want to have to fix all of the jail cells!"

Bryan got the key, and in a moment all three stood in the center of the station. A beeping alarm began to sound, coming from one of the computer consoles near the Police Captain's desk. From outside, in the distance, another echoed with a familiar squeal: the grocery store alarm was at it again.

Then a second distant alarm joined the first. The second was different, with a single, loud buzzing. A light flashed at the computer console.

"Oh," said the Police Captain. "That's both the store...and the First Federal Bank!"

Out the door of the station ran the fake Dr. Devious, the fake Mr. Mischief, and the real Police Captain. They loaded into the police cruiser. All three of them buckled up, and the Police Captain drove back toward the store. Night had fallen fully now, and the street lamps were on.

As the police car passed between two houses it was possible to see both the bank and the store at the same time. Fake Raceboy and Fake Super Qwok were running out of the store. And the bank... well, the Police Captain said some very un-police like words when he saw who was robbing the bank: it was the Police Captain. "This has got to be the worst day ever," he muttered as he turned toward the bank.

Pulling the car in front of the Fake Police Captain, he leapt from his car door, pulled his gun from its holster, and yelled, "Freeze!"

Racing away from the bank, the Fake Police Captain cackled in a very un-police-officerish way and did not freeze. He was holding a giant sack full of money. A trail of bills blew on the ground behind him, were it was being picked up by three shadows that stopped to stare at the Police Captain.

"Freeze, he says," the high pitched voice of the Fake Police Captain giggled. Then after a moment's laughter, he pointed his—wand?—and with an abrupt word the Real Police Captain stood frozen in a cube of ice.

"That could have gone better," Alex told Bryan.

Bryan didn't answer. Instead he moved to the Real Police Captain's side, lifted him up, and rolled him straight at the Fake Police Captain. Like a log rolling across a frozen river, the Real Police Captain blasted straight into the fake one, who squawked as the rolling police-sicle rolled atop him and then straight into the three dim shapes behind. "Oooh," groaned the Fake Police Captain. The three shapes screeched as the Police Captain rolled over them as well.

Tottering back to his feet, the Fake Police Captain looked in the direction of the car and said, "Oh, Mischief! You'll pay for that, my boy!"

"Who are you?" asked Bryan in his most Mischievous voice.

"You don't recognize me, do you?" asked the voice, a hint of pride and amusement coming through the irritation. Then the three shadowy shapes wobbled near enough to became clear: three monkeys, one rubbing its mouth, the next rubbing its ears, and the third rubbing its eyes. The boys knew that this was no man in disguise; they recognized the voice; it was the Wicked Witch.

"Yes, you darling meanies," she said, "I'm the Police Captain tonight on All Hallows' Eve, and it has been a good night for both tricks and treats! But this is only the start. Before the night is done, this whole town will be a ghost town ... in more ways than one!"

"What's that supposed to mean?" Alex, a.k.a. Dr. Devious asked.

"You'll have to wait to see. You won't have to wait long. Once the moon is out, oh, so very soon, you'll see. Just a little surprise." She cackled again, a long, loud laugh that echoed through the chill nighttime air. "And to show you how much I value the two of you, I'll make sure you're the first to meet my new pets!"

Around her the three monkeys giggled very dark, un-monkeyish giggles that promised discomfort and pain. Their chuckles did not foreshadow a walk in the park.

The bank's glass front door exploded, and the figure of a costumed hero stepped out into the street light. It was Fake Super Qwok. He was saying to someone following him, "—time I got to use these power gauntlets. I can't believe someone robbed the bank before—" and he stopped, staring at the scene before him. "You—" he said, though neither Alex nor Bryan could tell if the "you" he was talking to was either of them, was the Police Captain (still frozen like an ice cube statue), or the Wicked Witch in the guise of the Police Captain.

Fake Raceboy followed Fake Super Qwok from the shattered glass bank door and announced, "We left you in the slammer! What are you doing out!"

The Police Captain who had been in the slammer said nothing; he was trapped in an ice cube. The Police Captain who had just robbed the bank examined these heroes who had just exited the building. He (she) must have believed that the two were superheroes in pursuit of (his) her criminal activities, not villains bent on perpetrating the exact crime he (she) had just perpetrated. "Well," the Wicked Witch in the guise of the Police Captain declared, "if it isn't the dynamite dipsticks, Racebrat and Super Crap."

Both Alex and Bryan heard themselves say, "Hey!" but no one noticed because at that very moment, Fake Raceboy and Fake Super Qwok were yelling, "Get him!"

The melee that ensued involved everyone except the frozen chunk of police officer and the two costumed pseudo-super villains, who stood in mute fascination. Fake Raceboy was using his portable sonic boom, Fake Super Qwok was wielding some sort of power gauntlets, and the Police Captain/Witch was illuminated by flashes of heat lightning as spells went off with cracks and clatters. Seamus/Remus/Amos danced karate-style dances around the battle, striking here, punching there. Shouts, exclamations, oaths, echoed.

Then Alex and Bryan noticed the first of the ambling shapes that were not trick-or-treaters walking down the block. Although apparently costumed, the shapes did not walk in the same manner as children in pursuit of candy. In fact, their walk was hardly a walk. It was more of a limp, or a lurch, or a wobble. It was a disoriented walk, the rambling shuffle of a still-sleeping sluggard trying to find his way to the bathroom at three in the morning.

One shape with such a walk would have been funny, maybe someone trying to be "in character" on Halloween. Two was a ridiculous, unbelievable coincidence. Above that, three was noticeably disturbing, especially when the shapes became illuminated beneath the street lights. They included men and women, but in clothes decayed beyond recognition, mere rags that moldered upon bodies brown with putrescence. Sunken eye sockets hid beneath matted clumps of mossy hair; the clumps were falling out in chunks and patches. Sharp yellowed teeth clacked like sabers rattling against shields on some battlefield of antiquity.

Both Alex and Bryan said at the same time: "Zombies."

Yes, zombies. The walking undead. Reanimated corpses brought—not back to life, but back to movement through dark arts and terrible spells. The Wicked Witch had threatened Alex and Bryan, costumed as they were as Dr. Devious and Mr. Mischief. And she had told them that her "pets" would be arriving with the moon. Looking up, both Alex and Bryan could see the clouds part like a gash to expose the milky softness of the moon's face.

"This is going to take more than just the two of us," Bryan said. He looked around at the street which was filling up with the walking undead.

"Agreed," said Alex.

"And I'm tired of being a villain. It's just one problem after another."

"That's the truth. Let's show those fakes how real heroes act."

Bryan watched the blur that was Alex change from his Dr. Devious costume to his Raceboy outfit in less time than it takes to blink an eye. For the millionth time he envied his brother's speed, not because of its superhero qualities, but because of that quick change. Bryan looked down at the button on his Mr. Mischief trousers and sighed. Buttons. His trousers had buttons. Buttons really were worse than super villains.

* * *

"Gwa-unnngh," said a zombie as it snatched at Katherine's

trick-or-treat candy. This one was male, tall, and extraordinarily thin. With more life experience Katherine would have thought the zombie looked like Abraham Lincoln before he'd grown a beard.

"No you don't," Katherine said. "That's mine!"

"Hey, you! Stop that!" Mom said, and she stepped closer to the zombie. She pushed the front of its shirt and then the thing turned its undead eyes upon her and opened its mouth to expose its gumless teeth. "Oh my gosh!" Mom goshed, hands flying immediately to cover her mouth. "We've got to get out of here! That's…That's…"

"Not without my candy!" Katherine said. Taking aim, she swung her green purse with the pink flowers so that it struck the zombie in the face.

Moments later, Katherine's Flower-pager went off: that silent signal calling for her assistance as Flowergirl to fight criminals? Villains? Robots from space? She eyed the gray shapes in the moonlight, and she knew. She also knew what to do about them. But first, she had to get Mom home.

*   *   *

Super Qwok hauled off and punched a zombie in the face with his powerful strength. Had that particular zombie participated in that particular moment as a gymnast in the Summer Olympics, the unique twisting and turning its body performed while spiraling across the street may well have earned near perfect scores. Unfortunately, there were no Olympic judges nearby, and if there were, they should have been running for their lives because zombies don't care about gymnasts, unless they manage to catch one for dinner.

The zombie stood up, shook off Super Qwok's super punch, and continued its plodding march forward. Its face no longer had a nose. Its mouth no longer had teeth. Neither seemed to matter to the zombie, who mashed his gums together as he tramped with outstretched arms straight back at Super Qwok.

"What do we have to kill them?" Super Qwok asked.

"I don't know!" Raceboy exclaimed. "I've already tried punching, kicking, laser-swording, throwing. They just keep coming back!" Raceboy planted a karate kick straight into a zombie's gut. When the creature bent in half he kicked straight up, snapping the zombie's head back and forcing its legs to follow in a back flip that left it face down on the ground. It shook itself and rose to its feet again.

Raceboy yelled, "This is ridiculous! They won't die!"

"Of course they won't die!" said the witch-voiced Police Captain. Both boys turned to see that he stood atop the groaning figures of the two artificial superheroes. "Zombies are already dead!" The Police Captain cackled, and it was an eerie sight: the uniformed figure of the Police Captain with his head thrown back in laughter as a high-pitched giggle erupted from his mouth. Behind him the three monkeys danced in hilarity, their arms snaking up and down and their howls cutting the night. "I knew these weren't you two pajama-lovers! They were too easy." Fake Super Qwok tried to put his head up but the Fake Police Captain put a booted foot on his head and ground his face against the asphalt.

"Ung, ung, ung," groaned a zombie near the heroes' feet. Raceboy reached down and yanked the zombie from the ground and prepared to throw him. Except this zombie was covered with chunks of ice and hung shivering from Raceboy's fist. The Police Captain! Raceboy realized. He shook the Police Captain, shedding the last of the semi-melted layer of ice to the ground. The Real Police Captain tried to speak, "Wa-wa-wag owin' non-non-non?"

"We couldn't explain it if we had an hour," Super Qwok said.

Raceboy added, "Protect yourself. This will be messy."

A nearby zombie grabbed the Real Police Captain's collar and made a gurgling, gasping sound. The Police Captain screamed and fell to his knees. "Wah id dat!"

"Just one of the walking undead," Super Qwok said, and threw the zombie straight at the Fake Police Captain. The zombie knocked the Fake Police Captain back a step.

Raceboy grabbed another zombie—maybe the same zombie he'd already thrown once? It was hard to tell them apart—and threw it at the Fake Police Captain. Another direct hit. This time the Fake Police Captain stumbled. The first zombie was pulling itself up using the Fake Police Captain's pant leg.

"No, you, get off!" shrieked the Fake Police Captain. "I created you!"

The second zombie gurgled and pulled on the Fake Police Captain's leg.

"No, no, no!" screeched the Fake Police Captain. He bellowed a magic word that sounded inside out and backwards at the same time. A poof of smoke surrounded him, and in his place stood the Wicked Witch in robes of black with a black pointed hat. Her green skin hardly looked healthier than the zombies that had pulled themselves to their feet. "Gung," said one of the zombies as its zombie hand clenched her sleeve.

"No!" the Wicked Witch roared. "I created you! I created you all—" The zombie seemed to be embracing the Wicked Witch, pulling her down.

"I suppose..." Raceboy sighed. Then he zipped past, yanked the zombie away from the Wicked Witch and threw it into the broken facade of the bank. He was thankful for his superhero gloves and wondered briefly whether there was a detergent known to man that could get green zombie ooze out of blue fabric.

Super Qwok stomped up to the Wicked Witch, lifted the second zombie, and with a flick, a twist, a spin, he crafted a zombie pretzel. The zombie's vacant eyes stared at Super Qwok from under its shoulder. Super Qwok twisted the head so it faced away before throwing the zombie like a Frisbee against the bricks of the bank. The zombie splatted against the wall then fell into the evergreens where it lay twitching, caught and unable to extricate itself.

"Waid uv me!" exclaimed the real Police Captain, whose limbs seemed to have thawed slightly as he shambled after Super Qwok and Raceboy.

The street was full of zombies. They surrounded the group, dozens of limping, oozing figures without the ability to do much more than groan or click or gnash their long teeth together.

The three monkeys hooted and hollered, cavorting around the Wicked Witch as though appealing for her to save them. Fake Super Qwok and Fake Raceboy managed to gain their feet, but they wobbled and leaned against one another. The Wicked Witch looked back and forth between Raceboy, Super Qwok, and the Police Captain, as if daring a single one of the three to point out who had created the zombies to get them all in this predicament. No one did. All around the group, the undead shapes moved closer.

"Even if we can knock them back, they will just keep coming," Raceboy said.

"Fire," Super Qwok said. "Maybe fire will do it?"

"And burn the entire town down? There has to be a better way!"

The Wicked Witch said, "There is no other way to kill zombies: fire alone! And to save your town, you must destroy it!" She laughed, her long, slender body bent in the middle like a forked branch of a gnarly walnut tree. "Choose, choose! Destroy, or be destroyed!"

Zombie arms reached out. Zombies fought, pushing one another to be the first to reach the small group of living flesh that stood in front of the bank. Fake Raceboy smacked zombie wrists. Fake Super Qwok blasted zombies with power gauntlets, sending them skyward like cannon fire. Raceboy and Super Qwok both kicked and punched. There was no room to move, to throw punches, to throw zombies. Raceboy fell with a zombie's arms wrapped around his neck. Super Qwok tried to grab for him, found himself being pushed to the ground. In all their crime fighting days, they had never thought that the end would come fighting alongside the very villains they had so often fought with, surrounded and outnumbered by a mindless adversary.

Green flashed nearby. Thud. A zombie collapsed in a cloud of dust. A pink arc. Smash. Another zombie fell.

Raceboy and Super Qwok looked through limbs, listened over grunts and groans. Green and pink zinged and swooshed. Zombies thunked and thudded, falling like wheat before the thresher.

"What is that?" asked Raceboy.

"I don't know, but I want one," said Super Qwok.

Both boys pushed, freed themselves from the zombies, and bounced to their feet in time to see Flowergirl wield a cute green purse which she swung overhead and slammed into a nearby zombie's face. The zombie had time to fall backward before its body jerked as though experiencing a grand mal seizure.

"Hey guys," Flowergirl said. "I heard there was a party and we couldn't be left out!"

"We like to *dance!*" Dr. Destructo shouted as she wiggled her behind and snapped a different zombie in the face with a pink sequined purse, causing the zombie to writhe in agony for a moment before it collapsed.

"I brought some extras for you boys," Katherine said. She tossed a white purse with a chain—very dressy—to Raceboy, and a black dinner purse—small and with long black rope for a strap—to Super Qwok.

Raceboy looked at the white purse. It was fake snakeskin. "What was that you said? 'I want one!'" he said, holding the purse and shaking it at Super Qwok.

"Wha—" Super Qwok asked as he stared at the dinner purse in his own gloved hands.

"Just swing them at the zombies!" Flowergirl explained. "They can't stand it! It makes them go completely dead." She demonstrated by swatting a female zombie that was still wearing a dilapidated brown wedding dress. The thing covered its face with its hands, did a frantic jig, and collapsed like a discarded puppet.

"Here goes my pride," said Super Qwok. He twirled the purse like a cowboy's lasso over his head and proceeded to slam the purse into a zombie. This one must have still had quite a bit of tongue left, because it made a loud sob before it stopped writhing.

Raceboy kicked into Race-mode, spinning the gold chain and slamming the white purse into anything that moved.

"Ow!" yelled Fake Mr. Mischief. "That hurt!"

"Stop that!" yelled Fake Dr. Devious. "Pay more attention to what you're doing!"

Raceboy didn't apologize. He just made sure to swing his purse near the dastardly duo every so often.

The street in front of the bank cleared of moving zombies. Piles of the undead—re-dead would probably be a more appropriate term—littered the ground.

"There's more to do," the real Raceboy told the real Police Captain. "We'll finish the cleanup, but before we go I want you to take

care of these three." He motioned to the villains.

Raceboy pulled Fake Raceboy's mask off. Dr. Devious's wild hair stuck out in all directions.

"Dr. Devious!" exclaimed the Police Captain. "So that must be—" He pointed at Fake Super Qwok.

Super Qwok—the real Super Qwok—removed the mask. "You guessed it," he said.

"Bah!" Mr. Mischief spat. "I'm innocent. I want my lawyer."

"Where are those other two, the ones who tried to rob the store?" the Police Captain asked.

Raceboy looked at Super Qwok. "They were gone before we got here."

The real Police Captain had finally thawed completely. He stood, purse in hand, looking around East Fifth Avenue. "That's it! No more super villain Halloween costumes! And no more superhero Halloween costumes! And no more wicked witch Halloween costumes! And no more zombie costumes! And no more police man Halloween costumes!"

Super Qwok asked, "What are people going to dress up as?"

"Harmless things. Nothing. I don't know. No, I mean cute and soft and fuzzy and nice!" The Police Captain swung his arms.

"That sounds awful," Raceboy said.

"No, it sounds wonderful!"

Raceboy explained, "Face it, Captain. Even if you made dressing up as certain things illegal, it would just force Dr. Devious or Mr. Mischief to dress up as fairies or ballerinas or whatever. Next thing you know, you'd be chasing a band of bad ballerinas out of the bank with bags full of cash."

"Be good for a laugh," Super Qwok pointed out. "Don't get any ideas!" he swatted Mr. Mischief on the chest with his purse. Mr.

Mischief had a diabolical look in his eyes, as though the idea of bad ballerinas robbing a bank had never crossed his mind, but had potential.

The Police Captain shivered at the thought. "Oh, never mind. Who's going to clean up this mess? All these dead bodies around town? It's simply hideous."

"I can think of three possibilities," said Super Qwok, eyeing Dr. Devious, Mr. Mischief, and the Wicked Witch. "Maybe they won't get jail time, but a little community service is a distinct possibility."

"I can't understand it," Devious said as he looked at the denim purse someone had shoved in his hands. It had two pink flowers and a carefully embroidered name that was smeared with zombie ichor. "I can't understand how a piece of fabric can destroy mindless creatures like zombies."

The Wicked Witch heard him and scowled. "You always were a nincompoop, Devious. Zombies are born of violence and evil. No amount of violence can kill them unless it's the violence of fire burning them to nothing, to a pile of ash. But take something like a cute pink purse, maybe one with sequins, and hit them with it. It's so completely outside the realm of the possible, it's so completely unexpected, that it has the power to stop them cold. It's like it makes their brains explode or something. Or if you want to think about it magically, it breaks the spell that holds them together. Why are you always such a twit?" she asked and hit him in the head with the cute purse she had that was made out of recycled drink pouches. "See? I can hit you with something like this purse and you don't die because it's completely in the realm of the plausible."

"What about them?" asked the Police Captain as he pointed to the three monkeys.

Flowergirl tossed the Police Captain a white ball. Except it wasn't a ball. It was a homemade popcorn ball wrapped in plastic wrap. The monkeys started dancing back and forth, begging, appealing.

"They love popcorn balls," Flowergirl explained.

Although the zombie hordes covered Clifton, Raceboy was able to spread the word about how to defeat the zombies. Battles raged as residents gathered to fight off the undead. When dawn broke over the horizon, a weary cheer rose with the sun. The last of the zombies had been defeated, and Clifton was safe once more.

The next day the newspaper headline read, "Purses Kill Zombies." The picture on the front page showed Dr. Destructo, Flowergirl, Super Qwok, and Raceboy lined up smiling with purses in hand. They stood atop a pile of zombies.

"I am pretty sure I have a purse like that," Mom said to Dad as they looked at the cover of the Sunday paper.

"Probably," Dad agreed, "you could have single handedly saved the town with all of your purses."

"Hmph. I might hit you with one!"

Dad put his arms out, walking over to Mom, and grabbed her in a zombie embrace.

Alex and Bryan winced. They hoped Mom wouldn't look through her purses to see if she did, in fact really have a purse like that.

"Look, it's people cleaning up zombies!" Katherine yelled from the picture window. Anna, Alex, Bryan, Mom and Dad all came to the living room to look outside. They saw the Police Captain along with the Wicked Witch's monkey's guarding a crew cleaning up zombie parts. Dr. Devious wore an orange workman's uniform and pushed a wheelbarrow. Mr. Mischief wore the same type of uniform and carried a scoop. The Wicked Witch wore orange witch robes. She had a shop broom instead of her traditional cane broom. Outside the Winkels' house, the Wicked Witch stopped to sweep zombie parts into Mr. Mischief's shovel. Mr. Mischief tossed the body parts into Dr. Devious's wheelbarrow.

The Police Captain saw the family looking out the window and waved. He turned back to watching the villains, held up a popcorn ball, and took a bite. Beside him the monkeys danced, waiting for some crumbs.

Epilogue

Bryan mumbled, "It's been a long time since Dad told us a story." He leaned against the frame of his bed, peered over the worn library book he'd brought home from third grade.

"Seventy-eight days," agreed Anna as she stacked a wooden block atop a tower she was building.

Katherine added her own block. "I think it's more like infinity-two."

Alex looked up from his spot at the drawing desk. "He's always at work, or working on something." He finished penciling a jet-pack on a small humanoid robot.

Katherine reached for another block. "Or fixing things…except he still needs to fix my fairy wand that makes noise when you wave it and the jewel broke off."

"Dad gets my milky," Anna pointed out.

Bryan rolled his eyes. "You're too old to have milky. You're four now. Dad says you don't need sippy cups anymore."

Anna puckered her lip at him as if to say, "I'm the baby of the family."

Alex thought about it. "I guess being a dad takes a lot of time."

Katherine's eyes flashed, and she clapped her hands. "I know!" she cried. "*You* can tell us a Raceboy and Super Qwok Adventure!"

Bryan waved his book. "Not me! I don't know what to say."

    346

Alex shrugged. "We could tell the stories Dad told us. Like the time Raceboy and Super Qwok babysat you—" He pointed at Katherine. "That was funny!"

Bryan giggled. "I really liked that one. Or how about the time Mom found out our secret identities. That one was the best!"

"I like the one where Anna becomes Dr. Destructo," Katherine said.

Anna laughed. "Yes! Dr. Destructo! Ka-pow!" and she punched the blocks. They scattered across the bedroom carpet.

"Or," Alex said, "we could make up new stories."

Bryan wrinkled his nose. "Like what?"

Before Alex could say anything, Katherine said, "Mr. Mischief could steal all of the nightlights in Clifton. So all the kids are scared at bedtime."

"I'm not scared, I'm Dr. Destructo!" Anna said. Then she added, "But I do want Mom to lay by me when I go to bed."

Alex said, "I think we can do this. Let's see: our story needs some things. What should we put in it? Katherine said that Mr. Mischief steals all the nightlights to scare kids. That's good. That sounds exactly like something Mr. Mischief would do. What else?"

Bryan said, "Ninjas. We need a story with ninjas. Masked ninjas with swords and throwing stars."

"They're called shuriken," Alex explained.

Katherine said, "What about giant lily pads? Like we saw at the museum."

"I like princesses," Anna added.

Alex hit his forehead. "Oh, all right! But if this story is going to have Mr. Mischief, ninjas, giant lily pads, and princesses, I can't do it alone. We all are going to have to take turns telling it. Agreed?"

Everyone nodded.

"Good. I'll start. How about this:

Once upon a time
there were four kids,
Alex, Bryan, Katherine, and Anna.
But they weren't just kids,
they were

Superheroes...

CHB"

Author's Notes

On the Settings

Clifton, Illinois, does exist. It is one of many Cliftons in the United States. My Clifton is a typical Midwestern town: railroad tracks bisect the town into west and east sides; it has a Main Street; it has grain elevators, a public library, a hardware store, a grocery store, and a collection of taverns balanced by roughly the same number of churches. That Clifton is a typical rural town is essentially true, and I have not tried to change that fact in these stories. Aside from Main Street and the Clifton Public Library, the other locations in Clifton are invented. They may have parallels in our world, but the versions in this story are not intended to portray the actual people or businesses in any way. Some of the elements simply cannot be fictionalized because they are true anywhere and everywhere in the rural Midwest.

On the Characters

The real people portrayed in this book are my immediate and extended family plus a select group of intimate friends; however, I must stress here that they are portrayed fictionally. None of the actions, conversations, choices or thoughts described within this book really happened. The purpose of their inclusion was to create

350

entertaining stories for my children, and populating these tales with the people and places familiar to them was a part of the storytelling. Everyone else in this book, from the bank teller to the Police Captain, are all fictionalized. None represent actual people from our world.

While I did populate the fictional Clifton with family and friends, there are far more people whose names were omitted because, unlike the real universe, the Raceboy and Super Qwok Universe must fit between book covers.

The Epigram

Terry Pratchett's quotation of G. K. Chesterton is a curiosity. It occurs in an article available at

http://www.concatenation.org/articles/pratchett.html

However, no version matching Pratchett's supposed quotation from Chesterton exists elsewhere in the world. The closest original I can find that makes sense is from Chesterton's collected essays titled *Tremendous Trifles*, published in 1909: "Fairy tales do not give a child his first idea of bogey. What fairy tales give the child is his first clear idea of the possible defeat of bogey. The baby has known the dragon intimately ever since he had an imagination. What the fairy tale provides for him is a St. George to kill the dragon." (Essay XVII, "The Red Angel"). I prefer Pratchett's more succinct adaptation and identified it as a paraphrase.

Maddie the Wonderdog

Maddie, our family dog, died on December 19th, 2011, just three days after Chris completed the final illustration for this book. While not a main character, she is a presence within the book, and her loss changes the way readers who knew her will view the images or stories that refer to her.

Chris commemorated Maddie's personality—her pure, bouncy, puppy nature—with an additional illustration of Maddie the Wonderdog. Although we buried her beneath the apple tree, she will always be bounding within the pages of this book.

Acknowledgements

Ellen Tribe retired from teaching and immediately spent her first summer as a retiree proofreading this book. Any errors that remain after her discriminating eye pored over this draft are not examples of errors she missed, but are likely errors that I didn't catch while poring over the hundreds of suggestions she offered, or—as is more likely—added as I attempted to make things "better." Additional eyes that generously offered to do final copy-editing included my co-teachers, Dr. Ruth Reynolds and Amelia Hamilton, as well as my sister Sarah Winkel, and my wife Milissa.

Chris Brault could have turned me down when I asked him to illustrate this book. He could have rolled his eyes and told me that he was busy, that he had better things to draw, that he didn't share my vision for Raceboy and Super Qwok. Instead he committed more than six months of his life to draw hundreds of sketches that included character designs for dozens of monsters, creatures, robots, and devices. We collaborated online, generating hundreds of blog posts and comments on a website I set up. The result of this collaboration is a book that transcends anything I could have created by myself. The words are mine, but the face of the stories will always be Chris's illustrations. Because of Chris, *Raceboy and Super Qwok Adventures* can even be enjoyed by people who never read a word or story I've written.

Finally, thank you to Milissa, my wife, for her support over the last year as I focused on the creation of this book. You may imagine that you know her already from these stories, but the truth is that Raceboy and Super Qwok's mom is a caricature of a generic mother with sprinkles of my own mother's penchant for wooden spoons. The real Milissa never really sneaks into this book, except in hints; even then, it would be inaccurate to try to imagine that the character you've read about comes close to matching my wife.

The Future of Raceboy and Super Qwok Adventures

Superhero stories have lives of their own. They are descendants of the great hero tales of our ancestors; they fulfill a personal need for myth that exists within each of us; they propagate as naturally as dandelions, spreading through the imagination with what if's, new villains, new challenges, new adventures. One day I expect that there will be more *Raceboy and Super Qwok Adventures*. After all, I have a note that refers to the time the boys saved the world from an invasion of Tricknobots: tiny robots that look like common appliances that are trying to take over the world. There's also 3,000 abandoned words in which the heroes foil a plot of Dr. Devious, only to acquire the powers of an ancient sect of Egyptian warrior-priests whose totem creature was the velociraptor. How the boys get rid of this blessing—or curse—has yet to be written. And what about the Nursery Rhyme Bandit? He never talks in anything but nursery rhymes. And he hasn't had a chance to prance his way against our heroes. At least, not in this volume.

Those are just some of my what-ifs. Alex, Bryan, Katherine, and Anna may have their own. Inevitably superhero tales like these don't belong to just one person. The possibilities for Raceboy and Super Qwok are as infinite as the imaginations of those boys and girls who listen to these stories and personalize them. Raceboy and Super Qwok stories will not end. They will continue as the Raceboy and Super Qwok universe expands, blasting outward from the big bang that was its origin: that fusion of time-space where I became a father to four beautiful, amazing children.

ABOUT THE AUTHOR

Andrew Winkel and his wife, Milissa, live in Clifton, Illinois. They have four children: Alex, Bryan, Katherine and Anna.

He graduated from the Fiction Writing program of Columbia College Chicago in 1996. He earned his M.A. from Olivet Nazarene University in 2000, and has taught middle school language arts for over ten years in Bradley, Illinois. He has also been the part-time director of the Clifton Public Library since 2006.

In 2011 he founded Hierophantasm to publish *Raceboy and Super Qwok Adventures.*

He has known Chris Brault since fourth grade.

Keep up with him at andrewwinkel.com.

ABOUT THE ILLUSTRATOR

Born and bred in the wilds of Illinois, Chris Brault was raised on a diet of Monty Python, Transformers, comics, George Carlin, and animation of all breeds and shapes. He is chronically illustrating, with influences that include Jeff Smith, Frank Cho, Mike Mignola, and Jill Thompson.

Chris has single-handedly given more comic books, action figures, and animation DVDs to Alex, Bryan, Katherine, and Anna than all of their grandparents combined.

Raceboy and Super Qwok Adventures is his first book of illustrations.

Check out more of his distinctive artwork online:
rashomonchb.deviantart.com/

Raceboy and Super Qwok Adventures

Interior and Cover Design: Andrew Winkel

The text was set in Adobe's Garamond Pro, a typeface chosen for its preeminent readability and its unobtrusive capital Q.

Additional fonts used in this book include

League Gothic designed by The League of Moveable Type, www.theleagueofmoveabletype.com

HVD Comic Serif Pro by Hannes von Döhren, www.hvdfonts.com

Gladifilthefte by Tup Wanders, www.tupwanders.nl

Goudy Bookletter 1911 by Barry Schwartz, crudfactory.com

Bevan by Vernon Adams, http://code.newtypography.co.uk/

Cabin by Pablo Impallari, www.impallari.com, and Igino Marini, www.ikern.com

Dyspepsia by Ray Larabie, www.larabiefonts.com

Franchise by Derek Weathersbee, www.derekweathersbee.com/

SF WONDER COMIC BLOTCH by Derek Vogelpohl, www.shyfoundry.com/